"Suspense, intrigue, trafficking in stolen artifacts, blackmail, murder: they're all here in this fast-paced mystery thriller. Chloe Ellefson sets off on a journey to visit all of the Laura Ingalls Wilder sites in search of the truth about a quilt Wilder may have made, and in the process of solving several crimes Chloe learns a lot about the beloved children's author and about herself."

—John E. Miller, author of *Becoming Laura Ingalls Wilder* and *Laura Ingalls Wilder's Little Town*

TRADITION OF DECEIT

"Ernst keeps getting better with each entry in this fascinating series."

—*Library Journal*

"Everybody has secrets in this action-filled cozy."

—*Publishers Weekly*

"All in all, a very enjoyable reading experience."

—*Mystery Scene*

"A page-turner with a clever surprise ending."

—G.M. Malliet, Agatha Award–winning author of the St. Just and Max Tudor mystery series

"[A] haunting tale of two murders ... This is more than a mystery. It is a plush journey into cultural time and place."

—Jill Florence Lackey, PhD, author of *Milwaukee's Old South Side* and *American Ethnic Practices in the Twenty-First Century*

HERITAGE OF DARKNESS

"Chloe's fourth ... provides a little mystery, a little romance, and a little more information about Norwegian folk art and tales." —*Kirkus Reviews*

THE LIGHT KEEPER'S LEGACY

"Kathleen Ernst wraps history with mystery in a fresh and compelling read. I ignored food so I could finish this third Chloe Ellefson mystery quickly. I marvel at Kathleen's ability to deepen her series characters while deftly introducing us to a new setting and unique people on an island off the Wisconsin coast... It takes a skilled writer to move back and forth 100 years apart, make us care for the characters in both centuries, give us particular details of lighthouse life and early Wisconsin, not forget Chloe's love interest, and have us cheering at the end. A rich and satisfying third novel that makes me ask what all avid readers will: When's the next one?! Well done, Kathleen!"

—Jane Kirkpatrick, *New York Times* bestselling author

"Chloe's third combines a good mystery with some interesting historical information on a niche subject." —*Kirkus Reviews*

"A haunted island makes for fun escape reading. Ernst's third amateur sleuth cozy is just the ticket for lighthouse fans and genealogy buffs. Deftly flipping back and forth in time in alternating chapters, the author builds up two mystery cases and cleverly weaves them back together." —*Library Journal*

"Framed by the history of lighthouses and their keepers and the story of fishery disputes through time, the multiple plots move easily across the intertwined past and present." —*Booklist Online*

"While the mystery elements of this book are very good, what really elevates it are the historical tidbits of the real-life Pottawatomie Lighthouse and the surrounding fishing village." —*Mystery Scene*

THE HEIRLOOM MURDERS

"Chloe is an appealing character, and Ernst's depiction of work at a living museum lends authenticity and a sense of place to the involving plot." —*St. Paul Pioneer Press*

"Greed, passion, skill, and luck all figure in this surprise-filled outing." —*Publishers Weekly*

"Interesting, well-drawn characters and a complicated plot make this a very satisfying read." —*Mystery Reader*

"Entertainment and edification." —*Mystery Scene*

OLD WORLD MURDER

"[S]trongest in its charming local color and genuine love for Wisconsin's rolling hills, pastures, and woodlands... a delightful distraction for an evening or two." —*New York Journal of Books*

"Clever plot twists and credible characters make this a far from humdrum cozy." —*Publishers Weekly*

"This series debut by an author of children's mysteries rolls out nicely for readers who like a cozy with a dab of antique lore. Jeanne M. Dams fans will like the ethnic background." —*Library Journal*

"Museum masterpiece." —*Rosebud Book Reviews*

"A real find... 5 stars." —*Once Upon a Romance*

"Information on how to conduct historical research, background on Norwegian culture, and details about running an outdoor museum frame the engaging story of a woman devastated by a failed romantic relationship whose sleuthing helps her heal." —*Booklist*

"A wonderfully woven tale that winds in and out of modern and historical Wisconsin with plenty of mysteries—both past and present. In curator Chloe Ellefson, Ernst has created a captivating character with humor, grit, and a tangled history of her own that needs unraveling. Enchanting!" —Sandi Ault, author of the WILD mystery series and recipient of the Mary Higgins Clark Award

"Propulsive and superbly written, this first entry in a dynamite new series from accomplished author Kathleen Ernst seamlessly melds the 1980s and the 19th century. Character-driven, with mystery aplenty, Old World Murder is a sensational read. Think Sue Grafton meets Earlene Fowler, with a dash of Elizabeth Peters."

—Julia Spencer-Fleming,
Anthony and Agatha Award–winning author of
I Shall Not Want and *One Was A Soldier*

ALSO BY KATHLEEN ERNST

Nonfiction

Too Afraid to Cry:
Maryland Civilians in the Antietam Campaign
A Settler's Year: Pioneer Life Through the Seasons

Chloe Ellefson Mysteries

Old World Murder
The Heirloom Murders
The Light Keeper's Legacy
Heritage of Darkness
Tradition of Deceit
Death on the Prairie
A Memory of Muskets
Mining for Justice
The Lacemaker's Secret
Fiddling with Fate

American Girl Series

Captain of the Ship: A Caroline Classic
Facing the Enemy: A Caroline Classic
Traitor in the Shipyard: A Caroline Mystery
Catch the Wind: My Journey with Caroline
The Smuggler's Secrets: A Caroline Mystery
Gunpowder and Teacakes: My Journey with Felicity

American Girl Mysteries

Trouble at Fort La Pointe
Whistler in the Dark
Betrayal at Cross Creek
Danger at the Zoo: A Kit Mystery
Secrets in the Hills: A Josefina Mystery
Midnight in Lonesome Hollow: A Kit Mystery
The Runaway Friend: A Kirsten Mystery
Clues in the Shadows: A Molly Mystery

Fiddling
with
Fate

A CHLOE ELLEFSON MYSTERY
Fiddling with Fate
KATHLEEN ERNST

MIDNIGHT INK
WOODBURY, MINNESOTA
MIDNIGHT INK

First Edition
First Printing, 2019

Book format by Samantha Penn
Cover design by Kevin R. Brown
Cover illustration by Charlie Griak
Editing by Nicole Nugent

Midnight Ink, an imprint of Llewellyn Worldwide Ltd.

Library of Congress Cataloging-in-Publication Data
Names: Ernst, Kathleen, author.
Title: Fiddling with fate: a Chloe Ellefson mystery / Kathleen Ernst.
Description: First edition. | Woodbury, Minnesota : Midnight Ink, [2019] |
Identifiers: LCCN 2019017406 (print) | LCCN 2019018353 (ebook) | ISBN 9780738761091 () | ISBN 9780738760902 (alk. paper)
Subjects: | GSAFD: Mystery fiction.
Classification: LCC PS3605.R77 (ebook) | LCC PS3605.R77 F53 2019 (print) | DDC 813/.6--dc23
LC record available at https://lccn.loc.gov/2019017406

Midnight Ink
Llewellyn Worldwide Ltd.
2143 Wooddale Drive
Woodbury, MN 55125-2989
www.midnightinkbooks.com

Printed in the United States of America

DEDICATION

For Scott—
The best possible partner
on this grand adventure.

AUTHOR'S NOTE

Yankee settlers established Stoughton, Wisconsin, in 1847. However, immigrants from Norway followed in such great numbers that today the community is perhaps best known for its Norwegian heritage.

Some of those immigrants came from the Hardanger region in southwest Norway. This area is particularly known for its vibrant folk arts and culture, including the Hardanger fiddle music and textiles highlighted in the mystery.

To learn more about the featured places and groups:

Stoughton Historical Society
http://www.stoughtonhistoricalsociety.org

Sons of Norway Mandt Lodge
https://www.facebook.com/Sons-Of-Norway-Stoughton-WI-129998320406152/

Stoughton Norwegian Dancers
https://stoughtonnorwegiandancers.com

Hardanger Folk Museum
https://hardangerfolkemuseum.no

Voss Folk Museum
https://vossfolkemuseum.no

Utne Hotel
https://utnehotel.no/en/

CAST OF CHARACTERS

Contemporary Timeline (1984)

Chloe Ellefson—curator of collections, Old World Wisconsin

Roelke McKenna—Chloe's fiancé; officer, Village of Eagle Police Department

Frank Ellefson—Chloe's dad

Kari—Chloe's sister, married to Trygve

Aunt Hilda Omdahl—Chloe's Mom's best friend

Kent Andreasson—director, Stoughton Historical Society

Trine Moen—intern, Stoughton Historical Society Museum

Rosemary Rossebo—genealogist

Sonja Gullickson—curator, Hardanger Folk Museum

Ellinor Falk—director, Hardanger Folk Museum

Ulrikke—proprietess, Utne Hotel

Klara Evenstad—employee, Utne Hotel and Hardanger Folk Museum

Torstein Landvik—folklorist studying traditional dance

Reverend Martin Brandvold—retired minister, Utne Church

Barbara-Eden Kirkevoll—employee, Utne Hotel

Bestemor—elderly dance informant

Politi Førsteinspektør Naess—Police Inspector

Historical Timeline

Gudrun—Chloe's great-great-great-great-great-grandmother

Lisbet—Gudrun's granddaughter

Lars—Lisbet's husband

Torhild—Lisbet and Lars's daughter

Halvor—Torhild's husband

Gjertrud—Torhild's cousin

Edvin Brekke—musician and folklorist

*Mother Utne—proprietess, Utne Inn

Erik—Torhild and Halvor's son

Britta—Torhild and Halvor's daughter

Svein Sivertsson—Britta's husband

Helene—Britta and Svein's oldest daughter

Solveig—Britta and Svein's middle daughter

Amalie—Britta and Svein's youngest daughter

Jørgen Riis—Hardanger fiddle maker and player

Gustav Nyhus—fisherman

* *Real person*

ONE

April 1984

Chloe didn't cry until the fiddler walked to the casket suspended over the grave, settled the instrument beneath her chin, and began to play.

Roelke McKenna, Chloe's fiancé, took her hand. "Are you okay?" he whispered. He wore a black suit, which seemed as surreal as everything else today. But his fingers were warm and strong. She was glad he was beside her.

She swiped at her eyes and tried to swallow the salty lump in her throat. "The fiddle." She tipped her chin toward her Aunt Hilda, who was coaxing a haunting tune from her Hardanger fiddle. Hilda's eyes were closed as she poured everything she had into the music. "It's just so—so *Mom*."

"I expect Marit is smiling down, right now."

Maybe so, Chloe thought. The music concluded a memorial service for her mother, Marit Kallerud, who'd cherished Norwegian heritage. She and Dad had been active members of Stoughton's

Christ Lutheran Church for years. Many of the mourners were wearing *bunader*, traditional Norwegian clothing.

Roelke leaned close. "It doesn't matter what Marit did or didn't know about her birth. This would please her. You put together a perfect tribute."

Chloe glanced at her older sister. Kari stood with her husband, Trygve, and their two daughters. She was crying. She'd been crying pretty much nonstop since Mom had died of a heart attack in her sleep five days earlier. Dad was a shadow of himself, unwilling or unable to offer opinions. Chloe had found herself making calls, making plans, making decisions.

At least we have a nice day, she thought now. April in Wisconsin could be iffy, but they'd been blessed with sunshine. Robins hopped among the graves. Daffodils were blooming. It helped.

After the last poignant strains of Hilda's tune faded in the quiet churchyard, the pastor cleared his throat. "We will close by reciting the Lord's Prayer in Norwegian. *Fader vår, du som er i himmelen, La ditt navn holdes hellig…*"

Chloe's gaze locked on the dates printed above Marit's photograph on the bulletin. *May 20, 1920—April 4, 1984*. Mom had only been sixty-three. In good health, as far as anyone had known. But just like that, she was gone.

I'm sorry, Mom, Chloe thought, blinking against the sting of tears. I thought we'd have more time.

———

The pastor urged everyone to stay for the luncheon, and people drifted toward the church hall. The fiddler stood alone by the grave with fiddle dangling from one hand, her bow from the other.

"Come meet Aunt Hilda," Chloe murmured to Roelke. "Hilda Omdahl. She's not really my aunt, but she was my mom's best friend."

When they approached, Hilda started from her reverie. "Oh, sweetie. What are we going to do without your mother?"

"I don't know," Chloe admitted. She hadn't even begun to process the reality of life without her mother. "Hilda, this is my fiancé, Roelke McKenna."

"I'm glad to meet you, Roelke." Hilda managed a tremulous smile. She was a plump woman of medium height, with permed gray hair. She wore a long blue wool skirt and matching vest, both gorgeously embroidered, and a white blouse adorned with a traditional silver filigree brooch. "When's the big day?"

A tricky subject. "We haven't actually set a wedding date yet," Chloe said. Roelke was Catholic. She was not. They hadn't quite figured out how to handle things.

Hilda patted Roelke's arm. "Marit spoke highly of you."

"My mom and Hilda went way back," Chloe added.

"We met when we were five." Hilda's eyes became glassy.

"Your fiddle is beautiful," Roelke said. "I've never seen anything so ornate." Intricate black designs had been inked onto the fiddle body, the fingerboard beneath the strings was inlaid with mother-of-pearl, and the scroll featured a carved dragon's head. A talented rosemaler had painted delicate flourishes on the sides.

Hilda regarded her fiddle with affection. "I was playing for Marit today."

"I'm sure Mom heard you." Chloe put her arm around the older woman's shoulders. "It was the perfect way to close the memorial."

"Well, I thought it best to play outside." A tiny smile quirked the corners of Hilda's mouth. "Just in case the good pastor is a traditionalist."

Roelke frowned. "I'm sorry?"

"In the old days, fiddlers weren't permitted to play in churches," Hilda explained. "Ministers declared *hardingfeles* like this 'the devil's instrument.' Most people today wouldn't think twice about it, but I didn't want to be insensitive."

"No one could ever call you insensitive," Chloe protested.

"Chloe ..." Hilda glanced away. "Never mind." She wiped her eyes with a tissue.

"Come inside with us," Chloe told her gently. "I'm sure the ladies have put on quite a spread."

The ladies, actually, had outdone themselves. "Holy toboggans," Roelke breathed as they went into the hall. Long tables covered with white cloths were laden with platters and bowls. Servers wearing comfortable shoes bustled in and out of the kitchen with coffee pots and water pitchers. Round tables held centerpieces created with flowers, candles, and tiny Norwegian and American flags.

Chloe felt a surge of affection for these people, this community. "The church annually serves the world's largest *lutefisk* supper," she told him. "Dried whitefish soaked in lye, served with *lefse*, for two thousand people." These women could handle the memorial meal for a dear friend with one hand tangled in their apron strings.

Near the door, Mom's rosemaling friends had created a display of some of her painted pieces. It included a photograph taken after Mom won her coveted Gold Medal in the annual National Exhibition of Folk Art in the Norwegian Tradition, coordinated by Vesterheim Norwegian-American Museum. Mom looked grand in her favorite *bunad* of white blouse with beaded bodice insert, black skirt, and fancy white apron. She held the painted porridge container that had tipped her into the winner's circle, and she was beaming.

"I wish I'd seen that smile more often," Chloe murmured. Grief, she was learning, meant far more than missing a loved one. Grief also meant confronting regrets and the finality of unasked questions. It meant accepting sadness for a life not completely understood, with no more time to try.

While Hilda went to retrieve her fiddle case, more friends and neighbors greeted Chloe and Roelke. One woman expressed condolences before saying, "As you know, Marit was serving as vice president of the Mandt Lodge."

"The Stoughton chapter of the Sons of Norway," Chloe interpreted for Roelke. The group promoted fellowship and preserved Norwegian traditions through gatherings, workshops, travel, and other activities.

"Some of us were wondering if you might step in," the woman continued. "We need to bring younger people into leadership positions, and as Marit's daughter..."

"Unfortunately, my schedule would not permit that," Chloe said. No way could she even *begin* to fill Marit's shoes with the lodge, and she wasn't foolish enough to try. "Perhaps you could ask Kari."

A man about her own age was waiting to greet her. Although the younger woman at his elbow was a stranger, the man looked familiar. Then the years slipped away. "*Kent?* How nice to see you!"

Kent Andreasson was still tall and muscular. His tawny hair was still thick and wavy. His blue eyes still crinkled when he smiled—just as they had in high school. Chloe accepted his hug, then drew Roelke forward. "Roelke, I've told you how much I enjoyed being part of the Stoughton Norwegian Dancers in high school, right? Kent was a star. There's a demanding dance called the Halling that ends with a man kicking down a hat held high with a stick. Nobody could leap as high as Kent. And with a few back flips tossed in, he always stole the show."

Kent put a hand on Chloe's arm. "Oh, it wasn't such a big deal. Being on the gymnastics team helped."

Chloe realized that her smile might be misconstrued at her mother's funeral. Then she realized that she hadn't even made proper introductions. "Kent, this is my fiancé, Roelke McKenna."

"Good to meet you, Roelke." The men shook hands. "And this is Trine Moen." He drew his companion forward. "She's an exchange student from the University of Bergen, interning at the museum this semester."

"I'm so sad about your mother," Trine said earnestly. "Marit was kind to me." Trine was a pretty young woman with big eyes, a luminous complexion, and light brown hair captured in a complicated braid. Chloe could only imagine that she turned heads on either continent.

"Thank you," she said. "Kent, what are you doing these days?"

"I'm an accountant." He shrugged. "I'm also serving as the director of the Stoughton Historical Society. I think I was tapped because of my fundraising experience with the dancers."

"We washed a whole lot of cars that year we went to Norway."

"Yeah." Kent nodded. "Anyway, Marit was one of our star volunteers at the museum. Irreplaceable, really. She was *so* excited about the Norway trip."

"The Norway trip?" Chloe repeated, trying to place this in context. Mom had often traveled to Norway—usually with Dad, but not always.

"Because of the Sons of Norway grant?" Kent prompted. "Funding her research trip to one of Norway's folk museums?"

“The grant, yes,” Chloe said sagely. She had no idea what he was talking about.

Kent leaned closer. “Since you’re a curator at Old World Wisconsin, we thought you might go in her place.”

Ah. Now Chloe understood the build-up. “Unfortunately, my schedule would not permit that. Perhaps you could ask Kari.”

Kent looked disappointed, but didn’t argue. “Give my respects to your dad, okay? Take care.” He and Trine moved away.

“Your mother was one busy lady,” Roelke observed as they edged toward the buffet. “And I suspect we don’t know the half of it.” When it came to preserving and celebrating Norwegian heritage, Mom had possessed a bottomless well of energy.

I wish I understood what drove her, Chloe thought. She was one of the few people who knew that Marit Kallerud had been adopted. Chloe had learned that only inadvertently, and she’d spent the past five months dithering about when/how/whether she should ask Mom what she knew about the adoption. Kari had been against broaching the subject, and Chloe had reluctantly stayed silent.

Now I’ll never know what, if anything, Mom knew about her birth parents, Chloe thought. She craned her neck, hoping the desserts weren’t getting too picked over. “I need *krumkake*,” she said plaintively. “Maybe a piece of almond cake too.” Comfort food.

“You need something nutritious,” Roelke said firmly. He handed her a paper plate. “Do not skip straight to the treats.”

“I don’t know how I got so lucky,” she whispered. Roelke McKenna was a good-looking guy with dark hair, a strong jaw, and muscled shoulders. He was a cop, and could be a bit intense. Chloe had found herself squirming more than once when those piercing brown eyes focused on *her*. But he was a good man. Someone to depend on. Nothing was more important to Roelke than the well-being of people he loved. Lucky me, she thought again as she dutifully scooped up some cucumber salad.

Hilda joined the family at the head table, but not for long. "I've been on my feet too much today," she confided. "I'm giving tours during the historical society open house tomorrow night and need to rest up for that. Anyway, sweetie, you know you can call me anytime, right?"

Chloe's throat grew thick. "Thank you, Hilda." She held the older woman close. Hilda kissed her cheek before limping away.

The food and the friends and the gathering's Norwegian-ness helped Chloe get through the afternoon. She took solace in the knowledge that Marit Kallerud would be remembered for making an enormous difference in the community.

"Well," Kari said finally. "We have to get going." Kari and Trygve ran a dairy farm. Their routine was inflexible.

"We can go anytime you're ready, Frank," Roelke told Chloe's dad. She shot him a grateful look. They were spending the night at her folks' house before heading home to Palmyra tomorrow.

As Dad hugged his granddaughters goodbye, Kari pulled Chloe aside. "Make sure he's okay."

Chloe suppressed a sigh. Kari was only a year older than her, but she sometimes took the "big sister" thing a bit too seriously.

Or … maybe that wasn't fair. Perhaps Kari was just reacting to the metaphorical cloak of "family matriarch" settling heavily onto her shoulders. One of their maternal grandmother's sisters was still alive, but Great-Aunt Birgitta lived in a nursing home and was fading into dementia. Mom had been a force of nature. Maybe Kari felt a need to step into that void.

And in truth, Kari had always taken the primary responsibility for their parents. When I got the heck out of Dodge, Chloe thought,

Kari stayed. Kari had been the one to check on Frank and Marit during blizzards, to deliver Crock-Pots of homemade chicken soup in flu season, to invite them over for anniversary or birthday celebrations. Kari had gone bowling with Dad, taken rosemaling classes with Mom, made *lefse* and *krumkake* for Mandt Lodge dinners.

Sometimes, Chloe thought, I can be extremely self-absorbed. "We won't leave tomorrow unless we're sure Dad's okay," she promised.

Once Dad was in the truck, Roelke headed to Stoughton's old Southwest Side, a celebrated historic district. Chloe felt wistful as they drove past fine Greek Revival, Italianate, and Queen Anne structures. Her parents' less-grand house on South Prairie Street would always be *home*. She'd grown up here, playing with Kari in the yard beneath flapping American and Norwegian flags. The Ellefsons' friends had gathered here for coffee, their conversation speckled with Norwegian words because many had grown up with the language. A sign Mom had painted hung by the front door: *Velkommen til vårt hjem*—Welcome to our home. Norwegian culture had become part of Stoughton's thriving tourism boom. But behind the rosemaled park benches and glossy photos of Norwegian Constitution Day celebrations, countless families like the Ellefsons were proud of their Norwegian roots.

Was Mom? Chloe wondered for the umpteenth time as they went inside. Had she known she was adopted? If so, did she embrace this heritage because it was in her genes and marrow? Because she'd married a Norwegian-American man? Because she desperately wanted to belong?

No telling.

Dad got as far as the kitchen before halting, staring around the cheerful room as if he'd never seen it before. He was a tall man, quiet and calm, with gray eyes that could sparkle with mischief. He liked to refinish old furniture, he liked to putter in the yard, he liked to have breakfast every Tuesday morning at a local diner with a few lodge buddies. He'd checked his daughters' math homework. He'd beamed with pride when they'd performed with the Stoughton Norwegian Dancers or exhibited with 4-H in the county fair. Chloe's relationship with Mom had been complicated; with Dad, not so much. Chloe hated thinking of him fumbling around this suddenly lonely kitchen.

"Dad, how about a Wisconsin brandy old-fashioned?" she asked, as eager to busy herself as she was to offer him a cocktail. She knew where to find the Korbel's brandy and Angostura bitters, the sugar, the oranges and cherries, the muddler used to squeeze juice from the fruit. Taking three glasses from the cupboard, she got to work. "And I'll fix supper."

"Lord, no, don't cook. Your sister was here yesterday."

Chloe cracked the fridge door and saw stacks of neatly labeled Tupperware containers. "Um … yeah. You're set." She added ice cubes and a splash of Sprite to each cocktail, stirred, and delivered them. "Here you go."

Dad lifted his glass. "To Marit."

"To Marit," Roelke echoed. Chloe's throat seized up, but she raised her glass.

Dad tasted the concoction. "That's perfect. Thank you." Then he hesitated. "Chloe, I need to talk to you about something."

She felt an instinctive childhood-inspired flash of *Am I in trouble?* "O-*kay* …"

He went into the den and returned with an envelope in his hand. "Your mother wanted you to have this."

As she accepted the envelope, Chloe darted a quick glance at Roelke: *I have no idea what this is all about*. He raised his eyebrows:

Only one way to find out. Peeking inside, she saw multiple bills featuring Benjamin Franklin.

Chloe had never seen a hundred-dollar bill before. Heck, she had only passing acquaintance with fifty-dollar bills. She looked up, dumbfounded. "What's this?"

Dad swirled the liquid in his glass. "Your mother was saving money so she could take you to Norway."

"So she could take me to Norway?" Chloe repeated blankly. She and Mom had not been particularly compatible travelers on a weeklong trip to Iowa a while back, but Mom had been thinking of a much bigger trip? "Don't you mean Kari?"

"They went together, you know. Before Kari's girls were born."

Chloe looked back at the Franklins. She'd been living in Switzerland when Mom and Kari went to Norway, and she'd paid no attention. "But we did *all* go that time. When I was in middle school." She remembered visiting some distant relatives of Dad's in Oslo, and sailing north on a Norwegian Coastal Express ship. Crossing the Arctic Circle had been a big deal. "I got to go again with the Norwegian Dancers in high school. We danced for the king."

"But you were young." Dad studied the rosemaled woodenware displayed above the cupboards. Mom's work, all of it. "I think your mother always felt bad that she didn't have a chance to take you again later."

This still wasn't making sense. "Did Mom want me to go along on that research trip she had planned with Kent Andreasson?"

"No." Dad waved that away. "She just wanted to take you."

"Why didn't Mom ever talk to *me* about it?"

He lifted his palms in a weary gesture. "You know how your mother was."

She did, but that explained nothing. "I don't know what to say."

"You don't have to say anything. Just take it. It's what she wanted."

Chloe glanced at Roelke again. He tipped his head with an affirmative expression: *Clearly, it's yours.*

Well, okey-dokey, Chloe thought as she stuffed the envelope into her shoulder bag. The last thing she wanted to do was make anything harder for her father. She'd think about the money later.

Dad sat in a kitchen chair, tugged at his tie, and gestured for Roelke to join him. "And Chloe, I have a favor to ask. Your mother's cousin Shirley cornered me after the service and asked if she could have one of your mother's purses. Some little black thing with beads on it, she said."

This was safer ground. "Geez, Dad. It takes some nerve to make that kind of request at a funeral."

"I guess Shirley's always admired it." He waved a dismissive hand. "Kari already said she didn't want it. Unless you do, the easiest thing is to find it and send it to Shirley."

"I can't even picture it," Chloe said, "so I don't care." She fished a cherry from her glass and popped it into her mouth.

"I'd be grateful if you'd look for it." Dad studied one thumb. "It's probably in the guest room closet. But going through your mother's things…"

Ah, of course. "Sure, Dad. Glad to."

Chloe headed up the stairs. She paused in the doorway of her own old bedroom. Mom had never taken down a hideous purple macramé creation that Chloe had made in seventh grade, or the *Doctor Zhivago* poster reflecting her burgeoning love of period dramas. It all seemed a long time ago.

Mom had used the guest room for things she didn't need often. "Hoo-boy," Chloe muttered when she opened the closet door. The space was jammed. Mom's *bunader* hung on padded hangers next to the folk dresses Chloe and Kari had worn during their dancing days. Cardboard cartons labeled "Christmas decorations" and "School projects—K" and "School projects—C" were stacked neatly on the shelf. More boxes covered the floor.

Chloe sat down—gingerly, since she was actually wearing a dress and pantyhose—and began pulling out cartons. It was hard not to get diverted by boxes of gloves, Stoughton High School yearbooks from 1937 and 1938, a heart-shaped button box that she and Kari had been permitted to play with when channeling their inner Laura and Mary Ingalls. In another box Chloe found long-forgotten toys, including an Etch A Sketch, a Magic 8 Ball, even a Slinky. Really, Mom? Chloe thought. You saved a Slinky? Either Mom had planned *way* ahead for grandchildren or she'd been more sentimental than she'd let on.

A silk handbag embellished with jet beads turned up near the end of her quest. Not something Chloe could imagine carrying. You're welcome to it, Shirley, she thought, and set it aside.

There was only one box left in the closet, shoved into a back corner. She might as well find out what was in it before burying it again. The carton was sealed, but the tape had gone brittle with age and easily gave way. She lifted the flaps and found a *tine*—a bentwood box—oval, with a flat lid, and rosemaled in shades of blue, red, yellow, and green. The design itself was simplistic, but cheerful.

"Mom," Chloe said softly, "was this your first project?" Preserving the rose-painting tradition had been Marit's greatest passion, but she only put her best work on view. It tickled Chloe to think that her mother had been sentimental enough to save an early piece.

But the *tine* wasn't empty. Easing off the lid, Chloe discovered something small and lumpy wrapped in tissue paper. She turned the wrapping back to reveal a small porcelain doll with long blond hair. "Oh!" Her eyebrows rose in surprise, for she'd never seen the doll before. It was dressed in a costume approximating a Norwegian *bunad*—red skirt, yellowing linen blouse, apron with a lace edge. Beads stitched on red ribbon suggested traditional ornamentation. Most distinctive was an elaborate crown made of wire, clearly representing the crowns that, historically, many Norwegian women wore on their wedding day.

"Mom, was this yours?" Chloe struggled to imagine a young Marit sitting on the floor, playing with a dolly.

She set the doll to one side. In the bottom of the *tine* were two more tissue-wrapped packets—both soft and flat. The first held a gorgeous example of white Hardanger embroidery with cutwork. "A doily," Chloe murmured. The cotton piece was about seventeen inches square, probably intended to take the place of honor on a table, perhaps beneath a vase. Why on earth had Mom kept this amazing textile folded away in the back of the closet?

The final treasure was another textile, this one maybe eighteen by twenty inches. The fine linen featured geometric patterns embroidered in black thread, much of it delicate cross stitch. The workmanship was exquisite, for the most part, although a couple of the mirror images didn't quite match, and one or two motifs were off-kilter. Also, the maker had evidently been unable to finish the project, for half of the cloth was unadorned. It looked old.

And it seemed to represent ... *something*. I'd swear I've never seen this before, Chloe thought, but it seems familiar. The doll evoked curiosity; the doily, admiration. This cloth brought a tingle to her palms.

Since childhood, Chloe had occasionally experienced lingering emotions in old places. She couldn't explain or predict the sensations, but had accepted her ability long ago. Perhaps this cloth had come from a place still vibrating with events long gone. She closed her eyes, trying to open herself. But whatever the cloth represented glimmered only momentarily at the edge of her understanding before slipping away like a silver minnow darting into the shadows.

Chloe opened her eyes again. I wonder… she thought, but cut herself off before going too far. No point in speculating. She nestled the doll, the doily, and the embroidered cloth back into the *tine* and carried it downstairs.

"I was beginning to think you'd gotten lost," Dad said. His forehead wrinkled as he saw what she held in her hands. "Weren't you looking for a purse?"

"I found that, but I also found these." Chloe placed the oval box on the table between the men, removed the lid, and slid into a chair. She brushed nonexistent crumbs from the table before reverently displaying her finds. "Dad, have you ever seen any of these pieces before?"

Dad studied them. "Don't think so. No."

"They were buried in a carton in the back of the guest room closet." Chloe felt Roelke's questioning gaze. He was always quick to pick up on her mood. She tried to compose her expression to suggest offhand curiosity.

"Your mother probably found those things at a garage sale or something," Dad was saying. "She couldn't bear to see heirlooms like that forgotten."

But if that were the case, Chloe thought, why was the carton hidden away? She glanced around the kitchen—familiar blue curtains, blue teapot on the stove, blue-and-white dishtowels. A *krumkake* iron hung above the stove, and an antique *lefse* pin was displayed on the counter. It felt as if Mom had just stepped out.

Right that minute, Chloe wanted nothing more than to see Mom stride briskly into the kitchen, to offer a plate of Norwegian cookies, even to murmur some lightly veiled barb about her younger daughter's inadequacies.

Most of all Chloe wanted Mom to explain why she'd hidden the *tine* and its treasures in her closet, and why she'd set money aside for a trip to Norway, without mentioning it to *her*.

TWO

Dad trudged up the stairs to bed early, his shoulders bowed with grief and loneliness. It hurt Chloe's heart to see him so lost.

"How are you doing?" Roelke asked Chloe when they were alone. "Is there anything you need?"

Chloe hesitated. "I think I need to talk to Hilda Omdahl."

"Your mom's friend?" Roelke's forehead wrinkled. "What for?"

"I want to ask her about the things I found in Mom's closet." She glanced at the wall clock. "It's only a little after nine. She's probably still up."

He studied her. "Chloe, what is this all about?"

"I can't explain it," she admitted. "The *tine* I found might have been an early project of Mom's, and I suppose the doll might have come from a garage sale, but the doily is worthy of a museum collection. And *something* about that unfinished blackwork cloth seems important. I'll check with Kari, but I have this feeling she won't recognize the pieces either. The only other person who might is Mom's oldest friend."

"Want company?"

She grabbed his hand, profoundly grateful that she was engaged to this guy. Roelke could be wound a bit too tight, but he was surprisingly patient with her more inexplicable notions. She didn't take that for granted. "Thank you, but I think I should talk to her alone."

Fifteen minutes later Chloe parked the truck in front of Hilda's 1920s bungalow in East Park. Behind drawn curtains, light glowed from the living room.

Hilda was clearly surprised to find Chloe on the front step. "Honey, what are you doing here?"

"I wanted to show you something." Chloe held up the carton. "I hope I'm not disturbing you."

"I'm glad you're here," Hilda said. "I was feeling lonely. Please, come in."

Hilda's living room was a comfortable space with rose-toned furniture, and travel photographs on the walls. A carved *nisse*—a creature from Norwegian folklore—stood on the raised brick hearth in front of the fireplace. The television, on but muted, provided a hint of company.

Chloe was distracted by a cloth worked with Hardanger embroidery draped over a table in one corner. She'd seen it a thousand times, but suddenly she was more interested. Focus, she told herself, and settled on the sofa. Hilda moved a crewel project from a chair and took a seat.

"I found something in Mom's closet that I'd never seen before." Chloe put the carton on a coffee table and pulled out the *tine*. "I don't know if Mom painted this."

"If she did," Hilda said dubiously, "it was a long time ago."

"And these were inside." Chloe removed the doll, the doily, and the blackwork cloth. "Are these familiar?"

Hilda shook her head. "No."

Chloe realized that a part of her—apparently a big part—had wanted Hilda to smile nostalgically and say, "Of course! Marit saw those at the Mount Horeb antiques mall and had to have them. That was a fun day." But she didn't. Chloe felt herself teetering on the edge of something unknown.

"Why do you ask, dear?" Hilda leaned forward, her eyes shadowed with sudden concern. "Is it important?"

"I don't know." Chloe hesitated. "Aunt Hilda, did my mother ever tell you that she was adopted?"

"Adopted?" Hilda repeated blankly. *"Marit?"*

"Mom's aunt Birgitta told me."

Hilda shook her head slowly. "No. Marit never mentioned it." She was silent for a moment, staring at the episode of *Kate & Allie* flickering on the TV screen. Finally she said, "Does your father know?"

"He's never mentioned it, and I haven't asked. Kari doesn't know anything about it."

"Wouldn't Marit have said something?" Hilda looked bewildered. "She was a genealogist!"

"I've got copies of the genealogical work that Mom's done. It shows her birthday, but there's no mention of an adoption. I've also seen baby pictures of Mom and my grandma together." Chloe rubbed her palms on her skirt. "But Mom could have been an infant when she was adopted."

Hilda's brow furrowed thoughtfully. "Did you know there was an orphanage in Stoughton? The Martin Luther Orphanage. It dated back to the 1890s, I think."

"Really?" Chloe sat up straighter.

"At some point they transitioned from housing orphans to helping troubled youth, but the whole enterprise closed five or six years ago. Who knows what happened to the records."

Damn, Chloe thought.

"What does all that have to do with these?" Hilda gestured at the artifacts.

"Maybe nothing," Chloe admitted. "But I found this box buried in Mom's closet. Any of these items could be sixty years old. I thought that maybe I'd found a clue."

"I'm sorry I can't help you, dear."

"I'm probably way off-base anyway." Chloe picked up the doll, smoothed her miniature apron with a gentle finger ... and felt a little *something* under the cloth. She lifted the apron—nothing. Then she eased back the skirt, and saw a yellowed bit of folded paper pinned to the doll's petticoat.

Chloe removed the pin. The strip of paper cracked in half, and she gingerly laid both pieces on the table and leaned close. She could just make out the writing: *Vennligst gi dette til barnet.*

She sucked in her lower lip, mind racing. By 1920, when Marit was born, the earliest Norwegian immigrants had been in Wisconsin for ... what, eighty years? But if Marit's people *had* been early arrivals, most likely her mother, as a second- or third-generation American, would have spoken and written in English.

"What is it?"

"A note, written in Norwegian." Chloe could almost hear Mom chiding her for not learning to speak the language. Well, I've got backup at the moment, Chloe thought. With a fingernail she gingerly turned the pieces toward Hilda.

Hilda frowned, pulled a magnifying glass from her needlework basket, and tried again. "Gracious," she said softly. "It says, 'Please give these to the child.'"

Chloe caught her breath. "These things *are* clues! Whoever gave my mom up for adoption wanted her to have these mementos."

Hilda considered the doll, the *tine*, the doily, and the embroidered cloth. "It does appear that way."

"Do any of these items suggest something specific to you?"

The older woman pinched her lips together for a moment, then shook her head. "No. They all appear to be Norwegian, but I'm no expert on folk arts." Hilda looked up, eyes gone shiny. "If only Marit were here!"

But she's not, Chloe thought. I had a chance to talk with her about this, and I didn't, and I lost my opportunity.

She pressed her fingertips to her temples. She'd decided months ago that she needed to try to discover her mother's biological lineage. Something about the discovery of these personal artifacts in the depths of Mom's closet only added a sense of urgency.

Hilda seemed to sense her distress. She picked up the doily. "Well, we know this is Hardanger embroidery."

"So it comes from the Hardanger region, right?" Chloe summoned a mental map of Norway. The country's famous Hardangerfjord reached inland from the southwest coast.

"Hardanger is a district in Hordaland County, but Hardanger embroidery has come to broadly represent Norwegian heritage." Hilda tilted her head thoughtfully. "Same thing for the doll."

"The doll …?" It took Chloe a moment to catch up. "You mean her costume? Is this style from Hardanger? It's similar to what Mom often wore."

Hilda touched the miniature *bunad*. "It suggests the Hardanger region. And although simplistic, you're right—it does look like the *bunad* your mother wore most often."

"She must have been born in Hardanger!" Chloe breathed. "Or perhaps she was born here, but her birth mother or grandmother was."

"Not necessarily." Hilda held up one hand. "'*Bunad*' has become an umbrella term. It does refer to traditional clothes once worn in different rural areas, but it has also come to mean 'folk costume.' The Hardanger woman's *bunad* has evolved into a sort of a national folk costume—just like the embroidery now represents Norway as much as the Hardanger district."

Chloe tried to sort that through. "So … the fact that Mom wore a *bunad* once particular to the Hardanger district might not mean that she knew she had ancestors from that area."

"Exactly. And the same might be true of the doll's costume. For all we know, whoever purchased this found it in an Oslo gift shop."

"I suppose," Chloe conceded. Certainly Norwegian souvenirs and gifts were being sold in any tourist hotspot by the 1920s. "But it's a place to start, anyway." She cocooned the doll in tissue and nestled it back into the *tine*.

"Chloe," Hilda began, then paused.

Chloe tried to decipher the older woman's expression. Hilda looked uncertain, but there was something more too. Was that guilt flickering in her eyes?

Then Hilda blinked, and the flicker was gone. "Never mind."

"What's wrong, Aunt Hilda?" This was the second time today that Hilda had started to speak, then thought better of it. "Did you think of something else?"

Hilda rubbed one hand with the other. "No."

Silence settled on the room, thick and heavy. Chloe felt something important hovering just out of reach. What was Hilda thinking? What had Mom been thinking? What had Mom known?

Finally a clock chimed ten times, rousing Chloe from her reverie. "It's late. Thanks for indulging me, Aunt Hilda."

Hilda got up to see her out. Chloe was almost to the door when she paused by the table. The tablecloth's embroidery wasn't as fine as the workmanship displayed in the doily she'd found. The design scale was larger, the stitching less delicate. But it was still lovely. "Who made this, Aunt Hilda?"

"My mother," Hilda said with quiet pride.

"Was it a reflection of national heritage, or was she actually from the Hardanger district?"

"She was from Hardanger. Who knows, perhaps that's why Marit and I were friends!" Hilda smoothed an invisible wrinkle in the cloth. "It's not really an antique, but I treasure it."

Chloe felt a prick of envy. She wanted something like Hilda's tablecloth—a family heirloom, a lovely true story, certain knowledge of the people *behind* the object. Something that would remind her that even though she and Mom hadn't been especially close, she still had a place in a long chain of strong women.

"It is a treasure," she agreed wistfully. After kissing Hilda on the cheek, Chloe left.

The next morning, Roelke had some quiet time in the kitchen. Nice, he thought, savoring the stillness. Although he liked Chloe's family and wanted to be supportive, he'd felt a bit on display at the church yesterday.

But that's understandable, he thought. Chloe had deep roots in this town. Of course people were curious about her fiancé. And he'd liked everyone he'd met…

Well. Except for Kent Andreasson. Roelke didn't like the way Andreasson had made Chloe smile, and he didn't like picturing the two of them whirling around together in their dance costumes.

The stab of distaste surprised him, and not in a good way. Chloe was wearing his engagement ring, for God's sake. Was he really so insecure?

Yes. Apparently he was.

Well, he and Andreasson would probably never cross paths again. Roelke put the other man out of mind as he fixed a bowl of instant oatmeal and added a sliced banana.

He'd visited this house many times, but it felt different now. Marit's absence was almost a presence itself, hovering in the periphery of his vision. Chloe's relationship with her mother had been complicated, but Marit had taken to *him* from the start. He sent a silent message skyward: *Marit, I will take good care of your daughter.*

Roelke had realized long ago that he was best off staying out of mother-daughter dynamics, but now he worried that Chloe was left with regrets. She'd come back from Hilda's house the night before all excited about the note pinned to the doll's petticoat. The stuff Chloe had found in her mother's closet suggested that Marit's birth parents *had* been Norwegian. And the note did seem to validate Birgitta's story about Chloe's mother being adopted. But where all of this would take Chloe next, he had no idea. He just hoped that—

"Good morning." Chloe appeared in the doorway, yawning. She'd pulled on jeans and a green shirt and thick wool socks, but her long hair was loose. God, she was lovely. She'd insisted they sleep in separate bedrooms here, which struck Roelke as unnecessary, since her dad was well aware that they lived together. He was looking forward to getting back to their own home.

"Hey, sweetie," he said.

She kissed him. "Dad hasn't come down yet?"

"He's come and gone. Something about breakfast with the guys?" Roelke went to the stove. "I'll get you something to eat."

"Thanks."

He turned on the burner beneath a teakettle. As he reached for another banana he heard Chloe sigh, and glanced over his shoulder. "Something wrong?"

"Maybe. I don't know." She nibbled her lower lip. "Twice yesterday, when we were talking about my mom, Aunt Hilda started to tell me something, then stopped. I think she knows something she's not telling me."

"Why would she do that?"

"I don't know, but it's troubling her." Chloe rubbed her forehead. "I think I'll go see her again and try to find out what's on her mind."

"Are you sure? You might put Hilda in a difficult position. Maybe Marit told her something in confidence."

"My mom is dead," Chloe countered. "Nothing's going to trouble her now. I'm the one who needs help."

"Have you decided whether to tell Kari about the Norwegian heirlooms you found?"

Chloe sighed again. "Yeah, I think I need to. She deserves to know, even if she doesn't want to do anything about it, so—"

The back door opened and Kari walked into the kitchen.

"Freaky," Chloe muttered.

"What?" Kari deposited a cookie tin on the counter and kissed Roelke's cheek. "Good morning, Roelke." He'd done her a huge favor once. They got along just fine.

He was glad to see her looking more composed than she'd been at the funeral. "Hey."

Then Kari turned to her sister and folded her arms. Both women were blond and blue-eyed, and so close in age that people sometimes mistook them for twins. "Thanks a lot for volunteering me, Chloe." Kari's voice held both resignation and annoyance.

Roelke flashed back to yesterday's church hall conversations. It was clear from Chloe's expression that she realized that she might, just possibly, have spoken out of turn. "For volunteering you?" she repeated.

"I just got off the phone with Kent Andreasson. He wants me to go to Norway on a research trip in Mom's place. And he said it was your idea."

"I figured it might be a treat for you," Chloe tried.

"Are you out of your mind? I live on a dairy farm! I have two young daughters! I can't drop everything and go to Norway."

"Okay, okay. It was just an idea."

"A bad one."

Roelke poured Chloe a cup of coffee. He looked at Kari with a silent question: *Want some?*

She shook her head, but some of the stiffness left her shoulders. "How's Dad?"

Chloe sipped with obvious gratitude. "Doing as well as could be expected, I guess. He's out to breakfast with his lodge buddies." She took a deep breath. "Listen, Kari, I have something else to tell you. I found some things in Mom's closet last night." She fetched the box and displayed the heirlooms, including the note she'd discovered pinned to the doll's petticoat. "This was buried in Mom's closet. Have you ever seen any of this stuff before?"

Kari considered the objects without stepping up for a closer look. "No."

"I think we finally have a tangible clue to Mom's birth parents, and—"

"Chloe, I don't *care*! I just want to remember Mom the way she was."

Roelke opened his mouth but thought better of speaking. Everyone was extra-emotional right now. The sisters had to work things out for themselves.

"Sorry. Didn't mean to sound shrill," Kari said stiffly. "Anyway, back to Kent. When I turned him down on the trip idea, he hit me up for a donation for a bake sale they're having this evening." She patted the container she'd brought. "I whipped up some almond cookies, and I told him I was sure you'd be *delighted* to participate as well. Better get busy. And deliver mine at the same time, okay?"

"But …"

"See you later." Kari awarded Roelke a smile before letting herself out.

Chloe stared after her. "Well, *that* bit me in the butt."

"You love to bake," he observed mildly. "But eat your breakfast first." He sprinkled nutmeg over her steaming oatmeal and set it at her place.

"It's not just that." Chloe propped an elbow on the table and one cheek on her palm. "Kari spent a lot of time with Mom, and she made it look easy. I should have tried harder. But I'm trying to do something good now."

"It sounded like the subject of those heirlooms is closed with Kari."

"Yeah," Chloe said morosely. "I'm clearly on my own."

"How do you feel about that?" He was learning that asking Chloe questions was usually more helpful than offering advice. As illogical as that seemed.

"Liberated," she said. "And lonely."

THREE

Chloe baked a double batch of *snipp*, diamond-shaped cookies flavored with cardamom and cinnamon. If I'm lucky, she thought, the Sons of Norway won't call Kari about taking Mom's vice president slot until Roelke and I have gotten home.

"There," she said, settling the lid on a cookie tin. "Want to come with?"

"Sure," Roelke said.

Chloe tucked a few cookies into a small container. "I'm going to leave these with Hilda on the way to the museum. She deserves a treat."

Roelke filched a cookie and raised an eyebrow.

"I won't upset her," Chloe protested. "But if Mom did tell her something about her past, I deserve to know."

After Roelke pulled into Hilda's driveway, Chloe grabbed the cookies and led him up the walk. Suddenly he grabbed her arm, pointing ahead with his other hand. Hilda's front door was ajar. "That's odd," Chloe murmured uneasily.

Roelke stepped in front of her, mounted the steps, and knocked on the door. No answer. He banged harder. No answer.

Chloe leaned closer. "Hilda? Hilda!"

Still no answer. Roelke pushed the door open and stepped inside.

When Chloe crowded in behind him, the first thing that caught her gaze was Hilda's beautiful heirloom tablecloth. It was rumpled, slightly askew.

Then Roelke cursed beneath his breath and ran across the living room. "Call 911."

Chloe's pulse began to pound. Hilda lay crumpled on the floor in front of the fireplace.

"Chloe! Call an ambulance!" He crouched and pressed a finger against Hilda's carotid artery. "She's still alive."

"Do you think she's going to be okay?" Chloe asked anxiously as the EMTs whisked Hilda out to the ambulance.

"I don't know." Roelke's jaw was tight.

Officer Corvado, the young policeman who'd been first on the scene, approached. "You two are friends of the victim, correct? Do you have contact information for Mrs. Omdahl's family?"

Chloe winced as the ambulance pulled away with siren blaring. "Hilda didn't have any family that I know of. She's a widow. No kids." Even her best friend, Marit, was gone. It all seemed impossibly sad.

"Listen," Roelke said, "you need to know that when we arrived, the front door was standing open. It's chilly today. Why was the door open when she was on the far side of the room?"

As his meaning became clear, Chloe's mouth opened and her eyes went wide. She'd figured Hilda had tripped and fallen, or suffered a stroke or something. "Are you suggesting that Hilda was attacked?"

Roelke held up both palms. "I'm merely considering the possibilities."

"Let's not rush to conclusions." Officer Corvado's tone was calibrated to defuse tension. "Did you notice anything else amiss?"

"That." Chloe pointed to the off-kilter tablecloth. "It looks as if someone stumbled against the table and kept going."

"Perhaps one of the EMTs?"

"No," Chloe insisted. "I noticed it before they arrived. That's a treasured heirloom, and Hilda wouldn't leave it crooked. I was here last night, and it didn't look like that."

"Can you tell if anything is missing?" the officer asked.

Chloe gazed around the room. "Everything looks in place," she said finally, "but I couldn't say for sure."

Officer Corvado gave them each a business card. "Please call if you think of anything else. If you want to head to the hospital, I'll secure the house."

At Stoughton Hospital, Chloe and Roelke settled in the emergency waiting room with cups of bitter vending machine coffee. Officer Corvado arrived with Hilda's insurance card and several medications he'd found. "No sign of forced entry at the house," he told Roelke. "I'll talk to the neighbors, see if anyone noticed a visitor at Mrs. Omdahl's place."

A young woman in blue scrubs came to ask Chloe questions: "Has Mrs. Omdahl had recent vision problems? Dizzy spells? Headaches? Numbness? Does she have diabetes? Any history of seizures? Of strokes?"

"Not that I'm aware of," Chloe said over and over, wishing her mother was there. Marit would have known.

When she'd answered what she could, Chloe found a payphone and called her father and the pastor. Then she settled down to wait beside Roelke, whose knee was bouncing with suppressed agitation. Chloe hunched over, feeling numb.

When the doctor finally talked with them, she tried to listen, she really did, but she had a hard time taking in his words. "Nonresponsive … brain scan … depressed brainstem reflexes … coma."

How can this be? she thought. Just last night Hilda had been fine. Chloe needed Hilda to be fine again. She couldn't lose Mom *and* Aunt Hilda.

And … what had Hilda wanted to tell her? Had Marit shared something in strict confidence? I may never know, Chloe thought. Why hadn't she pressed the issue at the time? *Why?*

"You're welcome to stay, of course," the doctor was saying. He took off his glasses, rubbed the lenses on his coat. "But there's really nothing you can do for your friend. We'll call if there's any change."

"Thank you," Chloe managed, and Roelke shook the man's hand. As the doctor hurried away she rested her cheek on Roelke's shoulder.

"I'm so sorry," he said.

"I had trouble following everything the doctor said. Do they know what happened?"

"Not yet." Roelke rubbed his chin. "A bad stroke could leave someone in a coma. Or a traumatic head injury."

Chloe grimaced, picturing the raised brick hearth. "I hate to think of Aunt Hilda lying there, all alone, for God knows how long."

Roelke smoothed a strand of hair away from her face. "Look, let's take a break. Want to go back to your folks' place?"

"I guess so—oh, wait." Her shoulders sagged. "Hilda said she was giving tours during the historical society open house tonight. We should try to catch Kent at the museum. It would be best to talk in person."

They stopped at the house to check on Chloe's father, then walked to the museum. Right across Page Street from the Sons of Norway Mandt Lodge, which had repurposed an old Norwegian Methodist church, the Stoughton Historical Society had repurposed an old Universalist church made of cream-colored brick. Stoughton was best known for the Norwegian culture transported by immigrants who'd started farms on Dane County's fertile prairies, but a Vermont native had established the city. Other Yankee businessmen had built mills along the Yahara River and developed a well-to-do downtown. The historical society did a good job of telling all kinds of stories.

"I was about ten when the society formed," Chloe told Roelke as they mounted the steps. "I think that was in 1960."

"I expect your folks were involved?"

"Oh, yeah. Kari and I spent many an hour here. You should see their collection of Per Lysne pieces."

"Who?"

"He was a Norwegian rosemaler who worked at a wagon factory in town. When business dropped off during the Great Depression, he began rosemaling again, and generally gets credit for reviving the art."

"Well, hunh," Roelke said thoughtfully. "I didn't know it ever needed reviving."

The door was unlocked. Several volunteers were preparing for the evening event. Chloe surrendered the cookie tins to the women setting out paper plates and napkins. "Is Kent around?"

They found the director on the lower level, deep in conversation with intern Trine Moen. "I'm sorry to interrupt," Chloe began.

Trine's smile looked tired, but Kent grinned and hurried over. "It's no interruption. We're planning the next special exhibit. I'm really excited about this one—"

"Kent, I'm afraid we've got some bad news." Chloe took a deep breath and explained.

His broad smile faded. "*What?*" Trine gasped and clapped a hand over her mouth.

"I gave the hospital my dad's phone number," Chloe said. "Hilda doesn't have any family that I know of."

"But she has lots of friends. She's one of our most dedicated volunteers here at the museum." Kent ran a hand over his face.

"She's so sweet!" Trine's eyes filled with tears. "Excuse me."

Chloe watched the young woman hurry away. "I'm sorry to bear such bad tidings."

"Trine's having boyfriend trouble, so she was already a tad emotional," Kent murmured, sounding distracted. "I overheard a bit of a phone conversation." He waved a dismissive hand. "Dear God, I'm just sick about Hilda."

"Me too," Chloe said soberly.

"We need a tour guide for tonight," he muttered. "And … what are we going to do about the exhibit?"

"What exhibit?" Roelke asked.

Kent held up a clipboard, displaying notes and sketches. "We're planning a new special exhibit about Hardanger fiddles."

Hardanger fiddles, Chloe thought. *Hardanger*. The word sent a faint quiver down her backbone. It conjured the artifacts found buried in her mother's closet. It conjured the look on Hilda's face as she'd played her fiddle for Marit in the cemetery, and the plaintive tune itself.

"We have a rare opportunity to partner with the Hardanger Folkemuseum."

There was that word again.

"It was Trine's doing, actually," Kent continued. "She worked as a guide there last summer. She and Hilda started talking about music on both sides of the Atlantic. They wrote a proposal for an exhibit, I ran it by the board, and here we are."

No wonder the poor kid was so upset, Chloe thought. "Hilda must have been excited."

"Oh, yes." Kent nodded. "She insisted that we explore the music's social context. What fiddle music meant to the early Norwegian immigrants. How the traditions and tunes evolved over time."

Chloe felt a flicker of her customary passion for museum education, but it was bittersweet.

"We don't want visitors to just come and see Hardanger fiddles, as beautiful as they are." Kent studied his notes. "We want to do some interactive programming. Certainly some fiddle performances."

"How about incorporating folk dance?" Chloe asked. It was much more pleasant to spitball programming ideas than to think about Hilda's injury.

"I'm hoping that the Norwegian Dancers can premiere a new *bygdedans* when the exhibit opens."

"A regional dance," Chloe murmured for Roelke's sake.

Kent turned to him. "Many of the indigenous dances date at least to the nineteenth century, and some are older. Dances, like fiddle tunes, can be lost if care isn't taken to pass them on."

"I imagine so," Roelke said politely.

"Chloe, your mother was a key player in this project," Kent continued. "Trine's former boss at the Hardanger Folkemuseum is an authority on fiddle music. The museum has the best collection of fiddles in the world. Hilda and Marit got excited, and next thing I knew I was writing a grant application to send someone to visit the Hardanger Folkemuseum to learn about fiddling and dance traditions." Kent began to pace. "But we've lost Marit. And now with Hilda out of the picture, at least for a while..."

Chloe tried to think of something helpful. "Why don't *you* go to Norway, Kent?"

"My parents need a lot of help these days, so I can't get away. Hilda wasn't up to the trip. That's why I turned to Marit."

"But... my mother wasn't a musician. Or a dancer." This seemed a stretch, even for Mom. *Unless*... Chloe paused as a new possibility struck. Had her mother been enticed by the word *Hardanger*?

"After years in the Dancers' parents' group, she knew a lot," Kent was saying. "She had experience interviewing elderly informants. She spoke Norwegian. She was comfortable traveling in rural Norway. It would have been perfect... Well. We'll figure something—"

A loud crash echoed from above.

"Oh Lord, what now," Kent muttered. "Excuse me." He trotted from the room.

Chloe lifted a hand in vague farewell. Thoughts were flashing in her head like fireflies.

"Chloe? You coming?" Roelke was already halfway down the aisle. She caught up, but grabbed his arm. His eyes narrowed. "What's going on?"

"Roelke…" She hesitated, then plunged ahead. "Want to go to Norway?"

His eyebrows shot skyward. "Me?"

"Us."

"*What?*" He shook his head. "We can't afford to go to Norway."

"I think we can." Words tumbled out faster as the idea took hold. "My mom's money can pay your way, and Kent offered me the museum's grant money if I'd go do the research he needs."

"But—"

"*Hardanger*, Roelke! It's an omen."

Roelke didn't do omens. "It's a coincidence."

"What are the odds that Kent would be planning an exhibit about Hardanger fiddles right at the time I find evidence that suggests my mother's people came from Hardanger? What if my mom had decided she finally wanted to learn more about her roots? Maybe that's even why she wanted to take me to Norway—she thought my research skills might come in handy! She didn't live long enough to figure it out, but if *we* go…"

"Hold on." Roelke's dark eyes reflected concern. "You're moving awfully fast."

"But it feels like everything is falling into place. I want to go, Roelke, and I'd really like it if you come with me."

He looked away, gathering his thoughts. "What about your job? Isn't this a crazy time of year for you?"

"Well… yes," she admitted. This *was* a crazy time at Old World Wisconsin. The site officially opened on May first, and April days were crammed with training sessions for seasonal staff. She also faced the enormous job of de-winterizing all of the fifty or so historic structures—removing dustcovers from furniture, returning those pieces she had deemed too fragile to leave off-season in unheated buildings, rehanging pictures. "I couldn't go right this minute. But once the site is actually open, I'm over my biggest hurdle. I've got plenty of vacation hours."

"You think Petty would agree?"

Chloe rolled her eyes. Site director Ralph Petty, a misogynistic megalomaniac, was the bane of her professional existence. It wasn't a pleasant situation, but she could occasionally use it to her advantage. "Nothing makes Petty happier than seeing my taillights disappearing in the distance," she reminded Roelke. "How about you?"

Roelke tapped one thumb against his thigh. "I've got vacation time too. I'd have to talk to Chief Naborski, of course. But I can probably make arrangements."

Chloe stared at him, feeling the world turn upside-down. Was she being irrational? Hadn't she said just yesterday that a trip to Norway was impossible? But it did feel right. "Oh my God, Roelke. Let's go find Kent. I think we're going to Norway."

FOUR

ONE MONTH LATER, THEIR plane landed in Bergen and settled into a smooth taxi. Chloe felt Roelke, in the next seat, interlace his fingers with hers. "We made it to Norway," he murmured.

"We did." Chloe blew out a long breath. Even after their tickets had been purchased, she'd almost despaired of accomplishing what needed to be done—getting Old World Wisconsin open, planting her vegetable garden, driving to Stoughton for meetings with Kent and Trine.

She'd visited her dad as often as possible too. She'd summoned her courage and related what she'd heard and suspected about Mom's birth. "She never said a word to me," Dad had said slowly, clearly stunned. That was the end of the conversation.

Chloe had also visited Hilda, who was still in a coma. It had been caused, the doctor had concluded, by a traumatic head injury—probably a result of falling against the hearth—which had led to epidural hemorrhage. She might have tripped. She might have been pushed. The not knowing haunted Chloe. Had it been an accident? A random home invasion by a thief? She couldn't imagine anyone wanting to deliberately harm Hilda Omdahl.

The doctor had explained that most people emerged from comas within four weeks. "Of course, a coma can last for years," he'd said, "leaving the patient in a persistent vegetative state—"

"I've never liked that term." Chloe's voice was sharp.

He looked startled. "Well. We'll hope for the best."

On her last visit, Chloe had held Hilda's hand and told her all about the trip. "I'm going since you and Mom can't, Aunt Hilda. I'll learn as much as I can about Hardanger fiddles, especially the social history of fiddle music. We'll try hard to make the special exhibit and programming here in Stoughton everything you want it to be."

Hilda appeared to be sleeping peacefully.

Chloe had kissed the older woman's cheek. "I love you, Aunt Hilda. I'll see you when I get home."

Now, the plane came to a halt. Metallic clicks sounded as impatient passengers ignored the warning lights and unbuckled their seatbelts. Chloe wanted to, but figured Roelke would scold.

You'll be in Hardanger soon enough, she told herself. An anticipatory shiver skittered down her spine. She'd left the *tine* and doll at home, but the two textiles were cocooned in the yellow daypack serving as her carry-on. Chloe had wanted to show them to the curator at Vesterheim Norwegian-American Museum in Iowa, but she hadn't found time to make the trip. However, she'd called and described both pieces. "We have lots and lots of white Hardanger embroidery," the curator had told her. "And one piece of blackwork embroidery that sounds similar to yours. It was made in Aga." Chloe had checked a map and discovered that Aga was a hamlet in the Hardanger region—a nebulous clue, perhaps, but one more thing to suggest that she was on the right track.

And, she was arriving in Norway with one *real* piece of information. She'd finally tracked down the whereabouts of the Martin Luther Orphanage records, which had at some point been transferred to a Lutheran home for troubled children in northeast Wisconsin. She'd called and was lucky enough to find a staffer willing to dig through old files. "I didn't find much," the woman had reported just the day before. "But I did find a record of a Marit Ann, age almost four months, being brought to the orphanage on September 13, 1920. Three weeks later she was adopted by Nels and Maria Kallerud."

"So it's true," Chloe had breathed, a bit dazed to have Birgitta's story verified. "Is there any other information?"

"Just the name of the woman who surrendered her. Amalie Sveinsdatter."

Amalie, Svein's daughter, Chloe translated silently. Suddenly her mother's lineage felt more real. Was Amalie Marit's mother—her own maternal grandmother?

"And a note says that Amalie didn't speak English, only Norwegian. That's probably why the records are so minimal."

Chloe twisted the phone cord absently. A Norwegian woman in 1920 who didn't speak any English? Since the note pinned to the doll's petticoat had also been written in Norwegian, it seemed very likely that Amalie was newly arrived.

Chloe had thanked the staffer profusely before hanging up. She wanted nothing more than to drop everything and grab a metaphorical shovel so she could dig through records at the State Historical Society of Wisconsin and the Norwegian-American Genealogical Center. There was surely information to discover . . . but she was about to leave for Norway and simply didn't have time to scroll through miles of microfilm. In desperation she called another friend of her mother's, genealogist Rosemary Rossebo, and asked if she'd be willing to help.

"Of course!" Rosemary assured her. "I'm retired now, but I still love the hunt. Stoughton was long settled by 1920. Most Norwegians who arrived in the area during the teens and twenties settled in Madison, especially on the East Side where there were lots of factories. Perhaps Amalie only traveled to Stoughton to give her child to the orphanage. Or Amalie might have joined family there, or heard about work opportunities. Some women worked at the hospital as laundresses, for example."

Chloe was already overwhelmed.

"I'll search passenger lists for any ships traveling from Norway to the United States in 1920," Rosemary had said. "And if I don't find Amalie in 1920, I'll work backwards." Chloe had provided a fax number for the hotel in Utne, Norway, where she and Roelke would be staying.

Now she stared out the plane window, lost in thought. Had Amalie left Norway with Marit on the way or in her arms, and fallen on hard times in Wisconsin? Had Amalie been widowed? Or had she been a young unwed mother, unable to care for her child?

I might never know, Chloe thought, but I came here with a name. Someone specific to search for. It was a start.

The "Fasten Seatbelt" lights finally went out. Passengers surged into the aisles, dragging carry-ons and snapping open overhead compartments. Chloe felt a tingle of excitement. She loved digging for the stories of any women long gone, but this felt very different. She'd come to search for her own ancestors. She could hardly wait to begin.

After Chloe and Roelke cleared customs and claimed their baggage, she checked the local time. "We're a little later than expected, but the curator should be waiting for us."

Roelke yawned. "Are you sure a meeting is a smart idea? A little sleep would be good."

Exhaustion was pulling at Chloe too, but she tried to will it away. "Sonja is flying to Stockholm later this afternoon for some conference," she reminded him. "Once we get to the Hardanger Folkemuseum, I'll work with the director and a grad student studying traditional dances, but Sonja is the textile expert. This is my only chance to show her the pieces I found in Mom's closet."

When Chloe and Roelke had finally dragged their luggage to the designated airport café, Chloe was sorry to see that it was jammed. But a woman wearing the promised red sweater at a nearby table stood up and waved.

"That's her," Chloe said.

Sonja Gullickson was in her mid-thirties, and striking. Intelligent green eyes sparkled with self-assurance. Light brown hair wisped from a carelessly stylish twist behind her head to frame her face. The handshake she offered was firm. Her scarlet sweater featured an intricate lace design, and Chloe suspected Sonja had knit it herself.

"Welcome to Norway," Sonja exclaimed with only a slight accent.

After Chloe introduced Roelke, they all settled at the table. Sonja was sipping wine, and Roelke ordered coffee from a harried waitress. "It was kind of you to squeeze this meeting in," Chloe said.

Sonja waved that away with an elegant hand. "Two mysterious antique textiles that might have come from Norway? I'm eager to see them."

Chloe opened her daypack and retrieved the doily and the blackwork cloth carefully packed inside. "I understand your area of expertise is Norwegian textiles."

"By training and by passion."

A kindred soul, Chloe thought as she unwrapped the white doily. "As I said on the phone, this piece of Hardanger embroidery might have been made by one of my ancestors. My mother was adopted. The woman who surrendered her to an orphanage in Wisconsin was named Amalie Sveinsdatter, and I believe this doily was surrendered with her. I suspect my mother's family came from somewhere in the Hardanger region." She spread the protective cloth she'd brought over the table before displaying the treasure.

Sonja leaned close. "Oh, that's *quite* nice. As I'm sure you know, *Hardangersaum* involves both cutting threads and drawing threads together to create openwork designs. This piece balances both techniques beautifully. And ..." She turned the doily over. "The back looks as good as the front."

Chloe felt a flush of pride, as if she'd made the doily herself. "Any guesses as to how old it might be?"

Sonja tipped her head, considering. "The delicate work is reminiscent of older styles—mid-eighteen-hundreds, perhaps. But the gauge of the cotton suggests the first decade or two of this century.

After the Victorian period, when everything was fussy, designs began to simplify around 1920. The scale got larger. There was less filling in the little open blocks."

"Some of the open blocks here are filled in," Chloe observed, trying to keep up. She certainly recognized Hardanger cutwork embroidery when she saw it—the satin stitch kloster blocks, the pulled and drawn threadwork—but she'd never studied the design nuances.

"Yes, and the maker took the time to decorate the other open blocks with these delicate picots." Sonja pointed at a series of minuscule loops adding texture and depth to the doily's openwork areas. "My best guess? The piece is only fifty or sixty years old, but the maker was quite skilled."

"Cool." Roelke sounded impressed, although Chloe wasn't sure if he was admiring Sonja's analysis or the unknown stitcher's talent. Chloe was impressed with both.

"*Kaffe.*" The waitress arrived with a tray and delivered two steaming mugs. Chloe snatched the doily from the table and tucked it away, being careful not to reuse the same fold lines.

"First things first," Sonja said firmly, and carefully pushed the mugs and her wineglass to one corner of the table.

Chloe extracted the second package. "The workmanship on this one isn't on par with the doily, but I think it's older." She unfolded the linen rectangle decorated with geometric black designs.

"My God." Sonja's eyes went wide. "A *handaplagg.*"

Chloe had never heard the term. "A what?"

Sonja made an impatient gesture, as if everyone should know. "A hand cloth. Women once covered their hands with them when they went to church. Except for weddings, the practice died out in the mid-eighteen-hundreds."

"So ... this is pretty old, then?"

"I'd say so." Sonja hadn't taken her gaze from the *handaplagg*. "Look how fine the linen is—that's another clue. Maybe ... fifty count?"

"Yikes." Fifty threads to the inch, she meant. The last cotton Chloe had bought for an embroidery project was twenty-two count.

"This was likely made in the seventeen hundreds. It's a very valuable artifact."

Roelke whistled.

"Is this type of work especially known locally, or is it done all over Norway?" Chloe asked.

"I'd say this one is particular to the Hardanger region. Similar cloths have been found in other parts of Hordaland County, but most especially in Hardanger."

One more piece of evidence suggesting my family roots are in Hardanger, Chloe thought with a familiar quiver in her chest. Something about this piece affected her. Every time she took it from its tissue shroud she felt the same frisson of—of *something* undefined ...

"Do you mind if I snap a photo?" Sonja pulled a camera from her bag and took several shots before reaching for her wineglass.

Time is short, Chloe reminded herself. "The embroidery appears to be unfinished." She gestured toward the unadorned end of the rectangle.

"No, no, it's complete," Sonja assured her. "That plain part hung behind the hands, so there was no point in adding decoration."

"Oh." Chloe nodded. "What do you make of these errors?" She pointed toward the motifs that hadn't been properly centered.

"They only add to the charm of the piece." Sonja glanced at her watch, frowned slightly, and tossed back the remains of her wine. "My flight will start boarding soon. Anyway, the woman who created this *handaplagg* was expressing herself, yes? The ideas were more important than achieving perfection in the stitches."

Chloe frowned, perplexed. "The ideas ..."

"The symbols." Sonja was gathering her handbag and carry-on. "I'm sorry, I really must go." She glanced at Chloe, seemed to recognize her confusion, and paused. "It's as if someone wrote a brilliant essay, but the handwriting wasn't perfect. What does it matter, if the thoughts are clear?"

That made certain sense, Chloe admitted. "But what thoughts ..." she began, then swallowed the rest. Sonja was already on her feet.

"I hope we can talk again," Sonja said. "It was very good to meet you both." With that, she hurried away.

Roelke felt a little better after downing the coffee. "Was that helpful?"

"It was." Chloe swirled the dregs of her caffeine in her mug. "It was certainly nice to hear that the *Hardangersaum* doily shows good workmanship. And Sonja thought it was made about the time my mother was born."

Roelke wasn't sure what she was getting at. "Does that have some significance?"

"Well ... I don't know," Chloe acknowledged. "But it might. I'm not sure I totally understood what Sonja said about the blackwork piece, though. What ideas was the stitcher trying to convey back in seventeen hundred whatever?"

"How could we ever know?" Roelke considered the woman he loved. He still had some doubts about the trip. She was so enthused, so hopeful ... he didn't want her to be disappointed if she couldn't trace Marit's family here in Norway. "Maybe the museum director will have more information for you tomorrow."

"Maybe. One thing is clear, though. While the doily is special, the *handaplagg* is obviously a *real* treasure. Made in the seventeen hundreds!" Chloe's eyes glinted. "Can you imagine?"

"Not really," he admitted. He had a lot less experience imagining old times than she did. "But it's very cool."

"Well." Chloe pushed back her chair, shrugged into the yellow daypack, and reached for her suitcase. "You ready to head out? Let's go find the rental car place."

They eeled into the flow of business travelers trotting past with leather briefcases, jet-lagged tourists dragging bulging suitcases, harried parents trying to herd their children. Roelke veered to avoid a slow-moving toddler.

Chloe pointed ahead to a sign for ground transportation and raised her voice. "I think it's that way—" Her voice broke as she stumbled and crashed inelegantly to the floor.

"Chloe!" Roelke crouched beside her, his brain filled with visions of bones broken before they'd even left the airport. "Are you all right?"

"*O-ow*." Wincing she sat up and nodded. He offered a hand, and she gingerly staggered to her feet. "Someone knocked me down!"

A ring of the concerned or the curious was already forming. Roelke scanned the crowd without seeing anyone hovering with a guilty or apologetic expression. "Did you get a look at the guy?"

She shook her head. "Someone just grabbed my pack from behind and yanked it really hard."

An elderly woman, looking worried, said something in Norwegian. "Thank you, I'm fine," Chloe said. "Really." She smiled an artificial smile until the bystanders were again on their way, then looked grimly at Roelke. "It didn't feel like an accident."

Roelke did not like the sound of that. He should have been paying more attention.

"If I hadn't had the front strap hooked, I might have lost everything! My money, my credit card, my passport…" Her eyes filled with panic. "Oh my God, Roelke, he might have ended up with my family heirlooms!"

"Come on," he said, well aware that they were impeding traffic. "We should find a security guard and report this."

She shook her head. "No. It happened so fast…" The panic faded to a scowl directed down the corridor, evidently in the direction the SOB had disappeared.

In an odd way, that was reassuring. Roelke could deal with an angry Chloe better than an upset Chloe.

"And since they didn't get away with anything," she added, "there really isn't anything to report. Let's just get going, okay?"

Roelke hesitated. It went against the cop grain to just walk away. But… she was right. He could imagine a guard's polite response: *You didn't see what the man looked like? Perhaps he was trying to rob you, or perhaps it was just an unfortunate accident. Someone in a hurry…* Roelke contented himself with touching her cheek, giving the strap on her daypack a little tug to make sure it was still secure. "If you're sure."

"I'm sure. All I want to do right now is get on the road." She started walking again. But when he caught up with her, she gave him an anxious look, her lower lip caught between her teeth. "I know that losing my cash and credit card and camera on day one would cause colossal problems. But it's horrifying to think he might have gotten my textiles. They may be the only things left of my Norwegian ancestors."

FIVE

Gudrun—May 1838

Gudrun leaned closer to the window as rose streaked the sky over the western mountains. Her eyes were not as sharp as they'd once been, her fingers not as nimble with the needle. But she was almost finished updating the *handaplagg* she had received long ago from her mother's mother, adding a few special touches for Lisbet, her oldest son's youngest daughter.

Lisbet, Gudrun's favorite grandchild, was getting married tomorrow. They would no longer share daily chores and walks and whispered confidences. Is that why I'm sensing shadows? Gudrun wondered. She'd been filled with a sense of foreboding all day. That afternoon she'd carefully polished the silver bangles dangling from the family's bridal crown. When Gudrun had married seventy-three years earlier, everyone understood that the silver's soft tinkling would scare away malevolent spirits. Everyone understood that the pastor covered the right hands of the couple to protect the marriage from evil. Some people today scoffed at such ideas, which only compelled Gudrun to do what she could to protect her family.

She glanced across the room, where her daughter-in-law was organizing food for the wedding feast. Three other families shared a courtyard with theirs, and neighbors had been stopping by the farm all day with gifts of *lefse* and butter, salmon and sausages, many-layered almond cakes and sponge cakes made festive with beaten cream and fresh fruit. Lisbet's sharp-tongued mother was actually humming, clearly pleased with the contributions ... and oblivious to Gudrun's unease.

Gudrun had perceived things unseen since she was a young girl. Sometimes she felt strong emotions lingering in old buildings—anger, fear, grief, joy. Sometimes she sensed some momentous event that had yet to unfold. She couldn't explain, predict, or control such impressions. But they were very real.

Her own grandmother had experienced such things too, and told Gudrun secret stories about the old times. She had impressed upon Gudrun the importance of passing on this knowledge to the right female descendant. "Sometimes the gift passes a generation by," the old woman had explained. Gudrun hadn't glimpsed the gift in any of her own daughters, or in Lisbet's older sisters. She thought that Lisbet, always eager to hear stories about the old ways, might be the one.

Usually Gudrun accepted her gift without disquiet. But today, she thought as she squinted at the fine linen, I need to understand what's troubling me.

She wasn't worried about the couple, even though Lisbet and Lars had made the match themselves instead of letting their elders settle things. It had taken some time to convince Lisbet's parents of its suitability.

"He is the fourth son, with no prospects," Lisbet's mother had protested. "Don't be a fool! You will have to scrape and struggle for every mouthful."

Lisbet merely shrugged. "We'll manage."

"He has no land," Gudrun's son had added. "How can you marry with no farm?"

"Lars fishes in every spare moment to earn money of his own," Lisbet said quietly. "It will take time, but we *will* have a bit of land one day."

Gudrun saw the longing in the girl's eyes, so she'd stayed silent during the early months of discussion, sizing up Lars for herself. Lars was not a particularly handsome young man. He had a stocky build, a crooked smile, the big rough hands of a farmer. But his gaze was steady. He spoke of his ambitions with quiet assurance. He looked at Lisbet with a mix of affection and awe, as if he could hardly believe his good fortune.

In the end it had been Gudrun who settled things. "He'll do," she'd told her son. "Lars is a hard worker. He'll take good care of Lisbet." Gudrun admired Lars for daring to work for what he wanted despite the difficulties, and for proving himself.

And yet . . . she felt trouble gathering, like black clouds building before a storm.

Perhaps I've just lived too long, seen too much, Gudrun thought. Recent years had brought bitter rifts to the communities clinging to the steep land along the fjord, and she didn't want discord to taint the wedding. Just that afternoon a visiting neighbor woman had wrinkled her nose toward kegs of ale and *akevitt* other families had donated for the feast. She was a member of the new *totalafholdsforeninger,* a total abstinence society formed after a new law allowed liquor production at home.

Gudrun snorted as she knotted her black silk thread. She didn't appreciate belligerent drunkenness, and she'd seen brawls mar more than one wedding party. But how could a family celebrate a marriage without drinking to the new couple's health?

The abstainers were part of the religious movement that had been spreading through rural Norway for some years. Last month a wandering preacher proclaiming "the living faith," as some called it, had held a revival meeting in nearby Aga. Gudrun had heard tales of men weeping, women wailing, sober people condemning themselves. The movement was part of the Lutheran tradition—but it was also forbidden. Only one church was legal in Norway. Membership was mandatory, and it was against the law to gather for worship without a Church of Norway pastor present. Longtime neighbors quarreled about God's true intentions in hushed but strident tones on the fish docks, when hanging hay to dry—even in the Kinsarvik churchyard after service, when rural folk lingered to share news, conduct business, and settle accounts.

Gudrun spread the cloth she'd been stitching over her lap. It was old, but she'd cared for it well. The linen was still crisp; the original black embroidery silk still dark and even. Her own grandmother had stitched her blessings and fears into this cloth. Most of the symbolism Gudrun understood, but she'd been young when her grandmother died. Are there messages in the patterns that I've missed? she wondered, touching the old threads with a gnarled finger. Have I misinterpreted something I'm meant to pass on? Will coming generations understand what *I've* contributed?

Her own stitches blended well with what had been done so long ago. She'd added multiple tree motifs to symbolize the connections of all life—past and present, good and evil, pagan and Christian. And she'd added a female figure to honor the *disir,* spirits who guarded women and linked their families from one generation to the next throughout time.

Gudrun placed both of her palms on the cloth. Closing her eyes, she sent a prayer for protection into the fine linen…

Lisbet burst through the door, startling Gudrun from her reverie. The young woman's face glowed with happiness as she regarded the food, the bridal crown nestled in its box. She strode to her grandmother's chair so exuberantly that her braids swung back and forth. Gudrun barely had time to fold her gift away so it would be a surprise tomorrow.

"I can hardly believe the day has finally come!" Lisbet kissed Gudrun on the cheek.

By the time Lisbet had been born, six other children were already underfoot. Lisbet's mother had been too tired, too busy to spare particular time and attention to the new baby, so Gudrun had taken a primary role in raising the child. The old stories had always helped Gudrun make sense of the world, and she'd done her best to school Lisbet in those as well as practical skills.

I hope I did enough, Gudrun thought now, for I am out of time. She took Lisbet's hand and smiled, trying to hide her presentiment of disaster.

SIX

"Holy Mother of God!" Roelke yelped as a tour bus roared past with approximately three-quarters of an inch to spare. His mouth had gone dry and he swallowed hard, trying to regain his composure.

"Would you like me to drive?" Chloe asked.

"No."

"Your knuckles are white, Roelke. Take a break."

"No," he repeated, although he did ease his death grip on the steering wheel. He was not enjoying his first international driving experience. What had looked on the map like a relatively easy jaunt to the ferry that would take them to Utne was actually a narrow, twisting road clinging to the mountains plunging into a fjord. At times there was room for two vehicles. At times there was not. With luck there was a small pullout where one driver could swerve to avoid a head-on collision. If not, somebody had to back up fast.

"Maybe we should have rented a VW," she mused. "A Beetle would have been smaller."

"Smaller is not safer." Roelke had insisted on a boxy Volvo sedan even though it was more expensive. The rental agent had said that Norwegian police drove Volvos, which sealed the deal.

They'd also paid extra to put both names on the rental agreement, but he intended to do all the driving. Chloe had professional obligations. She was also on an intensely personal quest. He couldn't contribute to her research, but he could at least take the wheel.

"I'm sorry the driving is challenging, but at least the scenery is gorgeous." Chloe scooched down and propped her toes on the dashboard. "So many waterfalls."

Since Roelke didn't dare take his gaze from the road, he couldn't comment on waterfalls.

"Why haven't I ever come before?" she wondered. "As an adult, I mean."

He was pleased that she seemed to have forgotten the ugly incident at the airport. She hadn't fretted about Hilda during the drive, either. Chloe's voice was happy, tinged with wonder, validating his resolve to be chauffeur.

"Seriously," she was saying, "how could I have lived in Europe for five years and never bothered to explore Norway?"

He didn't mention the obvious—that she'd craved space between herself and her mom, Marit All-Things-Norwegian Kallerud. "Well, you're here now. And I'm glad I got to—oh, *hell*." He'd just rounded a curve to confront not only an oncoming truck, but a string of bicyclists wobbling up the hill.

Two hours later, from the stress-free upper deck of a car ferry, they watched Utne grow more distinct in front of them. "There's the Hardanger Folkemuseum!" Chloe pointed to a low brick structure overlooking the fjord. Most buildings in the little hamlet were lined along the shore, with a few nestled farther up the mountain. Many were painted a tidy white and roofed with what looked like gray slate, including the pretty church watching over the village. The slopes faded from the middle green hues of deciduous trees to darker conifers above, capped with treeless areas of stone and scree and snowy ridgelines. The early evening was tinged with blue, but in this place, with the summer solstice approaching, darkness was still hours away.

Roelke tried to remember what Chloe had told him about Utne. The village was situated in the Hardanger region of Hordaland County. It marked the northern tip of the Folgefonna peninsula between the Hardangerfjord and one of its branches, the Sørfjord. Now that he was out on the water, free to soak in their surroundings, he had to agree with what she'd said earlier. The Hardanger region was jaw-droppingly beautiful.

The ferry docked right in front of their hotel. He found a small parking lot down the street, and they grabbed luggage from the trunk. Almost at once, though, Chloe stopped walking.

"Something wrong?"

"This place feels familiar, Roelke. Like I just shrugged into a comfortable old sweater."

The Utne Hotel was a white four-story frame building fronted by a picket fence and roofed in red tiles. Roses climbed along the lower wall. Geraniums and petunias spilled from window boxes above. "This place looks old," Roelke observed as they started up the steps.

"It opened in 1722 as the Utne Inn. Some say it's Norway's oldest continuously operating inn."

When they stepped inside Chloe paused again, head tipped slightly to one side. Roelke watched her, knowing she was assessing the historic inn's … what was the word? Vibe? Aura? He couldn't explain it, but he'd seen her impressions proved true more than once. "Anything?" he asked, hoping she hadn't picked up on something bad.

But she shook her head. "Just a faint impression of busyness. And something … something pleasant. A sense of hospitality, maybe." She smiled. "Let's go check in."

The proprietress, a stately white-haired woman named Ulrikke Moe, welcomed them warmly. "Klara?" she called over her shoulder. A young woman with wheat-colored braids and a radiant smile appeared. She wore a dress vaguely reminiscent of a *bunad*, but much more practical, with an ornate silver necklace hanging over the blouse.

"This is Klara Evenstad," Ulrikke said. "She'll take you up to Room 15."

Klara grabbed Chloe and Roelke's daypacks and led them up two flights of narrow stairs. "This is the only room on the top floor that overlooks the fjords," Klara explained as she opened their door. "I hope this will suit?"

"We obviously have the best room in the inn," Chloe assured the young woman as they set their suitcases down. "It's exciting to know that guests have been staying here for over two hundred and fifty years."

The last of Roelke's drive-induced stress seeped away. He loved seeing Chloe so content.

"Do you like history?" Klara asked.

"It's my passion," Chloe assured her.

"I love history too!" Klara's *We are kindred souls* smile revealed a gap between her two front teeth. "I grew up in Utne, so please let me know if you need any information." She deposited the packs in the tiny closet and left them alone.

Roelke was dubiously eyeing the twin beds, pushed together to make a double. "Footboards. We're both on the tall side for footboards."

"Who cares, when we have the best room?" Chloe asked happily, as if the prospect of bruised toes was of no importance. "Look at this view!" She crossed to the open window and put her hands on the sill.

Then she jerked away as if the wood had burned her palms. "Geez!"

Damn. "What was *that*? Are you okay?"

"I—I'm not sure." She eyed the window. "I felt this overwhelming flash of sadness. No, it was more like … despair."

Roelke felt a sinking sensation as he imagined them packing up, trying to explain to Ulrikke Moe why they had to check out ten minutes after checking in, hitting the narrow road again in search of new lodging.

Chloe rubbed her arms. "It only lasted for a second, though. Just when I was right by the window."

He eyed her. "You're all right now?"

She took a deep breath, considering. Finally she nodded. "I'm good. It's not the whole room. I think I just need to stay away from the window." She took another step backward, nodded decisively, and smiled at him in a way that twisted his heart. "Oh, Roelke. Are we lucky, or what?"

———

When Chloe woke the next morning she was relieved to discover that she'd slept soundly. No further jolts of heartrending despair. She wondered if someone had climbed to this room to watch over the fjord for a husband or lover lost in a storm. Or maybe someone watched passengers disembark from the ferries without seeing their loved one. I'll likely never know, she thought, but I will stay clear of the window.

She and Roelke enjoyed a sumptuous breakfast buffet in the hotel's dining room. Klara was circulating among the guest tables, offering coffee and whisking away dirty plates. When she stopped to top off their mugs, the light glimmered on her silver necklace.

Chloe leaned closer. The necklace's main element was an engraved disc covered with delicate filigree work. A Maltese-style cross hung below, and a number of leaf shapes dangled from both pieces. "Your necklace is gorgeous, Klara! And it looks like an antique."

"It is. I don't know how old it is, though."

Fine silver wasn't Chloe's thing, but to women like Mom, ornate jewelry was essential when wearing a *bunad*. "Is it a family heirloom?"

"No, a gift." Her cheeks flushed pink as plum blossoms. "From my boyfriend."

"Well, your boyfriend obviously thinks the world of you."

Klara ducked her head shyly, but she looked pleased.

As the young woman moved on, Chloe spread cloudberry jam on a piece of homemade bread. "Roelke, you're welcome to come with me to the museum today, you know."

"I don't want to intrude on your meeting with the director. I thought I'd do some exploring on foot. After the flight and being in the car, a long walk sounds good." Roelke forked up some pickled herring, sniffed it, then tasted. "Well, hunh. Interesting."

After the meal, Chloe had only a short walk to the Hardanger Folkemuseum. Clouds hung low today, softening the terrain to an ombre mist of blues and grays. The mountains behind the village and across the fjords imparted a sense of haven and safety that she hadn't expected.

"Mom," she whispered, "I'm sorry we couldn't come here together." She let the sadness come, and wrapped it around thoughts of Aunt Hilda too. Then she walked on up the hill to the museum.

Director Ellinor Falk had a sleek cap of silver hair framing a round face. Her flowing green skirt and black clogs suggested a comfy-professional style. "I was so sorry to hear that your mother died," she said in greeting, clasping Chloe's hand. "We'd been corresponding as Marit planned her research trip, and I'd looked forward to meeting her." Ellinor's blue eyes held Chloe's gaze. "How nice that you could take her place."

As if I could ever take Mom's place, Chloe thought, but she appreciated the sentiment. "I'm glad to be here."

Ellinor beckoned Chloe into her office, a small space brightened by a row of potted plants in the window and posters from past exhibits. "There's a lot to keep you busy during your visit, but I haven't forgotten that you're also here to look for family."

"I know it won't be easy," Chloe said. "The whole naming thing..." There was no standard for surnames until the 1920s, when a law was passed requiring all Norwegians to choose a permanent family name. Before that, members of the same family often had different last names. Many surnames reflected a person's occupation or their farm name. If people moved, their name might change.

Ellinor smiled sympathetically. "It does create some confusion."

"What I need most is to identify a hometown for the woman I'm trying to find." Chloe lifted her palms, acknowledging that without more to go on, she was unlikely to get very far in the short time she had. "Her name is Amalie Sveinsdatter."

"You should talk with a friend of mine. Martin Brandvold was pastor here in Utne for many years. He knows everyone, and he knows what records are kept where. I'm sure he'll be glad to chat with you." She passed over a slip of paper with the name and phone number.

"Thank you."

"Before I forget ..." Ellinor picked up a book from her desk. "This is a local history written in English. You're welcome to borrow it."

"Thanks!" Chloe tucked it away.

"Were you able to connect with Sonja in Bergen yesterday?"

"Briefly." Chloe settled back into the guest chair. "We had a good talk, and I learned some things about the two embroidered heirlooms I mentioned on the phone."

"Sonja knows her textiles. My particular area of interest is folk music. How much do you know about Hardanger fiddles?"

"Not a lot," Chloe allowed humbly.

"Let me give you an overview." Ellinor looked pleased by the opportunity. "This region is, of course, the birthplace of the *hardingfele*—the Hardanger fiddle. They have understrings that resonate when the top four are played. That gives the instruments a unique sound."

"Haunting, I'd call it," Chloe offered.

Ellinor nodded. "The oldest known *hardingfele* dates to 1651. I believe it's safe to say that the tradition goes back even further. And while the fiddles themselves are valued for their sound, and worth study as works of art, what fascinates me most is the role fiddlers had in rural society."

"Me too." Chloe suppressed a wriggle of anticipation. "My Wisconsin colleagues want to explore how that role might have changed —or not—in the New World."

"In this region, talented fiddlers were vital members of any community. They played a ritual role in weddings and funerals and other gatherings."

Chloe pulled a notebook from her daypack and began scribbling.

"It is important to interview every *kilde* we can find…" Ellinor paused. "You would say a source, I think? Someone who passes tunes to others. Some have been played for hundreds of years, but never written down."

"That's amazing," Chloe agreed. "But… I've heard that some people branded fiddles as 'the devil's instrument.'"

"That's true." Ellinor picked up a pencil and tapped it against the desk. "Folklore from pagan times connected the *hardingfele* with evil. Many people believed that the best players learned their skill from the devil himself."

"Yikes," Chloe said soberly, picturing a superb musician being persecuted instead of celebrated.

"The real issue for the people objecting to fiddles in the 1800s, I think, was that music represented dancing and drinking, which presumably led to careless sex and drunken brawls. Fiddlers were condemned as godless. Fortunately a few musicians refused to be intimidated, which preserved at least some of the tunes and traditions."

"And for the fiddle makers, the skills."

"Exactly." Ellinor leaned forward with an eager expression Chloe recognized—the thrill of the historical hunt. "The names of many famous fiddle makers have survived: Ole Jonsen Jaastad, Isak and Trond Botnen, and of course the Helland brothers—"

"Who settled in Wisconsin," Chloe interjected, glad to have something to contribute. Kent Andreasson had shown her a photograph of Knut and Gunnar Helland posed jauntily in front of their Chippewa Falls fiddle shop.

"Yes." Ellinor nodded. "I want to document any makers who ended up in America, particularly if some of their instruments survived. Trine Moen is looking into that for me while she's in Wisconsin."

"She said to say hello, by the way. I understand that she worked as a guide here last summer?"

"Yes, and I miss her! She's a history major who got along with everyone. Visitors loved her."

In Chloe's experience, a front-line staffer who communicated well with both colleagues and guests trumped being a history major, although that was indeed a nice bonus. "Trine's doing a great job with her internship in Stoughton."

"I'm glad. I helped her with the scholarship application. If a cultural organization hadn't funded her year abroad, she never could have afforded it."

"Most college kids couldn't," Chloe observed. Even if living on ramen noodles and selling plasma twice a week.

"In addition to working here full-time, Trine did chores for some of our village elders. That speaks well of her."

"It does." Chloe knew what it was like to count pennies and juggle jobs, and she respected anyone who did so.

"Anyway, it would be exciting if Trine discovers a reference to any other Hardanger fiddle makers in Wisconsin." Ellinor hesitated, rolling the pencil back and forth in her fingers. "I do hope that next summer I can get her back here, though. She was helping me look for Jørgen Riis."

The name meant nothing to Chloe. "Jørgen Riis?"

"He's my research … um …" She groped for the right word. "Rival?"

"Nemesis?" Chloe suggested. "A constant challenge."

"Yes. Nemesis. Unfortunately, very little is known about him." Ellinor's mouth twisted wryly. "Still, oral tradition paints a vivid picture of a man who crafted exceptional instruments. He made only a few fiddles. Legend says that when he played one of his own instruments, listeners were moved to tears."

For a moment, Chloe thought she heard the faint echo of a Hardanger fiddle. She shivered appreciatively, then remembered where she was. Keep it professional, she told herself.

"Legend also says that Riis had indeed sold his soul to the devil," Ellinor was saying. "And his name is often mentioned in connection with a murder—"

"A murder?" Chloe blinked. "Seriously?"

"Who knows?" Ellinor lifted her hands, palms up. "I know for sure that he spent some time in the area, but he disappeared from the historical record at a relatively young age sixty-seven years ago. It's possible that he simply moved on—to other parts of Norway or Europe, or to America. Many of the fiddlers were itinerant, traveling widely to share their tunes and learn new ones." She looked pensive. "And yet..."

"And yet?" Chloe prompted.

"The stories didn't disappear with him," Ellinor mused. "I started interviewing local elders about Riis decades ago. Everyone had their own version of the story. One person said Riis committed murder. Another believed Riis was the victim. I've heard that the murder involved a lover, and I've heard that it involved a pastor."

Chloe was intrigued—who wouldn't be?—but decided not to dwell on the unsavory bit of Riis's story. "Do you have any of his fiddles in your collection?"

"We have one. Riis always included a tiny, elaborate *R* in the designs inked on his fiddles. This one was donated a decade after the museum was established in 1911. But unfortunately the provenance information is... limited."

Been there, Chloe thought. Nothing was more frustrating than discovering that an amazing artifact had been accessioned into a museum collection without complete records. Sometimes no information was available, of course. But sometimes early curator-types had been more interested in collecting objects than recording pertinent stories.

"I've also seen another *hardingfele*, still in private hands, that was made by Jørgen Riis. Other than his initial, it shows no real similarity to our fiddle... but that only supports the theory that he labored long over each instrument, making every one unique, instead of... what do you Americans say? Cranking them out?"

Chloe smiled. "Yes."

"The most persistent tale speaks of his finest fiddle, supposedly hidden away."

"Because some anti-fiddle zealots believed it was the devil's instrument?"

"So they say." Ellinor shrugged. "Let's go up to the music exhibit, and I'll show you the fiddle that was made by Riis." She rose and led the way.

Treasures beckoned in every direction. On the second-floor corridor a "Folk Art in Focus" exhibit displayed photographs featuring spectacular close-ups of decorated objects—the satiny kloster blocks of *Hardangersaum* cutwork embroidery, the intricate geometry of a chip-carved plate, the meticulous beadwork covering a *bunad*'s bodice insert, the astonishingly tiny pleats in a woman's headdress.

"Chloe?" Ellinor called.

You can come back later, Chloe promised herself, and scurried after the director into a permanent gallery. The Hardanger fiddles displayed in a long case made Chloe's jaw dangle. "Oh, *my*."

"This is the one credited to Jørgen Riis." Ellinor pointed. "The face is spruce, the sides and back are black alder, and the pegs are applewood. The mother-of-pearl came from local shellfish."

Chloe studied the elaborate designs inked onto the fiddle's sides, the exquisite inlay on the fingerboard. "It's remarkable."

"I agree." Ellinor glanced at her watch. "I'm expecting a phone call in about ten minutes. Why don't you take the rest of the morning to explore the museum exhibits. At two this afternoon a guide is taking an American tour group through the open-air part of the museum. You're welcome to join in."

"Great."

"On Thursday afternoon I'm meeting a colleague at our sister site, the Voss Folkemuseum. They're designing an exhibit about folk music for their new museum building. It will be a quick trip, but you're welcome to come along."

This is getting better and better, Chloe thought. "I'd like that."

"Also, Torstein Landvik, who's documenting regional music and dance traditions, is eager to meet you. He had a class this morning, but he's driving out from Bergen and should be here by three."

"It's kind of him to make the trip," Chloe said. Getting places by car in Norway took longer, it seemed, than it might appear.

"He has a cousin nearby, so he has a place to stay. And . . ." Ellinor smiled wryly. "His girlfriend lives here. They met last summer when she was one of our guides. This year Klara is working at the hotel and just helping us out as needed."

"Klara Evenstad? We've met. She seems sweet."

"She's scheduled to give the afternoon tour. And Torstein's organized an informal performance for tonight. He fiddles a bit, and knows all the local musicians."

My ale bowl runneth over, Chloe thought. She didn't mind having time on her own. From materials to social context to a murky tale of murder, Ellinor had given her a lot to consider about the *hardingfele* tradition. I'll need to take good notes, Chloe thought, if I want to translate Ellinor's knowledge into a meaningful exhibit and programming in Stoughton.

Before disappearing back downstairs, Ellinor pointed Chloe to a gallery focusing on the Hardanger region's rich textile traditions. "It's important to understand something special about Hardanger's folk arts. People here have always appreciated their heritage. They kept traditions alive, even when Norway was dominated by Denmark and Sweden."

Chloe knew that Norway had survived four hundred years of Danish rule, and almost a century of Swedish control. True Norwegian independence didn't come until 1905.

"Foreign rule muddied Norwegian culture," Ellinor continued. "By the late eighteen hundreds, people were trying to rediscover Norway's true cultural identity as a way to establish independence. But people in Hardanger had never lost it. They were often isolated, so traditions persisted. And to a large degree, those things were eventually embraced by Norwegians from other regions as well."

I hope Mom's people really did come from here, Chloe thought, as she explored the gallery. Examples of white Hardanger cutwork embroidery were displayed along one long wall, and she lingered over the glass cases. The other long wall featured mannequins attired in a dazzling array of traditional clothing. Chloe spotted several *handaplaggs,* including another worked with black geometric patterns, and concluded with satisfaction that the one she'd found in her mother's closet was definitely of equal quality.

A large wooden rowboat holding eight figures dominated the center of the gallery—a wedding party, Chloe realized. The bride and groom sat together, he in a red vest and black top hat, she with an ornate crown and flowing brown hair. Facing them were two women—mom and grandma, perhaps—wearing elaborately pleated white headscarves. A male mannequin in the bow held a fiddle.

Chloe had been trained to consider the past objectively, analytically, with a cool sense of scholarship. She all too often wavered in that regard, but never more than this moment. The romantic splendor of the bridal couple's clothing, the knowledge that this might represent something her own ancestors experienced ... it was impossible to stay detached.

Did one of my great-whatever-grandmothers wear such an elaborate crown? Chloe wondered. What was her wedding like?

SEVEN

Lisbet—May 1838

"Have a care, Lisbet!" Mother snapped. "You'll ruin the wedding feast before it begins."

Lisbet's cheeks burned as she steadied the bowl of cream she'd almost knocked from the table. Say nothing, she told herself. Once she married Lars that afternoon, she'd have a home of her own.

Gudrun beckoned. "Let's go to the *stabbur*, Lisbet."

Lisbet nodded gratefully. Yesterday's tingling excitement had been replaced by something more solemn, and the commotion in the house was jarring. Mother was barking orders to the local women who'd come to help. Lisbet's married sisters were decorating the house with greenery and wildflowers. Father and her brothers were debating where the ale should be served. Neighbors from the adjacent holdings darted in and out of the house with offers of help, of extra flatbread, of the loan of ale bowls for the toasts to come.

Lisbet surveyed the familiar room: hearth in one corner, carved box beds built into the other corners, table and benches, shelves crowded with tin plates and candlesticks, coats and cloaks on pegs. Colorful wool weavings hung on the log walls, fighting drafts and brightening the dark space. The new green tips of juniper trees she'd helped spread on the floors to protect the boards from mud added a fresh scent to the air. She'd been born in this room. She had never slept anywhere else. Still, she was very ready to leave.

If only Grandmother could come with her. Lisbet watched the old woman push slowly to her feet, knowing better than to offer help. Gudrun was small and stooped, her hair thin beneath its crisp white pleated headdress, her face wrinkled as a forgotten plum, her voice soft. Yet she still commanded respect. She still rolled out *lefse* in perfect circles for the griddle. She still earned a few coins selling her delicate white *Hardangersaum* embroidery, and occasionally blackwork embroidery too. She still could distract Lisbet with a well-told story, or comfort her with a knowing glance.

Gudrun led the way outside, across the yard, and up the stone steps of her family's *stabbur*. The storehouse held their grain and food supplies, and was locked, but Gudrun kept the key. Inside Lisbet inhaled the grain's dusty scent, the tang of souring milk, the faint fishy smell of dried cod, and the stronger reek of the last *rakfisk*—brown trout fermented in wooden tubs. They climbed to the loft, where the family stored wooden chests filled with rye and barley, her mother's silver jewelry, her father's savings, their best clothes. Those included Lisbet's bridal attire of black skirt trimmed with red braid, white apron with cutwork embroidery, white blouse, red vest with a beaded bodice insert, and the crown. Lisbet's grandmother had spent years assembling all the pieces. Some had been passed down. Some her sisters had worn for their weddings. Gudrun had made the apron, and she traded more embroidery with a friend who excelled at beadwork to make the bodice insert.

"It's all beautiful," Lisbet whispered as Gudrun solemnly laid out each piece. "Thank you, Grandmother." She turned to the old woman and was surprised to see shadows in her eyes. "Don't be sad! I won't be so far away. We'll still spend time together…" But the farm she was soon to share with Lars was an hour's row away, with a rough climb to follow. Gudrun wouldn't be able to manage the trip, and Lisbet knew that as mistress of Høiegård—High Farm—she'd seldom have time to visit.

Gudrun took both of Lisbet's hands in hers. "I want you to be careful. Promise me that."

"Careful about what?"

But the old woman shook her head. "Let's get you ready."

Surely I have no special need for care, Lisbet thought. Lars was a cheerful soul. He made her laugh. She loved the quiet optimism in his voice when he told her his dreams. And she loved the joy in his eyes when they danced. He had inherited an old *hardingfele* from an uncle, and he planned to learn how to play.

He also was a hard worker. It had taken Lars three years to acquire Høiegård, perched high above the more-established farms along the Hardangerfjord. An old, old cabin still stood, the birch-bark and turf roof rotted away, the walls blackened with centuries of smoke. It would do for now, and Lars had promised to build a new house as soon as he could. Father negotiated Lisbet's dowry—a cow, a set of linen sheets, a dozen grafted rootstocks for apple trees—and Lars's father agreed to help build a stable and repair the house for the new couple.

Father had announced the match as tradition dictated one Sunday in the Kinsarvik Church. She'd worn an empty sheath on her belt, and he'd led her around the sanctuary after the service reciting, "My daughter is getting married." Lars left his pew, came forward, and stuck a knife into the sheath. Finally, the wedding could be planned.

Father had hired Old Uncle Peder to help with arrangements. The skilled fiddler was the beloved local *kjøgemester*—a master of ceremonies. He'd gone from house to house to invite friends and neighbors to the wedding. He would organize the procession to the church. After the ceremony, when everyone gathered for a dinner at Lisbet's family farm, he would keep the toasts and songs flowing.

Lisbet planned to dance and dance and *dance*. She and Lars had met at a harvest dance, and he was surprisingly light on his feet...

"Stop daydreaming." Gudrun flapped the skirt at her. "Let's get you dressed."

It took time. When Gudrun was satisfied with the clothes, Lisbet fastened the belt, with Lars's knife in the sheath, around her waist. Gudrun undid Lisbet's braids and combed her long hair into a silky mass flowing down her back. Lisbet had not been permitted to leave her hair loose since she was a young girl, and after the wedding she'd be expected to wear the pleated headdress of a married woman.

Then Gudrun lifted the bridal crown and settled it in place. Lisbet felt a spurt of panic. The crown was heavier than she'd expected.

"You'll get used to the weight of marriage, child," Gudrun said, waving a hand to forestall further discussion. "Lisbet. I have something for you." She held out a linen cloth.

"Oh, Grandmother," Lisbet breathed. "It's *beautiful*." She held a *handaplagg*, a hand cloth, that had been embroidered with black silk thread.

"My grandmother made this cloth for my wedding," Gudrun told her. "And I added more designs for you."

Lisbet draped the cloth over her hands, feeling her stab of unease fade. Gudrun would always be an important part of her life, even if they no longer lived under the same roof. "Thank you, Grandmother. It's perfect."

The wedding procession was grand. Lars looked handsome in black knee breeches, a red vest over a white shirt, and black hat. Old Uncle Peder arranged everyone in a double line, began to bow a sprightly tune on his *hardingfele*, and led the way down to the cove below, where more distant neighbors were already waiting in two crowded church boats. Several empty ones, each with three sets of oars, sat on the beach. Lisbet and Lars sat together in the first, facing her mother and grandmother, while her father and brothers settled at the oars. Uncle Peder took the bow seat and launched into another tune. Everyone else crowded into the other boats for the trip to the village of Kinsarvik, as they did every Sunday.

But this is not any Sunday, Lisbet thought, as the men shoved the boats away from the shore. This was *her* special day, hers and Lars's. Uncle Peder's sweet tune floated over the fjord as the boat surged and slowed, surged and slowed. Sunshine glittered on the water, and a lone gull cried overhead. The cool breeze snapped the Norwegian banner flying from the stern. Lisbet clasped Lars's hand, somehow knowing she would live on memories of this day in the years to come.

Kinsarvik had been the meeting place for people in the inner Hardanger region's communities for centuries. When the procession arrived, men pulled the boats up on the beach, safe from the tide. Uncle Peder took them as far as the churchyard gate. Then

Lisbet and Lars led the others to the whitewashed church, a stone structure already seven hundred years old.

In the dim sanctuary, the service itself blurred in Lisbet's mind. The pastor in his black robe and white ruffed collar exhorted her and Lars to support each other and serve God. Lisbet was already resolved to help Lars, and she'd promised her faith when she'd been confirmed, soon after her fourteenth birthday. Her mind drifted instead to the feast and dancing to come, and the joy of making a home at Høiegård with Lars…

He moved beside her, and she realized they'd been bidden to stand. The pastor spoke of God's power to conquer evil. Then they pledged themselves to each other, and were married.

When they left the church, Old Uncle Peder was waiting by the gate, beaming. Lisbet's father produced a jug and an ale bowl, and everyone drank a toast to the new married couple. Uncle Peder tucked his fiddle beneath his chin and began to play, marching in step until Lisbet and Lars and their guests formed their column behind him. Then he led them back to the shore.

Lisbet was approaching the boats when she heard Gudrun's voice, raised and sharp: "Be gone!"

Lars muttered something under his breath and pulled away from her.

Then Lisbet saw a stranger striding toward them so forcefully his long gray hair bounced against the collar of his faded black suit. "Evil!" he quavered. A dozen or more people came behind him, mostly men, but a few women too.

The tune faltered to a halt. The joy in Uncle Peder's lined face faded to bewildered dismay.

The gray-haired man shook a long finger at the fiddler, marching closer. "You play the devil's instrument!"

Lars planted himself between the stranger and the *kjøgemester,* spreading his feet and fisting his hands. "Go on your way," he commanded. "Leave us in peace." Uncle Peder was still, his face now a heartache. Lisbet's heart thumped like a mallet.

A younger man tried to dart past Lars, who lunged and grabbed his arm. The gray-haired man snatched the fiddle from Uncle Peder's hands. He raised the glorious *hardingfele* high above his head. Sunlight glimmered on mother-of-pearl.

The man hurled it to the ground. The thin wood splintered into pieces with a jarring crash.

An outraged roar rose as male wedding guests charged the strangers. The afternoon dissolved in a fury of oaths and thrown fists.

"Stop it!" Lisbet shrieked, stamping her foot. *"Stop!"*

From beneath the shouts and grunts she heard another shriek, shrill with pain—this one from her new husband.

EIGHT

ROELKE ASKED THE HOTEL desk clerk about local footpaths. "I noticed a waterfall up the mountain behind the village. Is that accessible by trail?" Chloe liked waterfalls, so he thought he'd scope it out. Perhaps they'd have time to hike up together later on.

"There's a trail that will get you close," the man told him. "Local trails are graded easy, moderate, and hard. This trail is easy. Watch for red marks. You will have to go cross-country for the last bit."

Roelke acknowledged that going cross-country was okay by him, and left with directions to the trailhead. The daypack he'd brought to Norway was satisfyingly heavy with first-aid supplies and emergency gear. Chloe sometimes said he was a perpetual Boy Scout. There are far worse things, he thought as he clicked the hip strap closed.

From the hotel it was a short walk to the higher road above the village. He passed an apple orchard in bloom, each tree a cloud of white, buzzing with pollinators. He really did need to bring Chloe up here.

The tourist map he'd been given was frustratingly undetailed, but he finally discovered a faint path that crossed a field and led into the woods. A splash of red paint on a tree reassured him.

At first the trail climbed through a deciduous forest. Birches glowed in the dappled sunlight. Several openings offered impressive vistas of Utne, the fjord, and the mountains. *I hope Chloe's mom really did come from this area*, he thought. He wouldn't mind having relatives here.

As he moved into a mix of conifers and broadleaf trees, with ferns below, the trail got dimmer. Steeper, narrower, and rockier too. Roelke unfolded his collapsible walking stick, which helped, but eventually he found himself grabbing tree limbs and bushes to help haul himself up, step by step. Finally he paused, leaning against a tree while he uncapped his canteen. Then he eyed the trail ahead. He wasn't sure how far he'd come but he'd been walking for well over an hour without hearing the waterfall he was trying to reach.

"Well, hunh," he muttered. Clearly Norwegians rated trails on a different scale than Americans. This "easy" trail was doing him in. And he'd hiked enough to know that going down wouldn't be any easier than going up.

He was contemplating that when movement below caught his attention. Klara, the young woman who worked at the hotel, emerged on the path. Climbing swiftly, she was almost upon him before she noticed. "Oh! Hello."

Roelke couldn't help noticing that the girl wasn't even breathing heavily. *You've got ten years on her*, he told himself, but didn't feel any better. "Hi, Klara. Your shift at the hotel done already?"

"I was supposed to be off today, but they called me in for breakfast. I'm working at the museum this afternoon." Her hand unconsciously went to her ornate silver necklace, which provided an unexpected accent to her shorts and fleece pullover top. "I like to walk every day, so this was my best chance."

Walk, he thought. Not *hike*. Not *climb*.

She considered him. "Are you all right?"

"Fine," he assured her.

She gestured toward his bulging daypack. "You are camping?"

"Just out for the morning. I like to be prepared."

"That is wise." She nodded, although she didn't appear to be carrying anything except a sling holding a water bottle. And she wasn't wearing hiking boots, just well-worn blue athletic shoes with a white wing motif on each side.

"Say, do you know how close we are to the waterfall?" Roelke asked.

Klara's brow wrinkled. "Not close."

"Ah. Just wondering. Well, good hiking."

With another friendly gap-toothed smile she resumed the climb. She stepped with quick assurance, and didn't need to grab anything. Within moments she'd disappeared.

Roelke glanced at his watch and considered his options. He could walk for about twenty more minutes before he'd need to turn around. From what Klara had said, he evidently had no chance of finding the waterfall in that time, but according to the map another trail intersected with this one somewhere up ahead. Reaching that junction would be a feeble benchmark, but the best he could hope for. He capped his bottle, ate a couple of Chloe's Trail Mix Cookies from his snack stash, and resumed the climb.

He hadn't gone more than a hundred yards when he heard skittering ahead of him. A fist-sized stone bounced down the trail. More rocks were plummeting behind that one, pinging off larger stones and tree trunks. Then a rock the size of an engine block cart-wheeled toward him.

With a yelp Roelke stumbled sideways. He fell, landing hard and off-kilter on his right hip. He tried to roll to safety but the pack stopped him. At the last moment he curled into a tight ball, arms wrapped over his head, eyes closed tight. He felt a glancing blow against his right knee. A couple of small stones ricocheted against him and kept going. Finally the rock sounds faded away below him, and everything was still.

Well, that sucked, he grumbled silently. He opened his eyes but didn't move for a long moment, wanting to be sure no other projectiles were barreling his way. He tested his legs—both working properly, though he'd have one hell of a bruise on his knee. He lumbered to his feet and brushed a few broken fern fronds from his jeans.

Then he squinted up the trail. He was well below treeline, but the steep path was filled with scree. What had triggered the little avalanche? Had Klara inadvertently sent something tumbling? It would be easy enough to do, but at the pace she'd been hiking, she was probably a mile away by the time it started. Was he closer to the intersecting trail than he realized? Had some other hiker dislodged the first stone? A deer? A squirrel? Had it been one of those zen things stemming from a butterfly flapping its wings on top of the mountain?

No way to know.

Well, the one thing he did know was that he needed to turn around. If he didn't head back now, he'd likely keep Chloe waiting.

He began picking his way down the mountain. With any luck, Klara, having reached the summit or the waterfall or whatever she was hiking toward, wouldn't overtake him again before he reached the road.

———

Chloe found bread, *brunost*, and apple juice at the village market, and bought some strawberries from a self-serve stand. "I've got everything we need for lunch," she told Roelke when he returned from his hike and met her, as agreed, on the hotel porch. "Did you reach the waterfall?"

"Not even close," he admitted. "But I didn't want to keep you waiting."

They found a picnic table near the dock, and she laid out her goodies. He sat down. "That cheese is brown," he observed.

"It's supposed to be. Try it."

They ate strawberries and bread smeared with brown cheese, and watched ferries come and go. Clouds cast floating shadows on the mountains. Roelke told Chloe about meeting Klara on the trail. She summarized what she'd learned from Ellinor that morning, including whispers of a murder and a legendary missing *hardingfele*. Murder tale notwithstanding, she was pretty sure they were experiencing an absolutely perfect day. "What do you want to do this afternoon?" She reached for the almost-empty bottle of juice. "More hiking?"

Roelke considered, then shook his head. "I think not."

"Want to join me for a tour of the open-air part of the museum?" she asked, and was inordinately pleased when he agreed.

The Hardanger Folkemuseum's open-air exhibits were up a short but steep hill from the main building. "This would never fly in the States," Chloe murmured, trying not to pant as they reached the summit. She zipped her jacket as a light drizzle began to fall.

She spotted perhaps a dozen tourists gathered around Klara, their tour guide. When Chloe and Roelke wandered over, Klara smiled and nodded slightly: *I was expecting you two.*

When everyone was ready Klara welcomed the group. "The museum was established in 1911 in Utne, right in front of the hotel, but as the collection grew more space was needed. All of the buildings here came from Hardanger ..."

This property was a spectacular choice, Chloe thought. The twenty buildings restored on this high ground were presented with the fjord and mountains as backdrop. The combination of historic buildings and misty clouds was evocative.

And as Klara ushered them through the homes and outbuildings, some dating back centuries, Chloe's imagination kicked into overdrive. Her ancestors had surely lived in similar structures. "I'm going to see if they have any job openings here," she whispered to Roelke.

He smiled indulgently.

"No, I'm serious," she insisted. The view alone would have done it, but hey, it was her people represented here.

A man in a Baltimore Orioles ball cap asked about maintenance. "We take our responsibility seriously," Klara said, pointing at a pile of replacement roof slates. "That's our next project. And the turf systems on the older buildings are replaced regularly." She led them to a small log structure where grasses grew over a layer of birchbark to form a solid roof. "This is my favorite building. It's the oldest one we have, dating back to sometime between the thirteenth and fourteenth centuries. The style, with an open hearth in the center of the room, is called *årestove*. Let's go inside."

The door opened into a small anteroom, where an unusually low second door led on to the main room. Chloe was the last to step inside—and immediately felt something like an electric charge shoot through her. A barrage of emotions quivered in the air, hitting her with a force she'd never experienced. Sensate fragments whirled around her—joy, despair, grief, hope, fear. She couldn't think. Couldn't move. Couldn't breathe.

"Chloe?" Roelke gripped her arm and tugged her back outside. "Are you all right? What happened?"

She leaned over, hands on knees. The sensations faded, but it took a moment to regain her equilibrium. Finally, not wanting Roelke to call the Norwegian equivalent of 911, she straightened. "I'm okay," she muttered. "It was just that ... *geez*, I've never picked up on something so strong before."

"What was it? Good? Bad? Scary?"

"Well, that's the strange part." She was still trying to figure out where to slot the experience in her growing collection. "In all the other old buildings I just sensed the usual vague muddle of emotions. Like background noise, easily tuned out. Here, it was still a muddle, but everything was *really* strong." She stared at him, more unnerved that she wanted to admit. "My 'gift'"—she fingered air quotes to make clear it didn't always feel like one—"has gone haywire since we got here. I'm fine in our hotel room as long as I don't stand at the window. Now this."

Roelke frowned. "Let's just go back down."

Chloe sucked in her lip, looking from him to the log home. "No, I want to stay."

He looked distinctly unconvinced. She settled the matter by bracing herself and going back inside.

The mélange whacked her again, but she'd expected it. She forced herself to take in the antechamber, sussing out its use for temporary storage or a place for wood chopping in bad weather.

Then she bent low and stepped into the main room. It was dim, and the only decoration was a row of geometric patterns chalked on the walls. The tour group was seated on low benches built against three of the walls. Chloe and Roelke settled quietly. Her sternum quivered with the intensity of perceived emotions, but she willed herself to stay calm.

"... the only window in the house was probably added in the eighteen hundreds," Klara was saying, pointing to the eastern wall. "It replaced the original wooden hatch. In the old days, people believed that a dead person's soul would try to return to the house where it had lived, using the entrance where it last emerged. So bodies were removed through the hatch, which was kept closed at all other times. That way the soul couldn't return."

I'm glad I stuck it out, Chloe thought. She'd never heard of that custom before.

A man asked about the chalk decoration. "It's called *kroting*," Klara explained. "The designs were applied with a liquid chalk made from local minerals. Very few examples remain, all here in western Norway. Some designs may have been decorative, but others were intended to protect the home."

Chloe imagined living through a dark, cold winter in this dark, sooty room. Firelight flickered against the walls. Wind whistled through cracks, and sleety snow beat against the lone window. The air smelled of smoke and unwashed bodies. Somehow she understood that the designs brought comfort.

A red-haired lady waved a lime green umbrella to get Klara's attention. "The door into this room is unusually low," she observed. "Was that to discourage evil spirits, or because people were shorter back then?"

“Actually, there are other reasons for the low door,” Klara said. “It minimized heat loss. It was also a safety feature. If someone attacked the family, they'd be forced to bend low coming through the door, and …” She pantomimed striking a vicious blow to the back of an intruder's head.

Chloe exchanged a sideways glance with Roelke: *Yikes.*

Klara returned to more prosaic details. “This type of single-room dwelling, with an earthen floor and raised central hearth like this one, was once common in rural Norway. By the nineteenth century, most rural Norwegians lived in homes with chimneys and windows, but not everyone could afford those luxuries. This home was never updated. The smoke hole in the ceiling is a bit off center so rain didn't drip down into the fire. Imagine all the smoke swirling about! And imagine how bitterly cold this room must have been in the winter.”

“It's unbelievable that people actually lived like this,” a man muttered dismissively, as if farm folk seven hundred years earlier had a whole lot of choices. Chloe was tempted to say so but remembered just in time that she was not a museum representative.

But Klara had heard the comment as well. She did not observe that her ancestors' fortitude warranted respect, not derision, as Chloe would have done. “I'd like to share with you a different aspect to life in the old days on the fjord,” she said instead. “Music has always been incredibly important to Hardanger people. This is a lullaby that local women have sung to their babies for hundreds of years.”

She began to sing. The lullaby, offered in a clear soprano voice, was hauntingly beautiful … and familiar. Chloe closed her eyes, taking it in. Had Amalie Sveinsdatter sung this to baby Marit? Perhaps the lullaby was somehow imprinted in Mom, Chloe thought, and got passed down to me.

The group applauded when Klara finished. She nodded modestly in acknowledgment. "That concludes the tour. Your bus driver is waiting in the parking lot down the hill."

Chloe waited until the tour group had straggled from the building before approaching Klara. "That was amazing. Thank you *so* much for sharing your talent with us."

"My pleasure. Do you have any questions about the tour, or this building?"

"Probably." Chloe spread her hands in a helpless gesture. "But your song knocked everything else from my mind."

Klara laughed. "Well, you know where to find me. If I'm not here, grab me at the hotel." She fastened her coat and stepped outside.

Chloe wanted to linger, but Roelke tapped his wristwatch. "Didn't you say you were due to meet that grad student at three o'clock? It's ten till."

They descended to the formal museum building. In the gift shop, Klara was already engaged in an intimate conversation with a tall young man. "I believe that's the grad student working with Ellinor," Chloe murmured.

Klara noticed them and said something to her companion. He stroked her cheek with his thumb and kissed her. Then he bounded over to meet Chloe and Roelke, hand outstretched. "I'm Torstein Landvik. I'm excited that you're here!" His accent was a little thicker than his girlfriend's, but his English was flawless. Beneath a thick shock of dark hair, his gaze was an intense blue.

Oh my, Chloe thought. No wonder Klara seemed besotted.

They moved into Ellinor's office. Once introductions were complete, Torstein plunged right in. "Tell me how I can be helpful." He wore jeans, but also a reproduction linen shirt, and he wore a ring that looked as if had been hand-forged.

"I'm curious about your fieldwork." Chloe pulled out her notebook and pen. "I understand you're studying regional folk dance? *Bygdedanser?*"

Torstein nodded vigorously. "Some of the historical dances are endangered. For example, Springars are the oldest surviving couple dances. They were performed as early as the 1600s, with choreography specific to particular valleys or communities. But many disappeared when new dances, polkas and Reinlendars and such, became popular during the last century. We must document those that are left."

"They are important heirlooms," Chloe agreed.

"But it's impossible, of course, to study dance without studying music too. Do you know the Halling?"

Chloe flashed to her high school days, watching Kent Andreasson perform the challenging dance. "I do."

"The Halling must have an experienced fiddler. So much athleticism is demanded of the men! The fiddler must urge them on. And considering that the men were often trying to show off for the women watching ... well." He grinned. "Who knows how many engagements took place because a fiddler helped a man meet the challenge?" He abruptly turned to Roelke. "Is that how you won Chloe's heart?"

"I'm afraid not," Roelke said blandly. "I do not dance."

Chloe sent him a reassuring glance: *You had your own ways of winning my heart.* A crooked smile quirked his mouth.

"No matter." Torstein shrugged. "I've also been studying *Rammeslatter,* and—"

Chloe held up one hand. "That's a term I don't know."

"It's the name given to tunes with a hypnotic quality. Stories tell of fiddlers so skilled that they played dancers into a trance. Even themselves. Such men would play until most of the dancers had collapsed, and someone pulled the fiddle away from his hands. It still happens today—at least for the fiddler, who emerges bone-weary, with no memories of the music played."

Chloe felt her eyebrows rise. "Seriously?"

"It has not happened to me," Torstein said sadly. "But I aspire to such heights. Well." He shoved to his feet, as if sitting still any longer was impossible. "Tomorrow afternoon I'm scheduled to interview an elderly dancer. Would you like to join me?"

"Of course!"

Torstein grinned. "And did Ellinor tell you I've planned a musical evening to welcome you to Utne? Nothing big or fancy—we just put up a few posters around the village. Eight o'clock in the open-air area. You can come?" His hopeful gaze suggested that nothing was more important than her attendance.

"That sounds great."

"I need to see to some final arrangements, so I'll see you then." Torstein beamed at them and departed with an air of barely suppressed exuberance.

"Wow." Chloe blinked.

Ellinor had watched the exchange in what appeared to be amused silence. "He's a force of nature. He's passionate about local folklore, and carefully documents every detail he gathers. He's really made inroads with some of the elders who haven't felt comfortable sharing before." She tented her fingers beneath her chin. "Collectors appeared in Hardanger as early as the 1850s, determined to document what they called 'pure peasant culture.' Unfortunately, most were lofty academics who didn't find much success. Torstein's saving dances that would otherwise be lost."

"I look forward to working with him." Chloe slipped her notebook into her daypack and stood. "Will we see you this evening?"

"I wouldn't miss it," Ellinor assured her.

When Chloe and Roelke passed back from the office area into the gift shop, Klara was on duty behind the counter. Chloe paused to thank her again for singing the lullaby. "That house is now my favorite as well," she told the younger woman. "By the way, did the farm it came from have a name?"

"It did," Klara said. "It was called Høiegård."

NINE

Torhild—June 1854

Torhild arched her back, stretching out the kinks that came from cutting the first grass crop with a sickle. She and her mother Lisbet had climbed above the *seter*—the small isolated farm where they summered their cow and goats—which was high above Høiegård, so they were very high indeed. A golden eagle soared overhead. Far below, the fjord sparkled a deep blue. Several waterfalls plunged down the mountain face on the far side. Although snow still capped the peaks, it was Midsummer.

The sun sent a trickle of sweat down Torhild's spine, but she offered a quick prayer of thanks for the green grass, which grew quickly during these long days. Every single blade in every scattered patch of grass was important. If in fall her father judged they didn't have enough hay to see even their few animals through the winter, they'd have to butcher more than they wished.

Lisbet tucked a strand of damp hair beneath the kerchief knotted under her chin, and gave her daughter a sidelong look. "No daydreaming, Torhild."

There was no point in telling her mother that she'd been thanking God for the recent rains that might—just might—grow enough grass to feed their animals, and let them harvest enough potatoes and turnips from their garden below to feed the small family. Torhild turned away, grabbed a handful of grass in her left hand, and swung her sickle, letting the cut blades fall to the ground. It would have to be raked and bundled and hauled to the racks, then carefully spread to dry in the sun. But not today.

"I will have to head down soon, Mother," she said. "Remember? I'm working this afternoon at the inn."

Lisbet regarded her wearily.

"I did tell you," Torhild reminded her. "And I'm working tomorrow, so I'll sleep there." No one would mind if she bedded down in the *stabbur* behind the inn.

"And is sleeping all you'll be doing after your chores are done?"

Torhild's shoulders sagged. "It *is* Midsummer."

"Oh, child." Lisbet's eyes were concerned. "Music, dancing, drinking…"

"It's just a little fun."

"I want you to have more than I have."

"I *know*." They'd had this conversation many times. But I won't lie, Torhild thought. She wouldn't promise not to attend the dance when she had every intention of being there.

"Don't go," Lisbet said. "Please, Torhild. There's nothing for you there."

But there is, Torhild protested silently. She needed to dance like she needed to breathe. Losing herself to the music provided the only moments when she forgot the shadows in her parents' eyes, forgot the constant fear of going hungry. Every once in a while, if the fiddler was truly gifted, she danced to a place where she wasn't even aware of her partner, of the steps … as if she had disappeared into a trance. It was the most wonderful feeling in the world.

"Sometimes I think the zealots are right about the fiddles," Lisbet fretted. "That they are indeed the devil's instrument."

"Mother—"

"When you dance, you're dancing with the devil!" Lisbet's cheeks had flushed a ruddy red.

"*Mother*. You don't actually believe that."

"I did not when I was your age." Lisbet's eyes grew glassy. "But if the devil isn't involved, devilish people are. Please, Torhild. Do not go."

The grief in her mother's eyes pricked Torhild's heart. But I'm fifteen now, she thought stubbornly. She'd been confirmed a year ago. After making a solemn pledge to God, she was considered an adult, free to make her own decisions. And she had decided that tonight, she would attend the Midsummer dance with her cousin Gjertrud.

Torhild wished that the one thing that truly made her happy didn't represent what most upset her mother. Her mother should understand! Torhild's great-grandmother Gudrun had told her that Lisbet used to attend dances as well. "That's how she met your father, did you know? He was a wonderful dancer. Once. Before."

Before the wedding, Gudrun meant. Before a group of people who believed that fiddle music and dancing were evil had started a brawl just moments after her parents emerged from the church as a married couple. Before an angry zealot hurled Lars against one of the church boats so hard his thigh bone had snapped, and several bones in his left hand too.

The broken leg had not healed well. Lars couldn't walk without a stick even now, and he limped badly. His fingers mended poorly too, with permanent angles God had not intended. Adding to the tragedy, Old Uncle Peder, the community's beloved *kjøgemester,* had died that night. Folks said that after seeing his fiddle destroyed, and Lars badly injured, and the wedding feast ruined, his heart had simply given out.

"Your parents had such dreams," Gudrun had said. Her hands trembled with palsy, and her voice had grown raspy, but her mind was as sharp and her gaze as direct as ever. "They were no strangers to hard work, but they knew happiness too. Briefly. Be patient with them, Torhild."

Torhild understood. She truly did. Her father was a kind man who kept busy and didn't complain. But it was impossible for him to heft a hoe or scythe for very long. It was impossible for him to climb ancient trails high into the mountains to fish for trout in cold streams in summer, or to hunt for the reindeer or ptarmigan that would make such a difference in the winter. It was impossible for him to pass an hour without wincing, face muscles taut, eyes hooded with pain.

That left Lisbet to do all of her chores and half of his. She didn't complain either, but her shoulders were perpetually bowed with fatigue, her mouth pinched with frustration and worry. Torhild was an only child, and as she'd grown she'd tried to take up more and more of the burden, but times were very hard. The great herring fishery along Norway's western coast that for years employed many Hardanger men had collapsed. Crop yields were declining on the small patchwork plots along the fjords. Famine was spreading through Norway, and many desperate people were emigrating to America.

I don't want to go to America, Torhild thought as she sliced the curved blade through another handful of grass. I just want to go to the Midsummer dance.

And she would.

Torhild worked as long as she dared before hurrying down the steep path. She hated leaving her mother alone, but they had no choice. The coins Torhild brought home from the inn were sometimes all that stood between the family and starvation.

She began hearing the waterfall as she approached the small log building where she and her mother separated milk, churned butter, made cheese, and slept while at the *seter*. Her father's father and brothers had built the stone foundation and log cabin years ago. "You've got enough to do without hauling water from some distant stream," Grandfather had decreed gruffly. "And you'll need a pool to help keep milk and cheese cool."

"He pities us," Lisbet had said to Lars, Torhild's father. He had turned away without answering. Torhild had been very young, and it was the first time she recognized the disappointment in her mother's tone, and the regret in her father's eyes.

Well, I'm glad our *seter* is near the waterfall, Torhild thought now. Quickly she hauled water to the cow and their three goats, which they'd secured in the *seterfjøset*—a crude animal shelter—before leaving to cut hay. It was a shame to deny them pasture, but Torhild had no younger sibling to mind them, or the means to hire help. Then she packed their butter and started down the trail to Høiegård.

Torhild always loved the moment when she left the wooded path and could see the farm clearing below. The narrow meadow in front of the cabin ended on a cliff. The view made her want to dance.

Patches of rye and barley had sprouted behind the log barn, and her father was hoeing weeds. His forehead wrinkled as she approached. "What's wrong?"

She scuffed the toe of one shoe in the dirt and shot him a quick glance. "Mother was just talking to me about the sin of dancing."

Lars looked away. "Your mother was once a fine dancer. All the boys wanted to dance with her."

"Yet she scolds me. She said the *hardingfele* is the devil's instrument." Torhild pinched her mouth closed, wishing she hadn't said that last thing—not to her father, who had good reason to believe it. "I'm sorry."

"You have nothing to be sorry for." Lars hesitated, then seemed to make a decision. "Come with me." He hobbled inside and went to his corner cupboard. "Open the door."

Torhild hesitated. These special cupboards were considered private. "Are you sure?"

"Yes, yes," Lars said impatiently. "The bottom shelf, in the back…"

Peering inside, she saw something wrapped in an old blanket. She pulled it free and set it on the table. Lars pulled away the cloth to reveal a small wooden *hardingfele* case.

She eased up the lid and regarded a beautiful fiddle. "Father! Is this yours?"

"It is. It belonged to my uncle, and I once thought I'd learn to play." He regarded his crooked fingers, shook his head. "That never came to be, but I often loan it to a friend of mine. You know Big Gunnar."

"I do!" The fiddler's nickname was a joke, for he was short, and skinny as a scythe handle. He visited Høiegård every once in a while, and greeted Lars warmly after church. Torhild had often heard him play at dances. "He doesn't have a fiddle of his own?"

"He did." Lars's voice held an edge. "Some zealots came to his house and smashed it."

Torhild had heard the tales. Many fiddlers in Hardanger had been visited by fanatics determined to destroy the precious instruments. Rumors even claimed that one renowned fiddle maker lived in a stone cottage high in the mountains where the believers were unlikely to find him. "Does Mother know?"

"She knew I had it, back before we married. After ... after what happened, she told me to give it away. I couldn't bring myself to." His lips twisted in a deprecatory smile. "Then Big Gunnar lost his fiddle and couldn't afford another, so we worked out an arrangement. He's playing at the bonfire tonight, so he'll be by to pick it up. If you and Lisbet are at the *seter*, he comes to the house. Otherwise I've got a spot in the stone fence by the stable where I leave it." He fixed her with a steady gaze. "There's no need for your mother to know."

Torhild was astonished. How could her father have kept such a secret? Why was he telling her this now? She wanted to ask more questions ... but she was out of time.

"I must get to the inn," she said, "so I'll put this away." She quickly tucked the fiddle back out of sight. "And I'll fix you something to eat before I go." She found some *brunost,* and flatbread to go with the cheese, and poured her father a mug of ale. "You should eat outside. It's dark as night in here."

Lars accepted the plate and mug, but he didn't retreat from the gloom. After a moment he said, "I promised your mother that I would build her a new house. Before we wed, I *promised* her that."

Torhild had been about to fetch her good apron to take to work, but the pain in her father's voice made her pause. Their house was an old årestove, with a raised open hearth in the middle of the floor providing their only source of heat and place to cook. A little light filtered through the hole in the roof, which when not in use was covered with a pig's bladder stretched within a wooden frame. The upper parts of the windowless walls were black from years of accumulated smoke. Low earth-filled benches built against the walls were used for sitting or sleeping. Box beds had been built in two corners, short and wide and filled with straw. Torhild and her parents slept beneath sheep skins and rustling quilts filled with dried sedge grasses.

On every farm Torhild had ever visited, a newer log house with a proper chimney had been constructed decades earlier. If the *årestove* still stood, it was used only for big jobs like butchering or brewing. But Torhild had grown up in this house, and she gave it no particular thought. She'd helped her mother decorate the walls with fresh *kroting* each winter. One of Gudrun's beautiful *Hardanger saum* runners graced the table. Their home was not cheerless.

For a moment now she stood still, unsure what to say or do. Then she gave her father an impulsive hug. "We have a home," she said firmly. "Think of all those who are emigrating because they don't."

He kissed her cheek. "You're a good girl. You'll make someone a good wife one day. But I hope not *too* soon?"

The question embarrassed her. Her cousin Gjertrud, only a year older, was already eyeing every boy she met with interest. Torhild wasn't ready for that. "No, Father. Not anytime soon."

That seemed to satisfy him, for a smile twitched at the corners of his mouth. "Off you go. Have fun at the dance tonight."

———

Torhild hurried to meet a neighbor who'd promised to take her to Utne in his *Oselvar*, a small boat that could be rowed or sailed as weather dictated. He dropped her off in front of the Utne Inn and waved away her thanks. "I was going fishing anyway." Everyone used the fjord for errands and travel, and offering transport to those in need was a common custom.

To her surprise, Gjertrud was waiting on the shore. As daughters of sisters, Torhild and Gjertrud had grown up together. Gjertrud was employed full-time at the inn, and had recommended that the proprietress hire Torhild when extra help was needed. Torhild loved having someone to share her secrets with—not that she had many! Still, whispering and giggling together as they emptied night jars and hauled kitchen scraps to the pigs lightened the tasks. Gjertrud was a pretty girl with long, wheat-colored braids and bright blue eyes. Today her cheeks were flushed rosy.

"Come!" Gjertrud grabbed her hand and towed her toward the inn. "They're waiting for us in the kitchen."

"Then why are you—"

"I had to tell you about the new guest! He's come all the way from Bergen."

"What for?" Torhild asked as they scurried around the building to the back entrance.

"He wants to learn about our music and dance! His name is Edvin Brekke. And oh, Torhild, he's *so* handsome. And smart. You know how some of the guests act like they don't even see us? Well, Edvin stopped *me* just to say good morning."

"Why…" Torhild began, but they'd reached the kitchen. She'd have to hear the rest later.

Not many people visited Hardanger, and most who did traveled on foot. But Utne was a main stop on Norway's *skyss* route, a long-established boat-and-stagecoach web that linked a few rural communities to each other, and to Bergen and Christiania. The Utne Inn had been established well over a century earlier to provide hospitality to those hardy adventurers who did brave the fjord region. It was a white frame building with a steep roof—simple enough, but known for outstanding hospitality. That was ensured by Torbjørg Utne, who presided over her family's inn. Mother Utne, as she was called, had exacting standards, but she was fair—and often generous—with the girls she hired to clean, help cook, and serve.

This afternoon she set Gjertrud to shelling peas for Cook, and Torhild to cleaning cod. "Did you bring a clean blouse and apron?" Mother Utne asked.

Torhild nodded. "I did."

"Then you will serve our guest this evening."

Torhild pretended not to notice Gjertrud's frustrated pout.

Later, when Torhild carefully carried a plate of baked cod with *lefse* and peas into the dining room, she understood why Gjertrud had hoped to serve. The newcomer sat at a table by the front window. He was perhaps twenty-five, with a thin face and sandy hair worn long. The narrow white scar curving over his right cheekbone only added a mysterious hint of adventure. He was idly tapping the tablecloth with long fingers. His fine dark-wool suit looked expensive.

No wonder Gjertrud was so excited. This man looked nothing like Hardanger's husky, rough-palmed fishermen and farmers.

Torhild approached his table. "I have your dinner, sir."

"Ah, yes. Thank you."

She put the plate down and turned to go, but he circled her wrist with one hand. "No need to leave so quickly. What's your name?"

Torhild felt his grip like a hot iron, and pulled away. She didn't like his lazy smile any more than she liked his familiarity. "Torhild, sir." She grudged him that only because she didn't want him reporting a churlish serving girl to Mother Utne.

"You must call me Edvin."

"If you'll excuse me…" She backed away until she felt safe, then returned to the kitchen.

Gjertrud was waiting. "What did you think?" she whispered eagerly.

"He is handsome," Torhild allowed. "But he is also a bit too sure of himself."

Gjertrud flapped a dismissive hand. "You're just not used to his city ways. Men are different in Bergen."

And what do you know of Bergen men? Torhild wondered—but silently, because she didn't want to argue with her cousin. "Please, Gjertrud. Watch yourself."

When the dishes were scoured and the kitchen tidy, Mother Utne excused them for the night. Gjertrud and Torhild combed and re-braided their hair, straightened their stockings, and tied on their best aprons. Then they made their way up the hill behind the inn. A huge bonfire served as a beacon beneath the deep blue sky that would not, tonight, fade to black before brightening toward a milky dawn. It was the summer solstice.

Torhild heard Big Gunnar's *hardingfele*—her father's fiddle—calling as they approached the gathering. How sad that his own instrument had been destroyed! She felt a sudden shiver, wondering if the zealots might present themselves here to disrupt the Midsummer celebration. But she'd never seen them at a dance. Perhaps the tragedy of her parents' wedding dissuaded local believers from accosting fiddlers in public. Much easier, she thought with disgust, to surprise a man when he was home alone.

Well, tonight was not for gloomy thoughts. Several couples were already dancing on the wooden floor that had been erected on the sloping ground. The fiddler stood on the edge of the stage. His tune beckoned new arrivals as well as those who'd already stepped into an energetic Springar, a couples dance in triple time. People—some known, some strangers—were clustered in noisy knots nearby. Men were already passing jugs, but Torhild ignored them. She just wanted to dance.

"Torhild!" A boy she'd known all her life was grinning at her, holding out his hand.

She took it without hesitation. "See you," she called to Gjertrud, who laughed.

Torhild and her partner climbed the steps to the floor and joined the other dancers. He knew the figures well and they moved together effortlessly. She surrendered to the music, to the steps and figures, just as she always did. The music welled within her, taking her to a place without hunger, without worry, without grief.

She danced with several boys before, flushed and breathless, she declared the need for a break. Gjertrud had not appeared on the dance floor so Torhild searched the growing crowd. Finally she spotted her cousin sitting on a log near the bonfire. Torhild had drawn close before realizing that the man beside Gjertrud was Edvin Brekke. He held a small leather-bound journal on his lap, and was leaning toward the flames as if to illuminate whatever he'd written.

Torhild hesitated. It might be best to slip away.

But Edvin glanced up and saw her. "Please join us!" he exclaimed.

Gjertrud patted the log on her other side. "Yes, do. I've been telling Edvin about some of our dances." She turned to the visitor. "Torhild is one of the best dancers in the region."

"Wonderful!" Edvin scribbled something down. "What is the dance they're doing now?"

"Why, that's the Gammal Reinlendar." Torhild was surprised that Edvin didn't know such a popular dance.

His pencil scratched on the page. "I've never seen this Reinlendar variant before, although it's based on a schottische step."

Torhild couldn't imagine what had motivated him to come here. "Why are you writing all this down?"

Edvin shoved an errant lock of sandy hair from his forehead. "I play the violin myself. I also teach music and dance in Bergen, but of course we have many foreign influences in the city. I am traveling to the corners of Norway, documenting your pure peasant traditions."

"Isn't that exciting?" Gjertrud asked. "He thinks what we do here is important!"

Edvin leaned forward to look directly at Torhild. "Tell me, do you like *hardingfele* music?"

She shifted uneasily on the log. "Well, yes—"

"Even though some call it 'the devil's instrument'?" His eyes gleamed with humor. "I understand you country people are quite superstitious."

Torhild thought of the fiddle that had been destroyed on her parents' wedding day, and of the heartache that had followed. The local whispers pairing fiddling with evil had only intensified after the tragedy. "I do not believe in that evil," she said firmly. Any magic created by a talented fiddler came from his own skill, his own long hours of practice.

"Is that why you come to dances?"

Torhild twisted her fingers in her skirt. This man's curiosity made her feel as if she were a specimen to be studied. Dancing and *hardingfele* music had always been part of life. They just *were*, and everyone else here understood that. Even now, away from the platform, the sound of the fiddle quivered inside her.

Gjertrud nudged her. "I enjoy it," Torhild said finally.

"I'll want to speak with the fiddler later as well," Edvin added. "Some of these tunes … they are much more complex than I had expected. Say …" He straightened, looking expectant. "What can you tell me about the tune called 'Fanitullen'?"

Torhild wished Edvin Brekke had never traveled to Hardanger.

She stood abruptly. "I'm going back to dance. Gjertrud, will you come?"

Looking perplexed, Gjertrud shook her head. "No, I'm going to stay here and help Edvin."

Fine, Torhild thought, as she made her way back to the platform. Let Gjertrud waste her evening with the music teacher.

The fiddler ended his piece. "I need to re-tune," he shouted, "so wet your throats, boys. And when the break is over we'll have a Halling."

Some of the young men whooped with approval—perhaps for the invitation to drink, perhaps in anticipation of the exhilarating dance that provided them a chance to impress admiring young women. Torhild thought of her parents, and wondered if her father had won her mother's heart during a Halling dance. And when a boy with farmer's hands shyly invited her to join him on the platform, she nodded. With a bit of luck, the fiddler would take her to a place where Edvin Brekke's intrusive questions could be forgotten.

TEN

The rain stopped and shafts of sunlight pierced the clouds by the time Chloe and Roelke arrived in the grassy yard where the Hardanger Folkemuseum's historic buildings had been restored. A few dozen people were settled on lawn chairs or blankets, but Chloe's gaze went to Høiegård, the ancient log home where she'd experienced the overwhelming impression of complicated lives gone by. She put a hand on Roelke's arm. "I'd like to—"

"Chloe!" Ellinor beckoned from the edge of the crowd. Next to her, curator Sonja Gullickson wore sunglasses in artsy frames and a shawl knit from some luxury yarn in gorgeous shades of blue. Her brown hair was pinned up loosely, allowing a few curling tendrils to escape. Once again the whole look suggested casual elegance.

"Sonja, hello!" Chloe said. "I thought you were still in Stockholm."

"I've been trying to interview an elderly seamstress for months," Sonja explained. "She's one of the few people left who knows how to properly pleat and starch the traditional headscarf worn by married Hardanger women, but she has some health issues. Apparently she's doing better, and her son invited me to visit tomorrow. By good fortune, all of the conference sessions I was involved in, or wanted to attend, were scheduled for yesterday or this morning. I was able to catch an afternoon flight."

Ellinor slanted a smile at her colleague. "I could have covered for her, but Sonja didn't trust me to do the interview alone."

Chloe smiled. Any good curator was passionate about her specialty.

It was almost eight o'clock. Roelke and Chloe sat at a picnic table, and the performance began promptly. "Thank you for coming!" Torstein called. He introduced himself and the two other fiddlers—one a stocky man perhaps in his fifties, the other a younger woman with short spiky hair dyed garnet. They wore street clothes, but Torstein had donned a *bunad* of black knee breeches, white shirt, and red vest. "Yikes," Chloe murmured. His attention to detail included a ceremonial dagger in a sheath, silver buckles on black shoes, and what looked like hand-knit socks. Impressive.

"*Hardingfele* tunes once measured everyday life," Torstein continued. "Music was deeply rooted in rituals and traditions. There were specific tunes for every aspect of a Hardanger wedding. There were tunes for planting, for harvesting, for celebrating a good yield. Tonight we're going to play some old music, tell some stories, and hopefully get you on your feet."

The trio launched into a lively melody. "Oh, I wish Aunt Hilda could hear this," Chloe lamented. "She would love it."

"You'll tell her all about it when we get home," Roelke said, and the music was so uplifting that she couldn't stay sad for long.

It was a fun evening. Torstein deferred to the other two fiddlers, giving each opportunities to shine. He excelled as dance master, urging people to give the Norwegian Mountain March or a Springar a try.

"Are these the kind of dances you did in high school?" Roelke asked during a brief intermission.

Chloe nodded.

"How did you get started?"

"When I was ten I got picked to perform with the high school dancers for a fundraiser. People thought it was cute, but Roelke, I *loved* it. Dancing made me feel something I'd never felt before. You can't audition for the Stoughton Norwegian Dancers until you're a freshman. I wanted it so badly, and I was so nervous, I'm surprised I didn't fall flat on my face. I was accepted, though." She left it at that, but being a member of the Stoughton Norwegian Dancers for three years was one of the best experiences of her life.

Once the fiddlers had re-tuned, Torstein announced a Reinlendar.

"Want to dance?" Chloe asked Roelke.

"I do not," he said calmly, surprising her not even a little bit. "But you go ahead."

Chloe joined the willing and teamed up with an eager little girl who needed a partner. Chloe helped her practice the steps. Then Torstein had all the pairs form a double circle, and the fiddlers began to play. "Schottische step forward and back!" Torstein called. "Now step-hop!" The girl stumbled along, laughing with the fun of it all. Muscle memory led Chloe through the figures. She was sorry when the music ended.

Torstein was also a good storyteller. "Our next tune will be 'Fanitullen,'" he announced. "Do you know the tale? Legend says that long ago, a wedding dance was disrupted by a bloody brawl.

The young fiddler went to get a drink and discovered the devil himself sitting on the keg. The devil grabbed the man's fiddle and began to play, beating time with one cloven hoof. As long as the devil worked the bow, people at the party couldn't stop dancing. Even after they died from exhaustion, their bodies kept dancing."

Roelke's eyebrows raised. "That's a bit extreme."

"The fiddler was initially horrified, but the devil's music was too compelling to resist," Torstein continued. "'Fanitullen' is the tune that the fiddler learned from the devil himself that night. In order to play it for you, we're switching to what's known as 'troll tuning.'"

The three musicians plunked their strings, adjusting the pegs until satisfied. Then they launched into a frenzied piece.

"That's borderline discordant," Roelke observed. "But it's powerful."

Chloe's throat grew thick, and she blinked back unexpected tears. When she'd blithely decided to visit Norway, she hadn't known what it would be like to experience this music and dance *here*. People had been fiddling and dancing right here for hundreds of years. It suddenly felt quite different from dancing in the high school gym in Stoughton, Wisconsin. Or even for the king in Oslo.

Had similar feelings pulled her mother back to Norway, time after time? Chloe so wished she had ignored Kari's concerns and talked to Mom about the adoption. She wished Mom had told her about the trip she'd been planning for just the two of them. She wished they hadn't disappointed each other so often.

Roelke, ever prepared, passed her a tissue.

"Thanks." She sniffled. "I guess it all got to me."

"It's okay." He patted her knee.

Torstein brought the concert to a close after that, and the three fiddlers received enthusiastic applause. Some people began making their way back down the hill.

Roelke stood and stretched. "Ready?"

"Not really," Chloe admitted. The sky was smudged with cobalt, but the sun wouldn't set until ten or so. She felt too emotional to simply walk away. "I'd like to visit Høiegård. If you want to head back down, I'll meet you at the hotel."

"No, I'll wait." He sat back down.

Chloe had no idea how she'd gotten so lucky. "We really need to figure out where and when to have our wedding," she told him, "because I truly can hardly *wait* to marry you." That made him smile.

Høiegård was close by. It faced away from the fjord, and she walked around the building. The door would be locked, of course, but maybe that was fine. Maybe pressing her palms against the door would be easier than actually going inside—

Except the door wasn't locked. It was ajar.

A sense of foreboding prickled the back of Chloe's neck. She pushed the door open with one finger. "Hello?" Silence. She leaned inside, and her senses were walloped again. Emotive impressions buzzed in her head, quivered in her chest, seemed to shimmer in the air.

But this time there was even more to take in: the crumpled body, the dark pool of blood, and the stink of death.

Roelke heard Chloe yell his name and was up and running before she even rounded the corner of Høiegård. Boyfriend instincts and cop instincts crackled with alarm. "What?" he demanded, grabbing her arm.

Her eyes were huge, her skin pale. "In the house. Someone's hurt." She licked her lips. "Um, dead. I think."

Roelke glanced over the hillside. A few people lingered, laughing and chatting. "Go find Ellinor. Tell her to call for help, and to not let anyone else leave the grounds. The cops will want to know who was here. Can you do that?"

"Of course." Chloe sounded steadier already. "I see her—" She took off.

Roelke ran in the other direction, around Høiegård to the door in its western wall. A body was sprawled inside, partly through the low interior door to the main room. Visible in the antechamber were slim legs in blue jeans and—and oh, *damn*.

Beneath the jeans were well-worn blue athletic shoes with white wing motifs on the sides.

Maybe it's not her, he thought. The woman's head, arms, and torso were beyond the doorway, in the main room. He carefully stepped to the door, knelt, peered through … and clenched his jaw. It was indeed Klara Evenstad.

He snaked one hand to her throat, searching for a pulse, but he knew she was dead. The fair hair on the back of her head was matted with blood. Her right cheek was against the floor, but her left eye was open, already hazy with death. Her mouth was open too. But … what was on her forehead? It looked like a smear of ash. He leaned closer, contorting himself to see without further contaminating the scene. It wasn't a smear. It was a circle.

What the hell? Roelke glanced beyond her to the hearth-thing in the middle of the room. No way had Klara banged her head on that and landed back here, halfway through the door. It appeared that someone had drawn the circle with their finger. Why on earth would—

"Hva skjedde?"

Roelke jumped as someone behind him spoke in Norwegian. He got to his feet and stepped to the doorway before a concerned-looking bearded man could come inside. A few more guests, sensing trouble, were converging on the old house behind him.

"I'm a police officer," Roelke announced. He had no authority here, of course. But until Norwegian cops arrived, he was the best bet for keeping the crime scene—and he was sure it was a crime scene—as pristine as possible.

"There's been an accident," he told the bearded guy, exuding every ounce of command presence he could summon. "I need you to go see if anyone on the hill is a doctor." The man looked startled but nodded and turned away. "The rest of you, please, stay back from the house."

Ellinor appeared with Chloe in her wake. He frowned. "I said to—"

"Sonja is stopping the guests." Ellinor looked ready to charge inside. "I need to be here." Chloe made a helpless gesture: *I tried.*

Roelke blocked the door. "Did you call the police?"

"Of course. Closest station is in Odda, though. That's a forty-five-minute drive."

He cursed. That was a long time to wrangle people who wanted to go home. A long time to withhold what little information he had.

"I need to see what happened," Ellinor hissed. "Who is it?"

The bearded man returned, shaking his head. "No doctor."

Roelke asked him to keep people away before turning back to the director. Best get right to it. "Someone has died," he said. "I'm sorry to tell you that the victim is Klara Evenstad."

The hand Ellinor pressed over her mouth didn't stifle her shocked cry. She struggled visibly for composure. "What happened? How did she die?"

"The only thing that matters is what the Norwegian police conclude." He tried not to flinch from Ellinor's anguished face. "But unofficially, it looks as if someone struck her as she stooped to enter the main room."

Chloe gasped. Klara's earlier explanation for Høiegård's architecture flashed in Roelke's memory: *That inner door was a safety feature. If someone attacked the family, they'd be forced to bend low coming through the door, and* … Klara had pantomimed striking a vicious blow to the back of an intruder's head.

"But … but who would *do* something like that?" The director held his gaze, begging him to make sense of the insensible.

Roelke shook his head. "I have no idea."

"Everyone liked Klara!" Ellinor protested. She looked stunned.

Chloe put an arm around the older woman's shoulders. "I'm so very sorry. All we can do now is wait and let the police sort things out."

"But—"

"Ellinor? Ellinor!"

They all turned as Torstein ran across the lawn. "What's happened? Someone said …" He looked from one face to the next, wanting reassurances that no one could give.

Ellinor put a hand on his arm. "Oh, *Torstein*."

He clearly found more than he wanted to know in her eyes, in her tone, in her touch. "Not …" he began but couldn't complete the words. His face crumpled. Then his legs crumpled too. He fell to his knees, hands over his face, shoulders shaking with sobs.

Chloe felt bone-weary by the time she and Roelke got back to the Utne Hotel. She dropped onto the bed and stared up at him. "Dear God. Who would want to kill that girl?"

Roelke sat beside her and gathered her into his arms. Chloe nestled her head on his shoulder.

They sat in silence for a long time. She wished she knew how to turn off her brain. A movie flickered endlessly in her head: Klara smiling as she refilled their coffee cups that morning, Klara singing a centuries-old lullaby in Høiegård that afternoon, Klara glowing as Torstein kissed her in the gift shop, Klara lying dead in a pool of blood. It all felt like a bad dream … but it wasn't.

The police had finally arrived from Odda and taken charge. Volvos marked *Politi* parked among the historic structures, the first of the harsh intrusions. A medical person pronounced the death, and a detective—or whatever the Norwegian equivalent was—began his examination. Fluorescent tape was strung. Phone calls were made. More officials arrived—crime scene specialists, Roelke had speculated. An earnest young officer interviewed the audience members still on the hill. *Politi Førsteinspektør* Naess, an older, grim-faced officer with a square jaw and piercing gray eyes, had interviewed Chloe, interviewed Roelke, interviewed Ellinor and Sonja and Torstein. His black uniform displayed a fancy coat of arms on the sleeve and three yellow insignia of rank on the shoulder.

As darkness fell, someone brought bright lights and snaked power cords to Høiegård from a maintenance shop discreetly located in one of the historic structures. The harsh glare and bright colors and terse voices felt all wrong in that special place. Chloe had been profoundly relieved when Naess gave her and Roelke permission to go. "But don't leave the Hardanger area," he added, pinning her with that gray stare. "How long are you scheduled to be here?"

"For another week," Roelke told him.

"Well," the cop had said, "we'll see."

Now those simple words pinged in Chloe's mind. "Needing to stay in Norway for longer than we'd planned would be … difficult." For one thing, their money would run out fast. For another, their bosses—particularly hers—would not be pleased.

"Let's not worry about that quite yet," Roelke said. "A lot can happen in a week."

"Too much has already happened." Chloe pushed to her feet and plodded toward the bathroom. "I'm getting ready for bed."

Sunlight woke Chloe long before she was ready to get up—4:58, according to the clock. Roelke was sleeping beside her. She lay still, listening to his rhythmic breathing and trying to figure out why she felt so groggy. Then it all came flooding back—the body, the blood.

Chloe sighed. She'd never go back to sleep now. Might as well get up and go in search of coffee.

She padded silently across the room and, without thinking, went to the window. As her palm brushed the sill, she was again overwhelmed with a sense of unbearable despair. She whipped her hand away and just barely managed to swallow a squawk. What *was* that? It really was frustrating to have the best view in the hotel and not be able to lean out the window and enjoy it.

Roelke hadn't stirred. Moving silently, steering clear of the window, Chloe pulled on jeans and a green T-shirt. Then she eased the door open, slipped into the hall, and tiptoed down the stairs.

The hotel was quiet. She poked her head into the dining room, but no one was in sight. Geez, she thought with a sigh, it really was *way* too early to be up. The ground floor was divided into small rooms, each furnished with antiques. Not knowing what else to do with herself, she settled in a parlor … and tried not to think about Klara.

That part did not go well. Chloe was relieved to be interrupted by a red-haired teen carrying a broom and wearing the vaguely ethnic dress of an employee. "Pardon!" the girl gasped, clearly unnerved to see her. Behind wire-rimmed glasses her eyes were red and puffy.

"Sorry," Chloe said. "I didn't mean to startle you."

"You didn't." The girl pulled a tissue from her pocket and dabbed at her eyes. "May I bring you some tea or coffee?"

"Coffee would be absolutely wonderful," Chloe admitted.

The girl quickly returned with a mug, sugar bowl, and china pitcher of cream on a tray. "Here you are." She sniffled hard and dug for another tissue.

"Are you all right?" Chloe asked gently.

"It's j-just … Do y-you know about Klara?"

"I do." Chloe had to blink hard herself, and she tried to cover it by patting the sofa beside her. "Can you sit for a minute?"

The girl glanced toward the door before gingerly perching. Chloe put an arm around her shoulders. "I'm Chloe Ellefson. What's your name?"

"Barbara-Eden Kirkevoll."

"Oh!" Chloe tried to hide her surprise.

Barbara-Eden nodded wearily, as if used to the reaction. "It's hyphenated. My mother loved *I Dream of Jeannie*."

American pop culture at its finest, Chloe thought, remembering the blond actress in the starring role. Then she refocused on what mattered. "Were you and Klara friends?"

The younger woman began to cry unabashedly. "Best friends. I j-just can't think who w-would do such a thing."

"It's hard to imagine," Chloe agreed.

"If anybody had been bothering her, she would have told me." Barbara stared at the damp tissue she'd wadded in her fingers. "We've been best friends since we were five." Another tear slid down her cheek. She swiped it away with the back of one hand. "I'm sorry."

"You have nothing to apologize for," Chloe assured her. "I'm upset too, and I'd only just met Klara. She seemed very sweet."

"She really was." Barbara-Eden stood. "I have to get back to work. We'll open the dining room for breakfast at seven."

Chloe watched her go. Losing a best friend to illness or accident was horrid. Losing one to murder was brutal. And if the police hadn't already questioned her, they would soon. Chloe knew from experience that even informational interviews with police officers could be daunting.

And what about Torstein? Ellinor had said that he and Klara were "madly in love." Having seen him regarding Klara with glowing tenderness in the gift shop yesterday afternoon, Chloe believed it. But she'd heard Roelke say more than once that in cases like this, the lover/boyfriend/husband was always near the top of the suspect list. She remembered the exuberant joy in Torstein's face as he'd fiddled with his friends, all the while not knowing that the girl he loved was lying dead nearby.

Chloe poured cream into the fast-cooling cup of coffee and sipped, trying to stave off despondency. Love was a wonderful thing, but it could also lead to heartache.

ELEVEN

Torhild—August 1854

Torhild feared that Gjertrud was setting herself up for heartache.

Edvin Brekke had stayed in Utne after the Midsummer dance. Sometimes he brought out his *flatfele*—a violin—and sat in front of the inn, playing. He spent most of his days trying to find a *harding-fele* player who would talk to him—or, when that didn't work out, any elderly person who would tell him stories about dances and music.

"People have been quite rude to Edvin!" Gjertrud told her indignantly one hot day in early August. Plums and cherries were ripe in Hardanger. The first pears and apples too. After purchasing many baskets, Mother Utne had asked Torhild to come for a week and help set it all by.

Cook had ordered the two girls to have the kitchen tidy by the time she returned to make dinner, and left them to it. Now bees and flies buzzed at slop buckets brimming with pits and discarded bits of fruit, and the room smelled deliciously of cinnamon and cardamom.

"Rude?" Torhild echoed.

"Sometimes they won't even speak to him! Yesterday he wanted to talk with someone in Kvanndal. He paid a boatman for the trip, and the man shut the door in our faces—"

"*Our* faces?" Torhild looked up from the plum she was pitting, juice dripping from her fingers. "You went with him?"

"It was my off day, so of course." Gjertrud kept her gaze on some chopped fruit as she swept it into an iron kettle with her hand. "Torhild, Edvin and I are in love."

"In love?" Torhild blinked. "You only just met!"

"Sometimes people know at once," Gjertrud said loftily. "Since it hasn't happened to you, you can't understand."

Torhild groped for a response. "Are you happy?"

"Of course I am!" Gjertrud sighed with obvious pleasure. "I've never met anyone like Edvin. I've been helping him with his project, and the more time we spend together…" She sighed again.

Torhild reached for another plum. As an only child who lived high on a mountain, she had few close companions. She loved Gjertrud. She wanted to be joyful for her cousin… but she could not. It was more than the way Edvin Brekke had touched her in the dining room, and his obvious disdain for the very people whose help he wanted. Something told her that Brekke was not the man her cousin was meant to marry.

She wished she understood why Gjertrud's news prompted only apprehension. And she wished her great-grandmother Gudrun was still alive. She'd been a wise old soul, able to offer advice without offending. Torhild had loved and respected Gudrun, even if she hadn't always understood the old woman's stories. Gudrun had once asked if she ever anticipated events before they happened. "Like looking forward to a harvest dance?" Torhild had asked.

"No, child. I'm speaking of events you have no knowledge of."

Torhild laughed. "Then how could I anticipate them?"

"One day, I think you might." Gudrun gently cupped her great-granddaughter's face in her hands. "But I won't be here to guide you. Once I had hoped that your mother, Lisbet … well. She has been too burdened. But you, Torhild …"

"Yes?"

But Gudrun had said only, "Don't shut your heart to your gift, child. Promise me that. Watch for it in your own daughters and granddaughters. Nurture it." Three weeks later Gudrun's coffin was carried down to the shore while a fiddler played tunes for a death. The family had buried her in the Kinsarvik churchyard.

I should have asked more questions, Torhild thought now. For the first time, she thought she might understand what Gudrun had been trying to tell her. But it didn't feel like a gift. Her sense of foreboding was a dark burden.

Gjertrud dumped more sliced plums into the kettle on the new cookstove. Then she faced her cousin with hands on hips. "You're very quiet. Are you jealous of me?"

"No! No, it's not that, it's just that … I worry that Edvin might be … misrepresenting himself to you."

"You sound like my mother!" Two spots of color bloomed in Gjertrud's cheeks. Her eyes glittered with unshed tears. "You think I'm not good enough for Edvin?"

Torhild grabbed her hands. "*No*. I fear that he might not be good enough for you."

Gjertrud sniffled but smiled a forgiving smile. "I truly believe we are well matched. All will be well, Torhild. You'll see."

The next day, Mother Utne sent Torhild to a widow's home with a crock of plum preserves. Torhild found the woman sitting in a chair by the open front door. "A gift from Mother Utne," Torhild told her. "Shall I set it on the table?"

"That will be fine." The old woman looked pleased. "Take my thanks back to her. You work at the inn?"

"I help out when needed." Torhild turned to leave.

The widow held up one palsied hand, stopping her. "You've had a guest at the inn all summer."

Edvin Brekke, she meant. "Yes."

"He's a bad one." Despite the heat, the widow tugged at the worn wool shawl tucked around her shoulders. "All this talk of fiddles and collecting tunes! It's the devil's work. And that girl who goes about with him, she's the same. People see what's happening."

Torhild caught her breath. "'That girl' is my cousin," she flared. "She's a good Christian who doesn't believe in spiteful gossip. Good day to you." She marched away with chin held high.

But her annoyance couldn't mask her worry. Should I say something to Gjertrud? Torhild wondered miserably as she walked back to the inn. Let her know that people were talking? Would that do any good, or cause more harm?

When she stepped into the kitchen, Cook was berating Gjertrud, and her scowl quickly drew Torhild in too. "You girls left the floor sticky with juice. We'll have all sorts of vermin if we're not careful. I want it scrubbed, and scrubbed well."

They heated water in silence. But when they were both on their knees, scrubbing the slates, Gjertrud caught her eye and winked a saucy wink. Torhild bit her tongue to keep from snickering. Warning Gjertrud of ill-minded talk can wait until tomorrow, she thought.

That afternoon a cool wind blew dark clouds low before the mountains. Soon a steady rain was dappling the gray fjord, churning the street to mud, drumming against the roof. Several local men came to the inn in search of dinner and a dry evening before the fire. Edvin Brekke tried to introduce himself into the group, but when he received a cool welcome he fetched his *flatfele* and settled into a corner. "Bring me some *akevitt*, Torhild," he called. "I've grown quite fond of the wretched stuff."

When she brought the drink he was tuning his violin. It was an odd, ugly instrument, flat and unadorned, with a flimsy sound. "I didn't come to hear a squealing piglet," a scrawny fellow near the fire declared loudly. But Brekke nestled the instrument beneath his chin, picked up the bow, and began to play.

The other man scowled. "Another round of ale, then," he called to her.

Torhild poured the ale in the kitchen and fixed a tray. "I'll take it," Gjertrud said eagerly, almost elbowing her out of the way. Torhild didn't care. She'd rather wash dishes.

She'd just rolled up her sleeves and reached for a skillet when she heard Brekke cut off his tune, and new voices from the dining room. More people wanting haven from the storm, no doubt. She tugged her sleeves down again and went to see what they might need.

Just as she opened the kitchen door, Gjertrud cried, "Leave it alone!"

Half a dozen newcomers had formed a semicircle around Brekke, all men. "We want you gone," announced a man Torhild had seen selling fish on the shore. "And I'll take *that*." He made a grab for Brekke's violin.

Gjertrud lunged and grabbed the fisherman's arm. "No!" Torhild cried.

"For God's sake, man!" Brekke exclaimed, swinging the violin away—right into the chest of a younger man who managed to snatch it. Torhild watched in shock as he ran to the hearth and hurled the *flatfele* onto the crackling fire. It crashed in a sudden flare of sparks.

The other men were all on their feet. Torhild braced herself, certain they'd charge at the newcomers. They gawked—some at the fanatics, some at each other. But they didn't move. Didn't throw a single fist.

After a stunned silence, Gjertrud ran from the room. "Mother Utne! *Mother Utne!*"

Torhild felt a sinking sensation in her chest. It was happening again. After years of relative peace, of little beyond grumbles and dark looks from those who believed fiddles and drink and dance should be banned, of visits to fiddlers' homes that yielded no results, it was all happening again.

———

When everything had finally calmed down, when the dining room was empty and the last mug washed and dried, Torhild carried a candle to the storehouse. Gjertrud was not there. Torhild had not seen her since she ran from the dining room as Edvin Brekke's violin burned.

She is with him, Torhild thought, and berated herself for not telling Gjertrud that people were watching. People were talking. People were upset. Only a few … but enough to do the harm that had been done tonight.

Torhild didn't know how long she'd lain in bed, staring into the darkness, before the door creaked open. She saw a candle's glow, heard tiptoeing footsteps. "Gjertrud, I've been worried!"

Gjertrud slipped from her dress, blew out the candle, and climbed into the bed beside her. "Don't be. Everything is going to be fine."

"They burned Edvin Brekke's *flatfele*!"

"Oh, he's angry about it," Gjertrud conceded. "Very upset. In fact, he's decided to end his study and return to Bergen."

Torhild felt a flood of relief.

"And I'm going with him!"

The relief vanished. "You're … what?"

"We're going to be married! Edvin says a marriage can happen quickly in the city. We're leaving day after tomorrow on the morning boat."

"What about your mother?" Torhild could hardly believe what she was hearing. "She'll want to plan the wedding—"

"I'll write to her, of course," Gjertrud said. "But my mother tried to keep me from seeing Edvin. When I'm married and living in Bergen, she'll realize how wrong she was."

Torhild pictured Gjertrud's mother, a stern and implacable widow. If she had forbidden Gjertrud to spend time with the music teacher, nothing would change her mind.

"Edvin says this is the best solution," Gjertrud was saying. "I'll be a teacher's wife!" Her voice was filled with wonder.

"But… it's all so sudden. Why not wait until—"

"We'd leave tomorrow except he wants to go say goodbye to one of the few people who actually helped him, and he'll be gone overnight. And he wants me to have time to tell Mother Utne I'm leaving, and to say my own goodbyes."

"Oh, Gjertrud. Are you sure this is what you want?"

"I don't want to work at the inn all my life, or on a farm either. Edvin has offered me more than I ever dreamed of. *Please* be happy for me, Torhild. I couldn't bear it if you weren't."

"All right, Gjertrud," Torhild whispered. "I'll try." She rolled over and curled into a ball, but she couldn't sleep.

Two days later, shortly before nine o'clock, Torhild and Gjertrud walked across the lane to the dock. The rain had blown through. The damp air smelled of smoke and fish. The sloop that would carry Gjertrud and Edvin Brekke to Bergen was already anchored in the fjord. A boy, perhaps twelve, sat in a rowboat edged on shore, waiting to transport passengers to the sloop. Gjertrud set her bundle down and looked about.

"Edvin is cutting things short," Torhild murmured, then wished she hadn't.

Gjertrud shielded her eyes against the sun. "He'll be here."

The boy jerked his head toward the sloop. "You ladies coming?"

"I'm waiting for my traveling companion," Gjertrud told him.

Minutes ticked by. Torhild's sense of impending disaster balled sour in the pit of her stomach. At that moment she wanted to see Edvin Brekke running toward the dock as badly as Gjertrud did.

"They won't wait," the boy said. "Captain's got a schedule to keep."

"Have you already taken anyone on board?" Gjertrud's voice quavered. "A man going to Bergen?"

The boy shrugged. "Only man going to Bergen I've seen lately went out yesterday morning. A fancy city man with a scar on his cheek."

Gjertrud went very still. She stared at the boy, then looked blindly over the water. The cry of a gull soaring overhead sounded mournful.

Torhild opened her mouth, couldn't find words, and closed it again.

Finally Gjertrud said, "I won't be traveling today after all." The boy scowled in disgust.

Torhild reached for her. "Oh, Gjertrud—"

"Don't." She flinched away.

"Come back to the inn," Torhild said helplessly. Mother Utne would know what to do.

"How can I?" Gjertrud's voice was high and thin. She turned and walked away, leaving her bundle on the stony beach. Her pace was slow, unsteady, as if afraid she might lose her balance.

Torhild followed. When Gjertrud turned and passed the inn steps, Torhild grabbed her arm again. "Gjertrud! Where are you going?"

Gjertrud lifted her palms in a helpless gesture. "I've made a fool of myself."

"You didn't—"

"I gave notice. I said my goodbyes." She looked dazed. "My mother was already angry with me for spending time with Edvin. And other people are angry at me for helping him."

"It's not your fault!"

"He said he loved me." Gjertrud's gaze begged her cousin to believe it. "He said he wanted to marry me. And I … I lay with him."

She might be with child, Torhild thought. Something knotted in her chest. The bleak look on Gjertrud's face frightened her. "He is a liar, and not good enough for you. *Please* come back to the inn with me."

Gjertrud frowned as if confused to find herself in the middle of the lane. Finally she nodded. "Yes. All right." She let Torhild take her arm and lead her back to the inn.

Torhild didn't want Cook to be the first person they encountered, so she dared go in the front door. In the parlor she gently pushed her cousin onto a chair. "Sit here. I'll be right back."

It took Torhild several minutes to find the proprietress, who was working on accounts, and several more to stumble through the tale. Mother Utne shook her head and put her pencil aside. "That poor girl. She's not the first to be taken in by a glib tongue. Knowing that won't make her feel better, though. Time is what she needs. I had better see to her."

She hurried from the office with Torhild on her heels. But when they reached the front parlor, Gjertrud was gone. The sick knot in Torhild's chest jerked tight.

Mother Utne looked about, perplexed. "Where could she have—"

From the corner of her eye Torhild saw something—someone—falling past the front window.

The older woman ran to the glass, cringed, turned away. Torhild managed one step, but Mother Utne put up a hand. "Don't," she said, her voice like gravel. "You don't want to see."

TWELVE

Shortly after seven, Roelke woke and discovered that he was alone. Not good. Chloe never got up first.

He found her downstairs, staring at a portrait of an elderly woman in traditional Norwegian dress. "Hey," he said. "Nice painting."

"It's Mother Utne. She was a legendary innkeeper here." Chloe lifted her mug, noticed it was empty, set it aside.

"I hope you're having more than coffee."

"I'm not hungry."

"Eat something anyway. And not just a pastry. You need protein."

In the dining room, they passed through the buffet line and settled back by the window. Chloe picked at some scrambled eggs before pushing her plate away. Roelke was about to protest when a young red-haired woman with coffeepot in hand stopped by the table.

"Roelke, meet Barbara-Eden Kirkevoll," Chloe said. "Barbara-Eden, this is my fiancé, Roelke McKenna."

"Good to meet you," she said, then looked at Chloe anxiously. "Is something wrong with the eggs?"

"Oh—no. They're fine." She pulled the plate back and took a determined bite.

Apparently, Roelke thought, upsetting the waitstaff is worse than upsetting me.

The redhead leaned closer. "Did you sleep all right? Sometimes people in Room 15 don't."

"Why is that?" Chloe's forehead crinkled.

"Well, it's just a story."

Chloe glanced at Roelke, clearly perplexed. "We haven't heard it."

Barbara-Eden glanced over both shoulders. "They say a girl, someone who worked here, threw herself out of the window in Room 15 after her lover abandoned her."

Roelke leaned back, taking that in. Normally he would dismiss such a wild tale. But having seen how Chloe reacted to touching that window…

"Do you know her name?" Chloe asked. "Or when it took place?"

Barbara-Eden shook her head. "It happened a hundred years ago. Maybe even more."

"Thanks for letting us know," Chloe told her. "I hope the poor girl is resting in peace."

When they were alone again, she shook her head. "Well, now I know what happened at the window."

Roelke rubbed his chin. "You think?"

"I do. The heartbroken girl probably went straight to the window, then perhaps hesitated. That explains the overwhelming despair I felt—but only *there*. She didn't linger in the room, so the emotional residue was left at the window."

"Well, hunh."

"I talked with that young woman earlier," she told him, cocking her head toward Barbara-Eden as she disappeared back into the kitchen.

"Barbara-Eden? That's really her name?"

Chloe shrugged. "Her mother loved *I Dream of Jeannie*. Anyway, she was Klara's best friend. I asked if Klara had seemed upset about anything lately, and she said no."

"Well, hunh." Roelke spread some smoked mackerel on a cracker. Could Klara's death truly have been a random strike by some lunatic who just happened to be passing through the outdoor museum yesterday afternoon? It seemed unlikely. "We saw Klara in the gift shop at ... what, about four in the afternoon? After the tour?"

"Sounds about right." Chloe stabbed a slice of strawberry with her fork. "Maybe Klara went back to get something she forgot. Or maybe she noticed that the padlock was open and went inside to see why."

"And encountered a crazed killer who just happened to be waiting? That's a stretch. Perhaps she'd agreed to meet someone in that old house."

"Maybe."

"There's something I didn't have a chance to tell you." Roelke hesitated. "When I got close to check for a pulse, I noticed a smear of ashes on Klara's forehead."

Chloe stared at him blankly. "Ashes?"

"Yes. A circle, to be exact. No way did she hit that raised fireplace on the way down. And since it wasn't Ash Wednesday, all I can figure is that whoever killed Klara took a moment to put it there before leaving."

"That's … weird." Chloe rubbed her arms as if suddenly chilled. "And creepy."

"Yeah. I thought so too." Roelke tried again to make sense of the ashes. He could not, so he moved on. "There's something else. Remember I told you that Klara passed me yesterday morning when I was hiking up the mountain? Shortly after she disappeared there was a rockslide—"

"A rockslide?" Chloe looked horrified.

"Hardly an avalanche," he assured her, "but one of the stones that came bouncing down the trail could have done some damage if I hadn't jumped aside in time."

"Why didn't you tell me that?"

"It wasn't my finest hour," he said briefly. "And I'm not accusing Klara of causing it. Even if she did, it was probably inadvertently. But since we're considering what little we know about her, I thought I'd mention it."

"Why would she do something like that?"

"I don't know." He pulled an index card from his pocket and wrote *Klara Evenstad* on the top line.

Chloe sighed. "Do we have to start this? Can't we just leave things to the police?"

"It's what I do. I can't help it." In Roelke's experience, trying to sort through such things provided more comfort than simply stewing. "What do we know about Klara?"

"Not much." Chloe considered. "She was born and raised in Utne. She loved history. Barbara-Eden and Klara were best friends since they were young kids. Last summer Klara worked at the

Hardanger Folkemuseum, but this summer her main job is at the Utne Hotel, and she only helps out at the museum."

Roelke held up one finger, halting the flow as he caught up, then rolled his hand: *Go ahead.*

"Klara was romantically involved with Torstein Landvik."

He noted that, and added what Chloe had not mentioned:

- *was hiking up trail before rockslide*
- *found dead with ashes on her forehead*

He turned the card so Chloe could see it. "Anything else?"

She studied the card with distaste and shook her head. "No." They finished their meal in brooding silence.

As they left the dining room Chloe said, "I was supposed to go on a field visit with Torstein today, but I can't imagine that's still a go." She sighed. "Maybe we should go check in with Ellinor."

They walked to the museum. "Ellinor's in her office," the subdued woman at the ticket counter said.

Ellinor looked up from her desk when Chloe knocked. "Come in," the director said, rubbing her temples. She seemed to have aged overnight—the fine lines by her mouth deeper, the energy in her eyes muted. She wore a somber dark gray suit.

"Is there any news?" Chloe asked.

"Reporters keep calling, and the staff is upset, and I expect the police will be back. Høiegård is still cordoned off, so I'm keeping the whole open-air division closed for now." Ellinor picked up a file folder, stared at it for a moment, then put it down. "Sonja's off on her interview with the headdress maker. I haven't heard from Torstein."

"I wouldn't expect him to carry on as usual," Chloe said.

"Why don't you check back this afternoon?" Ellinor blew out a long breath. "I'm sorry to leave you with nothing to do."

Chloe considered. "Maybe I'll see if Reverend Brandvold might be available to talk."

Ellinor brightened. "I'll call him." She reached for the phone, and after a brief conversation in Norwegian, replaced the receiver again. "He was just on his way to the church. You're welcome to meet him there."

Chloe thought the Utne Church was quite lovely. It was a white, wooden structure with a red door. Slate tiles covered the roof and the commanding steeple. A sweeping lawn sloped toward the fjord below the church, and green and gray mountains rose above.

The front door was unlocked, the vestibule empty. Chloe paused inside, opening herself to the old building. The faint sense of faith and refuge she perceived was comforting.

The sanctuary honored Norwegian folk art with decoratively carved pews, doors, and pulpit; a model ship hanging from the ceiling paid tribute to the region's fishing heritage. I could happily worship here, Chloe thought. "Something about this place makes me feel at home."

Before Roelke could respond, a man wearing a black suit walked down the aisle to meet them. "You must be the American visitors! I'm Martin Brandvold." His voice was ponderous, as if he'd become accustomed to addressing a full sanctuary and hadn't adjusted to retirement. His gait was ponderous too, for he was a heavyset man. But beneath a still-thick thatch of white hair, the blue eyes in his weathered face were warm with welcome.

Chloe made the introductions. "It's kind of you to see us."

He waved that away. "I'm an old man who used to talk to people every day. I'm happy to talk with you. And to share this lovely church." He contemplated the sanctuary with obvious fondness. "It dates to 1895—very new compared to the Kinsarvik Church across the fjord. And it's hardly renowned, compared to Norway's famous stave churches, or even Ulvik's rosemaled sanctuary. But this one is beautiful too."

"How long were you minister here?" Roelke asked.

"Twenty-seven years. I do try to keep out of the new man's way, but it's a second home of sorts. I come here most days, just to rest and reflect. And today, after hearing the news..." He sobered. "Let's sit." He gestured to one of the pews.

Chloe sidled after the pastor and sat sideways to face him. "You're speaking of Klara Evenstad's death?"

"Yes." He rubbed his hands over his face. "I understand you found her? How dreadful."

Roelke leaned forward to catch the older man's eye. "Did you know Klara?"

He looked surprised at the question. "Of course! I baptized her. I celebrated her confirmation. I had hoped to... what is the word? Officiate? Officiate at her wedding."

Of course, Chloe echoed silently. Utne was a small village. Probably most residents attended this church. Reverend Brandvold had watched them grow, officiated at their baptisms and confirmations, conducted weddings and funerals. "I'm sorry for your loss, sir."

"Klara was born and raised here. Her father died long ago, so it's been just Klara, her younger brother, and her mother." He rested his palms on his knees and studied the hymnal rack. "I'll visit the poor woman, of course. She and Klara were close."

"We've met Torstein too," Roelke said. "Were he and Klara engaged?" His voice held a casual note that was most unlike him.

"Not officially," Reverend Brandvold said. "But sometimes he attended services here with her. That couple turned heads. Klara looked so happy when they were together! I think some of the other young women were envious. Her best friend … well."

Chloe hesitated, not wanting to pry. "Are you referring to Barbara-Eden? I spoke with her this morning. She's very upset."

"I think Barbara-Eden's friendship with Klara was a … a saving?" His hand moved as if groping for the right English word. "A lifeline, yes? Her home situation is not good. I'll see if she would like to talk, too." The pastor's shoulders hitched slightly, as if acknowledging the weight of his ongoing obligations. Chloe respected him for staying involved, and for caring, even after retirement.

Pastor Brandvold made a visible effort to rouse himself. "But you didn't come here to talk about Klara. Ellinor said you want to learn about traditional music and dance?"

"Well, that's the professional reason I'm in Norway," Chloe acknowledged.

"When I was called to this church, village people still used an old dance site up on the mountain. There was a wooden platform to dance on. They had bonfires too, especially on Midsummer." He smiled. "Some of my colleagues objected to such festivities, but I never did. It was all in fun."

"I wish I could have seen that," Chloe said wistfully. Her experience with folk dance had always been organized and performance-oriented—first with the Stoughton Norwegian Dancers, later with various folk dance groups. "Is it possible to visit the site?"

"I assume so, although I doubt there's much left to see. Keep going on the main road"—he pointed—"and look for a path that heads uphill just past the apple orchard." Reverend Brandvold rested one arm on the back of the pew. "But Ellinor also said there was another reason for your trip. Tell me, how can I help you?"

"I have reason to believe that my mother was either born somewhere in the Hardanger region or descended from people here," Chloe said.

"If your ancestors lived in the area, in the old days they probably worshipped in Kinsarvik. That was the main church in Hardanger for many years."

"All I know right now is that in 1920, my mother was surrendered to an orphanage in Stoughton, Wisconsin, by a woman named Amalie Sveinsdatter."

"Amalie Sveinsdatter?" His brow furrowed.

Chloe exchanged a quick glance with Roelke. "Is that name familiar?"

The older man rubbed his chin for a long moment, then shook his head. "It's a pretty name, but—no. I can't place it."

It couldn't have been that easy, Chloe thought. "Anyway, Amalie didn't speak English, so she was most likely an immigrant."

"Amalie's use of the surname Sveinsdatter also suggests that she might have been newly arrived in America," Reverend Brandvold mused. "She probably became known as Emily Swenson, or something like it."

"And even if I knew that she Americanized her name, I can only access Wisconsin census records through 1905," Chloe told him glumly. "And by law, the National Archives doesn't release federal records until seventy-two years after a census." That meant she had to wait eight more years to see if Amalie was listed in 1920 records, and *eighteen* years to search the 1930 information. The government officials who'd decreed it so no doubt had their reasons, but it seemed horribly unfair.

"And if Amalie was an unwed mother ..." The pastor spread his hands, indicating the enormity of Chloe's challenge. "She might have moved on. Started over in a new community. Even a new state. Between 1825, when the first organized group of Norwegians sailed to America, and 1920, over nine hundred thousand immigrants left Norway and settled in your country."

"Holy toboggans," Roelke said soberly. "That's a whole lot of Norwegians."

"Overpopulation here became a huge problem." Reverend Brandvold settled back in the pew. "The discovery of a smallpox vaccine, and the introduction of potatoes in the early 1800s, saved thousands from dying of disease or starvation. But in a family with ten or twelve children, most had to leave for America."

Chloe nibbled her lower lip. "We don't know exactly when Amalie departed, of course, but a friend of mine is searching ships' passenger lists, working backwards from 1920, in hopes of finding her name."

"That's a good strategy," the pastor said. "After Ellis Island opened in 1892, officials started collecting more detailed information about each passenger."

Chloe hoped that Rosemary Rossebo, Mom's friend and a genealogist extraordinaire, could find evidence of Amalie's departure from Norway. "I thought I could start searching church records during my visit, as time permits. Are the Utne records kept here?"

"I'm afraid not." Reverend Brandvold sounded grieved. "Parish records would include immigrant departures, but they're kept at the regional archives in Bergen. I could have borrowed them if you'd let me know in advance."

Chloe twisted her mouth with frustration. "I should have thought that through." Some researcher she was.

"You were kinda busy," Roelke observed. She gave him a grateful look.

"It doesn't mean I can't help," the older man assured them. "I've got friends in the city. Someone may have time to check church records for you. From 1867 to 1973, the Norwegian Police also kept emigration records. And pastors wrote recommendations for immigrants. I'll look through my own files at home."

"This is all *very* kind of you," Chloe said.

He waved that away. "I've been collecting local items for years. Letters, account books—anything I can find. It's become a … what do you say?"

"A passion?" Chloe tried. "An addiction? An obsession?"

"Yes!" Reverend Brandvold beamed. "An obsession." Then his smile faded, and his eyes grew shadowed. "I care deeply about the people who live here now, and about their ancestors. It's hard to read of tragedies and losses, even if they happened a century ago, maybe longer."

"But inspiring too?" Chloe guessed. She was often inspired by stories of people who had gone before.

"They persevered," the pastor agreed.

"I often wonder," Chloe said soberly, "if I would have done as well."

THIRTEEN

Torhild—February 1866

"Torhild! Torhild, wake up!"

Torhild struggled groggily to wakefulness. She blinked at the flickering light of a candle. Her mother Lisbet stood by the bed. "What's wrong?" Torhild mumbled, shoving hair back from her face. Halvor, her husband of six years, didn't stir.

Lisbet's face was an anxious white oval in the shadows. "Your father is gone."

Torhild pushed herself upright. "He likely went out to check the animals."

"I waited for him to come back. It's been too long."

Not good, Torhild thought. The night was bitterly cold. The howling wind knifed through cracks in the old house. Snow had been knee-deep when they'd all gone to bed, and surely it was drifted higher now.

"We'll go look. You build up the fire." She turned and shook her husband's shoulder. "Halvor, wake up. I need your help."

He rolled away from her. “Leave me be,” he grumbled.

“Halvor!” Torhild yanked back the sheepskins and shook him harder. Honestly, sometimes her man was as shiftless as Edvin Brekke…

She shivered, as she always did when thinking of her cousin Gjertrud’s disastrous relationship with the Bergen musician. Twelve years had passed since Gjertrud had thrown herself from the Utne Inn’s highest window. Not a day had gone by without Torhild remembering, grieving, struggling to cope with her anger.

Halvor had seemed to be everything that Edvin Brekke was *not*. Her groom was a stolid farmer she’d met at a harvest party. When he’d asked for her hand four months later, she’d been willing. Torhild had worn the ancestral bridal crown for their wedding and covered her hands with the blackwork *handaplagg* her mother had received from *her* grandmother Gudrun. Halvor was a younger son with no land of his own, so he’d moved to Høiegård. Torhild’s father needed help, God knew, and she’d felt optimistic about the future. Best of all, Halvor was a good dancer.

But Halvor was also a good drinker. Once they married he’d grown less careful, not bothering to pretend to be anything but stumbling drunk after an evening with friends. When he drank, he turned lazy and sharp-tongued. And he drank a lot.

Now Halvor blinked, then winced. “What?” he grumbled.

“My father went outside and hasn’t come back.” Torhild scrambled from bed, shivering. She glanced to the pallet where her two young sons slept peacefully, nestled between woolly sheepskins. At the hearth, Lisbet tossed kindling on the smoldering ashes and blew sparks into flames.

Torhild and Halvor pulled on coats and cloaks and thick mittens. "We'll find him," Torhild promised her mother, as Halvor lit a lantern. "He's probably waiting out the storm in the stable."

The night was a dark, whirling chaos of snow. Torhild staggered before the wind, head bent as tiny pellets lashed her cheeks. Halvor locked his arm through hers and they stumbled forward. Inside, the stable smelled comfortingly of cow manure and hay and the oily fleeces stored after the last shearing. It was a relief to escape the wind. But there was no sign of her father.

"He must have lost his way in the storm," Halvor muttered. "We'll never find his tracks now."

Torhild couldn't bear the image of her father limping through the storm, missing the house, confused and freezing. "Then we must search for him!"

Halvor hesitated, then nodded. "Do *not* stray from me." He found a length of rope, tied one end around his waist, and the other around hers. They pulled their scarves up over their noses and went back into the blizzard.

It took much too long to find Lars. If he hadn't worn a scarlet cap, they would have missed him altogether. He lay in the snow, well away from both stable and house. "Father?" Torhild cried, crouching beside him. His skin was white, his hair crusted with snow, his eyes closed. *"Father!"* His lips moved, but no words emerged.

She turned to her husband. "Help me! We've got to get him inside."

———

Two weeks later, Torhild pulled a stool close to the bed and settled the bowl of sour cream porridge in her lap. "I've made *rømmegrøt*, Father," she murmured. "I'll help you." She spooned a bit between her father's lips, then used a cloth to wipe away what had spilled. Her father managed a lopsided smile.

Somewhere behind her, Lisbet stifled a sob. Lars had suffered a high fever after getting lost in the storm. Even now he was too weak to leave his bed. His breath rattled in his chest. Lisbet's tears were understandable if not, Torhild couldn't help thinking, particularly helpful.

At least Halvor was trying to be useful. A steady *swish-swish* sounded from the chipping stool as he stripped bark from elm and aspen branches. Fodder was running low with spring still just a promise.

When someone knocked on the door, Torhild jumped, spilling the porridge. Høiegård was so difficult to reach that they rarely had visitors, especially in winter. As she mopped up the dribble, her mother went to greet their guest. Glancing over her shoulder, Torhild was surprised to see her father's fiddling friend, Big Gunnar.

He pulled off his hat. "I don't mean to intrude," he said respectfully to Lisbet. "But I heard about Lars. I thought to play him a few tunes. It might cheer him."

"Play a few tunes?" Lisbet sounded wary. "I don't think…"

"Yes," Lars croaked. "Please." He looked from his friend to his daughter.

"What's this?" Halvor murmured, one eyebrow raised speculatively.

This is something that will cause trouble, Torhild thought, but she couldn't deny her father's request. "I'll fetch the fiddle," she said, avoiding her mother's gaze. She retrieved the *hardingfele* from Lars's cupboard.

Lisbet gasped. "You dared have this in our home?"

Torhild offered the instrument to the fiddler. He accepted it like a beloved companion and lifted it gently from the case, a smile softening his weathered face.

"After everything that has happened?" Lisbet's voice climbed higher.

Torhild stepped between Lisbet and the bed. This was not the moment to bring up their tragic wedding day. "Mother—"

"What if someone hears?" Lisbet turned to her daughter.

Torhild went to her mother's side. "There's no one to hear. Let him play for Father."

Big Gunnar played with eyes closed, his body dipping and swaying as the music soared through the dark room. He bowed some of the new *lydarslåttars*, pieces intended for listening, not dancing. Torhild wasn't able to even tap her toes, for he often changed tempo and held notes longer than expected, making the music his own. Sometimes he sang along, sharing stories. How Great-Grandmother Gudrun would have loved this, Torhild thought.

Halvor fetched a jug of ale and filled mugs for the fiddler and himself. Lisbet retreated to a far corner and watched with mouth pinched into a tight line, arms crossed over her chest. Please, Mother, Torhild thought. No one will know. Forget your fears, the bad memories, just for this night. And perhaps Lisbet did, for she made no more complaints.

Lars closed his eyes. The muscles in his face—so often rigid with pain—relaxed. His lips curled into an easy smile. The eiderdown-filled quilt twitched, as if his body was sketching the movements of an old march or reel. He was a dancer, Torhild reminded herself. He'd won her mother's hand and heart with his stamina and grace.

Torhild's throat grew thick, and her eyes blurred with hot tears. She didn't know which hurt her heart more: that her mother was broken, that her father was dying, or that she'd never seen them dance.

FOURTEEN

As they left the Utne Church, Roelke could tell that Chloe had hoped for more encouragement about tracing Marit's people. "Are you okay?"

She twisted her mouth in a halfhearted smile. "Just wondering about my ancestors. Some of them might have attended church here, Roelke. Walked these roads. Listened to Hardanger fiddle tunes. Gone to dances. I just don't know."

"You're only getting started," he reminded her.

"I suppose. I just thought…" She heaved a sigh. "I was sure that coming to Norway and searching for ancestors was absolutely the right thing to do. Now… I don't know."

Roelke reached for her hand, trying to anchor her. Chloe wasn't a particularly practical person. She could be impulsive. She tended to plunge ahead when pursuing her passions without considering consequences. That was true when doing any historical research. Her mission here was intensely personal.

Worse, he sensed that her quest was motivated by more than finding ancestral records. Chloe's relationship with her mom had been strained. He suspected Chloe believed that learning about Marit's birth might atone for that. But although finding some basic record of the mysterious Amalie might be possible, finding actual relatives during their short time in Norway seemed like a tall order.

When Chloe tipped her head against his shoulder, his heart hitched. He was still amazed that she'd fallen in love with him. And in all honesty, he had to admit that Chloe's impetuousness—and her vulnerability—were two things that had attracted him from the beginning.

Those things also sometimes kept him awake at night.

"Let's head back to the hotel," Chloe said. "I want to see how my dad's doing and find out if Aunt Hilda has shown any improvement."

Back at the Utne Hotel, Chloe went in search of a phone. Roelke settled at a table on the front porch and stared over the fjord. The ferries coming and going didn't detract from the village's peaceful charm. Shadows shifted on the mountains, fragmenting the forested slopes and stone faces into geometric shapes. The water rippled restlessly at this junction between the Sørfjord and the Hardangerfjord.

Roelke felt restless too. He'd never been to Norway before and dammit, he wanted to be a tourist. He wanted Chloe's dreams to come true so she could relax and enjoy their visit. But neither of those things were going to happen before some problems got resolved. And frankly, to his mind, there were too many problems stacking up.

He reached into his shirt pocket and retrieved the stack of index cards. On top was the one he'd labeled *Klara Evenstad*. The problems, though, hadn't started with her death. He plucked a blank card from the pile and began to write.

<u>*Trouble:*</u>

- *Someone tried to snatch Chloe's daypack at the Bergen airport*
- *Rock slide on the trail when I was hiking up the mountain*
- *Klara Evenstad murdered at the folk museum in Utne*

Roelke tried to find some link between the incidents. If there was one, he couldn't see it. The attempted daypack snatch had happened what, eighty miles away? Something like that. And they'd only just met Klara Evenstad—

"Whatcha doin'?"

He jumped, startled to find Chloe standing beside him. "Just collecting my thoughts. Did you reach your dad?"

"Yes, and he sounded glad to hear from me, but there's been no change in Aunt Hilda's condition. I had a fax waiting from Rosemary Rossebo, the genealogist who's helping me, but so far she hasn't found Amalie Sveinsdatter on a ship's passenger list."

Roelke could tell that his beloved was more discouraged than ever. "Has Rosemary given up?"

Chloe managed the ghost of a smile. "Heck, no. She's tenacious."

"So maybe you'll get better news next time."

"Maybe." She shrugged before leaning closer to peer at the index card. Her eyebrows went up. "Do you honestly think there's some connection between those incidents?"

"It seems unlikely. But..."

"But what?" She slid into the chair across from him.

He rested on his elbows. "Chloe, why would someone try to grab your pack at the airport? It would have been much easier to target some elderly woman with a dangling pocketbook."

She sucked in her lower lip as she thought that over. "Because my daypack was bigger? Possibly holding more stuff of value?"

"I can't help wondering if someone was after more than a tourist's wallet. What if somebody wanted to steal that embroidered thing you found in Marit's closet?"

Chloe had set her yellow daypack on the ground by her chair. Now she pulled it protectively into her lap. "But who?"

"I have no idea. But you did pull it out in the middle of a crowded café at the airport. Sonja Gullickson did talk in detail about how rare it was. I remember her saying that your piece with the black embroidery—what did she call it?"

"It's a *handaplagg*. A hand cloth."

"Right. She said it was probably made in the seventeen hundreds, and very valuable." Roelke had been hanging around with Chloe for long enough to know that some people went nuts over antiques like that.

Chloe's gaze went distant. Finally she said, "It's hard to imagine that by chance, someone eavesdropping from the next table in an airport café was the kind of person who'd try to make a grab for it."

"Unless Sonja Gullickson had set something up with an accomplice."

"Roelke!"

"Sonja did come back from Stockholm early, too. She could have been back in Utne by the time Klara was attacked."

Chloe looked stricken. "*Surely* Sonja had nothing to do with Klara's murder. Or with whoever tried to grab my daypack."

"I'm not accusing her." He held up both hands. "But you have to admit, it's possible." He wrote *Sonja Gullickson* on a clean index card. "And when we talked to her before the concert, she never took off her sunglasses. Sometimes people do that if they have something to hide."

"Or if they like looking stylish. Which Sonja does."

Okay, further debate wouldn't accomplish anything. "You're probably right," Roelke admitted. "What happened at the airport probably had nothing to do with Klara's death. Even so, I suggest we ask the innkeeper if there's a safe where you can leave your heirlooms."

"But … they're talismans." Chloe patted her daypack. "I like having them with me."

He waited, giving her time. Telling Chloe what to do usually prompted her to do the exact opposite.

"Oh, all right," she conceded, sounding aggrieved. "The most important thing is to keep the doily and *handaplagg* safe." But she still hesitated, nibbling her lower lip.

"What?"

"I was thinking about the conversation about Klara we had this morning. One thing strikes me as unusual. Why did she go from working full-time at the museum to working full-time as a maid and waitress at the hotel? There's nothing wrong with hotel work, but based on the tour Klara gave us, she was a fantastic guide."

"Maybe she wanted to work with her friend."

"Maybe." Chloe sounded doubtful.

"Or maybe Klara wasn't invited to return full-time this year."

Chloe's brow furrowed. "Why wouldn't she be?"

"I don't know." He shrugged. "Some conflict with Ellinor, maybe?"

"But if that were the case, why would Ellinor bring her in at all?"

"Because the museum ended up short-staffed?"

"I think we're drifting into pretty wild speculation."

Wild speculation can lead to unexpected answers, Roelke thought. But he sensed Chloe had done all the brainstorming she was going to do, just now. He wrapped a rubber band around his index cards and tucked them away. "How about we get some lunch," he suggested, and was rewarded with a smile.

After a meal of open-faced Norwegian sandwiches—Jarlsburg cheese for Chloe, roast pork for Roelke—they stopped at the hotel desk. Barbara-Eden answered the bell and, when Chloe explained what she wanted, summoned proprietress Ulrikke Moe.

"I'd be glad to secure your things in our safe." Ulrikke accepted the tissue-wrapped textiles from Chloe. "Barbara-Eden, I believe your help is needed in the kitchen." When the younger woman had disappeared, Ulrikke turned back to her guests. "Is everything all right? Has Barbara-Eden said something inappropriate?"

Where did that come from? Roelke wondered.

"Everyone is upset about Klara, of course," Ulrikke was saying, "but Barbara-Eden can be … impressionable."

"She hasn't said anything inappropriate," Chloe assured her. "And all of you must be in shock. I'm so sorry."

Ulrikke nodded and disappeared into the office behind the counter. Roelke felt better when Chloe's heirlooms were locked in the hotel safe.

Then he and Chloe walked back to the museum. Ellinor was talking on the phone in her office, leaning on one elbow as if to keep herself upright. "Yes … of course … yes. I will." She hung up and waved her visitors inside. When the phone rang again, she rolled her eyes. "I'll let the gift shop take that one."

"I just wondered if you'd heard anything from Torstein," Chloe said.

"Torstein. Yes. He stopped by." Ellinor ran her hands through her hair. "He's devastated, as you can imagine. Said he didn't have the heart to think about fieldwork just now."

"Of course."

The man's feelings were perfectly understandable, but Roelke couldn't help wondering what Torstein's absence might mean for Chloe's obligation to the Stoughton Historical Society. He also couldn't help wondering what Torstein had told the Norwegian cops when interviewed.

"He said that you were welcome to go without him. You can borrow our tape recorder, and…" Ellinor picked up a manila envelope and held it out. "He left contact info for you."

That idea obviously appealed to Chloe. She tore open the envelope. "Yep—name, phone and address, some background." She glanced at Roelke. "Up for a drive?"

Roelke opted against speculating about just what kind of roads they'd encounter on this particular jaunt. "Sure."

"I wish I could come with you, instead of being chained to this office." Ellinor pressed fingertips to her temples. "Sorry. I've never been in this kind of situation before. And I hope I never am again."

Chloe called the informant's granddaughter from the hotel. "You work with Torstein?" the woman asked.

"Yes. Unfortunately he's not able to visit this afternoon, but he suggested that I come anyway. If that still suits."

"I'd much rather do that than postpone, actually. My grandfather doesn't speak English well, so I missed work to interpret for him."

Chloe was doubly glad Torstein had suggested that she keep the appointment. "I look forward to meeting you both. I'll have to look at a map. I'm not sure how long it will take to drive to your home."

"We're in Kinsarvik, so from Utne, there's no need for a car. Just hop on the next ferry."

Twenty minutes later Chloe and Roelke were on their way. The puffy cumulous clouds dappling a brilliant blue sky above were reflected in the water below. Along the shore, flowering apple and plum trees misted orchards pink and creamy white. But standing beside Roelke at the upper deck's rail, Chloe felt an ache inside. Klara would never again hear birds call as they flew over the water. She would never again inhale the damp air, or watch the light change over the mountains.

"What's wrong?" Roelke asked.

"I'm just feeling a little..." She tried to find the right word. "Emotional. Overwhelmed."

Roelke tucked a wind-whipped strand of hair behind her ear. "Try to focus on your meeting this afternoon."

Chloe exhaled slowly. "I'll try."

The ferry entered a small bay and chugged toward the dock. Kinsarvik hunched on the shore, embraced by mountains. The most prominent village feature was a white church near the water, enclosed by a stone fence. That looks familiar, Chloe thought, gripping the railing. Had Amalie Sveinsdatter known this view? Had she been eager to emigrate, or had her heart broken as she watched the landscape of home fade into the distance behind her?

Roelke cocked his head toward the stairs. "Let's go down."

After they disembarked Chloe suddenly felt so confused that she abruptly stopped walking. "A lot has changed." She gestured toward the cars parked in a line, waiting to take their places on the ferry. "That's where the church boats used to beach."

Roelke pulled her out of the traffic flow. "Um … what church boats?" His voice sounded oddly hollow, as if they were speaking by telephone with a bad connection.

"The *tioerings*." She squinted, trying to stabilize a wavering landscape: cobbled shore and empty boats. She heard the faint strains of a distant *hardingfele*.

"Chloe!" Roelke barked.

The fuzziness faded. She stared at the concrete seawall, the asphalt car lanes, the powerboats moored in a nearby marina, the neatly manicured picnic area beside the church grounds.

Roelke gripped her arm. "What's going on? You sorta zoned out there for a minute. What's a *tioering*?"

"A boat with ten oars," she explained, although she didn't know why she knew that. "People used them to travel from their village or farm area to church on Sundays. And for weddings." That would explain the fiddle.

Roelke's piercing gaze didn't waver.

She took a deep breath. "Roelke, I know this place. I could swear I've been in Kinsarvik before."

"Like you felt in Utne?"

"This is different. Much stronger."

"You must have come through here on one of your earlier trips."

"No." Chloe shook her head. "I have never been here. But … remember what Reverend Brandvold said? If my ancestors lived in this area, they probably attended church here in Kinsarvik for centuries before later churches, like the one in Utne, were built."

Roelke glanced at the church, then over his shoulder toward the ferry. "Maybe this field visit isn't a good idea after all. Maybe we should go back to Utne—"

"I don't want to go back!" Chloe felt an unexpected smile tug at her lips. "I think I just had a flash of genetic memory." Something she'd read about, thought about, but never experienced.

Roelke eyed her for so long that Chloe almost regretted her words. Although he'd been remarkably accepting, maybe this was too personal. Too *much*.

Finally he nodded slowly. "Cool."

Tension eased from her shoulders. "Thank you," she whispered, and gave him a quick kiss.

"What does it feel like? Is it like what happened at that old cabin at the museum?"

She considered. "That was overwhelming. This sense of familiarity, here and in Utne, is sort of comforting." She kicked a stone from the walkway, trying to find the right words. "It feels like … like I might remember things I never actually experienced. It feels like important memories are hovering right outside what I know." She rubbed her temples. "It makes me think that if I just reach out quickly enough, I might capture something. Something specific. But … I don't know how."

"Holy toboggans." Roelke looked away, briefly diverted by two boys racing around the picnic area before catching her gaze again. "I think you should keep trying. Don't get frustrated. I can't imagine that would help."

Chloe snapped some pictures but was eager to learn if the sanctuary felt familiar too. "Let's see if we can go inside the church!"

"Um … isn't someone expecting us?"

"Oh, *geez*." Chloe felt chagrined. How could she have forgotten her plans to meet an octogenarian rumored to have learned local dances from his grandparents? She dug the address and directions she'd been given from her daypack. "Okey-dokey. Let's go."

Roelke kept a surreptitious eye on Chloe, but she didn't zone out again as they navigated Kinsarvik. They soon reached a frame home painted bright red with green trim. A yellow picket fence enclosed the small yard. Somebody cheerful lives here, Roelke thought.

They were warmly welcomed inside by the gentleman and his granddaughter, a plump woman in her forties. "Call me Bestefar," the old man told them.

"I'm honored!" Chloe said, then murmured to Roelke, "That means 'Grandfather.'"

Bestefar seemed mentally sharp and was obviously delighted that Chloe had traveled from America to learn about regional dances. He walked as if his knees hurt, but when he unexpectedly grabbed Chloe's hand and twirled her around, his wrinkled face glowed and years slipped away. Roelke enjoyed seeing Chloe energized and enthused, chatting with an elder about a pastime they both loved.

Still, as an hour passed, the lengthy discussion of dialectical forms and *vendingsdels,* promenades and *gameldansers,* made him antsy. He didn't realize his right knee was bouncing until Chloe put her hand out, gently stilling it.

"Why don't you take a walk?" she suggested. "I'll meet you down by the ferry dock when we're through."

"You're sure?"

"I'm fine, Roelke. See you later."

"Well ... okay." Roelke thanked their hosts and let himself out the front door feeling guilty but liberated.

He wandered, taking his time, until he came to a gracious old white building near the harbor. A big sign said *Kinsarvik Brygge.* He didn't know what that meant, but it appeared to be a tourism office. He went inside and picked up some information about nearby waterfalls and the Hardangervidda National Park. It seemed unlikely that Chloe would be able to spend a day hiking, but hey, he could dream. And be prepared with maps and trail descriptions.

As he emerged, the first cars puttered from a just-docked ferry. A stream of pedestrians emerged too, most dressed in casual hiking or sightseeing clothes. Then he saw a woman walking quickly, head down, angling away from the others. It looked like Ellinor, which didn't make sense since Ellinor had said that she'd be "chained" to her office all day. But it definitely *was* the museum director. He recognized the silver hair, the gray suit.

What was Ellinor doing in Kinsarvik? Had she come to surreptitiously check up on Chloe's interview? Roelke frowned. No, that made no sense either. Ellinor was dealing with a murder investigation. Besides, the envelope Torstein left for Chloe had been sealed. Ellinor hadn't seemed to know the details, which meant she had no idea that Chloe was even in Kinsarvik.

Ellinor paused, glanced over both shoulders, then turned onto a side street and disappeared from sight. Roelke followed, careful to keep his distance. She strode along the walk at a brisk pace, head still down.

When she made another turn, Roelke stopped at the corner. Just ahead, Ellinor dropped onto a bench in front of a shop advertising *Hardanger's Best Selection of Souvenirs* in half a dozen languages. A man was already seated on the bench—maybe thirty years old, maybe thirty-five, with thick brown hair swept back from his forehead and black-framed glasses resting on his nose. He wore jeans and a black jacket over a tan shirt. Roelke had no idea who the guy was. Ellinor apparently did, for although she didn't turn to face him, she began to speak.

The man didn't look at her, either. But after a moment he extracted something from his vest pocket and placed it on the bench between them. Roelke cussed silently, wishing he could see what it was. He edged closer, taking cover behind a food cart where a man was selling sausages. Two women who'd emerged from the souvenir shop looked at him warily as they passed. He unfolded his new map and studied it. Nothing to see here, ladies, he said silently. Just another lost tourist. The women walked on.

Roelke considered his options. He could give Ellinor the benefit of the doubt, acknowledge that her errand was none of his business. But he discarded that choice at once. One woman was dead, and too many odd things had happened since he and Chloe had arrived in Norway. Ellinor was acting furtively. He wanted to know why.

So that left only two courses of action. He could stay here and, if she moved on, keep following her. Or, he could ever-so-casually wander by, express *great* surprise upon seeing her, and try to get a glimpse of—

Too late. Ellinor shook her head vigorously and pushed whatever the man had shared back at him. Her rigid posture suggested irritation, maybe anger. Then she was on her feet, marching toward Roelke.

He held the map higher. She passed by. He waited a few moments before following.

Ellinor strode straight back to the ferry landing. The boat she'd arrived on had already departed, so she stood with her back to the village, arms folded, to wait for the next. He stepped inside the tourism office's small portico, where he could watch Ellinor without being easily seen. But she didn't move.

Half an hour later the next ferry rumbled to the dock. Ellinor didn't even wait for the current load of cars and walkers to disembark before boarding. She never looked back.

Well, hunh, Roelke thought as he stepped back to the sidewalk. Ellinor's behavior was curious. And … unsettling. Something about the stealthy exchange he'd just witnessed made him uneasy. He wished—

"Hey, sailor!"

He whirled and saw Chloe sauntering toward him with a saucy grin on her face. She blew him a kiss, and all Roelke wanted to do was protect her from all ills and evils.

FIFTEEN

Torhild—July 1870

Torhild straightened and swung one leg back over the goat she'd been straddling. The goat leapt indignantly away. Torhild stretched, rubbing her back. She sat on a stool when milking the cows, but most of the boisterous goats needed to be firmly held. She was always glad to finish with the goats.

When the evening's milk was strained and set in pans to separate, Torhild turned to her son Erik, a sturdy seven-year-old who was spending the summer with her. "I'll haul water to scour the pails. You go see to the animals."

He looked worried. "Will you be all right?"

Torhild's heart constricted. When had her little boy become her defender? Erik took his *seter* duties seriously, and she was grateful. Harder to bear was his growing concern for *her*. She suspected that not all the ills and evils he imagined came from wild animal attacks or avalanches or storms. Halvor and I must try harder not to argue in front of the boys, she thought.

When the buckets were scrubbed, she left the building that doubled as dwelling and dairy storage house. Erik was squatting on his haunches in the distance, watching over their two cows, several sheep, and half a dozen goats. The cows' bells clanged dully as they nosed here and there in search of mushrooms. The frolicking goats' bells added a lighter jingle.

She walked out to join him. "No sign of your father?"

The boy shook his head. He didn't appear to be surprised or disappointed that his father had not arrived this Saturday night to see them, and to take the week's butter and cheese back down to Høiegård. It would be nice to believe that Halvor was too busy with the farm below to make the climb, for since Lars had died, there was more work to do and fewer hands to do it. But Halvor was drinking more and more. He sometimes disappeared from the farm for days on end.

"Well, perhaps he or your brother will come tomorrow." Torhild gently ruffled Erik's hair. "I'll come back to help when it's time to bring the animals in for the night."

She retraced her steps slowly, contemplating the low log-and-stone building. Rain dripped through gaps in the moldering logs. The turf roof leaked. Some people built their summer farms close to their neighbors' *seters*, clustering the buildings so heavy chores like replacing logs or roofs could be shared. But Høiegård was isolated, so its *seter* was as well.

"I can't do everything myself," Torhild said. She thought about the wooden tubs of cheese waiting inside—sweet and salty brown *brunost*, soft goats' milk *gjetost*, cooked *kokeost*. She had butter, too. Her cows and goats produced about two-thirds of their milk in the summer. She spent the long days transforming it into food they could sell in the village. But nothing could be sold if her husband didn't come every Saturday, as promised, to leave empty containers and transport what she'd made. And make sure we're safe and well, she thought, with a humorless laugh.

But perhaps, she thought, I should be grateful he hasn't come. She liked being here, liked being mostly on her own. She liked watching yellow primroses and purple foxgloves bloom among the grass, and going to sleep to the waterfall's lullaby. She liked watching baby swallows poke their heads from the row of nests beneath the eaves, and hearing stonechats' clicking song when they perched on the rock walls. Her mother still ruled Høiegård. Being at the *seter* gave Torhild a taste of independence, and a break from Lisbet's sadness.

"Torhild!" Halvor was trudging up the path, walking stick in one hand and a tall, sturdy pack basket strapped to his back.

So, she thought. He's come after all.

She waited until he'd approached before speaking. "Is everything well? I expected you earlier."

"I was delayed," Halvor said. That was all, and he didn't meet her gaze, staring instead at a buzzard circling lazily overhead.

Torhild stifled a sigh. "Come inside. You'll want to spend the night—"

"No." Halvor raked one hand through his hair. "I'll pack up what you have and walk back down."

Either Halvor didn't want to spend time with his wife and younger son, or he already had other plans for the evening. Torhild really didn't care which. "Come along, then."

The log building was cloaked in shadows, but there wasn't much to see—one box bed in the corner where she slept, a pallet on the floor for her son, a corner hearth, table, two churns, buckets, a few dishes, shelves holding bowls and butter paddles. A row of *ambars*, the wooden tubs where she stored butter, waited near the door.

Halvor shrugged from the pack and began removing empty containers, every one carved by Torhild's father and scoured after each use by Lisbet. For a moment Torhild's parents and the relative security of childhood felt very close—Lars bent close to the fire on a winter night, quietly carving; Lisbet vigorously attacking the woodenware with hot water and soap and a handful of rushes.

"What do you have for me?" Halvor was clearly impatient to be back on his way. Torhild silently fetched the week's bounty. "Not as much as I'd hoped," he grumbled as he began settling the containers into his pack.

Torhild didn't answer. The animals produced what they produced.

"One more thing." Halvor shifted his weight from one foot to the other. He was still well-muscled, although the beer and *akevitt* were softening his middle. "Torhild, things are bad. The boys will need new shoes—"

"I can't cajole the animals into increasing their milk."

"But you can give over to me anything of value."

"I have nothing of value to give," she protested, but her heart beat faster. They'd had this conversation before. Halvor was looking for something to sell. Lisbet kept the family's bridal crown and silver jewelry locked in the *stabbur* and slept with the key beneath her pillow. That left only one thing.

Halvor's face hardened. "You have your father's fiddle!"

"I don't. And if you didn't spend so much on ale—"

With the back of his hand, Halvor knocked Torhild against the shelf. Pain exploded in her left cheek and jaw.

Amid the cacophony of tumbling tin and wood she heard a wordless cry. Erik, her little boy, hurtled across the room and knocked his father off-balance. Only the table kept Halvor from falling to the floor.

Torhild snatched Erik's arm and pulled him away. "Don't you dare strike him," she hissed at Halvor, cheek throbbing, eyes narrowed. "Do not *dare*." She gave the panting boy a little push toward the door. "Go back outside." Erik hesitated, then scurried away.

Then Torhild and Halvor stood alone, glaring at each other. Telling him she didn't have the fiddle was a lie, and she knew that *he* knew it was a lie. But she'd decided years ago to protect the fiddle.

After her father died, Torhild had hidden his *hardingfele* in the stone wall. She wanted Big Gunnar to keep it in thanks for the pleasure he'd given her father at the end of his life. But her father's friend had never returned, and she'd never again seen him playing at a community gathering. Finally she'd brought the fiddle up to the *seter* and hidden it in an old butter churn that, needing repair, had been shoved into a back corner. She hoped Lisbet had forgotten about the fiddle altogether.

But clearly Halvor had not. "I know you have it!" He scowled.

"Go." Torhild reached toward the table and curled her fingers around the handle of a knife. "*Now*. And do not *ever* raise your hand to me again."

Perhaps it was the knife, or perhaps it was shame, or perhaps something else entirely. For whatever reason, Halvor hefted the pack and walked out. Torhild stepped to the door and watched her husband walk across the clearing and disappear down the trail.

Erik had returned to the grazing animals. She started to go to him, then realized that she was shaking. Her knees bent and she sat abruptly on the doorstep, staring at the knife still clenched in one hand. I wouldn't have used it, she told herself.

She touched her cheek and winced. Things with Halvor had not been good for some time, but he'd never hit her before. They had reached a new place in their marriage. She instinctively knew there was no going back, and she had no idea what to do now.

Torhild forced her fingers to let the knife fall. Was there anything she could say to convince Halvor to drink less and work more? Perhaps she should ask her mother for advice…

No. She couldn't confide in her mother, for she knew what Lisbet would say: *Give him the fiddle. It's the devil's instrument.* A fiddle had brought anguish to Torhild's parents. A man trying to "discover" Hardanger music had indirectly caused Gjertrud's death. Now a fiddle represented heartache for *her*.

But fiddle music had also, once, brought her parents together. It had eased her father's final journey. It had given her great joy at dances. She would never give the fiddle to Halvor. It's hiding place would remain secret.

Suddenly she smiled, remembering her other secret. She hadn't yet told Halvor that she was pregnant.

Although Torhild adored her two sons, she had always longed for a daughter. This time she knew, simply *knew*, that she was carrying a girl. She smiled, imagining herself showing her daughter how to make cheese and spin wool. She would share Great-Grandmother Gudrun's stories of the old days. She would advise her girl to heed unexplained impressions. And she would teach her daughter to dance.

SIXTEEN

I MUST SPEND MORE time with elders, Chloe thought as she rejoined Roelke. Especially elders who still loved to dance. Bestefar had demonstrated steps he'd learned as a child, moving unsteadily but with joy. The visit hadn't made Chloe forget Mom's death and her own tangled family history, or Aunt Hilda's injury, or Klara Evenstad's death. But it had provided some balance, and at least partially filled a depleted inner well. She felt ready for the next challenge.

"Something weird just happened," Roelke muttered.

And there it is, she thought. "Okay, tell me."

His story left Chloe incredulous. "You *followed* Ellinor? You actually tailed the director of the Hardanger Folkemuseum?"

"I didn't have a whole lot of options," he observed testily. "Don't you think it's strange that Ellinor complained about being 'chained' to the office all day, and then finds time to visit Kinsarvik?"

"She must have had a good reason. Maybe she just needed a break after dealing with the cops and the press and everything."

“This wasn’t ‘a break.’ The guy she met was waiting for her. It was prearranged.”

Chloe opened her mouth, then closed it again. A mom nearby shrieked at her children, who were chasing gulls. A boy threw a Frisbee for his joyful dog.

Finally Roelke asked, “So, did you get what you needed from the interview?”

She was glad to change the subject. “More than I could have hoped for, actually. I’ll have to write up my notes to share with Torstein while everything’s still fresh in my mind. He believes that different isolated areas in Hardanger have produced unique variants of the same dance. That’s what he’s trying to document. And in theory, I might be able to discover if immigrants from different communities brought their variants to Wisconsin, or if the New World dances are distinct.”

“Well, hunh.”

“And guess what? We were invited to attend a dance being held on Saturday, up in the mountains. It’s not a public event, so the invitation is a real honor.” Chloe remembered belatedly that Roelke did not dance. “The music should be good,” she tried, “but if you’d rather not go …”

“No, I’ll go.” He reached for her hand.

She nodded toward the trail map he was holding. “What’s that?”

“I was hoping we might find a bit of spare time to forget all the trouble and just enjoy ourselves.”

Chloe imagined picnicking with Roelke by some remote waterfall. “That would be heavenly,” she agreed wistfully.

“But not right now,” Roelke said. “Do you still want to see the church?”

“Definitely.”

As they walked through the gate in the stone fence surrounding the churchyard, Chloe made a conscious effort to open herself to whatever might be hovering unseen in this place. She sensed a mélange of emotions, centuries of grief and joy and devotion. When they entered the church, she was struck again by a sense of familiarity. I do *know* this place, she thought, and if I try hard enough …

"Good afternoon!" A diminutive white-haired lady tucked knitting into a basket by her chair and popped eagerly to her feet. "You are Americans? I'm a volunteer. It will be my pleasure to give you a tour."

Chloe felt Roelke's questioning gaze. She responded with a tiny shrug: *No, I'd rather wander through on our own.* That didn't seem to be an option.

The guide was enthusiastic and informative. "Because of the sheltered harbor, Kinsarvik has been a gathering place since the days when Vikings sailed the fjords. There has been a church here since the twelfth century. The first wooden church was replaced with this stone building about a century later, making it the oldest stone church in all of the Hardanger region …"

Chloe trailed silently in the woman's wake. The church was both humble and magnificent. Plastered walls and heavy wooden beams balanced ornate carvings and painted biblical scenes. As she admired rosemaled panels, Chloe wondered if her mother had ever visited Kinsarvik.

"And here in the nave we have the remains of medieval frescoes." The guide pointed to a faded figure looming on the wall. "The painting was done on wet plaster, and depicts St. Michael weighing souls …"

Chloe caught her breath, suddenly transfixed. Not by St. Michael, but by what appeared to be two devils lurking at the man's feet. "I've seen these before." These two creatures ... she knew them in detail.

"I beg your pardon?" The docent looked nonplussed.

"A photograph," Roelke interjected. "Pictures in a guidebook."

"Ah." The woman nodded and resumed the tour.

Chloe tried to appear attentive, and when the guide wound down, she thanked her profusely. "Is it all right if my fiancé and I sit here? Just for a little while."

"Of course."

Chloe and Roelke settled into a pew. "What's going on?" he asked quietly.

"More of the same. I know this place. Most especially that." She gestured to the faded fresco.

He rubbed his chin, eyeing the painting. "Not the most pleasant of images."

"No, but ... it's all right. The devils seem important, somehow, but they don't scare me. I just sort of feel like I belong here."

He looked startled. "You belong here?"

"I don't mean I want to move here. But even if I don't learn another thing about my mother's birth family, I'll always believe that she descended from people who worshipped here. And that's pretty amazing."

He nodded. Chloe leaned her head on his shoulder, soaking in the memories of a place she'd never been before.

Then Roelke said, "Maybe we should get married here."

That brought her upright again. "What?"

"We haven't known how to handle the wedding. Well, maybe this is why. Maybe we're supposed to get married here."

Chloe had *not* seen that coming. "But ... what about our families?"

"I don't know." He spread his hands. "Maybe we could have a private ceremony here, and then do something else when we get home. A reception for everybody."

"A private ceremony here," she repeated. "Roelke, that's an amazing idea. I love it. But only if you're truly sure." He was Catholic. He had no Norwegians on his family tree. Their wedding couldn't be all about her.

"I'm sure. I can tell it would make you happy. Besides, St. Michael is on the wall."

Chloe caught her breath. "That's right! I didn't make the connection." After learning the previous autumn that St. Michael was the patron saint of police officers, she'd given Roelke a medal bearing the archangel's likeness.

"So, there you go. I won't be left out."

"Then ... let's do it." Chloe felt a little breathless. She wanted to linger in the moment ... but more practical thoughts were already pinging through her brain. "Do you think we can pull it off? We don't have a lot of time. I expect there's paperwork. Getting a license or something. I have no idea what will be involved."

"Me neither."

Chloe nibbled her lower lip, thinking. "But you know who *would* know? Reverend Brandvold. Maybe we could even ask him to perform the ceremony."

"Well, we better head back to Utne, don't you think?" Roelke got to his feet. "We've got a wedding to plan."

Chloe had wanted to wander through the cemetery, see if any of the old gravesites let off any particular vibes, but the sudden urgency of exploring the procedures required to marry in Norway took precedence. Another time, she promised herself, and turned to the ferry dock.

Back at the Utne Hotel, Chloe stopped at the desk and rang the bell. After a moment Barbara-Eden appeared. "I was wondering if there are any messages for me," Chloe explained.

Barbara-Eden rummaged beneath the desk. "Yes, a fax came in." She produced a shiny, curling piece of paper. "And you have a couple of phone messages, too. One from Pastor Brandvold, and … one from Torstein Landvik." Her eyebrows rose in surprise as she handed the slips over. "You know Torstein?"

"We're collaborating on a research project."

"Oh. That sounds interesting." Barbara-Eden's expression changed as Ulrikke Moe, the proprietress, joined them. The girl bobbed her chin before scurrying away.

Ulrikke watched her go before asking Chloe, "Do you have everything you need?"

"Yes, thank you." Chloe smiled politely and turned away, eager to read her messages. She retired to the front parlor and started with the message from Torstein Landvik: *I'll be at the ferry dock tomorrow at 12:30. Hope we can meet.*

Maybe he has another field assignment for me, Chloe thought. It sounded promising.

She turned next to the fax from Rosemary Rossebo, Mom's genealogist friend, which was not promising:

Chloe, I'm still unable to find any reference to Amalie Sveinsdatter in records of ships leaving Bergen. I started with 1920 and have gone back five years. It's possible that Amalie lied about her identity.

Great, Chloe thought.

It's also possible that Amalie didn't leave from Bergen. In 1920, fourteen ships carrying immigrants left Kristiania (Oslo), and only three from Bergen. She might have even left from Trondheim.

Ju-u-ust great, Chloe thought.

Rosemary signed off with a promise to keep searching. Chloe blew out an aggravated sigh. She'd hoped to have at least a nugget of new information by now, but Amalie was proving elusive.

The message from Pastor Brandvold was cryptic: *I might have something for you, but can't find it. I'll be home this evening if you wish to come by.* He'd included his phone number and address.

Perfect timing, Chloe thought, and headed for the payphone.

Pastor Brandvold lived up the hill from the church in a small white home with gray slate shingles. Chloe and Roelke arrived just as the sun was languidly sinking. "Pretty," Chloe observed, for the small yard was neat as the proverbial pin. Lamps glowed behind lace curtains hung in the windows. Crimson geraniums bloomed in yellow ceramic pots flanking the front step.

The pastor opened the door before she could knock. "Thanks for the call," Chloe said as he ushered them inside. A black cat appeared from a side room and rubbed against her ankles.

"Katt, don't be a pest," Reverend Brandvold scolded.

"He's not." Chloe crouched to pet Katt. "You said you might have something…?"

"First, I've looked through my copies of the Norwegian Police's emigration records. I started in 1920 and worked backwards for four years without finding a listing for Amalie Sveinsdatter."

Chloe stifled an inappropriate expression of disappointment. "My genealogist friend back home hasn't found a ship's listing for her either."

"We had reason to think she was newly arrived in Wisconsin when she surrendered her baby," Brandvold said thoughtfully, "but perhaps she actually traveled much earlier than 1920."

If that's true, Chloe thought, we might never find record of her passage. She exhaled slowly. "Well, thank you for looking."

"There's one more thing." He rubbed stubby fingers together, looking suddenly ill at ease. "When we talked earlier, the name Amalie Sveinsdatter sounded vaguely familiar, but I couldn't place it. After thinking about it, I decided I saw the name on a letter from America—"

"A letter from Amalie?" Chloe gasped. "From America?"

The pastor waved his hands as if trying to tamp down her burst of excitement. "I bought a collection of regional materials at an auction last fall. I *think* I saw the letter there. I remember thinking that Amalie was a lovely name. But I spent the afternoon searching," he concluded sorrowfully, "without finding it."

"Oh." It was all she could manage.

"Given how important it is, I thought you might want to look yourself."

"But if you haven't found it . . ." Chloe glanced uncertainly from the pastor to Roelke and back again.

"Come to my study." Pastor Brandvold led the way.

Chloe stepped inside and contemplated the messiest room she'd ever seen. A desk, file cabinets, and bookshelves were barely visible beneath all the *stuff*. Piles of papers, old books, photograph albums, and God-knew-what-else covered every horizontal surface. Cartons, evidently awaiting excavation, were stacked on the floor.

Roelke, who had followed her into the room, looked horrified. Officer Roelke McKenna did not like clutter. At least it's not teddy bears and knickknacks, Chloe thought. Those would have sent him running.

"I know, I know." Pastor Brandvold walked heavily to his desk, moved a shoebox from the chair, and sank down. "It's overwhelming. I *try* to be organized. I sometimes hire students to catalog what's here, but they never stay long enough to do much good."

Can't imagine why, Chloe thought.

"I started collecting pastors' accounts of early tourists. There weren't many travelers until the late 1800s, but those who had money often stayed with clergy. But my collection kept growing. I just can't bear to see anything relating to the local area thrown away. Often parishioners bring me things. It's all important, don't you think?"

As a collections curator, Chloe had faced her share of tearful would-be donors begging her to accept beloved heirlooms they no longer had space or resources to keep. I've got to admire his spirit, she thought. "Yes, sir. I'm sure it's all important." She nudged her fiancé. "Right, Roelke?"

He swallowed. "Absolutely."

"I've gone through those things already." Reverend Brandvold gestured toward a heap near his desk. "I was sure that the letter bearing the name Amalie Sveinsdatter was in that batch. But I didn't find it. I must have filed it away somewhere. I thought that if you have time …"

"Sure!" Chloe said brightly, ignoring Roelke's pointed stare. Her first real glimpse of Amalie might, just might, be somewhere in here.

She wouldn't have blamed Roelke if he bailed on the endeavor but he, bless his heart, waded in too. Several hours later, though, no letter or anything else bearing Amalie's name had surfaced. Katt was snoring, the pastor looked tired, Roelke had started sneezing, and Chloe was frustrated. Much as she wanted to keep going, common sense prevailed. "I think we should call it a night."

"I'm sorry." The minister looked chagrined. "I'll keep searching."

Chloe took a deep breath. "Before we go, Roelke and I wanted to talk with you about something else. If we may."

"Certainly, but let's go into the living room. We'll be more comfortable."

Once he was ensconced in an easy chair, and she and Roelke had settled together on an overstuffed sofa, Chloe leaned forward, elbows on knees. "Pastor Brandvold, Roelke and I went to Kinsarvik today and toured the church, and I felt a real … well, I'll call it a kinship with the building. And Roelke liked it too." She glanced at him: *Feel free to jump in any time*. He shook his head: *You're doing fine*.

"Ah, that building is quite the treasure, isn't it?" The pastor seemed more at ease now. "A fine example of Romanesque architecture, complete with Norman arches."

"Roelke and I wondered if it would be possible to get married there before we leave. And if you'd be willing to officiate …" Chloe's voice trailed away. Reverend Brandvold was already shaking his head.

"I'm truly sorry," he said, "but it is not easy for two foreigners to marry in Norway. You must have a residence permit or something similar. I could not officiate a marriage without a certificate from the Tax Administration verifying you meet all requirements. And getting one would take some time."

"Oh." Chloe studied her knuckles. She'd known it might not be possible to pull a wedding together so quickly. But she was still profoundly disappointed.

"You could get things started, and then come back," Reverend Brandvold suggested. "I'd be honored to help in any way."

Chloe glanced at Roelke, and she knew they were both thinking the same thing. It was miraculous enough that the fates—and Mom—had conspired to get them to Norway once. No way could they afford a second trip in the foreseeable future. If ever.

"That won't be possible," Chloe told him. "Thank you, but I guess it just isn't going to work out."

As if sensing that she needed solace, Katt jumped onto the sofa and settled on Chloe's lap. She petted him softly, returning in her mind to the Kinsarvik Church as she'd imagined it for a wedding day—the faint aroma of wood polish, the narrow windows glowing in the sun, the echoes of ages past suggesting comfort and companionship. The peaceful sense of reverence and faith she'd tried to soak in. *I can't marry where you might have married,* she told her female forebears, *but wherever you lived and wherever your worshipped, I hope you also found comfort.*

SEVENTEEN

Britta—November 1886

Britta took no comfort from her mother Torhild's funeral. The November wind knifed through the Kinsarvik churchyard. Her brother Erik was leading the hymn-singing and graveside scripture-reading, but he paused every few minutes to wipe his running nose. The few mourners stood in a miserable ring around the lampblack-stained coffin resting beside the grave. Britta's father Halvor was long dead, and her oldest brother too. Drunks, both of them. Halvor had passed out on the way home to Høiegård one frigid night four years ago, when Britta had been just twelve, and died of exposure. Two years later her older brother had stumbled from a pier and drowned.

She turned her head toward the old Kinsarvik Church. She wished they could say goodbye to her mother inside, but that luxury was reserved for dignitaries, not a widow from a struggling farm like Høiegård. And perhaps that's well, Britta thought, picturing the painting of St. Michael weighing souls with devils at his feet. How would the saint weigh Torhild's soul? Britta blinked hard against threatening tears. More than anything else, Torhild had loved to dance. Maybe, Britta thought, that's where Mother found her strength.

There were some, even now, who found fault with dancing and music. But Britta and Erik were observing a ceremonious burial. They'd led the small procession down the long trail from their farm to the shore. From there the mourners went by church boats to Kinsarvik. Bells had been rung. Psalms had been sung. On Sunday the pastor would toss some dirt on the grave and say his own words.

Erik stopped speaking. They'd brought a keg of burial beer, and he offered a toast to Torhild before drinking from a carved bowl. When he handed it to Britta, she gripped the horsehead handles, sipped, passed it on. She hoped the drink would last until the bowl came back to Erik. Running out before everyone got a swallow would disgrace the family.

Not that my mother would have worried about such a thing, Britta thought. Torhild had managed the farm and kept her small family fed when Halvor had not. No matter how tired or worried, Torhild always found time for her daughter. Torhild had told stories during days-long flatbread baking sessions or as they sat spinning wool by the fire. Some were family stories. Some were old tales she'd learned from her mother, Lisbet, who'd learned them from *her* grandmother, Gudrun. "We honor them by remembering their stories," Torhild had explained. "One day you will share them with your daughters and granddaughters."

But Britta wasn't sure if her mother had died proud or with regrets. The day before she succumbed to a long, lingering illness, she'd spoken of something never mentioned before: fear. "It will all be up to you and Erik," she'd whispered. "You must keep Høiegård going. It's a poor farm, but if you lose it, you will have nothing. That frightens me."

Britta, who'd been sitting on a stool pulled close by her mother's bed, didn't say that she was terrified of that as well. "I'll try, but Erik..." There was no need to finish the thought. At heart, Erik was not a farmer. He was a musician, a fledgling *kjøgemester* who'd already been called to perform at several weddings. He played the instrument that had belonged to their grandfather, Lars. It was smaller than the newer fiddles, but it served him.

Many men fiddled and farmed. *Bondekunster*, folks called men like Erik—Norwegian farmer-artists. But Erik was working less and less on the farm, wandering away for days or even weeks at a time to meet other fiddlers, learn new tunes, play for new audiences.

"Erik has a bit of his father in him," Torhild had agreed. "But his heart is good. I should have been harder on him, perhaps." She lifted one hand in a gesture of futility. "You're the youngest child. And a daughter. But it's up to you now, Britta. Keep an eye on Erik. Remind him of his duties. And find a good man to marry."

Now Britta looked around the circle of shivering mourners. There wasn't a man among them she could imagine marrying. A young man she knew only slightly had surprised her with his presence here, but he was a loutish fellow who loved to fish, not farm. Even now he was staring out over the fjord as if impatient to be away. The only other single man in attendance was Svein Sivertsson, a widower ten or more years older than she was. Britta didn't know him well, but she saw him here at weekly Sunday services. The big man was a *husmann*—a farm laborer—and as a younger son with no right of inheritance, he would likely never be more. Big hands and broad shoulders suggested that he was a good worker.

He was also quiet and dull. I hope to do better, Britta thought, glancing at Svein.

He was staring at her across the circle, over Torhild's coffin. The intensity in his hooded eyes made her uncomfortable, and she quickly looked away.

Rituals completed, her brother cleared his throat. "We will now recite the Lord's Prayer ..."

When the coffin had been lowered, Britta cast her fistful of soil upon the lid and sent a silent farewell to her mother: *I will do my best to honor your wishes and your memory.* Then she turned away, almost breathless, fighting a sudden surge of panic. She bowed her head, trying to calm her racing heart ... and realized she was standing near Gudrun's grave.

Britta walked over and placed one mittened palm on the moldering wooden marker. She'd never met Gudrun, but somehow, thinking about her today brought the comfort she'd been craving.

I come from a line of strong women, Britta reminded herself. They'd done what they needed to do. She could do the same.

EIGHTEEN

ROELKE WAS GLAD TO escape the pastor's study. "I was afraid some pile might collapse and bury us all," he told Chloe as they started walking back toward the hotel.

"I appreciate your help." Her voice was subdued.

"Hey." He stopped by the side of the road. "We didn't get the news we wanted about getting married while we're here, but at least now we know. We'll come up with another plan." Although they'd had six months to come up with another plan, and had not. Roelke had suggested getting married at the Kinsarvik Church mostly because he thought it would make Chloe happy. Now he realized that he was disappointed, too.

"I suppose. But it's discouraging." She hitched one shoulder up and down. "Aunt Hilda is still in a coma. My genealogist friend hasn't found a trace of Amalie, and Reverend Brandvold has apparently lost whatever clue he had. Finding Klara dead was horrid, and the murder has everyone at the museum twisted into knots. And we finally came up with a wedding plan that appealed to both of us, only to learn that it won't be possible."

Roelke put one arm around her. The mountains stood black against an evening sky streaked with deep shades of blue. Lights blinked out in the nearest house.

"Sorry," Chloe said finally. "Whining doesn't help anything."

He squeezed her shoulder. "Here's what I know: we want to get married, we *will* get married, and—wherever and whenever—the wedding will be wonderful."

Chloe kissed his cheek. "I believe that too. You're absolutely right."

They started walking again and soon approached the Utne Church. Its steeple was silhouetted against the sky, its white walls clear in the lingering twilight. When a stealthy figure slipped around one corner of the building, the shadowed profile stood in stark relief.

Roelke switched from boyfriend to cop. "Wait here," he whispered. He hurried away before she could protest. Maybe whoever was down by the church was simply a resident taking a shortcut home, but he wanted to be sure.

As he silently hurried toward the churchyard, he eased free the flashlight kept in his jacket pocket. He emerged from the drive just as the person reached the end of the wall. Roelke thumbed on the light. The lurker cringed, raising an arm to block the beam. Roelke made a quick inventory: Jeans. Dark jacket with hood pulled up. Small stature. No sign of a weapon.

"I'm Roelke McKenna," he called. As if that would mean diddly to whomever had been creeping around the church. "Is everything all right?"

The guy slowly lowered his arm. Except it wasn't a guy. It was Barbara-Eden Kirkevoll, the redhead who worked at the hotel.

"Mr. McKenna?" she quavered. "You scared me!"

He hurried to join her. "Scaring you was not my intention," he assured her. "I was surprised to see someone here at this hour, and wanted to—" He whirled when he heard footsteps behind him.

"What's going on?" Chloe asked.

He shot her an exasperated look: *I told you to stay where you were!*

Ignoring it, Chloe turned to the younger woman. "Is everything okay?"

"I … It's … *no*!" She pulled off her glasses and swiped at her eyes.

"What are you doing here?" Roelke asked. He glanced at his watch. "It's after eleven."

Barbara-Eden sniffled.

"Why don't we sit down." Chloe put a gentle arm around the girl's shoulders and walked her to a nearby bench. Roelke had no choice but to follow.

Barbara-Eden sniffled harder. "I just came t-to sit in the church for a while. That's all."

Roelke didn't think that was all. "Is there something you need to tell us?"

Chloe shot him a disapproving glance, but it was too late. Barbara-Eden dissolved into tears. "I w-wasn't doing a-anything wrong!" She scrabbled frantically in one pocket, found a tissue, and blew her nose. "And I haven't *done* anything wrong!" With that she shot to her feet and ran up the drive.

Roelke and Chloe watched her disappear into the shadows. "That could have gone better," Chloe observed.

"My fault, I guess," Roelke admitted. "But *something* was off about her being here. Call it instinct."

"That may be, but when you go all cop on somebody, you can be a wee bit … intense." Chloe sighed. "I know that serves you well. But I suspect that the only thing wrong was that Barbara-Eden's best friend was just murdered. Maybe she came here to pray."

"Maybe." Roelke knew that grief provided a rational explanation for the girl's behavior. Still, there had been something about the encounter that left his cop antennae quivering.

"Well, there's nothing more we can do." Chloe shoved to her feet. "Let's go. No, wait. Shine your light over here again." She pointed, and when he obliged, she crouched and picked something up from the ground behind the bench. "What's this?"

Roelke kept the beam on her hand. She'd retrieved a small drawstring bag made of black velvet.

"Was Barbara-Eden carrying this?" Chloe asked.

"I didn't notice it. But it could have slipped from her pocket when she pulled out the tissue. Or someone could have dropped it earlier."

"Let's see what's inside." Chloe loosened the string. She poked one finger into the bag and withdrew an ornate silver necklace. She stared from the jewelry to Roelke and back again. "Oh my."

"Is that …" Roelke frowned, trying to remember.

"Yes." The dangling antique silver swung gracefully from her finger. "This is definitely Klara's necklace."

The corroboration made Roelke's jaw tense. He quickly scanned the shadowed churchyard. "Slide the necklace back into the bag. Be careful not to handle it. Let's go back to the hotel before we discuss this any further."

They didn't speak again until they were back in Room 15. "What do we do now?" Chloe plopped down on the bed. "Ask Barbara-Eden if she dropped it? Or ... talk to Torstein about it? He's the one who gave it to Klara in the first place."

"No." Roelke shook his head. "Not under these circumstances. First thing in the morning we'll turn it over to the cops."

"Was Klara wearing it when she died?"

He thought back. "I don't think so. Since she fell forward, I suppose it might have been hidden beneath her, but I think I would have noticed the chain around her neck when I checked for a pulse." He thought back farther. "I do know that Klara was wearing it when I saw her hiking yesterday morning." The combination of hiking garb and antique necklace would have been hard to miss.

"Oh, Roelke," Chloe said sadly. "Torstein cared so much for Klara that he spent, presumably, a whole lot of money for this token of his feelings. Klara held this gift so dear that she wore it even while working. Even while hiking! It's hard to imagine her loaning it to someone. Do you think Barbara-Eden stole it?"

Roelke had been entertaining that thought but didn't want to say so. "We don't know enough to draw that conclusion. It's possible that someone else dropped the purse in the churchyard. I'm guessing that necklace is pretty valuable?"

Chloe held the drawstring bag to her nose and sniffed.

His eyebrows lifted. "Um ... what are you doing?"

"Real silver doesn't smell like anything. If a silver piece has a strong smell, it likely contains a lot of copper. This one doesn't smell, so it's probably sterling. If I had ice cubes, or a magnet, I could test that theory."

He decided against asking what ice cubes or magnets had to do with anything.

"The point *is*, based on my extremely limited understanding of silver, I do think this necklace is good quality. The workmanship is exquisite, and it's in beautiful condition. And it's antique. So yes, it's valuable. Women today pay small fortunes for good Norwegian silver jewelry to wear with their *bunads*."

That was pretty much what Roelke had figured.

"This necklace has gone from being a love token to a clue in a murder investigation." Blinking hard, Chloe handed Roelke the velvet bag. "Here. I'll let you handle things with the police. It's all just unbearably sad. I'm going to get ready for bed and try to distract myself."

She soon slipped beneath the sheet and picked up the local history book she'd borrowed from Ellinor. Almost immediately she returned it to the nightstand. Roelke watched her curl into a tight ball. He felt an ache in his chest, and another in his jaw. He made a concerted effort to unclench tense muscles. But his heart would hurt as long as Chloe was struggling. The anxiety about finding Marit's roots during this short visit to Norway … Klara's murder … Barbara-Eden's possible role in *whatever* was going on … it was all taking a toll.

Dammit, he thought. He added a few notes to his index cards. Then he slid into bed and put an arm over Chloe's shoulders, hoping the presence would ease her.

Some time later a warning screech jolted him from sleep. Smoke alarm. He leapt to his feet, grabbed his flashlight, and checked the clock—not quite one a.m.

Chloe hadn't moved. He grabbed her arm and shook it. "*Chloe!* Get up!"

She stirred, blinking groggily. "What's the matter?" she mumbled.

"There may be a fire. And we're on the top floor." He hauled her to her feet.

"Ow!" she complained, but she was awake now. She jerked on jeans, stamped into shoes, grabbed her daypack. He did the same. At the last minute he grabbed the little bag holding Klara's necklace too.

As they left the room and hurried down the stairs he heard other voices, other footsteps as guests joined the exodus. Lights were on in the hallways. The siren was still blaring. No smell of smoke yet, though. That was good.

On the ground floor, proprietress Ulrikke Moe, wearing an ankle-length bathrobe over her nightgown, directed the evacuation in English and Norwegian. "Please leave quickly and calmly. Wait across the street… No, we don't know yet what's happening."

Roelke felt better as soon as they were outside. An interesting assemblage of perhaps two dozen guests gathered near the ferry dock. Some were barefoot, clad in pajamas, shivering in the cool night air. Others had dressed and appeared with suitcases clutched in their hands.

Chloe stared at the hotel. "My heirlooms are in there," she moaned. "I don't see any flames. Maybe I could just—"

"You are *absolutely* not going back inside until we get the all-clear." She nodded reluctantly.

Over an hour passed before hotel staff herded the guests back inside. "It was a false alarm," Ulrikke announced. "We will be serving tea and toast for anyone who would like some."

Roelke and Chloe decided against the snack. "I just want to go back to sleep," Chloe said as they plodded up the last flight of narrow stairs. "But thank goodness there wasn't actually a fire—"

"Stop," Roelke hissed, halting so abruptly that she bumped into him. The door to their room was ajar. "I left the door closed."

"They probably sent someone around to check all the rooms."

"Maybe. Wait here." He stepped to one side of the door and eased it open. When nothing happened he leaned forward to look—and felt something inside go hard.

"What the hell?" Chloe was right behind him.

He pushed her away from the door before stepping inside. The small room and bathroom were empty. No one was hiding beneath the beds. "All clear."

But that wasn't quite true. Both suitcases were open, their contents flung on the floor. The drawers on both bedside tables were open too. Their room had been tossed.

"Oh my God." Chloe gazed at the mess, eyes wide. "Who would do this?"

"I don't know." He had to unclench his teeth to force out the words. He didn't know why, either. Had someone, during the chaotic evacuation, decided to take a chance and loot for valuables? Or … had the person come looking for something specific in his and Chloe's room? If so, *what*? That idea might have seemed far-fetched if someone hadn't tried to snatch Chloe's daypack at the airport.

Well, the first thing to do was report what happened. He reached for Chloe's hand. "Come on. We need to contact the police."

The hotel was already quiet. Downstairs, the reception desk was deserted. Roelke checked the dining room, where half a dozen people were enjoying the promised tea and toast. The proprietress was talking to one of them, a reassuring hand on the gentleman's shoulder. Roelke caught her eye and beckoned her to join them in the adjacent parlor. Once they were out of earshot, he told Ulrikke what they'd found upon returning to their room.

Her eyes flared with shock. "I will call the police at once."

They followed the older woman back to the desk, where she placed the call. After hanging up she said, "An officer is on the way, but it will take a while. I'm *so* sorry this happened. Do you know if anything was taken from your room?"

"We didn't do a thorough check," Roelke said, "but there wasn't anything of value in the room." Both he and Chloe kept their wallets in their daypacks, which they'd taken with them. Thank God he'd grabbed the silver necklace they'd found in the churchyard, too.

Then another thought struck. "Ma'am, would you be so kind as to check the hotel safe, and make sure the valuables we put in there are secure?"

Her patrician brows furrowed. "I can't imagine … but of course. I'm happy to put your mind at ease. One moment." She disappeared into the office behind the desk.

Chloe uneasily hugged her arms across her chest. Roelke tapped his thumb against his thigh as worry ratcheted tight inside. It seemed to take Ulrikke longer to return than it should.

When she did rejoin them, the reassuring smile he'd hoped for was absent. Instead she looked stricken. "I don't know how this happened," she said hoarsely. "But the safe is empty."

Roelke clenched his teeth to keep from swearing.

"My heirlooms are ... *gone*?" Chloe asked Ulrikke blankly. "Someone stole them?"

Ulrikke nodded miserably. "It seems so."

Chloe turned to face Roelke, and the anguished look on her face sent a dagger beneath his ribs. "My *Hardangersaum* doily! And ... oh my God, Roelke, the *handaplagg*!"

NINETEEN

Britta—March 1887

Britta put her hand on the corner cupboard, took a deep breath, and opened the door. And there it was: the *handaplagg*.

It was the first time she'd opened the cupboard since her mother Torhild had died four months earlier. Erik had raided their father's cupboard right after the funeral, finding little beyond some tobacco and spare socks and Halvor's knife. Britta had been loath to invade Torhild's private cupboard, as if opening the door would finalize the loss.

But today, she needed to see the hand cloth that had been passed down, mother to daughter, for generations. She lifted it gently from the shelf, carried it to the table, sat down. In the soft glow of a cod-liver oil lamp she contemplated the black designs embroidered on the linen cloth. Trees of life connected earth and sky. Female figures honored the *disir* who guarded women. Sun symbols summoned all that was good and warm and holy. Square fields, dotted with seed stitches, represented the hope of a bride's fertility. Sharp angles whorling in opposite directions were intended to confuse evil spirits. Torhild had explained the meanings inherent in the symbols. She'd also explained that Britta might sometimes understand things, feel things, without explanation.

Britta hadn't grasped everything her mother had tried to teach her. Now she grieved her inability to ask questions. Sometimes she *did* sense something unknown. But lately, since her mother died, she'd been floundering. "I am in need of guidance," she whispered, trying to tap into whatever wisdom had been stitched into the cloth, whatever knowledge had seeped into the threads from her ancestors' hands.

There was no sound in the old cabin beyond the crackle of low flames in the hearth, and the wind's incessant howl. After a long, dark winter, Erik had taken advantage of the first thaw to take his fiddle and hike down the mountain in search of friends and a chance to play his tunes. Britta had no idea when he'd return. Or even if, she thought, for winter had roared back to the isolated farm, packing snow around the cabin and hurling sleet against the window. Erik wasn't a hard drinker, as their father had been. But if the storm had surprised him …

Britta sighed. She wasn't ready to give up on her brother. She understood that Erik needed to get away from time to time. She'd spent many cold winter evenings cleaning fleeces, carding wool, spinning yarn, and listening to him play his fiddle. He'd progressed from sounding out familiar tunes to composing his own. When a piece pleased him, he closed his eyes, looking truly happy. She wouldn't deny him that.

But she also wasn't ready to give up on Høiegård. Her grandparents, Lisbet and Lars, had managed to keep the farm going despite Lars's injury. Her mother, Torhild, had managed to keep the farm going despite Halvor's neglect. It was a poor piece of land, but it was *theirs*.

Britta touched the *handaplagg*, tracing shapes ancestors she'd never met had stitched and additions made by her own mother and grandmother. Once, women in her family had used it to cover their hands when attending weekly church services. That practice had faded, but it was still traditional for women to carry *handaplaggs* on their wedding day.

And will I? Britta wondered. She liked the idea of using the cloth that her mother and grandmother and more had used. And if she married a strong man without a farm of his own, and bore lots of sons, Høiegård could improve.

But the idea of getting married did not appeal, even though she'd recently received her first proposal.

It had come as a surprise. During the warm spell that had sent Erik wandering, Britta had left the lonely cabin and gone to church for the first time in months. It had been good to leave the high farm, to worship, to chat with friends after the service. When she realized she might be lingering in the churchyard overlong, keeping her boatmates waiting, she quickly said goodbye to the Kinsarvik ladies and turned away.

Svein Sivertsson had been waiting for her by the gate. "*God dag*," he'd said, and launched into what appeared to be a well-rehearsed speech. "As you know, my good wife died last year. I am looking to marry a pious woman. You are in need of a husband. I have no property, but you do. I believe God intends us to wed."

Astounded, Britta had groped for words. Finally she managed, "Thank you, but I am not ready to wed. Please excuse me. I mustn't keep the others waiting." And she'd fled toward the beach.

I'm only seventeen, Britta thought now. Plenty of girls her age were wed or promised by now, of course, but she still had time. Slowly she draped the cloth over her hands, trying to imagine Torhild and Lisbet and Gudrun on their wedding days.

And as she stared at the delicate black embroidery, she sensed an affirmation: *No. Not yet.*

Perhaps it had come from one of those women. Or perhaps it came from her own heart. It didn't matter. I must make Erik mind his responsibilities here, Britta thought. She carefully folded the *handaplagg* and tucked it back away.

TWENTY

The instant Chloe opened her eyes the next morning, one thought filled her consciousness: her blackwork *handaplagg* and the *Hardangersaum* doily were gone. She felt empty. Exhausted.

Well, no wonder. It had been a difficult night. *Politi Førsteinspektør* Naess, the policeman who'd interviewed them after Klara's death, had finally arrived. He and a colleague had taken notes, photographed their room, dusted the safe, promised to do everything possible to return her precious heirlooms. But honestly, Chloe didn't hold out much hope. It seemed that someone knew exactly what they were looking for, which explained both the frantic search of Room 15 and the theft. Chloe couldn't imagine who that person was. The aghast proprietress couldn't explain who, other than a few trusted staffers, knew the safe's combination.

I should never have brought the pieces with me, Chloe thought now. She had somehow believed that they might help her find Mom's ancestors. She'd been a fanciful idiot. Traveling with the treasures had been worse than foolish. She remembered the frisson of something intangible she'd felt every single time she'd touched the hand cloth. The textiles held stories she hadn't yet discovered. Now they were *gone*.

The double loss weighted Chloe's chest, making it hard to breathe. She lay still for a few minutes, curled into a fetal ball, blinking back tears. Finally she eased back the covers and slipped from bed.

"Did you get any sleep?" Roelke asked quietly.

She paused in the bathroom doorway, hand on the frame. "A little."

"Chloe, I am more sorry than I can say."

"It's not your fault."

He sat up and scrubbed his face with his palms. "What do you want to do today? No one would mind if you took some time off, you know. Maybe we should try to get away from—from all of this."

The idea of driving away from Utne was appealing. Maybe she and Roelke could go for a long hike in the mountains. But… no. Even the mountains wouldn't make her forget this.

"I need to go to the museum. I want to type up my interview notes before meeting Torstein at twelve thirty. I don't know if Ellinor still wants to go to the Voss Folkemuseum this afternoon or not."

In the dining room, a young woman they hadn't met was stocking the buffet table. Was this Barbara-Eden's day off? Or had a police interview interfered with her work schedule? Chloe had no idea. Barbara-Eden had become an enigma. She'd most likely been the one who'd dropped the bag holding Klara's silver necklace in the churchyard. She'd also been the one who summoned her boss when Chloe had asked to lock her antique textiles in the hotel safe. It was certainly possible that Barbara-Eden had come across the combination somehow, or observed Ulrikke working the lock. Had the young woman been dazzled by the opportunity to sell antique jewelry and textiles?

"I was hoping Barbara-Eden would be here this morning," Chloe muttered. "I want to talk to her."

"Not a good idea," Roelke said. "Leave it to the police."

Chloe didn't want to leave it to the police. She wanted to see what might be hidden in the younger woman's eyes. But Barbara-Eden did not appear.

Roelke wanted some quiet time, so after picking at her breakfast, Chloe kissed him goodbye and set out for the museum. The morning felt different. The village felt different. The delight she'd felt earlier, the sense of familiarity and comfort, were gone. She quickened her pace, feeling absurdly uneasy.

She found Sonja and Ellinor in quiet conversation in the director's office. Both women looked up, clearly startled, when she knocked on the door. Sonja was stylish as ever in a silk shirt of vivid teal worn with black trousers and high heels. Ellinor, by contrast, had dark circles under her eyes and wore a rumpled skirt that suggested she'd either been too busy to iron or too overwhelmed to care.

"Am I intruding?" Chloe asked.

Ellinor beckoned. "No, come in. I fear we are neglecting you. I haven't heard from Torstein today."

"I'm meeting him later," Chloe explained. "Perhaps he'll have another suggestion for some fieldwork I can do on my own." She certainly hoped so. She needed something to occupy herself.

"I imagine all he can think about is Klara." Ellinor rolled a pencil between her fingers.

"Oh, I doubt Torstein will be lonely for too long," Sonja murmured.

Chloe's eyebrows shot skyward. "Sonja!" Ellinor hissed.

"I'm just being honest. Torstein Landvik is a man who turns heads."

Ellinor frowned at her colleague. "Honestly, Sonja. Show some sympathy."

"Sorry." Sonja held up both palms in surrender. "I meant no disrespect."

Sonja may not have meant to be disrespectful, Chloe thought, but she also does not look repentant. There had been an edge in her voice that argued against casual observation.

An unexpected possibility wormed into Chloe's brain. Could it be? Had Torstein once turned Sonja's head…?

An awkward silence filled the room. Then Chloe remembered why she was there. "Ellinor, I'm guessing our afternoon trip to Voss is off?"

"No," Ellinor said firmly. "The police said there's no reason I had to cancel. I'll meet you here at one."

"Excellent." Chloe was pleasantly surprised—and she'd have just enough time to see Torstein at twelve thirty before meeting Ellinor. "And I do have a favor to ask. Is there a transcription machine I might use?"

In short order the machine was produced. "You can use my desk," Ellinor said. "We still need a few more guides for the summer season, and I've got several interviews scheduled this morning." She sighed. "Assuming they weren't scared away by the news of Klara's death on the site. Anyway, I'll find a quiet spot upstairs for those."

Sonja stood. "And I've got to pack a few pieces of *Hardangersaum* we're loaning to the Norsk Folkemuseum in Oslo for a temporary exhibit. Chloe, have a good day."

Alone in the office, Chloe sat thinking about her stolen treasures. Then she straightened her shoulders, pulled out the mini-cassettes, put on the transcribing machine's headphones, and positioned the foot pedal so she could start and stop. At first she paused every few seconds to type what she'd heard, but in time she found a rhythm and was able to make better progress.

She finished with twenty minutes to spare before she was due to meet Torstein at the ferry dock. She made a photocopy of the transcription for herself. Then she tucked the cassettes and recorder back into her daypack, ready for another interview.

She was about to take her leave when a fat file folder on the corner of Ellinor's desk caught her eye. A name was inked on the label: *Jørgen Riis*. Ellinor's research nemesis, Chloe recalled. Jørgen Riis had been a master fiddler and fiddle maker who'd left behind his reputation, a few superbly crafted fiddles, and whispers of an unsolved murder.

Chloe opened the file, which was stuffed with pages of notes and photocopies of journal articles. All were in Norwegian, of course. She did find a couple of photographs of fiddles presumably made by Jørgen Riis. She knew nothing about fiddle construction, but they were gorgeous.

She looked for additional photos but found only more scribbled notes. She was about to move on when two words leapt from a page: *Amalie Sveinsdatter*.

A jolt of electricity struck Chloe's core. What on *earth* did Amalie Sveinsdatter have to do with Jørgen Riis? What had Ellinor discovered? And ... for the love of God, why hadn't she said anything about it? Chloe stared open-mouthed, trying to will the words on either side of the name to magically transpose themselves into English.

Ellinor's voice drifted down the hall. Chloe slapped the file closed just before the museum director walked in. "Ah, you're still here. Any trouble with the machine?"

"None." Chloe strove for a cheerful, calm, and professional tone. "Thanks for your help. I've got to go meet Torstein." With that, she fled.

She began berating herself before she reached the parking lot. Trembling, she stopped at a stone bench on the hill's edge and dropped down. Stupid, stupid, *stupid*! Why had she run away like a frightened rabbit? She hadn't done anything wrong. Snooping in a file on a colleague's desk was inappropriate, but hardly a crime. Why hadn't she just said *Hey Ellinor, I wanted to learn more about Jørgen Riis and couldn't help noticing that some notes in your handwriting included the name that brought me to Norway. The name I shared with you on my first day here. The name that's the only clue I have about my mother's birth family. So… what's up with that?*

Rubbing her temples, Chloe gazed over the village and waterway below. Ellinor had been searching for information about Jørgen Riis for many years. Maybe that particular notation had been scribbled long ago, and she truly had forgotten that the name was in there.

Or maybe, for some reason Chloe could not fathom, Ellinor hadn't wanted to share whatever it was she'd captured in black ink on that page.

Now, having am-scrayed out of Ellinor's office, it was too late to casually ask a question. At least not without looking more idiotic than she probably already did.

Chloe had no idea what to do.

With a frustrated groan, she leaned back and tipped her face to the sky. Clouds were building, and the gray skies matched her mood. “Mom, you were absolutely right,” she muttered. “I should have learned Norwegian a long time ago.”

After Chloe left for the museum, Roelke found a corner chair in one of the hotel’s deserted parlors. He wanted to organize his thoughts without fear of anyone seeing, but found himself glaring at the wall instead of working the problem. He didn’t want to work the problem. He wanted the Norwegian cops to identify the SOB who’d stolen Chloe’s family heirlooms. He also wanted to beat the SOB senseless.

Chloe blamed herself and had assured him that the theft wasn’t his fault. Roelke’s rational mind accepted that. Still, he was the one who’d urged her to surrender the family treasures to the hotel safe. If he hadn’t, the old textiles would have been with her, safe in her yellow daypack, when they’d evacuated the hotel.

He’d had to listen to Chloe cry herself to sleep. He’d never heard Chloe cry like that before. Not when she’d been on the verge of being fired at Old World Wisconsin. Not when her sister Kari had let her down. Not even when Marit died. Chloe had cried quietly at the funeral, sniffling and wiping her eyes. But last night she’d sobbed, first against his shoulder, later into her pillow.

I never want to hear that sound again, he thought. Never, *ever.*

So. That meant he had to stop brooding and do whatever he could to help Inspector Naess discover the thief and the killer who’d murdered Klara Evenstad. Maybe they were one and the same. Maybe they weren’t. It didn’t matter, as long as the guilty were identified and arrested.

Roelke blew out a deep breath and pulled his index cards from his pocket. The *Problems* card was updated first: *Someone pulled fire alarm, tossed our room, stole Chloe's family heirlooms from hotel safe.*

Then he updated Ellinor's card: *After saying she couldn't leave museum, went to Kinsarvik for prearranged meeting with unknown man.*

Finally, the *Barbara-Eden Kirkevoll* card received a new notation: *Possibly dropped Klara Evenstad's silver necklace after Klara's death.* If Barbara-Eden *had* dropped the silver necklace, she'd catapult to top-suspect status. The idea of her killing her childhood friend and stealing the necklace from the still-warm body was grim … but Roelke had been a cop for way too long to believe even a teenaged girl was incapable of crime.

Roelke had taken advantage of Inspector Naess's two a.m. visit to describe the churchyard encounter and produce the black velvet bag. "My fiancée is sure that the necklace inside belonged to Klara Evenstad."

Chloe, who'd been listening in silence, nodded.

Naess slipped the necklace into an evidence bag and filled out a form, presumably verifying what it was and the chain of custody. Then he nodded. "Thank you." It felt like a dismissal.

Well, there's nothing to stop me from thinking, Roelke thought now. He spent the next half hour shuffling the cards, considering, brooding … without even the spark of a new idea. He didn't have enough information to connect the many different problems and suspicions in any meaningful way.

When Chloe joined him, her expression suggested a new calamity. "What's wrong?"

She took a seat and leaned close. "I was working in Ellinor's office, and I looked inside a folder of notes about this famous fiddler she's researching. It was all in Norwegian, of course, but on one page I saw the name Amalie Sveinsdatter."

"You did?" That had not been on his list of possibilities. "What did Ellinor say about that?"

Chloe massaged her temples. "I didn't ask her."

"You didn't ask her?"

"I panicked! I had no business looking in that folder, so when I heard Ellinor coming down the hall I kind of… bolted."

Not the best choice of action, he thought, but managed not to say so. "And now it will be even more awkward to ask her about it."

"Exactly! I can't ask her now."

He beat a staccato rhythm with his pen against the arm of his chair.

After a moment she pressed her hand over his. "Stop it. That chair's an antique."

That response was so *Chloe* that he felt a teensy bit better. "I think you're making too much of it. Ask Ellinor about what you saw, and you'll both probably end up having a good laugh."

She nibbled her lower lip. "Nobody likes a snoop. And the fact that I ran out instead of confessing just makes it worse."

"But you'll drive yourself crazy with wondering if you don't find out why Amalie's name was in her file," he observed. That did not sound good. Not for her, and honestly, not for him either.

She planted elbows on her knees and her face in her palms. "I don't know."

Roelke remembered Ellinor's surreptitious trip to Kinsarvik. "Maybe you're right," he admitted. "There's something's hinky about Ellinor."

———

Chloe felt better for confiding her folly in Roelke, but she still wasn't sure what to do about it. First things first, she thought with a sigh. After grabbing and gobbling a quick cheese sandwich with Roelke, it was time to meet Torstein.

She spotted him at a picnic table near the ferry dock, staring over the fjord. He somehow looked thinner, his features already whittled down by grief. During their first meeting Torstein had bubbled with enthusiasm and energy, but now he was oddly still. At the performance he'd been charming, drawing the audience into the music that brought him joy. Now he seemed like a brittle husk, emptied of everything meaningful.

"Hey," she called softly as she approached.

"Oh!" He jumped. "Sorry."

"No need to be." She settled on the bench across from him, trying to banish a sudden mental movie linking him with Sonja. "Torstein, I didn't know Klara well, but ... I'm just so, so sorry."

His eyes welled with tears. "Who would do such a thing? *Who*?"

"I don't know," Chloe said helplessly. "I can't imagine."

He nodded dully, sniffed hard, set his shoulders. "Anyway, thanks for meeting me here. I see Klara everywhere I look. I'm not ready to go back into the museum or hotel yet."

"Is there something I can do to be helpful?"

Torstein made an obvious effort to focus. "First, tell me about your visit yesterday."

"It went very well." Chloe summarized what she'd learned from Bestemor. "I was able to transcribe the interview this morning." She handed him the pages. "Oh—and I almost forgot. Roelke and I, and you, have been invited to a dance on Saturday at a place called Tollef's Danseplass—"

"We have?" Torstein's eyes flashed with a hint of his old energy. "Are you *serious*? I've been wanting to get there forever. Ellinor has too. It's invitation only, primarily just a social event for the locals. You must have made a good impression."

Chloe shrugged, pleased but a bit bemused. "I'm glad it worked out. I'm sure no one will mind if Ellinor comes too."

"I'll ask her. And I'll try to pull myself together," Torstein added, almost to himself. "I might not get another chance."

Chloe wasn't surprised that the prospect of the community dance roused Torstein from his grief. Dancing was transportive and healing and, for a folklorist, endlessly fascinating. Besides, sitting alone and brooding wouldn't help him. "Let's touch base Saturday morning, all right?"

"Sounds good." The spark of interest flickered out. "Listen, Chloe, I'm very sorry that … that this happened while you're here. It's not fair to you, but I'm just not able to face fieldwork and interviews right now."

"Don't worry about that. And if there's anything else I can help with, I'm glad to."

"Thanks," he said. "But honestly, nobody can help me now."

The trip to Voss took about an hour and a half—less time than Chloe would have guessed. After taking a ferry to Kvanndal, Ellinor drove with easy confidence. Despite steady rain, she not only navigated the narrow lanes with ease, but passed slower cars with aplomb. Roelke would be appalled, Chloe thought, pressing her foot against an imaginary brake pedal as the older woman careened around a delivery van just as a truck appeared in the oncoming lane. Ellinor veered calmly back to her side of the road with at least a foot to spare.

Any thought of broaching the awkward topic of finding Amalie's name in Ellinor's file disappeared. This was obviously not the right time.

Chloe was still in one piece when they arrived in Voss, a small city beside a glittering lake between the Sognefjord and Hardangerfjord. "You'll have to come back when you have more time and see the church," Ellinor said as she took a hairpin turn and began climbing the steep hill rising behind the town. "Olav Tryggvason, King of Norway from 995 to 1000, imposed Christianity on his Norse subjects. By force, if necessary. There's a beautiful stone church near the lake that was built in 1277, which replaced an earlier wood structure, which supposedly replaced some type of so-called heathen gathering spot."

Americans don't know the meaning of "old," Chloe reflected. When she thought about genealogy, about finding her mother's ancestors, her imagination generally quit a few generations back. But her roots disappeared into time much longer ago.

Ten minutes later they passed a sign welcoming them to the Voss Folkemuseum. Ellinor parked in a small lot behind a cluster of old buildings. "Mølstertunet," she said, waving a hand toward the log structures. "The Mølster Farmstead. In the old days, the dwelling houses, animal barns, storehouses, and other functional buildings were arranged around a farmyard. What I love about this place is that all of the buildings were preserved right where they'd been erected. The oldest is from the 1500s, and the last residents moved out in 1927."

"Will there be time for a tour?" Chloe asked hopefully. They'd come for a meeting, but seriously, she could not *imagine* driving away without at least a quick look.

"Maybe." Ellinor turned toward a modern building. "Come on. Let's go find my colleague."

Soon they were seated at a table in the small reception/ticket/gift shop area with Ellinor's counterpart, a gray-haired man with half-glasses perched on his nose. A plump young woman in period clothing produced cups of steaming coffee. "*Takk*," Chloe said gratefully. At least she knew how to say *thanks* in Norwegian.

Ellinor explained the reason for Chloe's visit to Norway. "Voss has been a gathering place for centuries," the man told her. "Dancers and fiddlers met here. Fiddle makers brought their instruments here to sell. Unlike fiddlers in the isolated valleys and hills near Utne, fiddle players here interacted with musicians from other regions. Ellinor and I are working to understand how that interaction affected Voss fiddlers, and how the relative lack of interaction affected fiddlers and dancers in more remote areas."

"And in Wisconsin, we're hoping to document how some of those tunes and dances evolved in the New World." Chloe pulled her notebook and pen from her yellow daypack.

They spent over an hour discussing local musicians, exhibit themes, and special events. Chloe scribbled copious notes, confident that both the content and the interpretive ideas being discussed would be relevant to the exhibit and programming being planned back home in Stoughton.

It was good to see Ellinor forget the murder investigation she'd left behind. She grew animated, sometimes breaking into Norwegian if she wasn't able to process English quickly enough. She'd brought photographs and accession information about a few artifacts that might support the Voss Folkemuseum's efforts. "And here's the prize," Ellinor said, pushing a black-and-white photo across the table. "This is the fiddle attributed to Jørgen Riis."

That name knocked Chloe from her note-taking. And what did Jørgen Riis have to do with Amalie Sveinsdatter? she demanded silently. All right, that was it. She was definitely going to ask Ellinor about the name on the way home. Traffic be damned.

As the meeting wound down, Ellinor glanced at her watch. "We should leave in about half an hour, but Chloe was hoping for a quick tour of the farmstead . . . ?"

"Of course," the man said. He beckoned to the young woman who'd served them coffee.

The guide pulled on a heavy sweater, and Chloe zipped back into her hooded jacket. "Meet me back here," Ellinor said.

The guide slogged across the muddy lane. "Let's start in the barn. We'll be out of the rain and we can see the whole farmyard from there." She headed toward a large barn with side bays for hay and grain, and a central drive-through/threshing floor. "There have probably been two families farming here since before the Black Death in the thirteen hundreds. They shared a yard but maintained their own homes . . ."

Chloe tried to listen, she really did, but on this cloudy day the deserted old homes and cowsheds and storage houses—their logs weathered almost gray, with roofs of slate or turf—seemed especially evocative. She followed the guide into the barn . . . and dual emotions hit her like a boxer's punch.

Raindrops drummed against the roof and pelted the earth. The young woman's voice grew distant.

Focus, Chloe ordered herself, but the palpable rage and joy lingering in the barn were too strong to ignore. She pressed one hand over her rib cage, trying to subdue a buzzing in her chest. Mist blurred her vision. And from a distance, she heard a *hardingfele's* irresistible call…

TWENTY-ONE

Britta—April 1888

"Britta?" Erik called. "Stop dawdling."

"I've never been to Voss before," Britta reminded her brother. Erik knew the town, a frequent gathering place for fiddlers, quite well. Dances like the one they were attending that evening attracted talented musicians from the Hardanger region and beyond.

Her brother folded his arms. "You can see the sights another time." He'd stepped from the walkway to avoid being jostled by pedestrians in the village center's narrow street. A railroad line had connected Voss with Bergen in 1883, bringing trade and tourists. "I need to get to Mølstertunet and get my name on the list to play. If too many fiddlers come, I won't get a chance."

Britta sighed. She'd never been this far from home. She wanted to visit the town's famous stone church. There had been a Christian church on this spot for hundreds of years, but in ancient times, the old religion had been practiced here too. Both traditions are part of me, Britta thought, remembering what she'd heard about her great-great-grandmother Gudrun.

But Erik was clearly out of patience. "And there's a competition for best original tune, you know. The prize is ten *kroner*!"

An enormous sum for them. "All right. Let's go."

They made their way to a footpath tracking up a steep hill. "How many fiddlers will be there?" she asked, holding her skirt up with one hand and a basket piled with thick Hardanger *lefse* in the other.

"Hard to know," Erik said over his shoulder. "A dozen, maybe more. You'll be able to dance all night."

As enticing as that sounded, dancing wasn't what had compelled Britta to accompany him. Leaving their own farm overnight was no small thing. But when Erik had first spoken of the trip, she'd sensed shadows gathering. "I'm coming too," she'd announced. Now that they were on the road, her sense of foreboding had only grown.

Erik paused to look back over the village and lake below. "Even if I don't win, with luck I'll attract new business. I can't earn a living unless I move beyond our own area."

"And what about Høiegård? Mother wanted us to—"

"It's a miserable patch of barren ground." Erik scowled. "There is nothing for us there. You should leave that place. Maybe go find work in Bergen."

And wouldn't that be convenient for you, Britta thought crossly. If she went to the city, Erik would be free of all responsibility—to her, to the farm. Before leaving for Voss they had shoveled cow dung over the soil to hasten the final thaw. There was much more to do before they could plant: breaking clods with hoes, tossing frost-shoved stones from the fields, raking more manure into the earth. And soon it would be time for her to take their animals to the *seter*.

Erik was older than her and, by law, the man of the house. But Høiegård was *theirs*.

She bit back a retort, shoved past her brother, and resumed the climb. After a moment Erik caught up to her. "Sorry," he muttered. "For a musician, an evening like this isn't about fun. Fiddlers aren't always kind to one another."

"You'll do well," Britta told him, because he *was* good.

Mølstertunet, home to two families, was an old farm perched on the hill. In the courtyard, women were setting out baskets and bowls of food. Shrieking children chased each other in circles. A *hardingfele* cacophony drifted from the barn as fiddlers tuned and practiced. Erik disappeared toward the barn, fiddle case in hand.

Britta carried her basket to the feast tables, where an old woman was scolding a bearded man in a fancy suit. "… come here looking to make a profit? Our heirlooms are not for sale. Be gone."

The man's smile was patronizing. "Oh, come now. I'll pay well for any of those." He gestured to a row of ale bowls standing ready. Some, intended for strong drink, were small. Mid-sized bowls would pass from hand to hand, while the largest would be filled for people who had cups to dip. All were beautifully carved, and most were rosemaled. "In Kristiania I've got buyers eager for your primitive country antiques."

"I said they're not for sale!" the woman snapped.

The man snorted with derision. "Your loss."

As she watched him walk away, the old woman shook her head. "That's the third time this month someone's come sniffing around, wanting to buy anything old. We could use the money, but it doesn't feel right to sell things my grandparents made to some stranger."

Britta thought of her own heirlooms back at the farm—the *handaplagg* and other linens, the ornate cupboards her grandfather had carved. She wouldn't dream of selling her treasures, either.

Soon the first fiddler was announced, and the program got underway with a Rudl, a popular couples dance. Courting pairs smiled flirtatiously, the women's skirts flaring with every whirl. Children skipped and hopped among them. Older men and women joined in, their steps more practiced. The fiddle's melody rose over the sounds of heels stomping the floorboards and laughter from men clustered near the ale barrel. The barn smelled faintly of sweet hay and horse sweat.

It was pleasant to be among strangers who expected nothing from her, and Britta was soon tapping her foot. When a grinning blond man wearing farmer's boots offered a calloused hand, she took it. She had almost forgotten the pleasure of moving in tandem with a good partner, almost forgotten how it felt to lose her worries, almost forgotten the pure joy of being buoyed by the music. Moving from partner to partner, she danced until she was breathless.

Chest heaving, she treated herself to a cup of ale. Then she spotted Erik standing with the other musicians, all holding fiddles and bows. Some were at ease, joking with friends seen only infrequently. But her brother's face was hard.

She joined him. "What's wrong? Did you get your name on the list to play?"

"I did. But I had hoped *he* would not be here." Erik jerked his chin toward a young man leaning against a beam, legs crossed at the ankles, the picture of ease. He wore old-fashioned knee breeches and a red vest over a white shirt. The fiddle he cradled in his arms was old-style too, small with a curved back.

Britta wiped sweat from her forehead. "Who is it?"

"A well-known thief," a young man standing nearby muttered. Beneath a shaggy thatch of sand-colored hair his face was pitted with smallpox scars.

She didn't understand. "What?"

Erik waved a hand to silence her. "Perhaps he won't try again."

The performer brought his tune to a close. The *kjøgemester* stepped up to the small performance platform and announced the next musician. The man Erik had been glaring at sauntered to the front. When he launched into his first piece, Erik growled.

After a few measures, Britta understood why. "But that's—"

Erik shoved his fiddle and bow at her before elbowing his way into the crowd, with his friend right behind. Britta's unease turned to dread as she rose on tiptoes. Some people kept dancing; others paused.

Erik reached the platform. *"Stop!"* he yelled. "That is *my* tune!"

A perplexed murmur rose from the crowd. The fiddler lowered his instrument and bow. "I don't know what you mean." A smug smile quirked the corners of his mouth. "This tune was born in my own home, friend."

"That's not true! You heard me play it in Aga last fall, and—"

"Did you steal the tune?" a musician on the sidelines demanded.

"Let him play!" one of the dancers bellowed.

"That tune is my brother's!" Britta exclaimed. She'd heard him develop it as autumn had blazed down the mountain—experimenting with this fingering, that tuning, practicing until he'd perfected the rippling melody. But a growing roar drowned her out.

Suddenly mothers were dragging children from the floor. Unmarried girls tugged their young men's arms in an effort to keep them from the brawl. A man near her sent another stumbling with a thrown punch. Britta had no idea if the antagonist had a stake in the competition or simply liked a good fight.

"Erik!" Britta shrieked, trying desperately to see. He'd disappeared into the melee of blows and shouts and oaths. She bit her lower lip until pain made her whimper.

An eternity passed before a few wiser heads prevailed, and several sturdy farmers waded into the fray. They grabbed whoever was handy, dragged them to the big doorway, and shoved them outside. Waiting women with arms akimbo unleashed their own verbal assault: "Shame! There's no excuse for brutish behavior! Don't you *dare* go back inside until you sober up!" Grousing or subdued, the men obeyed.

As the brawl died down Britta waded into the throng with the fiddle clutched against her chest. Erik and his adversary were at opposite ends of the platform, panting, each held in check by friends. "You're bleeding!" she cried, horrified by the dribble of blood on Erik's cheek and a spreading stain on one arm. Someone had drawn a knife.

He swiped angrily at his face. "It's nothing." He snatched his red knit hat from the floor and slapped it against his thigh.

The *kjøgemester* mounted the steps. He had the look of a working man, not easily intimidated. "That is enough. There will be no more fighting. Still, a serious charge has been raised." He glowered from Erik to his adversary. "Is the tune you started playing your own?"

The smug smile had been wiped from the young man's face, but he had some bravado left. "It is."

Erik's eyes narrowed. "It is *not*!"

Britta understood why Erik was furious. Many tunes were widely shared, each fiddler adding embellishments to make it his own. But it was disgraceful to claim another man's melody—especially in a competition for original tunes! "It is my brother's," she insisted. "I was with him as he coaxed it to life over many evenings."

"Of course his sister would rise to his defense," the thief crowed sarcastically.

"Enough!" the *kjøgemester* yelled. "Let me confer with the judges." He huddled briefly with several other officials before returning to the platform. Dancers and fiddlers pressed close. In the sudden stillness Britta heard doves cooing from the rafters.

"We have no way to determine the truth," he began, "so I announce a *kappleik.* A formal, judged contest of skill and talent will be held in three weeks. It will be open to these two fiddlers and anyone else who wishes to enter." The *kjøgemester* gestured to one of the judges. "My friend here has offered his farm in Telemark..."

Telemark! Britta thought with dismay. Telemark was a neighboring county. Erik's participation in the contest could take him much farther away from home than Voss. She needed him on the farm, not traipsing off again!

Erik lifted his chin and addressed the *kjøgemester*. "I will be there." Only then did Erik look at her: *Please understand. I must do this.* There was desperation in his gaze, and yearning too.

I've lost, Britta thought. Erik's music meant more to him than the farm. More than her. It was his passion, his calling. There was nothing left to say.

She nodded and produced a shaky smile, trying to hide her presentiment of disaster.

June 1888

"Thank you," Britta said to the fisherman as she stepped from his boat at the dock in front of the Utne Inn. The basket of spun and skeined wool she carried down from Høiegård hung from one arm.

"I can stop after I lift my nets," he offered. "I'd be glad to take you back again."

Britta shook her head. "I appreciate the offer, but I'm not sure how long I'll be." She'd have to take her chances.

After snugging her shawl around her shoulders, Britta strode toward the stone seawall. Just beyond, sunshine gleamed a welcome on the freshly painted inn and its picket fence. She didn't often visit the inn. It was difficult to leave the farm, and besides, she'd grown up hearing about Gjertrud. Her mother's cousin had thrown herself from the inn's highest window after some cruel city man had disgraced her. The image gave Britta shivers.

But by the middle of June, the trail was clear of snow, she had wool to sell, and she'd been alone for six weeks. She'd had no word from Erik since he left for the *kappleik* in Telemark. She'd soon have to take the animals to the *seter*, and then she'd be even farther from Utne—from other people, from news. Finally she'd hiked to her closest neighbor's farm and bartered an offer to help make soap for the loan of a young son to watch her livestock overnight.

Now she went inside and asked for Mother Utne, who would pay a few *kroner* for the yarn. Britta planned to buy coffee and a little sugar before heading home.

Mother Utne fingered a skein the color of charcoal. "I'll take everything you have. It's a pleasure to knit with such fine yarn."

Britta hadn't realized how hungry she'd become for an encouraging word. "Thank you. And … I also came in hopes of getting some word about the fiddle *kappleik* in Telemark." She assumed that everyone up and down the fjord had heard about the challenge. Mother Utne talked with every passing traveler. If anyone would have news, it would be her.

But the older woman's eyes crinkled with sympathy. "I've not heard a thing."

Britta tried to stifle her disappointment. "Well, I'm sure Erik will be home soon. I'll hear all about it from him."

"Must you head home right away?" Mother Utne put a hand on her arm. "I believe we have a bit of cod soup left in the kitchen. It would be a shame to waste it. You go sit down."

Mother Utne was every bit as generous as Torhild had said. "That's kind of you," Britta said gratefully.

She heard voices as she approached the dining room. Two men she didn't recognize, one fat and one skinny as a fence rail, sat at the window table. Both were dressed in black suits. Their hands were not broad and scarred as fishermen's and farmers' were. Their clothes were not threadbare, like those of the drovers and peddlers who sometimes came through Hardanger. City men.

Svein Sivertsson was also relaxing at the Utne Inn. The big man was sitting in a corner with a newspaper, a plate of buttered *lefse*, and a tankard. Perhaps his landlord had sent him on some errand. At least I could make my own decision to leave the farm, Britta thought. As she'd tried to impress upon Erik: Høiegård might be a poor holding, but it was theirs, and they were their own masters.

Britta wasn't sure if she should speak to Svein. They hadn't spoken since his awkward proposal two years ago. Apparently sensing her presence, he looked up from the newspaper. She thought he was going to speak, or perhaps wave her over, but he only nodded. The gesture was polite, although Britta saw a hint of regret in his blue eyes. She returned the silent greeting and chose a table far enough away to discourage conversation.

A maid brought the soup, delicious with chunks of cod and bits of dried onion and dill. However, even that couldn't distract Britta from her worries. What if Erik decided that he wasn't coming home? Could she manage everything herself?

No. She could not.

She was grateful when the two city men's spirited conversation intruded on her depressing thoughts. "But what is Norwegian culture?" the skinny man asked his companion. "After centuries of Danish rule and decades of Swedish influence, does pure Norwegian culture even exist?"

"It does." The fat man spoke with confidence. "But it is difficult to find, and harder still to document. That's why this survey expedition is so important! We must seek out the mountain farmers. Rustic peasants who have not been exposed to foreign customs, and who still practice traditions dating back to ancient times."

I hope those two don't climb to *my* mountain farm, Britta thought. She knew that Denmark had ruled Norway for almost three hundred years, and that Norway had been passed to Sweden in 1814. She'd heard men in the Kinsarvik churchyard speaking vigorously of the need for "true Norwegian independence." But she didn't fully understand the issue.

"I hope you're right," the first man said dubiously. "I fear we've lost it all—folk costumes, speech patterns, handicrafts ... the very character of true Norwegian heritage."

"We can find it. Right here, in the Hardanger region," his companion insisted. "And when we do, we must revive it. Winning true independence will be a hollow victory if the very character of our beloved Norway slips from our fingers!"

The kitchen door opened. Mother Utne caught Britta's eye and beckoned. Something in the older woman's expression curdled

Britta's unease in the pit of her stomach. She pushed back her chair with sudden care. Dread slowed her steps. All too soon she had crossed the room.

Mother Utne drew her into the kitchen, where a man stood with hunched shoulders and head bowed. But she recognized the pox scars on his cheeks, the sandy hair. This was Erik's friend.

"Britta," Mother Utne began, "this young man came to the kitchen looking for directions to Høiegård."

Britta advanced on the fiddle player. "What's happened to Erik?"

"I'm sorry to tell you that…" The fiddler dared glance at her, quickly looked back at the floor. "Erik is dead."

A thumping sounded in her ears. "Tell me."

"We went to the *kappleik* together," the young man mumbled. "Erik played very well and was judged the winner of the competition."

How happy that must have made him, Britta thought. She should have been there to share his triumph.

"Most of us spent the night at the farm, but Erik was eager to start for home," the fiddler continued miserably. "He said you'd be worried."

Something hard and sour filled Britta's throat. She hadn't expected Erik to spare her a thought.

The fiddler shifted his weight from one foot to the other. "I left early the next morning. And not an hour down the road, I… I found him. His body. He'd been stabbed."

Britta put a hand to the wall. Had death been quick, or had Erik been left to suffer alone in the dark? Had he known that someone was following him, or had the killer been waiting? She had the odd sense that if she tried to imagine what had happened, the image would form. Her mind shied away.

Erik's friend stooped and picked up something she hadn't noticed—a familiar wooden fiddle case. "This was lying nearby."

Britta didn't want the fiddle. Fiddles had brought heartache to her family, over and over and over. But the young man shoved it at her, and she found herself cradling the wooden case in her arms. She managed to whisper, "Thank you for coming." The fiddler fled.

"My dear, I'm so sorry." Mother Utne spoke softly. "Go back and sit by the fire. I'll bring hot tea."

Britta felt numb. She put down the fiddle case, afraid she would drop it. It took effort to pivot, to walk back into the dining room. The city men were still jabbering.

Then she turned and approached Svein Sivertsson. He folded his newspaper with a rustle and pushed to his feet.

"Pardon me," Britta said woodenly. "Can we talk?"

TWENTY-TWO

When Roelke stopped at the hotel desk after lunch, a staffer handed him a message: *Reverend Brandvold called. If possible, he'd like you to visit this afternoon.* Should this wait for Chloe? Roelke decided against it. The minister might not even be available by the time Chloe got back from Voss.

Fifteen minutes later, Roelke presented himself at the little house on the hill. "Hello!" the minister boomed when he opened the door. He leaned to one side, as if expecting to see Chloe hiding behind Roelke. "You are alone?"

"Chloe went to Voss with Ellinor Falk," Roelke explained. "Something to do with fiddles and folk dance. She won't be back for hours."

Reverend Brandvold gestured Roelke inside. "I'm glad you came anyway. I've got something."

Please, *please* let it be good news, Roelke thought. "Something about Amalie Sveinsdatter?"

"My archivist friend in Bergen found her baptism record." The pastor looked triumphant. "And, she was baptized right here in the Utne parish church."

Utne, Roelke thought. Of all the places the Stoughton Historical Society could have sent Chloe, it had been to Utne. *Something about this place makes me feel at home*, Chloe had said. She'd been right all along.

As if reading Roelke's mind, Pastor Brandvold said, "I imagine Chloe will be pleased. Scholars came to this area a century ago in search of the cultural heart of Norway. And," he added wryly, "any pieces of folk art they could find."

Roelke thought of Chloe's stolen heirlooms with another wrench of anger. Chloe's ancestors hadn't sold those antiques when they might have. But now …

"Anyway, it seems certain that Chloe has roots in Hardanger. My friend is mailing the information, but he called with the basic details." Reverend Brandvold picked up a tablet by the telephone. "Amalie Sveinsdatter was born on March 11, 1905, and baptized two weeks later. Her parents were listed as Britta Halvorsdatter and Svein Sivertsson Fjelland."

"Amalie would have been fifteen years old when Marit was born. A young unwed mother?"

"Perhaps."

"That last name is new," Roelke mused. "Fjelland, I mean." He still got confused about the whole Norwegian naming thing.

"The third name was the farm name. 'Fjelland' means 'mountainous.'"

Which in this vertical landscape narrowed things down not a bit, Roelke thought. "So … Amalie wasn't from right here in the village, then?"

The older man shook his head. "Not likely."

As nice as it would have been to have the pastor link Chloe's ancestors to a local, well-known Utne family, Roelke reminded himself that this was still profoundly good news. Amalie was real, he thought. And she attended church in Utne.

While traveling back to Utne, Chloe didn't make good on her vow to ask why Ellinor had written Amalie Sveinsdatter's name in her notes about fiddler Jørgen Riis. Ellinor said little on the drive, and she drove more sedately, as if reluctant to return to the museum where one of her favorite employees had been killed.

Chloe was okay with the silence. She was having a hard time shaking the vestiges of what she'd experienced in the barn. The anger and happiness had both been so strong, so tangible, that she'd almost lost herself. Only the tour guide's voice, first distant, then growing louder—"Miss Ellefson? Miss Ellefson!"—had pulled Chloe from her fog. Yes, she'd assured the young woman, she was just fine. "I'm fighting off a migraine," Chloe had lied.

But she couldn't ignore what she'd perceived in the old barn at Mølstertunet. At the Hardanger Folkemuseum's Høiegård house, she'd felt a powerful jumble of emotions. This barn's double whammy was new. What did it mean that she'd felt both hot fury and, simultaneously, that ebullient joy? Her "gift" was stronger here in Norway. She didn't know if that was a good thing.

This could seriously get in the way, Chloe thought, remembering just in time that propping her toes on Ellinor's dashboard was not something a responsible professional would do. And that was the problem: professionalism. She'd chosen to work in the museum field. She had no other particular skills. She'd always managed to keep these unexpected jolts from causing colleagues notice, much less alarm.

Until today.

Lovely, Chloe thought. Ralph Petty, her micromanaging boss, already disliked her. Hopefully the Atlantic Ocean would keep rumours of her odd behavior from spreading on the museum grapevine. She was developing a for-real headache by the time she and Ellinor got back to the Hardanger Folkemuseum.

"I've got a few things to do inside," Ellinor said as she parked. "You can check in with me tomorrow, if you want."

If you want, Chloe thought. Was Ellinor just tired? Or was she tired of trying to keep the American curator busy? Who knew. "Thanks for including me on the trip to Voss," Chloe said, avoiding the question. "It was an interesting day." In more ways than one.

Ellinor disappeared inside the museum. Chloe hesitated, weighing her options. After Klara's death, she'd never had a chance to revisit the ancient restored home in the folk museum's open-air division. The hilltop collection of restored buildings would be deserted at this hour. Maybe she should make a brief detour now, see what happened. But after glancing toward the path, Chloe shook her head. Not today. Someone had killed Klara Evenstad in that house. Further exploration would wait until Roelke could accompany her. I'm becoming a weenie, she thought, but even that sad assessment didn't change her mind.

She shoved her hands into her pockets and started down the drive. She and Roelke had made a late dinner reservation at the hotel, so she had plenty of time. Soft evening light slanted through the small apple orchard between the museum and the village, and lit the mountainsides beyond. The landscape felt peaceful again. I need peaceful right now, Chloe thought, and decided to take a longer-than-necessary route back to the hotel.

Her stroll took her past tidy homes with well-tended gardens, a smiling elderly couple walking hand-in-hand, the Utne Church. She paused there, remembering what she'd said to Roelke when they'd gone inside: *Something about this place makes me feel at home*. She decided to linger on the bench outside—then noticed that a young woman with red hair was already there, hunched over with elbows on knees and face in her hands. She wore the Utne Hotel's costume/uniform of ethnic-inspired dress and comfortable black shoes. Barbara-Eden.

Keep walking, Chloe told herself sternly. As Roelke had emphasized, the girl's possible role in criminal acts was a matter for the Norwegian police.

But Barbara-Eden's shoulders were shaking. Chloe sucked in her lower lip, debating. Compassion won, and she hesitantly approached the bench. "Are you all right?"

Barbara-Eden jerked erect, snuffling hard. Her pink-rimmed eyes widened. "*What?* What do you want from me? I told you last night, I haven't done anything wrong!"

"I didn't accuse you of doing anything wrong," Chloe said, as mildly as humanly possible. "I just wanted to make sure you're all right." She held up both hands in placating gesture. "I'll go if you want. But if there's anything I can do to help ..."

Two girls sped past the church on bikes. Somewhere in the distance a dog barked twice, then subsided. Finally Barbara-Eden scrubbed at her eyes and blew out a long, shuddery breath. "I think I dropped something here last night. Something important. But I can't find it."

Oh my, Chloe thought, processing that admission. First, Barbara-Eden *was* the one who'd dropped Klara's silver necklace. And second, Inspector Naess had not told her that he had the necklace. The police were probably trying to see what Barbara-Eden might reveal, or do, on her own; maybe trap the girl in a lie.

This is why Roelke didn't want me talking to her, Chloe thought. But it was too late to walk away now.

Barbara-Eden filled the awkward silence. "I got questioned by the police today!" She started to cry again. "They came and got me at work. It was humiliating. I think *they* think I killed Klara. Probably everyone at the hotel does too, now. But I didn't!"

Chloe tentatively stepped closer, eased down on the bench, and put her arm around the girl's shoulders. "I'm so sorry. Sorry that your friend died. Sorry that you can't find... whatever it was that you lost."

"It w-was an antique s-silver necklace," Barbara-Eden wept. "One that b-belonged to Klara."

"I see." Chloe was still striving to map a safe path through this conversational minefield. She almost asked if Barbara-Eden had borrowed the necklace from her friend, because she really wanted that to be the case. *Don't lead the conversation!* Roelke barked in her head, so she bit her tongue. "Um... how did you come to have Klara's necklace?"

"I didn't steal it." Barbara-Eden crossed her arms defensively. "I found it."

"Where did you find it?"

"There's a room at the hotel where employees can change. We each have a small locker. I got a run in my stocking, and I thought Klara might have a spare pair, so I looked in her locker. We know each other's combinations. Knew." She shuddered convulsively. Chloe unzipped her daypack, found a packet of tissues, and handed it over. Barbara-Eden blew her nose before continuing. "I noticed this little black velvet bag on the floor of her locker. I knew what it was, and figured Klara must have dropped it by mistake."

"Why by mistake?"

"Because she would never have tossed the necklace on the floor! She *cherished* it."

Remembering Klara's shy but obvious pride as she fingered the delicate silver, Chloe agreed with the assessment. Still … something wasn't adding up here. If Barbara-Eden had thought the necklace ended up on the locker floor by mistake, why hadn't she simply locked the door and let her friend know what she'd seen? Chloe knew what Roelke would probably say. *It's an antique, right? Valuable? Barbara-Eden probably decided to sell it.*

But that didn't feel right either. "Did you tell the police that you'd picked up Klara's necklace?"

The girl shook her head. "No."

"Oh, Barbara-Eden," Chloe said with a groan. She just couldn't help it. Lying to the cops, or even being evasive, would only make a bad situation worse.

"That has nothing to do with *anything*. After hearing that Klara was dead, I wanted to give the necklace to her mother." Barbara-Eden pulled another tissue from the packet and began shredding it. "But now I've lost it."

Chloe stared blindly at the church, trying to remember anything helpful about Barbara-Eden. Ulrikke Moe had referred to her employee as "impressionable," and seemed concerned that she might have said something innappropriate. Earlier, Barbara-Eden had given Chloe the fax from genealogist Rosemary Rossebo, and the messages from Reverend Brandvold and Torstein Landvik. *You have a couple of phone messages, too. One from Reverend Brandvold, and… one from Torstein Landvik. You know Torstein?* Barbara-Eden had seemed surprised that Torstein had called for Chloe.

Torstein, who was vibrant and virile and in love with Barbara-Eden's best friend.

Tortstein, who had prompted a caustic observation from the urbane Sonja Gullickson: *Oh, I doubt Torstein will be lonely for too long… Torstein Landvik is a man who turns heads.*

At the time, Chloe had wondered if Torstein had turned Sonja's head at some point. But… what if he had, knowingly or not, turned Barbara-Eden's head? Hadn't Reverend Brandvold speculated that some of Utne's young women were envious of Klara?

Frost formed in Chloe's marrow as she realized that *if* Torstein and Barbara-Eden *had* shared some kind of clandestine relationship—or even if Barbara-Eden had simply experienced a fierce but unrequited attraction—the girl had a motive for murder.

Chloe had to moisten her lips before daring the question. "Are you in love with Torstein Landvik?" She half expected Roelke to burst from the shrubbery to terminate this conversation by any means necessary. But she's opening up, Chloe argued silently. As she did *not* do when being interrogated by the police.

Barbara-Eden had sucked in a harsh breath. After a long moment she sagged, as if all fight was gone. "I… I guess so."

"Was he attracted to you?"

Barbara-Eden winced. "I thought he might be. He flirted with me sometimes."

"Does the fact that Torstein flirted with you have anything to do with why you took the necklace from Klara's locker?"

"Well ... maybe." The girl shrugged, still avoiding eye contact. "I guess I wanted to pretend that he'd given it to me. Just for a little while! I really was going to give it back to Klara." She swiped at a tear. "But I never got the chance."

What a colossal mess, Chloe thought. She silently thanked the universe for bringing her and Roelke together, effectively removing them both from this type of romantic wretchedness.

She took a deep breath. "Barbara-Eden, if you had anything to do with Klara's death, you have to say so. The police will find out anyway, and it will go much better for you if—"

"But I didn't!" Barbara-Eden pinned Chloe with a wild-eyed stare. "I swear to God. You've got to believe me!"

Chloe held her gaze for a long, anguished moment. Then she nodded. "I do believe you."

The girl's shoulders slumped with relief.

"*But*, you withheld information from the police. You have to set that straight. You must tell them everything you know, including how you came to have the necklace, and that you lost it." It was hard not to squirm with the discomfort of *not* blurting out that the necklace was safely in police custody.

Barbara-Eden's sigh held the weight of mountains. But she nodded. "I will."

"Right now," Chloe added, in case she hadn't been clear. Leaning over, she began picking up the tissue scraps Barbara-Eden had dropped. "In fact, I'll come with you."

Roelke forked up a morsel of salmon. It was lightly herbed and grilled to perfection.

He wasn't used to having dinner at eight p.m., so his stomach had been growling by the time Chloe returned to the hotel. She'd looked tired but also distinctly guilty about something, which always blipped his radar. When she'd confessed to initiating a conversation with Barbara-Eden, he'd gotten a little cranky.

Now, twenty minutes later, the fine meal was improving his mood. Chloe's vegetarian dish, something white covered with a bright green sauce, was also provoking sighs of contentment. "I don't know what this is, but it's fantastic," she marveled. "Anyway, I swear I didn't do anything that will rouse the ire of the Norwegian police."

"You really think Barbara-Eden was telling the truth?"

"I do. She was indulging in a romantic fantasy, not trying to fence valuable antiques. And I stayed with her until she'd called the police."

At least Chloe didn't reveal anything that she shouldn't have, Roelke thought. Instead, she'd gotten Barbara-Eden to reveal and report new information. Inspector Naess couldn't complain too loudly about that. He hoped.

"Here's what I don't get." Chloe pointed her butter knife at him. "Knowing how Klara treasured that necklace, it seems unlikely that she wouldn't notice dropping it on the floor of her locker. Why did she even take it off?"

He gave her a pointed look. "I'm quite sure that Naess will pursue that question himself."

"Yeah, yeah." She smiled at the young waiter who'd appeared to refill her goblet with sparkling apple juice. "From here on in, I'm staying out of police business."

I can only hope, Roelke thought. "Listen, I haven't even had a chance to tell you about my afternoon."

Chloe leaned back in her chair, considering him as she sipped. "Did something come up?"

"You could say that," Roelke acknowledged, and grinned. "Something about Amalie."

TWENTY-THREE

Solveig—June 1912

"Amalie!" Britta called. "Don't chase the chickens! Did you finish hoeing the garden?"

Solveig saw her mother Britta standing in the cabin doorway, knitting basket in hand. Solveig's younger sister, Amalie, stopped racing about. "Almost." Clucking indignantly, the brown and yellow *Jærhøns* scurried away from the seven-year-old.

"Please get back to it."

Solveig shook her head indulgently. It was the first warm day of summer. Bluebells blossomed in the woods and tender fiddleheads uncurled from the damp soil. Spruce trees were tipped with bright new green. The lambs and calves were safely born, already cavorting in their fenced pasture. She could hardly blame her sister for playing—especially since their father was not at home to beat such a "willful indulgence" from Amalie with a switch. But today Svein had taken his son fishing. His absence felt like a field of purple heather had burst into bloom.

Solveig bent over her laundry tub, closing her eyes as she often did to better listen, better hear. A gentle breeze sighed through the apple trees, suggesting the faintest of melodies. Solveig knew she could capture it, shape it—

"Solveig!" It was Britta, standing right beside her. "I've been calling you. Sometimes you're no better than Amalie."

"I wasn't daydreaming," Solveig protested mildly. She'd learned long ago that no one else experienced the world in music, as she did. "Do you need something?"

Britta's exasperation faded, and she smiled. "Come sit with me."

Mother must feel peaceful too, Solveig thought. She draped the last wet shirt over the line and followed Britta through the front meadow to the cliff edge. They settled on a stone ledge where yellow saxifrage bloomed, thread-thin roots clenching tight in any crevice. Sunlight glinted on the snow still streaking the ravines.

Britta pulled a small leather-bound book from beneath her wool and held it out.

Puzzled, Solveig accepted it. "What is this?"

"It's a book to capture stories."

"Stories?"

"I grew up hearing stories from my mother, Torhild, who'd collected them from her mother, Lisbet. Lisbet learned them from *her* grandmother Gudrun, and some are even older. Some of them reflect the old ways." Britta paused before adding, "The old religion."

Solveig's eyes widened. This was dangerous territory. Father would take a switch to Mother if he heard her speak of such things.

Britta gazed at the distant waterfalls, swollen with snowmelt, cascading down the mountainsides. "I want the stories to be written down. They musn't get lost. And you're the best one to do it."

The charge made Solveig feel a little breathless. "But where did . . ." She gestured at the blank book.

Although Britta's cheeks flushed, she held her head high. "Last time I sold wool in Utne I held a few skeins back and traded them for the book. I got it from a peddler who doesn't know us."

So he can't carry tales to Father, Solvieg thought. She was amazed at her mother's daring. To her knowledge, and growing annoyance, Mother had never crossed her husband. Never argued.

"You're seventeen," Britta continued. "Surely you'll marry and leave the family farm before too long."

Solveig's flicker of admiration faded. "Oh, Mother. I have no such plans."

"You need a man, Solveig. A woman does."

"*I* don't."

"Your older sister was married and gone by your age."

"And she's already a widow." Solveig's brother-in-law had drowned just a year after the marriage.

Britta fixed her with another exasperated look.

I do not need a man! Solveig thought. Trading life in her father's house for life with a husband she didn't truly love held no appeal. Besides, she was too quiet for the local young men. Too different.

Britta may have discerned her daughter's thoughts, for she abruptly changed the subject. "Solveig, have you ever felt that you understood something without knowing why?" Britta hesitated as if groping to find the right words. "Perhaps you sometimes get a sense of things long gone, things unseen?"

Solveig sucked in her breath. She knew all too well the snatches of prescience her mother was trying to describe. As a child, she'd been bewildered to realize that she sometimes sensed things that her companions clearly did not—overpowering sensations of long-ago happiness or grief or anger. The feeling of joyful anticipation or uneasy forboding that occasionally consumed her, and were always born out.

"I understand what that burden feels like," Britta said. "But your father ... well. This conversation is not for his ears." She tapped the book in Solveig's hands. "And you understand that he must never know about this."

"I understand." Solveig watched a golden eagle glide silently past the cliff. "Mother? Why did you marry him?"

Britta caught her breath. She glanced over her shoulder at Amalie, dutifully hoeing weeds from between fledgling rows of peas and turnips. Finally she said, "As you know, my brother Erik was killed by a rival fiddler in 1888. My parents were dead, and my other brother was already dead too. I was alone, and desperate to keep this farm from being sold. Without Erik, I could not survive here. I needed a husband."

There must have been other choices, Solveig thought. Better than taking marriage vows with someone like Svein.

Britta picked up her knitting and began a new row. "Twenty-four years have passed since Erik was killed. I've been married to Svein for almost as long. He had no property of his own, so of course he moved here."

Solveig had always known that her mother's marriage was not a good one. Svein's religious beliefs were more fervent than those preached by the pastor at the new Utne Church. "You would have been better off without him."

"Not here, all alone. And in fairness, Svein has worked hard. This farm has produced more since our marriage than it ever did before. He's carried logs here on his back, and soon we'll have a new home." Britta nodded. "I came close to losing this place, so I am grateful."

"You could have left here, found work," Solveig dared. It seemed so obvious.

But Britta looked shocked. "I couldn't abandon this!" Her expansive gesture took in the house and barn, the fjord and ring of mountains. "I promised my mother to safeguard this holding. The thought of letting everything go was unbearable."

"But … was keeping this farm really worth sacrificing your happiness?"

"Do not judge!" Britta snapped. Then she sighed, and let her knitting fall to her lap. "This place makes me happy. I am rooted here."

Solveig tried to imagine how it might feel to be so rooted. Did her mother truly not dream of new possibilities? Or did she simply not dare?

"You don't understand." Britta's gaze grew distant. "Erik never understood why I stayed, either. He longed to wander."

Solveig knew well the urge to wander. To wonder what lay beyond everything comfortable and familiar.

"I do regret Svein's harshness toward you children," Britta added. "Your brother is lost to me, already molded in Svein's beliefs about good and evil. But you girls … I didn't know how it would be. You're a clever young woman who knows how to avoid trouble. But Amalie isn't sturdy like you older girls. I know you've often shielded her. I'm grateful, Solveig."

Solveig waved that away. Keeping an eye out for Amalie's welfare was a deeply ingrained habit.

"I wish ..." Britta began, then bit her lip. "Solveig, I wish you could go to dances. I know you've missed things, simple harmless things, that would have made you happy."

Music, Solveig thought, with a familiar ache of longing. More than anything she wanted to learn how to play the fiddle. But Father believed that the *hardingfele* was the devil's instrument. And in her family, the topic was not philosophical. Fiddle music had been at the heart of several tragedies.

Just as frustrating, fiddling was a man's occupation. Women might play a *langeleik*, a rectangular instrument with only one melody string contrasting the drone strings. A *langeleik* was placed flat on a table to play, unlike *hardingfeles*, which seemed to become an extension of the musician's body. Playing the *langeleik* had never appealed to her.

But her mother's acknowledgment of Solveig's unattainable dream was an unexpected comfort. Although part of her was still frustrated with Britta, another part—a new part, tender as the first sprouts poking through the earth in spring—was pleased to be having such a conversation.

"That child," Britta murmured. Solveig followed her mother's gaze and saw Amalie squatting in the dirt with hoe lying idle.

"That's enough talk for now," Britta said. She stuffed her knitting away and got to her feet. "But we will look for another opportunity to talk. I don't want to waste time, especially since you will soon leave for the *seter*."

Solvieg held up the book, savoring their shared secret. "Until then, I'll hide this away."

When Solveig's father and brother returned to the farm that afternoon, an unexpected guest was with them. "You've met Gustav Nyhus," Father said.

"Welcome, Gustav," Britta said. "You'll want to spend the night, I imagine. It's a long walk back down the mountain. Amalie, set an extra place at the table." The words were right, but Solveig heard the sudden tension in Mother's tone. Gustav was perhaps fifty or fifty-five years old, with a long gray beard and deep-set eyes. He had the wide tough hands of a boatman, and he always smelled of cod. The fisherman was a widower who sometimes attended the Utne Church. He and Father were friends. She'd seen them deep in conversation in the churchyard after services. And when her father held his own meetings, preaching from a stump to whomever was passing by, Gustav often joined him.

Gustav was a dour man. During the meal he showed no interest in the farm or the family. He didn't make eye contact when Solveig served the brined herring and flatbread. Her father steered the conversation from the weather to the changing price of stockfish to the local pastor's inadequacies. "I've heard plans for a Midsummer dance above Utne," Svein said grimly. "And the pastor says nothing!"

"It's a disgrace," Gustav agreed.

When the table was cleared and dishes washed, Solvieg reached for her shawl. "I'll tend the animals," she murmured to her mother.

Gustav rose. "I'll come with you."

Startled, Solveig groped for words. Finally she stammered, "But—I—there's no need to . . ." Then she noticed her father's scowl. "Very well."

They walked to the barn in silence. Solveig crossed her arms uneasily over her chest. I don't want this, she thought, even though "this" had yet to be defined.

She didn't expect Gustav to help milk the cows and goats, and he did not. Instead he grabbed a pitchfork and tossed animal waste onto the pile waiting to be spread on the barley and wheat patches. Neither spoke until they were walking back to the house. "Your father," Gustav said abruptly, "believes we should marry."

Solveig clutched the shawl more tightly around her shoulders. She waited until they had reached the house before speaking. "Thank you," she said carefully, "but I have no wish to marry at this time." She went inside.

That night she lay awake, listening to Amalie sleep beside her, and to the snores coming from the pallet of sheepskins and blankets Mother had made for Gustav by the raised hearth. Solveig didn't regret what she'd told him. But she knew the matter was not closed.

When she woke the next morning, Gustav was gone. Solveig slipped from the house to begin morning chores.

This time her father followed. "*Solveig*," he snapped. He grabbed her arm and jerked her around to face him. "I brought Gustav here for a reason."

Solveig forced herself to meet her father's furious gaze. "I do not wish to marry him."

Svein gave her arm a hard shake. "You want to be a burden for the rest of your life? I feed you. I clothe you. One day your brother will take over this farm, and his wife will take charge. What will you do then?"

I'll fly away, Solveig thought. I'll find work in Bergen. I'll emigrate to America. I'll—

"God intends you to marry," Svein muttered.

She blinked, willing back tears as his fingers bit into her skin. The wild look in his eyes frightened her. "Father, I—"

"Your perversity is a sin!" He pulled her, stumbling, to the small rowan tree growing beside the barn and broke off a narrow branch.

———

Ten days later, Solveig and her brother took their livestock up to the summer farm.

"It will be nice for you to be away," Mother whispered when Solveig said goodbye. "I will come up when I can, and Amalie too."

Solveig grabbed their oldest cow's halter and led her to the trail. The backs of her legs still hurt, but she'd managed to wrench away from Father before he'd struck too many blows. All she wanted to do was leave the main farm, and her father, behind. The cows were eager, knowing fresh grass awaited. The sheep bleated with apparent happiness as well. The goats danced and pranced.

The procession moved up the mountain with a constant jingle-jangle of the animals' bells. When they arrived in the high meadow, Solveig felt something tight inside ease. She loved the *seter*, and this year she'd been given responsibility for the summer farm.

Her brother stayed only one night. "I'll be back on Saturday to pick up your butter and cheese," he told her the next morning as he shrugged into a pack basket. He lifted one hand in farewell and strode down the trail.

"Well." Solveig turned back to the low log building where she would work and cook and sleep this summer. Everything needed cleaning, but soon enough she'd have her buckets and churns, strainers and paddles, bowls and *ambars* arranged on the shelves just where she needed them.

First, though, she wanted to hide the book her mother had given her. In the past week or so they'd snatched a few quiet minutes when Svein was elsewhere. Britta shared a story, and Solveig wrote it down. It took a long time. But these stolen moments with her mother made Solveig content. And her mother's ability to save a bit back from the family account, and secretly buy the notebook, had given Solveig an idea. In the fall, after she closed the *seter*, she'd be expected to take some of the cheese and butter to sell in Utne. If Mother can take some money for herself, Solveig thought, I can too. The prospect of saving even a few *kroner* was tantalizing. And she would ask the pastor for an *attest*—a letter of recommendation she could use if she one day looked for work in Bergen … or even America.

Now she considered where to hide the book of stories. Her father might visit the *seter* at any time to bring supplies or check production or patch a leaky roof. Best to get into the habit of securing the book out of sight.

The back room of the cabin had been built against the mountain wall, which helped keep cheese and milk cool. Over the years a few broken domestic tools had been shoved into a far corner, including an old churn with dry staves. "This will do," Solveig murmured. She lifted the dasher and lid, peered inside … and her jaw dropped with astonishment. Standing inside the hollow churn was a small wooden fiddle case.

She pulled the case free, carried it into the main room, and opened the lid to reveal the *hardingfele*. Where did you come from? she demanded silently. But almost as quickly, she knew. This must be the fiddle once owned by her long-dead Uncle Erik, who'd inherited it from his grandfather, Lars. Her mother must have hidden it here when she married Svein. Solveig had always assumed that Erik's fiddle was long gone, perhaps even destroyed. It pleased her to imagine her mother defiantly tucking away Erik's *hardingfele*.

And now, Solveig thought with a sense of awe, it is mine. The spruce fingerboard had been overlaid with horn, and she traced a finger over the precise pattern formed by imbedded pieces of clam shell. She turned the fiddle to better see the intricate designs inked on the curving sides.

But after so many years of neglect, the instrument was warped. The thin wood held several small cracks. The brittle strings had snapped. Solveig had no idea how to bring the instrument back to life.

Nonetheless, she was determined to try.

TWENTY-FOUR

Hardingfele music haunted Chloe's dreams. The final chord didn't fade until she woke that morning.

It was very early, but sunlight was streaming through the window and she felt restless. The news about Amalie that Roelke'd shared the night before had kept her awake. Most exciting was establishing Amalie as a one-time resident of the general Utne area. But the farm name listed—Fjelland—was meaningful too. Mountainous, Chloe thought again. The name conjured high meadows and stupendous views. It explained why she'd chosen to go to college in West Virginia, why she'd loved Switzerland, why the Hardangerfjord felt like home.

She had a new plan. Her primary goal had shifted from finding some record of Amalie to connecting with a living relative. Chloe wanted to identify the location of the farm where Amalie had been born. That meant finding a *Bygdebok*—a book written about the history of a specific Norwegian community. Her mom, *über* genealogist, had often talked about the wealth of information contained in *Bygdebøker*, including who lived where, and when they lived there. With luck, Chloe thought, the local library will have copies of *Bygdebøker* for the region.

With more luck, Amalie's childhood home might still be in the family.

But the library wouldn't be open for hours. Chloe sat up and considered her sleeping fiancé. She didn't want to disturb him, but after five minutes of fighting the twitchies, she gave up. "Roelke? Are you awake?"

"Not really," he mumbled. But he stretched, knuckled his eyes, and sat up with his usual *Let's go* alertness. His ability to wake up quickly was a trial for Chloe, who preferred to hit the snooze button four or five times before accepting the inevitable.

Today, though, it came in handy. "I can't sleep, and they haven't started serving breakfast downstairs yet. Want to go for a walk? I'd like to go up to the old dance site Reverend Brandvold told us about. I can go by myself if—"

"Nope." Roelke tossed the sheet aside. "Let's go."

They left the hotel dressed for hiking and, once on the high road, had no trouble finding the path. It skirted an orchard where apple trees had been pruned into narrow columns. The air was perfumed by creamy pink-tinged blossoms, and a small bird lilted a song nearby. The still morning felt fresh. "I'm going to start getting up early every day," Chloe vowed.

"Sure you are," Roelke said, but without malice.

Beyond the orchard the trail wound into the forest, easing into a series of switchbacks. Fifteen minutes later they emerged into a rocky clearing. "This must be it!" Chloe said.

"There's the platform." Roelke strode over to inspect the crumbling wooden structure. "What's left of it, anyway. Do *not* try to climb on that."

Already enchanted, Chloe didn't need to climb on anything. She quivered with the joyful energy left by generations of people who'd barely scraped a living from the rugged landscape. This is what I need to capture back in Stoughton, she thought. How important music and dance were to rural people who worked hard for every morsel. Closing her eyes, Chloe heard a *hardingfele*'s call, heavy shoes pounding against the wooden floor, laughter and voices. She smelled woodsmoke from a crackling bonfire, sensed the anticipation of courting couples exchanging knowing glances in the blue twilight—

"You still with me?" Roelke's voice penetrated the vision.

She blinked back to the moment. "Yes. I was just imagining everything." She pointed beyond the dance floor to a spot overgrown with ferns and shrubby evergreens. "The men built bonfires there."

"It's happening again, isn't it. Just like in Kinsarvik."

"Yes." She nodded. "And at the barn at the Voss Folkemuseum. I think some of my ancestors might have come here to dance."

"Do you want to linger, or head back down?"

Much as she did want to linger, Chloe cocked her head toward the trail. "Let's go get some breakfast, then head to the library. I want to identify Amalie's farm!"

Two hours later, Chloe checked her watch for the seventeenth time. "They're late."

"It's three minutes till the hour," Roelke said. "Try to be patient, sweetie."

The Utne Library was a gracious white frame building just down the road from the hotel. Chloe and Roelke waited on the front step. Amalie may have stood right here, Chloe thought. She was getting closer and closer to some real answers.

Finally the door opened and an elderly gentleman who walked with a cane welcomed them inside. "I'm from America, looking for family records," she explained.

He clearly wanted to help, but when his English proved inadequate, he enlisted the aide of another librarian, a pretty young woman with a funky asymmetric hairstyle. She wore a linen suit, impossible heels, and the assured confidence of a recent college graduate.

Chloe showed her Amalie's baptism information. "I'm hoping to find her farm. Is there a *Bygdebok* for the area?"

The librarians led them to a shelf, and the young woman pulled out a book and read the title page: "'Odda, Ullensvang, and Kinsarvik, in old and new times.' There are nine volumes."

"Nine?" Chloe echoed, hoping she'd misunderstood.

"The series covers the whole district," the young woman explained. "They didn't do a book for each little parish. And there's a *lot* of information. Each study began with the earliest available tax records, and then church records were added."

The older gentleman said something and hurried away. "He's getting the index," his colleague said.

While waiting, Chloe pulled a volume from the shelf, flipped through … and was instantly distracted. The book included old black-and-white photographs of families and farms, maps showing individual buildings on a property, pages and pages and *pages* of genealogical records. "Roelke, look," she murmured, pointing to a woman wearing a black dress and the area's distinctive white headscarf who stared stiffly at the photographer. "This wasn't my grandma, but she might have known my grandma." Chloe felt as if she were inching closer to her goal.

The gentleman returned, plucked Volume 5 from the shelf, thumbed through, then planted the open book on the counter. "Here. The family."

Chloe honed in on a single name: *Amalie Sveinsdatter, b. 1905.* "That's her!"

The man looked delighted. "So ... this is the farm name." He moved his finger. "Fjelland."

"Fjelland," she repeated with a renewed sense of wonder. "Can you show us the farm on a map? We need to check this out."

———

"Checking this out" turned out to be a bit more complicated than Roelke had hoped. Reaching Fjelland would require another ferry ride to Kinsarvik, then a drive north. "Twenty minutes?" the librarian guessed. Roelke automatically doubled the estimate.

After more research and a couple of phone calls, the librarians identified the current Fjelland occupant as H. R. Valebrokk. "But no phone," the man said.

"No phone?" Roelke repeated. In this day and age, that seemed unusual.

Chloe spread her hands with a *Watcha gonna do?* look. "We'll go anyway, and take our chances. I don't have time to write a letter and wait for an answer."

"Weren't you expected at the museum today?"

"Not really. Ellinor said I could 'check in with her if I wanted.'" Chloe hooked air quotes with her fingers. "She thought Torstein was going to keep me busy, so I can't blame her."

At this point Roelke didn't know what to make of Ellinor. Truth was, though, he didn't know what to make of most of the people they'd met since arriving in Norway.

When they left the library, Chloe looked ready to do a schottische or whatever, right there in the street. "Soon I'll be walking the ground my ancestors walked!"

"I hope so." Roelke didn't want to kill Chloe's joy. He also didn't want her to be disappointed.

As they neared the hotel they saw a line of vehicles waiting to board the next ferry to Kinsarvik. "I want to change into nicer clothes," Chloe said. "If I'm quick we should have enough time to catch the 9:55 boat."

As they hurried through the hotel lobby, though, a young staffer called after them. "I have a phone message for you. It actually came in last night." She handed over a note: *Please call home.*

Not good, Roelke thought, watching the excitement in Chloe's eyes turn to fear.

"Oh God," she exclaimed. "It's probably about Aunt Hilda. I've got to call my dad."

"It's only..." Roelke checked his watch and did the math. "Four a.m. in Wisconsin. Are you sure you want to—"

"Yes! I need to know."

At the pay phone, Chloe impatiently went through the steps of placing an international call. Finally she slammed the receiver back. "Dad didn't answer," she muttered. "Now I'm *really* worried. I'm going to call Kari."

Chloe's sister answered on the third ring. "It's me," Chloe began. "What?... Yes, I do know what time it is. What's wrong?... I got a message to call home, and Dad didn't answer, and ... what? Oh." She glanced at Roelke with a mystified shrug. "And there hasn't been bad news about Hilda?... Oh. Okay, I'm really sorry I bothered you." She hung up. "Everything's fine at home. My dad's staying with Kari and Trygve for a few days for a change of scenery. I don't understand ..."

Roelke grabbed the note. No name had been written on it, just *Room 15*. His gut clenched. "Maybe it's for me. I'm calling Libby." Except for Chloe, Roelke's cousin Libby and her two children were pretty much all the family he had.

When he made the call, though, all he got was Libby's groggy assurance that all was well. Roelke forced himself to loosen his grip on the receiver. "Sorry I bothered you, Libs. Give the kids a kiss from me."

They took the note back to the desk. "I think there's some mistake," Chloe explained. "We both called home, and nobody on that end made the call."

"I'm so sorry," the staffer said apologetically. "I suspect whoever took the call put the wrong room number down. Since Klara was killed, everybody's been ..." Her voice trailed away. "I'll look into it."

By this point, they'd missed the 9:55 ferry. "We lost a whole hour!" Chloe lamented as Roelke pulled into the parking line at the dock. "I'm glad everything was okay at home, of course. It's just that ... I might be about to discover a whole new family!"

Roelke hazarded a glance at the woman he loved. "You know the farm's probably passed out of the family, right?"

"Of course." Her scoff was so quick, so hearty, that he suspected she hadn't even briefly entertained that possibility. "But Roelke, I'll be *there*. The farm where my mother's people lived. I can't even imagine what that will be like, but . . . I bet it will be powerful."

Powerful in a good way, God willing, Roelke thought. They could only wait and see.

After arriving in Kinsarvik, they followed the librarian's directions. The route passed red barns and mustard-colored or white houses, all framed prettily against the mixed green of deciduous trees and conifers. Stone walls, sometimes bulging with the effort of containing the hills, often lined the roads. The day was overcast but dry, thank God. They didn't need rain to bollix the trip.

Chloe was wired, practically thrumming beside him. "Okay, slow down," she said some time later. "I think we're getting close. Supposedly there's a sign on the left side of the road."

"That seems unlikely." The terrain on that side was a wooded and almost vertical rise.

"Nope, there it is." Chloe pointed to a fading sign at the base of a narrow gravel track: *Fjelland*. "Pull over, okay? There's small print in Norwegian and English beneath the farm name."

He did. She got out, peered at the lettering, checked her watch, and slid back into the car. "Well, it's a little complicated."

Of course it is, Roelke thought.

"The drive to the farm is a single lane. You can drive up during the first half of every hour, and down the second half."

Roelke frowned at the lane disappearing into the trees. "That does not sound—"

"We can't turn back now!" She turned to him, beseeching. "We can start up in ten minutes. Please, Roelke. I'll take the wheel if you want."

He did *not* want. "No. I'll drive."

The lane was barely wide enough for one vehicle. Slowly they snaked their way up the mountain in a white-knuckle series of hairpin switchbacks. There were no handy pull-outs, no guard rails. On the Volvo's uphill side the rock face passed inches from the window. On the other, just beyond the tires, the ground fell away with gut-churning abruptness.

After about fifteen minutes Roelke rounded a turn and confronted a tunnel disappearing into the mountain. "Good God," he muttered.

"Surely we're almost there."

There was nothing to do but keep going. The tunnel was steep and narrow, lit only by widely spaced light bulbs dangling from the low ceiling. No paved or tiled surfaces, just craggy rock left by the dynamite that engineers had used to blast through the mountain. They did pass a few pull-outs in the tunnel, which was reassuring only until Roelke noticed the rubble piled into them. Apparently the pull-outs were intended not for driver comfort, but to provide an easy dumping ground for rockfalls. Great, Roelke thought, gritting his teeth. Just great.

By the time they emerged into daylight a mile or so later, his hands ached from clenching the steering wheel. He braked long enough to flex his fingers.

"Okay, that was a little intense," Chloe admitted in a small voice. "Thank you for driving."

Five minutes later a sign appeared: *Velkommen til Fjelland.* The road appeared to continue but another sign warned of a dead end. Roelke parked in a gravel lot and flexed his fingers again. Holy toboggans. He saw no sign of habitation. "Someone actually lives up here? How is that even possible?"

She didn't respond.

He turned to her. "Hey, are you okay?"

"I don't know. Now that we're here, I'm getting a bad feeling."

That was not what he wanted to hear. "What do you mean?"

"I don't know!" She shrugged helplessly. "What if whoever lives here doesn't want to meet an American relative?"

"We don't even know if the farm is still in the family," he reminded her. "And we've come a long way to find out." He opened his door. "Let's go look around."

They followed a footpath that wound through the trees before abruptly emerging into a clearing. *"O-o-oh,"* Chloe breathed reverently.

Roelke couldn't find words. Down a slope were several log buildings with stone foundations and slate roofs. Beyond the narrow meadow in front of the farmstead, the land disappeared altogether. A deep turquoise fjord was visible far below the cliff. Mountains thrust toward heaven on the distant shore. Roelke counted four ... no, five waterfalls plunging down the rock faces.

Chloe grasped his hand. "I've never seen anything like it ... and yet ..."

"It feels familiar?"

She nodded. "It truly does."

At least she's forgotten her bad feeling, Roelke thought. "Come on. Let's walk around to the front."

The place appeared deserted, but someone was taking good care of it. Pansies and geraniums bloomed in pots. A vegetable garden beside the house showed tidy rows of green sprouts. Several sheep were grazing in a fenced pasture. They lifted their heads, staring with momentary curiosity before returning to the grass.

The house was long and low—not new, but probably built earlier this century. "Look." Chloe pointed at a mark carved in the lowest log near the back corner of the house. Two snail shell swirls created a stylized heart.

"What is that all about?"

"I think it's a property mark." She leaned closer. "*Bumerker*, they're called. I read about them in that book Ellinor loaned me. They originated from the old Viking runic alphabet. People who couldn't read or write adopted a symbol to identify their land or belongings."

Roelke nodded thoughtfully. "Well, hunh."

"This is sweet. I like it." Chloe traced the figure with one finger. "Most of the samples I saw were geometric, not curved like this one. But this one seems familiar."

"Family memory stuff?"

She shook her head. "No. I'm sure I've seen this symbol, or something very similar. Not too long ago, either." She nibbled her lip, then shook her head. "I can't place it."

They continued around the building. Boxes spilling petunias were mounted beneath the front windows. On a small patio, a wrought-iron table and chairs were perfectly positioned. Chloe stopped and pressed one hand over her chest.

Roelke climbed the front steps and knocked on the door. He waited a minute or so, then knocked again. Please be here, he thought. *Please*. But no one came to the door. The yard remained still and silent.

Finally he rejoined Chloe, who'd been taking pictures. "Nobody's home," he said reluctantly. "And I don't think we should wander around without permission. If we leave now, we can drive down at the right time."

"I don't want to leave."

He put an arm around her. "I know. We can come back." If time allowed.

"Let me just write a little note." Chloe dug in her daypack for her notebook and pen. After composing the note she read it aloud:

Hello H.R. Valebrokk,

My name is Chloe Ellefson. I believe my mother Marit was connected to the family that lived here in the early 1900s, specifically Amalie Sveinsdatter. I would be grateful for any information about the family you can provide. I can be reached at the Utne Hotel until next Thursday.

"I'll add our home address too. If nothing else, maybe H. R. Valebrokk will write to me." Chloe left the note by the door, pinned with a small stone.

Then she paused, looking out over the meadow and fjord. She opened her arms as if embracing this place, this farm's story. Finally she sighed, dropped her arms, and turned toward the path.

Roelke fell into place beside her. "I'm sorry no one was here to talk to." He knew it was an enormous disappointment.

"Me too."

Once in the car, Roelke made a three-point-turn and headed back down the mountain. Before entering the tunnel he turned on the high beams and down-shifted the Volvo into second gear to help maintain a safe speed. He didn't want to ride the brakes all the way through the tunnel. The lower gear would, he hoped, help keep the speed down on the descent.

"I'm glad we came," Chloe said.

Already the car was picking up speed. He gently pumped the brakes.

"... really hoping we can squeeze in another trip ..."

He pumped the brakes again ... and there was no response. The pedal thumped to the floor.

Roelke's mouth went dry. Sweet Jesus. Had he lost all the brake fluid?

"What's going on?" Chloe swiveled on the seat. "Roelke?"

"I need you to be quiet." He had to focus. The car was already going too fast to shift into first gear. He reached between the seats and yanked up the parking brake. But after only a tiny hesitation the car continued accelerating.

Think. He had to slow down. The tunnel was straight. He could keep the car under control as they barreled through. But once out in the open, they'd quickly hit one of those monstrous hairpin turns and fly off the mountain.

Okay. Maybe he could slow the Volvo by scraping the car ever so carefully against one wall.

He slid left—his side, of course, not Chloe's. Holding his breath, he eased the Volvo against the wall. The car shuddered. His side view mirror disappeared. Metal screamed against stone in a shower of sparks. Chloe gave a terrified squeak.

Roelke steered the car back to the tunnel's center. His heart pounded in his chest. Sweat rolled down his forehead. Riding along the wall wouldn't work. The rock faces were too uneven to calculate. He didn't want to blow a tire and lose what scrap of control he had left.

Think, dammit! They had to be nearing the tunnel's lower end. They were about to sail off a cliff and Chloe was in the car. Chloe ...

The high beams picked up the edge of a pullout on the left. He had two seconds to consider trajectory. At this speed the car would spin when he jerked the wheel. So—not here. Not with Chloe on the side that would hit the wall.

Hadn't the first pullout they passed on the way up been on the other side? Yes. He strangled the steering wheel, trying to steel himself. No choice, he had no choice—

The right-side pullout flashed into view. *Now*. "Don't brace," he barked. He wrenched the wheel. Tires skidded as the Volvo's nose careened into the pullout. *Don't brace-don't brace-don't brace*. He glimpsed rubble piled in the pullout, heard the screech of skidding tires.

His side of the car slammed into the wall. "Oh, *Chloe*," he said, because he understood the profound wrongness of her dying on the mountain where her ancestors had lived.

TWENTY-FIVE

Solveig—August 1919

Solveig was skimming pans of milk, listening to the soft sounds of her paddle moving cream, when she heard her younger sister shout her name. She hadn't been expecting a midweek visitor. "Amalie!" Solveig called from the doorway. "Is there some trouble at home?"

Amalie shrugged out of the pack basket she'd carried and rolled her shoulders. "I wanted to tell you that Gustav came to talk to Father a few days ago."

"Gustav Nyhus?" Solveig asked slowly. Seven years had passed since she'd had the awkward exchange with the older man, declining his wish to marry her. Aside from murmuring *God dag* if she passed Gustav in the churchyard, she hadn't spoken to him since. A year later he'd married a young Kinsarvik woman. Solveig had said prayers for her happiness, but she'd also been relieved that Gustav was no longer looking for a wife.

Amalie's eyes clouded with concern. "Gustav's second wife died in childbirth last month, did you know?"

"No," Solveig said slowly. "I hadn't heard."

"He and Father had a long talk by the woodpile. Mother and I couldn't hear what they were saying, but…"

"Yes, I see." Solveig rubbed her temples. This wasn't good.

"And I won't be able to help here at the *seter* anymore," Amalie added. "Mama has made arrangements for me to work at the Utne Inn. Hotel, I mean."

Solveig's eyebrows rose in surprise. The old inn was a hotel now, and busier than ever because steamships were bringing more tourists every year. But when Britta had broached the idea of Amalie working there months earlier, Svein had opposed it: "She'd mix with all sorts there. Many wouldn't be God-fearing folk."

Amalie turned, looking wistfully over the landscape. She was fifteen now, an ethereal beauty with fair hair and luminous blue eyes. She was still fanciful, still inclined to daydreaming. "Idle hands do the devil's work!" Svein thundered whenever he caught her.

Now Solveig asked cautiously, "Father approved of this?"

"Not right away." Amalie glanced over her shoulder as if fearing that Svein might be on the path behind her. "But Mother insisted you could manage alone here, and that the money I'll earn will be useful."

They went inside, and Solveig made *rømmegrøt*. The porridge was a summertime treat. While she stirred barley flour into sour cream, Amalie settled at the table with a *Hardangersaum* project. Solveig had no patience for the painstaking work, but Amalie had become well known for her delicate cutwork embroidery.

"How do you feel about working at the hotel?" Solveig asked. "You remember the story about Gjertrud…"

"Of course." Amalie waved her hand. "Don't worry. I don't plan to let any city man have his way with me."

Solveig was ten years older than Amalie, and at moments like this, felt even older. "It isn't always easy to say no."

"I'll be fine," Amalie assured her. "There is nothing to worry about."

Solveig nibbled her lower lip uncertainly. "Just take care of yourself, Amalie. Please." And she had to leave it at that.

An hour later Amalie disappeared back down the trail. Solveig leaned against the doorframe. The goats and cows were grazing nearby. A willow warbler sang its descending whistle. In truth, she thought, I like being alone. Up here, she was free. Solitude gave her the freedom to revisit her little leather book. She'd kept her writing tight and small, but the book was almost full. Here at the *seter* she often flipped through the pages, re-reading tales that linked her to ancestors she'd never met. Sometimes they helped her understand things about herself that defied explanation.

Best of all, at the *seter* she was free to play the fiddle.

The old butter churn had kept it secrets for years now. When Father climbed to the *seter* to mend a sagging fence or to fetch cheese and butter, he never entered the women's workspace. Which was good, Solveig thought now, for Father must never know about the notebook, or the leather pouch holding the coins she'd set aside over the years, or the *hardingfele*.

Once the animals were penned that evening, Solveig tucked the fiddle case under her arm and walked to the waterfall. She settled on a rock ledge close to the pool where the plunging water collected itself before coursing on down the mountain. It was her favorite place to play.

Not that "play" is a fair word, she thought. She'd done what she could for the neglected instrument—polishing the wood with beeswax, filling the cracks with resin, gently removing clots of dried-out hide glue and adding fresh. Replacing the strings had been a taller task. She sliced pieces of a butchered sheep's intestine and experimented with stretching, drying, and twining the threads. It took several more butcherings, several more years of solitary work, to produce workable strings. She'd taught herself to play, after a fashion. Between her ignorance and the fiddle's defects, the results were nothing to be proud of. But she'd never given up.

That evening she played for an hour or more, trying to find a tune reflecting the rhythms of buttermaking that she'd been composing in her head. When darkness finally fell, she returned the fiddle to its case and stepped to the edge of the pool. "Thank you," she murmured, as she always did—just in case a *fossegrim* was hiding beneath the torrent. The water spirit was said to be an exceptional *hardingfele* player, willing to teach his skill in exchange for some smoked mutton or beef tossed into the falling water. If the offering was satisfactory, the *fossegrim* would impart an inhuman talent to the pupil.

Solveig had never tried to summon a *fossegrim*. The very notion evoked her father's thundering voice: *Heresy! Evil!* But someday I might, she thought defiantly. As she walked back to the cabin the sound of rushing water faded behind her.

She was almost to the door when she heard a *hardingfele*.

The back of her neck prickled. She froze, holding her breath, straining to hear. She didn't recognize the melody. The rippling tune displayed a skill far beyond hers. Far beyond any music she'd ever heard.

Solveig slowly turned. Was the fiddler hidden among the shadows on the rocky slope above the *seter*? In the woods? Or … did the music emanate from the waterfall? Part of her wanted to run to the cabin and bolt the door. But the greater part couldn't bear to leave the music behind.

Finally the tune ended, leaving only the breeze sighing through the trees. Perhaps it's *natt frieri*, she thought. Night courting. But … night courting usually took place in late fall or winter, when farmworkers had more time. And she didn't know anyone who might be inclined to climb up here at this hour.

"Hello?" Her voice sounded harsh in the sudden stillness. No one answered.

I'm not ready to leave the *seter*, Solveig thought three weeks later, even though summer was coming to an end at the high farm. Moss flowing over rocky ledges was already mottled red and orange. Chanterelles clustered yellow beneath the conifers, and she'd spotted patches of gold emerging among the birch groves at lower elevations.

She'd wandered into the woods that morning, looking for leaves and slender twigs and nuts to save for winter fodder. But clouds hid the mountain peaks this drizzly morning, and a damp chill was creeping through her wool cloak. If she didn't head back to the cabin, she'd soon be wet through.

After checking the animals she paused, head cocked, but heard nothing. Perhaps tonight, she thought hopefully. She'd stopped feeling spooked about the intermittent and mysterious evening serenades. Whoever was playing the *hardingfele* was so skilled that—

"Solveig!"

Whirling, she saw her father, Svein, marching toward the cabin from the lower trail. Even worse, Gustav was with him.

She struggled to compose herself as the men approached. "I didn't expect visitors today," she said.

"I'm ready to rig up the hay wire." Svein's eyes were narrow, inscrutable. "Gustav offered to help."

Solveig suspected that something other than kindness had motivated this trip. "You've both had a climb. I'll get you something to eat." She laid out flatbread and butter, cheese and sour milk, and oatmeal mush served with lingonberry jam.

Svein peppered Solveig with questions over the meal: Are the animals fit? Is milk production starting to slack? How many tubs of butter are set aside? Is the coffee gone? Solveig answered calmly, but couldn't stop thinking about the old churn in the corner. What would Father do if he knew she'd taught herself to play the devil's instrument? She kept her left hand curled in her lap, afraid he'd notice the tiny calluses marking each fingertip.

Gustav didn't speak until she started clearing the table. "That was good." He looked as if he wanted to say more, but he did not. His face seemed thinner than she remembered, his eyes more hooded.

He's lonely, Solveig realized—reluctantly, because she didn't want to understand that about him. Perhaps he'd truly cared for his young wife, and deeply grieved her death. Perhaps he was eager to marry again because he couldn't face the coming winter alone. She felt sorry for him.

Still, that didn't mean she wanted to marry him. "I'll send some jam with you," she promised. A bachelor fisherman was unlikely to have much fruit put by.

Solveig scoured and scalded her wooden buckets in the cleansing sunshine while her father and Gustav worked on the hay wire. Svein had been working for years on his rig, hauling heavy coils of wire to precarious ledges, building the wooden framework. The stout cable ran from their main farm up to the *seter*. Instead of sledding hay down in the winter, he'd now attach bundles of hay to the wire with long, supple osier branches. Once released, the bundle would whip down the mountain with terrifying speed—allowing Svein to fill the barn before snow fell.

By mid-afternoon, Father announced the task complete. "We'll try it out another day," he said. Then he looked at Gustav. "I'll wait at woods' edge." Father slung the sack of foraged fodder over one shoulder, nodded at his daughter, and walked away.

This was the moment Solveig had been dreading.

In the awkward silence Gustav shifted his weight from foot to foot. "My wife died in childbirth last month."

"I was very sorry to hear that."

"A man needs a wife," he said simply. "You have not yet married, even after all these years. And your father wants to see you wed."

She didn't need the reminder. If she told Gustav she didn't want to marry him, would Father beat her again? I won't be caught by surprise this time, she vowed silently, clenching her fists in her apron. I will *not* . . .

Gustav turned and walked away.

Solveig watched uneasily as he joined her father. Even across the meadow Father's gaze sent a chip of ice down her backbone. Then he turned and the two men disappeared down the trail.

Her shoulders sagged. She'd been unable to make her feelings clear to Gustav. How had he interpreted her silence? With a heavy sigh, she went back inside.

That evening Solveig paced the room, arms crossed. Finally she brought out her leather pouch and counted the *kroner*. She loved the *seter*, and she'd been reluctant to leave her mother and Amalie, but perhaps it was time to leave Høiegård altogether. She had enough money to travel to Bergen. Finding work as a maid or cook's helper wasn't appealing, but being on her own was. And in the city she could attend dances and concerts.

Once darkness fell over the mountain, she walked to the waterfall with a lantern and wooden club. The fine rain had ceased. She listened hopefully, but heard only the sound of falling water and a distant owl's call.

Since springtime, when snowmelt roared over the rocks, the river's flow had gradually slackened. Earlier that week she'd repaired the small dam built from stones below the fall every autumn. Now she put the lantern on a rock at the pool's edge, hoping the light would lure a trout or perch to the shallows. Kneeling, she picked up her club. She'd never perfected the skill of snatching fish with her bare hands.

Against the steady rush of water the plaintive chords of a *hardingfele* slipped through the night. Solveig forgot about fish. The fiddler must be *quite* close.

She put the club down as the melody strings and drones became more clear. Tonight's tune felt sad. Was the fiddler lamenting summer's end as she was? She got to her feet slowly. Turning, she stared into the darkness. Her heart beat too quickly.

The fiddler stepped from the trees, stopping just short of the lantern. Solveig held her breath. After the last quivering chord died away, he lowered the bow. In the dim light the stranger appeared to have dark hair, a narrow build. He was about her age, or perhaps a few years older. Finally she licked her lips and said, "Who *are* you?"

TWENTY-SIX

THE SILENCE IN THE tunnel was overwhelming. Finally, as if from a great distance, Roelke became aware of a metallic ticking as the engine cooled. He still gripped the Volvo's steering wheel. Blinking, he tried to make sense of the insensible. Quite unexpectedly, he was alive. He summoned every ounce of courage before slowly turning to his fiancée. "Chloe?"

"I . . . yeah." She stared forward. Her chest was heaving as if she'd just run up the mountain.

"Are you okay?"

"I think so." Her voice was shuddery. "Banged up, but—yeah."

Thank you, God, Roelke thought.

"But—you're bleeding." She touched her temple to indicate the spot.

He brushed his forehead. Sticky. "I don't think it's serious. Head wounds bleed a lot." He closed his eyes.

"What do we do now?"

Roelke opened his eyes again. Stay in control, he ordered himself. Do not give in to shock. He started with a preliminary assessment of the car. The left door was crumpled. The window had shattered. His lap was full of shards of glass. The Volvo's headlights, still on high, glared against the rock wall. He managed to loosen one hand and turn them down. It seemed important.

He looked at Chloe. "You're sure you're okay?" She nodded. "Then I need you to get out of the car."

Her eyes seemed enormous in the dim light. "What about you?"

"You first. I'm guessing the workers who built this tunnel had an emergency telephone installed in at least one of the pullouts. See if you can spot one." There was more to think about—emergency flashers, the first-aid kit in the trunk. But calling for help—the cops, an ambulance—came first.

It seemed to take a long time, but Chloe managed to unlock her seat belt and climb from the car. "Be right back."

Chloe's okay, he told himself over and over. Chloe, is, *okay.* Nothing else mattered.

After a few minutes he heard her voice. He couldn't make out the words, and decided she wasn't talking to him. Hopeful sign.

She'd left the passenger door open. When she got back the first-aid kit was in her hands. She knelt on the seat to face him. "I found a phone," she reported. "Help is on the way."

Hours later, after full examinations and multiple X-rays at a hospital in Odda, doctors agreed that Roelke and Chloe could leave. That was good, because he was in no mood to linger. Blossoming bruises gave evidence of the battering Chloe had taken. He'd needed three stitches on his left temple, and he had a mild concussion. But a scan didn't show any signs of serious swelling, and he knew things could have been much, much worse.

When they finally got back to the Utne Hotel that night, they dragged themselves up two flights of stairs. "I think we're eating bread and water for the rest of the trip," Roelke said. The fare for the cab ride from the hospital in Odda had almost sent him back into a medical state of shock.

"My dad will wire us money if we need it." Chloe was looking around the room as if she'd never been there before.

"Let's just go to bed," Roelke said. "Things will look better in the morning." He didn't really think so, but it seemed like a reasonable thing to say.

Once in bed, Chloe rolled close. He gingerly pulled her into his arms. "All that matters to me is that you're safe," he murmured into her hair.

"And you." She shivered. "I was so scared."

"You did good, though. It all happened so fast … I couldn't talk and think at the same time."

"Once I figured that out, I just wanted to be helpful. All I came up with was sliding my water bottle behind my back so it wouldn't fly around when we crashed."

I will never think of this woman as impractical again, Roelke vowed.

"Why did you tell me not to brace myself?"

"It goes against instinct, but bracing makes it more likely that bones will break in a crash."

She nuzzled closer, settling her face against his shoulder. "Roelke, what *happened*?"

There was nothing to be gained by evasion. "One of the cops told me they found hydraulic fluid in the tunnel, above the point where we crashed. I'm hoping that some mechanical issue caused that problem, but … it's also possible that someone tampered with the brakes."

She went very still.

"The car is totaled," he added, just in case she hadn't figured that out. "We'll have to deal with the rental agency in the morning."

Chloe was quiet for so long that he thought she'd fallen asleep. Finally she said, "I give up."

"What?"

She pulled away and sat up. Her long blond hair was loose and she looked extraordinarily beautiful in the moonlight. "I said, I give *up*. I don't know what's going on, but I've had it."

Roelke sat up too. In the ambulance, through all the waiting and exams and scans and more waiting at the hospital, he'd had plenty of time to think. If the brake line had been deliberately compromised, it seemed likely that the sabotage and the theft of Chloe's heirlooms were related.

"Someone stole my precious family textiles. Now someone might have tried to kill us." Chloe rubbed her palms over her face. "I can't imagine who, or why. But at this point, I don't even want to find out who my mom's people were anymore. It's led to nothing but trouble. I've never been so terrified as I was in that tunnel."

Roelke had no idea what to say.

"You were amazing. If I'd been at the wheel, I'm sure we'd both be dead." Her voice trembled. "It's not worth it, Roelke. Whatever is going on, it's not worth it. I quit. I want to go home."

Hearing Chloe say "I quit" was a shock. He opened his mouth, then closed it again. Trying to talk her out of her feelings never worked. Besides, he understood her feelings. In the end he just hugged her again.

After they settled back down, Chloe's breathing eased into sleep's quiet rhythm. Roelke lay staring at the ceiling, reliving what had happened in the tunnel, trying to figure out what the hell was going on. Someone had tried to grab Chloe's daypack in the Bergen Airport the day they arrived. Someone had managed to break into the hotel safe and steal Chloe's textiles. If the trouble had started because someone was after those embroidery pieces, it should have ended with the theft. Instead, someone had tried, he believed, to cause a car wreck in a manner that *should* have been fatal. Did that mean that some SOB wanted to harm Chloe? Or were there two people trying to get their hands on the textiles, and SOB #2 didn't realize that SOB #1 had already snatched them?

Either way, the fact that Chloe had survived the crash meant that the person responsible was probably getting desperate. Desperation might make that person careless, easier to catch. But desperation might also make that person even more dangerous. If Chloe wants to go back to Wisconsin, Roelke thought, that's probably for the best.

As for him, well … he did not want to leave Norway. Maybe he could put Chloe on a plane, but stay behind. He was *way* too angry to fly back home.

The next morning, Chloe woke with a groan. Everything hurt. Worst was her right forearm, which was green and purple from wrist to elbow. Right before impact she'd cradled her head in her arms. After the car hit the stone wall she'd slammed back against the side window. It could have been worse, she reminded herself as she staggered to her feet. It was nothing short of a miracle that Roelke had managed to stop the car.

Someone must have been looking out for us, she thought. Had it been Mom? Chloe had no idea what happened to souls once the body had died, no idea what heaven actually looked like. But an image formed now in her mind: Mom, standing at the end of a row of women, all watching out for those they'd left behind. It was comforting.

Roelke stepped from the bathroom with toothbrush in hand. "How are you doing?"

"Yesterday I thought I'd gotten off easy." She attempted a smile. "Today I feel like I got hit with a battering ram."

Once they'd made themselves as presentable as possible, they plodded down the stairs for breakfast. Ulrikke hurried over to their table, fussing over their visible bruises and Roelke's stitches. He took the proprietress's solicitous concern for about two minutes before politely excusing himself to make a phone call.

The two women watched him go. "You are having a terrible time," Ulrikke fretted. "Please let me know if there's anything we can do to make you more comfortable."

Chloe was touched. "You're very kind. I can't imagine a better place to be."

She'd made her way through the buffet line and was watching brown sugar dissolve on her steaming bowl of oatmeal by the time Roelke returned. With one glance she knew the call had not gone well. "What's up?"

He slid into his chair. "I was able to speak with one of the cops who responded to our crash yesterday." He nodded at the waitress who appeared with coffeepot in hand, and took a bracing sip before continuing. "They've already gone over the Volvo. Apparently, while we were looking around the farm, someone slid under the car and cut partway through a section of the rubber brake line. Every time I pumped the brakes near the top of the tunnel I lost more hydraulic fluid."

Chloe's gut twisted. Someone really *had* tampered with the brakes.

Overwhelmed, she focused on a detail. "Why cut just partway? Do you think someone was trying to scare us?"

Roelke shook his head. "No. If the line had been cut all the way through, the fluid would have leaked out in the parking area. We probably would have seen it. Even if we hadn't, I would have figured out that we had no brakes *before* we headed down. This bastard knew exactly what he was doing. The brakes didn't fail until we were in the most dangerous place."

Chloe put her spoon down. It would take a whole lot more than melting brown sugar to restore her appetite. "Why would someone do such a thing?"

"As you said, it's got to have something to do with your family research," Roelke muttered. "First someone tried to grab your day-pack at the airport. Then someone managed to get into the safe and steal your heirlooms. Then, right after we've identified a farm that appears to have been owned by your ancestors, our car is deliberately damaged in a way that should have killed us."

"All I'm trying to do is find my mother's roots." Chloe leaned back in her chair. "I wish I knew why Ellinor wrote Amalie's name in her notes. Although I have to say, I can't picture Ellinor scrambling underneath our car with bolt cutters or something." Or Sonja, in her expensive clothes. Or Torstein, who was grieving his fiancée and cared so passionately about folk dance and music. Or Reverend Brandvold, or Ulrikke, or Barbara-Eden, or anyone else they'd met.

Another thought struck. "Besides, how was the sabotage even possible? There was no one else up the mountain while we were there!"

"It's possible that someone was in the house and just didn't answer my knock. I suppose someone could have slipped up to the lot without us noticing while we were out front." Roelke's knee was bouncing so hard the table was vibrating. "It's also possible that someone parked a vehicle up that dead end that branched off from the parking area, where we couldn't see the car."

"But no one knew we were visiting the farm yesterday," Chloe protested.

"Not true. The librarians knew."

Chloe pictured the elderly man who'd limped through the library with a cane. It was impossible to imagine him shimmying under the Volvo. Then she pictured the young woman's high heels, the linen suit. Equally impossible.

"And don't forget that telephone message we received. By the time we'd both called home, we'd missed the ferry. That could have given somebody time to get up to Fjelland before we did." Roelke's eyes were hard as granite. "And there's something else to consider. Your family textiles were stolen *before* we had the car crash. Either somebody has it in for *you*, or two different people are after your heirlooms. It's possible that someone doesn't know you're not carrying them around anymore."

Chloe folded her arms, trying to think everything through. "Do you think this is connected to Klara Evenstad's death?"

"If so, I don't see how," Roelke admitted. "At least not yet."

Chloe didn't see how either.

"I'm going to get some breakfast." He headed for the buffet and returned with a laden plate. He used a fork to slide half of a mound of scrambled eggs into a small dish and pushed it in her direction. "Eat."

They finished the meal in silence. Chloe tried to imagine someone damaging the brake line, presumably hoping it would send her and Roelke either headlong into the tunnel wall or sailing over some cliff to their deaths. The image was horrific. But it also triggered something hot and sharp and welcome. I, Chloe thought, am royally pissed off.

Roelke forked up his last bite of smoked salmon. "Whenever you're ready we should go call the rental car place. If we can figure out how to get back to Bergen, we can look into changing your flight—"

"No."

He blinked. "No?"

"I do remember what I said last night. But I am not going to let somebody keep me from looking for Mom's people."

He hesitated, his fingers making a whispery noise as he rubbed the light stubble on his chin. "I really think that the best plan is for me to stay, and for you to—"

"No."

He eyed her for a long time. Chloe met his gaze. Finally he sighed, nodded. "Okay, on one condition. If I feel it's necessary, I get to pull the plug."

Once, Chloe might have reminded him that she had a brain and free will, thanks all the same, and needed no one to set conditions. But she understood that he did know that. He was just trying to keep her safe.

Roelke called the car rental company, and Chloe listened as he explained what had happened. The decibel level didn't rise when the agent learned that the caller had totaled one of their cars, which was encouraging. "That seemed to go okay," she hazarded when Roelke hung up. "Are we screwed?" She couldn't remember the terms of their insurance.

"We'll pay a deductable, but it could have been a lot worse." He exhaled a long, slow breath. "Good thing we got the top coverage possible."

"And that we didn't rent that little Volkswagen," Chloe added humbly. "Your 'be prepared' proclivities, at home and abroad, have been completely vindicated. Feel free to remind me I said so."

That made him smile. "The agent is looking into what other vehicles might be available, preferably somewhere closer than Bergen. Once we know our options, we can decide if we want to rent again or if we can rely on public transportation."

They stopped at the desk, and a staffer handed over messages from Torstein and Reverend Brandvold. "Maybe Reverend Brandvold found something else about Amalie," Chloe said hopefully. "I'm calling him first."

After connecting, though, the conversation went in an unexpected direction. Reverend Brandvold had already heard about their accident, and expressed concern for their well-being. "We're all right," Chloe assured him. "And immensely grateful that it wasn't much worse."

"I thank God for that," he boomed over the line. "Do you need a car? Mine's available."

Chloe blinked. "Reverend, that's incredibly kind of you, but … don't you need it?"

"I rarely drive anywhere. I'd be pleased if you borrow it."

"Thank you. I'll let you know." She replaced the receiver to its cradle and shared the offer with Roelke.

"That's generous, and it could come in handy," Roelke said. "Although at this point I'd want to take an extremely hard look-see at any car before getting in and driving away."

"*Surely* Reverend Brandvold isn't involved in …" Her words died when she glanced at Roelke's implacable expression. Clearly the retired pastor was on Roelke's suspect list just like everyone else.

Moving on, she scrabbled in her pocket for more coins. "Torstein is no doubt calling about the dance."

"The … *oh*. Right." Roelke leaned against the wall and folded his arms. "You don't still want to go, do you?"

"I do. It's an amazing opportunity."

He frowned. "But … surely you don't feel ready to dance the night away. I certainly don't."

She frowned back. "Since you'd rather play jacks in traffic than step onto a dance floor, that doesn't seem entirely relevant."

"It's not a good idea."

Chloe was too stiff and achy for strenuous activity, and she didn't want to bicker with Roelke. But dancing had always lifted her from worries, transported her to a place where nothing existed but the music and the steps. And for reasons she couldn't entirely articulate, attending this particular dance felt especially important.

"Roelke, I need to go. For my own sake, not just to learn. Even if all I do is listen and watch. Besides, I was the one who got the invitation. It would be awkward for Torstein and Ellinor to go if we don't."

"Maybe Torstein has decided he's not up to it," Roelke said hopefully.

"He'll want to go."

"Then I vote for borrowing Reverend Brandvold's car and driving separately. That way we can leave if you get overtired, without worrying about whether Torstein and Ellinor are ready to go."

"Good thinking." Chloe made the calls, concluded the arrangements, and reported back. "We can pick up the car anytime after lunch, and we'll meet Torstein and Ellinor at the dance at three."

With that decided, she and Roelke considered the intervening hours. "With the offer of Reverend Brandvold's car," Chloe said slowly, "I suppose we could try going back to ..." Her voice trailed away.

"Are you seriously considering going back up that mountain to Fjelland?" Roelke sounded incredulous.

Chloe rubbed at a loose thread on her jeans. Part of her was desperate to try again. Maybe today someone would be home! Honestly, though, when she thought about driving into that tunnel again ... no, not yet. "I *want* to, but after what happened yesterday, I don't think I can go back again. Not right away."

"We've still got a few days. Maybe we'll have another chance."

"Maybe." She tried to swallow a sudden lump in her throat. "Anyway, today I think I'd like to go back to the museum. Do you remember that symbol we saw at Fjelland, carved into one of the logs? It's been nagging at me. I could swear I've seen it before. It's the kind of design that might decorate a Hardanger fiddle, so I'd like to check the instruments on display."

Roelke shrugged. "Okay."

"Also, so much has happened that I haven't had a chance to try and figure out why I had that strong reaction to Høiegård on Tuesday. I'm sure lots of information about the building was collected when the museum acquired it. I'd like to see the file."

They set out into a misty morning. Clouds drifted below the mountain peaks and the fjord was a dull gunmetal gray. First stop, the library.

The elderly librarian was not working that day, but they found the young woman who'd helped them yesterday alone at the reference desk. She wore a bright blue pantsuit today, and had combed and sprayed her hair into little spikes.

"Pardon me," Roelke said. "We were wondering if, by chance, you happened to mention our trip yesterday to anyone else."

The young woman reached for a file folder. "Why would I do that? We respect patrons' privacy."

"So you did *not* mention our visit to anyone."

Look out, Chloe thought. She recognized the signs of his suppressed anger: slightly narrowed eyes, tensed jaw muscles, the uncharacteristically friendly tone.

"Of course not." The librarian rubbed the sides of her mouth with thumb and forefinger. "Is there anything else I can help you with? It's a busy morning."

Roelke waited until they were back on the street before speaking. "She was lying."

That seemed a bit declarative. "How do you know?"

"She had trouble making eye contact. She felt a need to busy her hands. And she literally covered her mouth when she denied telling anyone about our trip. I can always tell when someone's lying."

Chloe tried to remember the last time she'd lied to Roelke. Note to self, she thought. Don't.

At the museum, they found two tour buses parked in the small lot and the reception area jammed with visitors browsing for gifts and mementos. Chloe waved at the young woman behind the front desk before leading Roelke upstairs. His eyebrows raised when he saw the Hardanger fiddle display. "Holy toboggans."

"They're awesome, aren't they?" Chloe walked slowly along the case, squinting at the mother-of-pearl and inked designs on each. At the end, she twisted her mouth in frustration. "Nothing here looks just like the symbol we saw at Fjelland. I must have been mistaken." She crossed her arms, trying to remember where she might have seen the motif. "I don't think it resembled any of the symbols on my *handaplagg*, but since it got stolen, I can't check."

"I'm truly sorry, sweetie." Roelke touched her cheek. "I'm still hoping the police recover it."

Chloe wanted to believe that too, but she didn't feel optimistic. "Let's look at the hand cloths on exhibit in the textile room. Maybe I saw it there."

Several stunning hand cloths featuring black embroidery were on display. None of the motifs duplicated the design Chloe remembered from the high mountain farm, but they reminded her of something she'd almost forgotten. "Do you remember what Sonja said about my hand cloth when we met her at the airport?" She closed her eyes, wanting to get it right. "Sonja said, 'The woman who created this *handaplagg* was expressing herself, yes? The ideas were more important than achieving perfection in the stitches.' The design motifs embroidered on the old cloth had some symbolic meaning."

"Let's see if she's here today," Roelke suggested.

When they asked after the curator, however, the receptionist shook her head. "Sonja isn't working this morning. She will be here later, though."

Later, when we're at the dance, Chloe thought. "How about Ellinor?"

"Ellinor's with one of the tour groups. She's leaving right after finishing up with them."

"I wanted to take a look at whatever research file exists about the oldest building in the open-air division. Høiegård." Chloe hoped the receptionist wouldn't ask what Høiegård had to do with her study of folk music and dance. "Do you have a staff library?"

"Ellinor keeps master files for the restored buildings in her office. I'm sure she wouldn't mind if you took a look."

Back in the staff area, Ellinor's office door was open. Chloe stepped inside and flicked on the light. "Maybe I can get another look at that *Jørgen Riis* file," she whispered hopefully. If she could photocopy the page that included the reference to Amalie, she might learn something important.

But the bulging folder was gone from Ellinor's desk. "Dagnabbit," Chloe muttered.

Roelke considered four file cabinets standing against the wall behind the desk. "Maybe she filed it. I'll start on the right." He slid open the top drawer and began rifling through the folders.

Chloe did the same on the left, fighting a growing sense of anxiety. The files were clustered and neatly labeled: *Budget, Summer Staff 1984, Maintenance, Special Events, Temporary Exhibits*. "Everything in this first cabinet relates to operations," she reported, and moved on. The second cabinet contained the research files, and she found reports about the museum's restored buildings in the second drawer.

"I found the Høiegård info," she reported, extricating a thick file—commendable, but it would take a while to wade through everything.

"I have not found Jørgen Riis." Roelke crouched in front of a lower drawer. "You?"

Chloe sighed. "Not a trace."

TWENTY-SEVEN

SOLVEIG—AUGUST 1919

WHEN THE FIDDLE PLAYER who'd presented himself didn't speak, Solveig repeated her question. "I said, who are you?"

"My name is Jørgen Riis."

Solveig had never heard of Jørgen Riis. "I thought you might be a *fossegrim*."

Riis seemed pleased. "I'm no *fossegrim*, but I'll accept your words as a compliment. The old people say that particular water spirit can play with unheard of skill and grace. They say a *fossegrim* captures the sounds of the forest and the sea and the wind, and that when he plays his enchanted fiddle, the trees themselves start to dance."

"They also say that the *fossegrim* only shares his talent with a human if he makes an acceptable offering," Solveig countered. "Have you made such a deal?"

"I have not." Riis stepped closer. "My music is my own."

In the lamplight his hair looked black, with an untidy shock hanging over his forehead. The intensity of his gaze made Solveig grateful for the shadows.

"Is your music your own?" he asked. "I've heard you playing tunes that are unfamiliar to me."

Blood warmed her face. "I can hardly claim to make music. Not compared to …" She waved a hand at the instrument and bow dangling from his left hand.

"I believe more fault lies with the fiddle than the fiddler."

Solveig shook her head. "I'm no fiddler."

"I could teach you."

She caught her lower lip between her teeth.

He took another step. "Would you like that?" His smile was beguiling.

Solveig felt herself slipping—perhaps into his eyes, perhaps into the promise of his music. She didn't know. She didn't care.

"Think about it," Riis said. "You can give me your answer tomorrow." With that he turned and disappeared back into the trees.

The next day, after finishing her late-day chores, Solveig sat on a bench in front of the cabin. She felt secure here, leaning against the old log building as it leaned against the mountain. It was too late in the day to worry about any family visitors.

Maybe, she thought, Jørgen Riis won't want to come across the meadow and show himself at the cabin. But before long she heard his *hardingfele* singing hello from the trees beyond the clearing. Riis appeared with his fiddle beneath his chin, playing a lively tune.

With perfect timing, he stopped in front of her just as he bowed the final note.

Solveig pressed a hand over her chest, the music still quivering in her bone marrow. "I wasn't sure you'd come."

He grinned and made a courtly bow. "I said I would, Solveig."

"You know my name?"

"I heard one of the men who came here yesterday call you that."

So Riis had been watching even then? He'd seen Father and Gustav visit, but hadn't shown himself? Daylight provided her first good look at the fiddler, and she tried to gauge his secrets. His clothes were plain—heavy shoes, wool trousers, white shirt, a knit sweater inexpertly darned. But his eyes … his eyes were the color of the fjord on a sunny day. She had to look away.

"May I sit?" He gestured to the bench.

She nodded. He settled beside her, and seemed comfortable with the silence between them. Finally she asked, "Where do you come from?"

"Higher up the mountain."

"Higher?" She frowned, perplexed. "At a *seter*?"

He smiled, leaning on his forearms. "No. Just a little stone cottage up among the cliffs."

Every tale Solveig had ever heard of men who escaped personal or legal trouble by hiding themselves high in the mountains flashed through her memory. "Why are you living up the mountain?"

"I don't always live there. I'm a wanderer."

Like Uncle Erik, Solveig thought. Like I might have been, had I been born a man. "You're not from around here."

"No. But I always come back to Hardanger." He shrugged. "This area is the richest source of fiddle tunes. My grandfather built the cottage years ago, and my father first took me there when I was a boy. I loved the wildness, the solitude. This summer I decided to stay there."

"Why?" She watched a brown hare hop into the meadow, freeze, hop on.

"To listen. And to play music." Riis patted his *hardingfele*.

"But … someone of your skill should surely be spending the summer playing for audiences, not hiding away."

"I play in the winter, enough to earn my keep. I need the summer for myself." He shrugged without apology. "People can be exhausting, don't you think?"

She did, although she wasn't sure if she should admit it.

"The last time I played, at a big dance near Odda, several men broke up the party." His tone remained light, but his narrow face took on hard lines. "It wasn't the first time someone tried to tell me that my fiddling is the devil's mischief."

Solveig thought of all the times she'd heard her father rail against dance and music and hard drink. She thought of her mother turning away, disagreeing but never arguing.

"It isn't," Riis added fiercely. "The music comes from in here." He tapped his chest. "And it comes from out there." He swept one arm open wide to embrace the mountains' grandeur. "I think you understand that." He leaned back against the wall. "Although I'd like to hurl your wretched fiddle off the closest cliff."

"I'm lucky to have it," Solveig retorted. "It belonged to my uncle, and to his grandfather before that. But it's been hidden up here for years. Nobody knows I have it."

"Your secret is safe. But if you want to play well, you need a new fiddle."

Solveig thought of the coins she'd saved, hidden away in hopes of one day escaping the farm. Did she have enough to purchase a fiddle? She eyed Riis's instrument. Not one like his, which had obviously been made by a master. Perhaps a simpler instrument—

Abruptly, she came to her senses. "I can't really play, ever. Women don't. And my father—"

"None of that matters." He impatiently waved her words away. "Here." He offered his fiddle.

She was afraid to take it... but she couldn't resist. The wood felt warm in her hands.

"Take the bow."

She accepted his bow in her right hand, and raised the fiddle.

"Not against your arm. Try it on your shoulder, under your chin... yes. Just so. Now, play. Play anything. Get to know the instrument."

It occurred to Solveig belatedly that she had not, in fact, given Jørgen Riis permission to teach her. Her father's harsh voice echoed somewhere in the back of her mind. She almost balked.

But somehow the bow slid across the melody strings. The tone was haunting and rich. She glanced at Jørgen, saw only encouragement in his blue eyes... and she knew she was done for.

"You are a quick learner." Jørgen smiled, and tiny lines fanned from the corner of his eyes.

They were sitting in front of the *seter* cabin as the sky faded toward night. Solveig lowered his fiddle, more pleased than she could remember. He'd been visiting every evening for a week now. Already she felt more confident. "It is a joy to play such a fine instrument. Where did you get it?"

"I made it."

"You did?" It hadn't occurred to her that such a skilled musician might also be a superb craftsman.

"My father taught me when I was a boy." He shrugged. "I don't make fiddles as some do, dozens and dozens a year just to sell. I won't make a fiddle for someone without a musician's heart."

"Did your father teach you to play as well?"

"He did."

Solveig wanted to ask more questions, for there was still much that she didn't know about Jørgen Riis. What she *did* know was that winter was creeping closer day by day, and that would bring an end to her fiddle lessons. She would soon have to leave the *seter*, and surely he wouldn't spend the dark months of blizzards alone on the mountain. She tried to smile, and handed back his fiddle. "Thank you for the lesson."

Jørgen stretched out his legs, crossed his ankles, and shoved hair away from his forehead. The gesture was already familiar. Astonishingly, many things about Jørgen already seemed familiar: the long nimble fingers, the sparkle in his eyes when she did well, the way he tipped his head when hearing night sounds, the faraway look on his face when he played, the smoky-sweet scent of him …

He reached out and gently tucked a stray strand of hair behind her ear.

"I'm so grateful to you." The words burst from her. "For teaching me. I've longed to play the fiddle since I was a girl, but I never dreamed I'd have the chance."

"It's so silly. The idea that women shouldn't play the *hardingfele*, I mean."

"It's not just that." Solveig cupped her elbows, watching the cows graze. Jørgen had done nothing to encourage secrets, but she felt a need to explain. "My father is one of those who believes the fiddle is the devil's instrument. If he knew that I … well. He must never know. So you see, it will all come to an end when I go back down the mountain."

Wind sighed down the slope, rustling the meadow grasses. Jørgen said simply, "I'm sorry."

"I am too." Her voice caught in her throat. She wouldn't have missed these visits from Jørgen for anything in the world. But now that she knew how it felt to play such a fine *hardingfele*, and to listen as he played just for her and the cows and the night birds … how could she return to her father's house?

"What do you yearn for?" Jørgen asked.

The question surprised her, and her eyebrows arched as she considered. "To play well." She wanted to lose herself in the music, forgetting all sorrows. She wanted listeners to do the same.

And she wanted to spend more time with Jørgen. "What do you yearn for?"

"I want to learn from fiddlers who come from different places. Different traditions." He rubbed his chin pensively. "I've been thinking of going to America."

The mention of America made Solveig's heart skitter like a tumbling leaf. "I've thought of emigrating too. I've been saving money, but I don't have nearly enough." She gave a little shrug, trying to suggest that it didn't really matter.

Jørgen studied her. Then he touched her face again, tracing the curve of her cheekbone. Solveig raised her palm and trapped his hand against her face. She felt the heat of him. Her skin tingled.

"You know," he said, "there are many ways to make music."

She felt a teetering sensation, as if she stood dizzy on the edge of a mountain cliff. She was twenty-four years old and had decided long ago that no man was meant for her. But Jørgen's astonishing appearance in her life made her reconsider.

"Solveig," he said hoarsely, "let's go inside."

When Solveig woke the next morning, Jørgen was gone.

A flash of disappointment was almost immediately replaced with an intangible joy. Life suddenly felt luscious, ripe with promise. She had met the man she wanted to marry.

Then her contentment seeped away. Jørgen had said nothing about marriage. He was a wanderer, letting music shape his days. She had no reason to believe he had room for her in his life. Had she been a fool?

Worse than that! her father thundered.

She curled into a ball, considering. She didn't know how much time she'd have with Jørgen . . . but he'd already given her more happiness than she'd ever imagined. However things ended, she could not regret a moment spent with him.

With that resolve she stretched and threw off the blankets, shivering as her bare feet hit the floor. The cows and goats were waiting. After dressing quickly, she stamped into shoes and headed for the door.

Humming, her mind on other things, she almost stepped on the gift left on the front step. "Oh!" She blinked at the wooden mangle, embellished with detailed fish and flowing vines. Her initials were carved at one end. Such mangles, once used to iron linens, were old-fashioned betrothal gifts.

For an instant she thought Jørgen had left it for her. She was reaching for the board when she saw the small initials carved by the handle: GN.

GN. Fish. Of course. Gustav Nyhus, fisherman.

She snatched her hand away and studied the meadow. When a man left a mangle for a woman he usually waited, crouched behind a woodpile or thicket, to see if she accepted his proposal by taking it inside. She saw no sign of anyone.

When had Gustav left the offering? The mangle had definitely not been on the front step when she and Jørgen had gone inside the night before. Had Gustav started his hike before dawn that morning, wanting to come and go and still salvage some time with his nets on the fjord?

And … when had Jørgen left? Dear God, what if Gustav had seen Jørgen leave her cabin with fiddle case in hand? What if Gustav was even now hurrying down to tell her father? Solveig's mouth went dry. She pressed one hand against her chest, trying to calm her racing heart. Trying not to panic.

Then she tamped it down. Gustav wouldn't have left the mangle if he knew that she'd not spent the night alone. She remembered the loneliness in Gustav's eyes, imagined him creeping to the cabin, still hopeful. She was sorry to disappoint him—again.

But I will not marry Gustav Nyhus, she thought. Most especially after last night. She picked up the mangle and leaned it gently against the front of the cabin.

She spent much of the day roaming the woods with a burlap sack, gathering fodder. When she returned to the meadow, the mangle was gone.

That evening she waited for Jørgen by the waterfall. He found her just as deep blue shadows began stretching across the mountain.

She'd been watching, but still jumped when he stepped silently from the trees, holding his fiddle case. He grinned and kissed her, and by the time he stepped away she was shivering with pleasure.

Jørgen sat on the flat rock by the pool and opened his case. "I want to teach you a new tune."

"Before that—I need to talk about something." Solveig settled down and told him about Gustav and the mangle.

"You're not going to marry him?" Jørgen's voice was uncharacteristically sharp.

"No." Solveig shifted as the stone's cold leached through her skirt. "I will have to leave, though. Find work in Bergen."

Jørgen drew up his legs and wrapped his arms around his knees as if he felt the chill, too. For a long moment only the waterfall's constant song filled the evening. Finally he said, "You should go to America."

She caught her breath.

"That is ..." he amended, "*we* should go to America."

Yes, yes, *yes*, she wanted to say. But it was not so simple. "I don't have enough money for the passage."

"The same is true with me. And autumn is not the time to make the trip. But I plan to go to Kristiania for the winter."

"Kristiania?" she echoed, dismayed. That city was much farther away than Bergen.

"There are more opportunities for me there. I'll play as many dances and concerts as I can, and travel if I need to. If you get work in Bergen, we should be able to leave in the spring."

"But ... how will I know where you are?"

Jørgen nodded as if he'd anticipated the question. "Every Midsummer I play for a big dance held at Tollef's Danseplass, near Kinsarvik. We can meet there. From Kinsarvik it's just a two-day trip to

England by steamer. From there we can arrange passage to America."

Solveig had dreamed of leaving Norway for years. Still, the reality was overwhelming. "America is big."

"I have a friend there who'll help us. A fiddler. He lives in a place called Stoughton, Wisconsin. There are many Norwegian people there." Jørgen picked up a small stone and tossed it into the pool.

Solveig waited, pinching and unpinching her skirt, wondering if he had anything else to say.

Finally he asked, "Will you come with me?"

"I want to. But there is something you have not mentioned." She moistened her lips with her tongue. "Marriage." Jørgen was the only person she could ever love. She was willing to leave her mother and sisters, eager to leave her father and the farm, excited about the prospect of emigrating. But she was not willing to do all of those things if he was unwilling to wed.

He leaned close and kissed her temple. "Forgive me," he whispered. "I have gone about this badly. Of *course* we will marry. But you must let me propose in my own way."

Solveig wasn't sure what that meant, but it was enough. She leaned against him, savoring his smoke-sweat scent, lulled by the waterfall, trying to imagine life as a fiddler's wife.

TWENTY-EIGHT

So THIS IS WHAT it means to be a dancer's spouse, Roelke thought as—against his better judgment—they set out on the road. After taking the ferry to Kinsarvik they followed a narrow lane that wound up a mountain. Nothing about his driving-in-Norway experience advocated throwing caution to the proverbial wind. They'd get there when they got there. He braked on a turn and was relieved to feel Reverend Brandvold's old sedan respond. He'd been gently testing the brakes ever since they left Utne. Evidently he was still a bit freaked.

"I think this is it." Chloe pointed ahead. There was no sign for Tollef's Danseplass, but two dozen or so cars were lined up in a mowed field.

He pulled off and parked. "So, where's the dance?" All he saw was a family on a path that disappeared into the trees. A little boy ran ahead while a little girl rode on her father's shoulders.

Chloe checked her directions. "It's a short walk from here." She unclicked her seat belt and grabbed her daypack.

"'Short' is a relative term in Norway." As Roelke got out of the car, though, he ordered himself to quit grousing. Chloe had worn her hair loose, and she looked especially lovely. She'd traded jeans for a red blouse and full denim skirt, too. She was looking forward to this.

His job was to make sure that no one harmed her. He felt the way he did when serving a warrant to someone likely to start shooting—tense, hyper-alert. He wasn't letting Chloe out of his sight.

After crossing the field the trail ascended, of course, but soon the strains of a rollicking tune reached through the trees, and they emerged into a clearing.

Chloe stopped, hands clasped joyfully. "Oh, *look*!"

Dancers young and old already crowded the wooden floor. On a raised platform at the far end, two young men bowed fiddles and a grinning woman played an accordion. Onlookers had settled into folding lawn chairs, or were munching goodies from picnic hampers. Two little blond girls were blowing bubbles.

Torstein and Ellinor beckoned from a bench they'd claimed near the trailhead. Torstein wore his fancy *bunad* but still looked like hell, Roelke thought. His cheeks seemed hollow. Dark smudges showed beneath his eyes. But of course it had only been a few days since his girlfriend, Klara, had been killed.

As if reading Roelke's thoughts Torstein said, "I almost didn't come."

"We're glad you did," Ellinor said.

"Good thing you could get away from the museum, Ellinor," Roelke said. "We stopped by this morning, and the place was hopping."

"I asked Sonja to come in mid-day and take charge." Ellinor's smile was distinctly guilty. "We've got a special evening tour, so it was kind of her. But I wouldn't have missed this for anything."

Chloe was watching the dancers. "I'm used to seeing performances, you know? People in folk costume entertaining an audience."

"This is the real deal," Ellinor said. "Local people gathering to entertain themselves."

"Is the accordion typical?" Chloe swung her daypack from her shoulder and pulled out a notebook and pen.

"Accordions began appearing at regional dances in the nineteenth century," Ellinor began. "New dances like the waltz and polka were becoming popular. Even then, some people worried that the old dances would fade away ..."

Chloe scribbled notes, nodding as Ellinor and Torstein detailed the complexities of local music and dance traditions. Roelke didn't even pretend to pay attention. Instead he assessed the clearing, trying to suss out any possible threat.

All he saw, though, were happy people. Among the throng on the dance floor were senior citizens, stooped with age but beaming. Toddlers held hands with siblings as they bounced back and forth. Parents with babies in their arms bobbed to the rhythm. When the musicians began a waltz, even teens paired up and joined the flow with unexpected skill.

Roelke scratched one earlobe. Well, hunh. Lots of people in Wisconsin grew up dancing the polka, but he'd never seen kids waltzing before.

Bestefar, the elderly man Chloe had interviewed in Kinsarvik, soon joined them with his granddaughter. They were clearly delighted to see Chloe. She greeted them with hugs before introducing Torstein and Ellinor. "Thank you *so* much for inviting us." Bestefar beamed.

Roelke felt a ripple of pride. When he'd first met Chloe, he hadn't had an inkling of what her career was about. Her enthusiasms still sometimes bewildered him. But even after the ugly incidents that had plagued their trip, here she was making an old man feel good about his knowledge. Watching her doing what she loved... well, it all made sense.

One of the fiddle players shouted an announcement. "The next piece will be a Springar," Torstein translated. He and Chloe watched avidly as the dance began. "I've never seen the promenade start before the music!" he marveled.

Chloe pointed with her pen. "And the speed of the women's orbiting turns..."

The Springar was evidently a favorite dance, because several tunes later, another one was announced. "Chloe?" Torstein said. "Do you want to try?"

"Sure!" She tucked her notebook away and kissed Roelke's cheek. "Be back soon." Ellinor spotted a friend and excused herself too.

Roelke crossed his arms and watched the dance. Even he could tell that Chloe and Torstein were good at this Springar thing. They seemed to have different steps—Chloe's graceful and flowing, Torstein's showing more bravado. There also seemed to be a flirtatious element to the dance that Roelke hadn't noticed before.

He realized that one knee was bouncing like a jackhammer. Then he realized that he was feeling the way he had while watching Chloe and Kent Andreasson reminiscing about *their* dancing days.

Well, hunh. Apparently he wasn't thrilled with his fiancée sharing her passion for folk dance with other guys.

So suck it up, buddy, he told himself. Chloe was glowing. No one would suspect that she'd been in a car wreck the day before. Bottom line: folk dancing made her happy. Either *he* took up dancing—which was *not* going to happen—or he had to learn to live with moments like this.

Torstein gave Chloe a final whirl, making her tiered skirt balloon prettily around her legs. They laughed and joined in the applause. Chloe tipped her head up and said something that prompted Torstein to put one arm around her shoulder. He kept it there as they started down the steps.

Roelke growled and looked away as his good intentions fled. All right, that was enough of *that*. He'd been a good sport, but he was reaching the limit. He took a couple of deep breaths, watching some big bird circling in the distance, trying to tamp down his irritation. When he felt capable of pleasantly greeting Chloe and Torstein, he stood to meet them.

Just one problem. Chloe and Torstein didn't appear.

Roelke frowned, moving closer as some dancers left the floor and others took their place. No sign of Chloe and Torstein.

What the *hell*? Roelke's hands clenched into fists. Every nerve tingled to full alert. Where could they have gone?

Okay, he told himself. Calm down. They had to be here. Somehow he'd just lost them in the crowd. He began a slow circle of the dance floor, dodging people laughing, people chattering in Norwegian, people calling to friends. He made another circle, this time focusing on the dancers.

He didn't find Chloe and Torstein.

He checked the two old-fashioned outhouses in the woods nearby, banging on the doors, yelling for Chloe. No joy.

Had she gone back to the car? Roelke couldn't imagine her leaving without speaking to him first. Besides, he had the only set of car keys in his pocket. Where else was there to go?

He stepped up on a bench, ignoring the startled looks of people nearby, and scanned the crowd again. Still no sign of them.

"Roelke?" It was Ellinor, regarding him with a puzzled frown. "Is something wrong?"

"I can't find Chloe and Torstein." He jumped down.

She scanned the clearing. "They must be here somewhere."

"I've looked. They're not."

"But—"

"When the Springar ended I saw them turn toward the steps. Then they were gone. I only glanced away for a second." Except… it had been more than a second.

A cold dread leached into Roelke's bones. This was *his* fault. He wouldn't have lost sight of them if he hadn't been struggling with grade-school jealousy. He'd vowed to keep his gaze on Chloe. And he hadn't done it.

"Hey." Ellinor put a hand on his arm. "Don't panic. I'll help you look for—"

"Roelke!" Torstein shoved through the crowd. Alone.

"What?" Roelke grabbed the other man's shoulder, gave a little shake. "Where's Chloe?"

"She fell—"

The cold in Roelke's bones turned to ice. "Where? Is she—"

"I'll show you." Torstein whirled and darted away.

Roelke grabbed his and Chloe's daypacks and followed. "Excuse me—sorry—pardon me," he panted. "*Unnskyld meg,*" Ellinor echoed behind him. "*Unnskyld…*"

Torstein followed a faint path that left the clearing beyond the dance floor, skirting underbrush and plunging between trees before making a sharp turn. They emerged on a rock outcrop so abruptly that he put up his hand to slow Roelke and Ellinor.

There was no sign of Chloe. "Where *is* she?" Roelke demanded.

Torstein's eyes glazed with tears. "She fell over the edge."

As Roelke imagined a tiny broken body at the bottom of a mile-high free-fall, an intense heat boiled inside. Chloe was an experienced hiker. She had never, to his knowledge, fallen off a cliff. He grabbed both of Torstein's shoulders. "What, did, you, *do*?"

"Stop it!" Ellinor snapped. She leaned gingerly over the edge. "I see her."

Roelke dropped to his belly, scraped up his courage, and peered down a steep, irregular slope. The woman he loved sat maybe fifteen feet below the outcrop, her bright shirt sharp against the grays and browns and greens. "Chloe!" he bellowed.

Chloe looked up. "Roelke?"

"Are you okay?"

"Yes!"

She was okay. Roelke's muscles went limp with relief. Chloe, was, okay. Again. No thanks to *him*.

"But I gashed my leg," she called. "And I'm afraid that if I try to move, I'll just slide farther."

"Hold tight!" he hollered. She lifted a hand in acknowledgment.

"I was going to go down and help her up, but it's so steep …" Torstein had backed away, hands raised defensively. "If Chloe and I *both* got stuck down there, you wouldn't have known where to look. That's why I ran to get you."

Which was, Roelke had to admit, the most responsible strategy. Well, he'd apologize to Torstein later.

Roelke considered the terrain below. Most of it was loose scree. He could see a track where Chloe had slid after landing below the outcrop. She huddled now at the base of a stunted evergreen that had, evidently, stopped her descent. Just a few yards beyond her was the final drop-off of his nightmares. If Chloe hadn't stopped herself, she almost certainly would have plunged to her death.

Hell, he thought, considering his options. Traction in that rubble would be difficult. But here and there a few other shrubby trees clung stubbornly to the mountain. If he started the descent off to the right, and zigzagged from tree to tree, it should be manageable. He narrowed his eyes, mentally mapping the safest possible route.

Then he scrambled to his feet. "I'm going down."

Ellinor looked uncertain. "Maybe we should—"

"I'm going to get Chloe. You can do whatever you want."

Ten minutes later Roelke eased from the side of the outcrop and began picking his way down the slope. The descent wasn't easy. He didn't take a step without first gouging his walking stick into the rubble. Even so he fell on his ass twice. But step by sideways step, aiming from one flat spot or shrub to the next, he managed to reach Chloe.

She was dusty and disheveled. Blood seeped between the fingers she'd clamped over her right calf. He'd never been so glad to see her.

"You're a sight for sore eyes," she said fervently.

"What were you *thinking*?" The outburst surprised them both, but he couldn't stop. "Why did you disappear with Torstein? Did it even *occur* to you that I'd be frantic?"

"I'm sorry!" she flared. "But can you yell at me later? I'd really like to get out of here."

"I was frightened," he admitted, already feeling contrite. Sometimes he really could be a jerk. "You're really all right?"

"Well, I've got a whole new layer of bruises." She managed a shuddery smile. "And I haven't been able to stop the bleeding here. I didn't think I could scramble back up on my own. But I'll survive."

Roelke cleaned and bandaged the gash with first-aid supplies from his pack, and took the time to clean and cover the worst of her scrapes. Finally he helped her to her feet. She put one arm over his shoulders, and he gave her the walking stick. Then they slowly, *very* slowly, crept back up the slope. Torstein grabbed Chloe's hand to help her the last few feet.

"Thank God," Ellinor exclaimed. "Should we call for medical help? What do you need?"

Chloe looked around. "Actually, what I need most right now is to take a pee."

"I'll go with you." Ellinor clearly wanted to feel useful. "Here. Lean on me."

Roelke waited until the women had hobbled out of earshot before turning to Torstein. "So, what happened?" His voice quivered with relief and residual anger. He just couldn't help it.

"When the dance ended I started thinking about Klara." Torstein blinked as tears welled in his eyes. "All of a sudden I just needed to be alone, so I took off. Chloe followed me."

Chloe will answer for that later, Roelke thought, but he nodded.

"I spotted that faint trail leading from the clearing. We got here, and…" Torstein spread his hands helplessly. "Roelke, I honestly don't know what happened. She caught up with me here on the ledge. She started talking, trying to comfort me, but all of a sudden she went quiet. She got this sort of faraway look on her face…"

Roelke felt a sinking sensation beneath his ribs. He knew that look. He'd seen it on the shore in Kinsarvik. He'd seen it when they visited the abandoned dance site near Utne. It happened when Chloe had a flash of… what had she called it? Genetic memory. He wasn't clear on exactly what happened at such moments. But for a few seconds, maybe longer, she was somewhere else.

"I saw her swaying," Torstein was saying. "She started pulling at her shirt. I thought she was having a heart attack or something! I reached for her, but she just—just fell over. It was horrifying."

Knowing he'd made an ass of himself, Roelke held out his right hand. "I'm sorry for losing my temper earlier, Torstein. I got scared."

Torstein accepted the handshake. "Believe me, I was scared too."

Dammit all. The entire situation, the entire trip, really was *completely* out of control.

Like I wasn't worried enough about bad guys, Roelke thought. Evidently he needed to worry just as much about Chloe's interactions with her ancestors.

TWENTY-NINE

Solveig—August to October 1919

When Solveig woke the next morning, Jørgen was lying on his side in the narrow bed beside her. He'd planted one elbow and propped his cheek on his hand, watching her.

She smiled and stretched. "You didn't leave," she said lightly. It was a first.

"I will never leave you, Solveig." He held her gaze, willing her to understand. "I'll need to travel. That's a fiddler's lot. But I will *always* return, because you're part of me"—he tapped his chest—"in here."

They said goodbye on the front step. Jørgen was happier than she'd ever seen him, more animated. "I will gather my things at the cottage, then start for Kristiania," he said. "But I will see you in June. Meet me at Tollef's Danseplass outside Kinsarvik on Midsummer." He pulled her against his chest, holding her tight as he kissed her again.

"I'll see you in June," Solveig echoed as she melted into him, wanting to store up his warmth, his scent, the music that framed his every moment.

Finally, reluctantly, he pulled away. She kept one hand on his arm, fingertips unwilling to break contact even as she forced herself to turn away—

Then she froze. Someone stood at the edge of the meadow.

"Who is that?" Jørgen asked quietly.

Not Father, but Amalie. Solveig pressed one hand against her chest, willing her racing heart to slow. "My younger sister." It was too late to pretend, so she lifted a hand in greeting.

Amalie walked through the meadow to join them, assessing Jørgen with open curiosity. She looked especially pretty with her blond braids wrapped coronet-style around her head and her cheeks flushed from the climb. She wore the *bunad* that most women saved for special occasions these days.

"Amalie, this is my friend Jørgen." Solveig managed a calm tone.

Jørgen offered a hand, and Amalie shook it politely. "How do you do, Jørgen." Then her gaze dropped to the fiddle case on the step.

"Good to meet you, Amalie." He nodded, picked up the case, and gave Solveig one last look. His piercing blue eyes repeated his promise: *I will see you at Midsummer.*

Amalie watched him walk away. "Who was that?"

"I told you. A friend."

"More than a friend, I think."

Solveig's cheeks flamed. "Well ... yes."

"But where is he going?" A perplexed frown furrowed Amalie's forehead.

"He has a summer cottage higher up the mountain."

"He had a fiddle."

"Yes." Solveig raked her fingers through her hair. Her sister was guileless. Could she keep a secret? I pray so, Solveig thought. "Amalie, you *must* not tell anyone about meeting Jørgen up here. Promise me. If Father—"

"I would never tell." Amalie was still staring after Jørgen. "He's very handsome, isn't he."

Solveig realized that her sister was not surprised or upset, but intrigued. The situation probably seemed romantic. "He is," Solveig agreed briefly, and changed the subject. "What are you doing here?" She gestured at Amalie's attire. "Is there a wedding I don't know about?"

Jørgen had disappeared, and Amalie finally met her sister's gaze. "What? Oh, no. I'm expected at the Utne Hotel this evening. We have to wear traditional clothes. The tourists like it."

"If you're going to Utne, this is quite a detour," Solveig observed.

Amalie nodded soberly. "I wanted to warn you. Gustav visited again yesterday. He and father had a long talk outside. Father was furious when he came back to the house."

Solveig sucked in her lower lip. You have a plan, she reminded herself. As soon as she was no longer responsible for the animals she would go to Bergen, work, and count the days until Midsummer. Already the missing of Jørgen was a brooding silence inside.

Events had been set in motion, but Father didn't climb to the *seter* that day. He wants me to wonder, Solveig thought as she milked, churned, scrubbed. He wants me to worry. She could do nothing but wait for the storm.

When Solveig stepped from the cabin the next morning, an oblong parcel wrapped in canvas lay on the step. Surely Gustav wouldn't try again.

Had Jørgen carved a mangle for her? She crouched and pulled back the canvas to reveal not a mangle, but a fiddle case. She opened it with trembling fingers. Inside was the most beautiful *hardingfele* she had ever seen. Jørgen had adorned the fingerboard with glowing pieces of mother-of-pearl. He'd carved a dragon's head above the pegs. He'd inked delicate designs on the front of the fiddle.

Overwhelmed, she picked it up.

Only then did she see the ornamentation on the fiddle's narrow sides: a row of dancing devils, drawn by a clever hand.

Solveig's sullen brother climbed to the *seter* every Saturday to fetch the dwindling loads of cheese and butter. He said little and never lingered. For the first time the solitude weighed on her. She shivered through her chores with two woolen shawls knotted over her shoulders, hands chapped with the constant scrubbing, wondering where Jørgen was. When might he reach Kristiania? Would he make haste, or look for opportunities to perform along the way?

"Midsummer," she whispered, making the word a talisman. And she remembered the look in his eyes that last morning: *I will always return, because you're part of me...*

He lived in the fiddle, too. Only Jørgen would poke defiant fun at those who believed that fiddlers did the devil's work. Despite her lack of skill, the new *hardingfele*'s tone and depth took her breath away. In the evening, when her ears strained to catch the faint echo of his music, she pressed her cheek to the polished fiddle. At night, when she couldn't sleep and her fingers longed to trace the knobs of his spine, she sat by the hearth and played. The music connected her to him, and was a comfort.

And she needed comfort. By mid-October, when her father finally appeared, Solveig knew she was in trouble.

Svein stalked across the meadow to meet her, contemptuous disdain burning in his eyes. Was he angry only because she'd rejected Gustav again, or did he know she'd kept company with a man? She forced herself to hold his iron gaze. Finally he turned and stalked to the barn.

He spent the rest of the day sending bundles of hay hurtling down the mountain on his new cable to the main farm. That evening he ate his flatbread and cheese in silence. He read aloud from the Old Testament before going to sleep in the barn.

That night Solveig wrapped a handkerchief around her little leather journal and settled it deep in her pocket. She couldn't take the fiddles, but she hid them well. She'd come back to fetch Jørgen's gift when she could.

Her brother arrived the next morning. The three of them shouldered pack baskets and herded the animals back down to Høiegård. Britta greeted her with a tight hug, but she didn't look happy to see her daughter. "Oh, Solveig," she whispered. "Stay out of your father's way." Then, with an anxious glance toward her husband, she scuttled back into the house.

Solveig had every intention of staying out of her father's way that evening—the last she meant to spend at Høiegård. She was sitting on a milking stool, cheek pressed against the cow's warm belly, when he grabbed her arm and jerked her to her feet. She hadn't even heard Svein approach. But she wasn't surprised to see the switch in his hand.

That night she lay in the straw, inhaling the familiar blend of cows and dung and hay, trying to will away the welted pain in the back of her legs. Trying to think. The plan she and Jørgen had agreed to couldn't work now. Once her pregnancy became obvious, any employer would almost certainly turn her out. Her father would do the same.

She had never felt so lonely.

But she had another life to think about now. I shall be, Solveig vowed fiercely, a mother who will do *anything* for her child. That resolve helped her focus and come up with a new plan.

She rose and groped for the lantern kept on a nail by the door. Once it was lit, she carefully tore a blank page from her leather-bound book and wrote a note: *I am going to America.* She folded the paper and left it in the bottom of a milk pail, where her mother would find it.

She considered taking the lantern but decided against it. She considered tiptoeing into the house to fetch her winter clothes but decided against that too. The burlap sack holding the summer clothes and essentials she'd taken to the *seter* was in the barn, and she'd make do with that. She patted each cow goodbye, slung the sack over her shoulder, and crept from the barn.

By sunrise, she was well on her way to the *seter*. When she reached the summer farm she fetched the precious fiddle Jørgen had made—her betrothal gift, offered because he understood her fiddler's heart.

Climbing down the mountain took longer, for she didn't dare take the main trail past Høiegård. She considered going first to Utne and stopping at the inn to say goodbye to Amalie. But handing Amalie another heavy secret would burden her, Solveig thought, and be a risk for me.

She caught a ride a short way along the coast with a fisherman, then kept walking. It was cool but sunny. Her feet began to hurt, and her stomach growled, but every passing kilometer made her feel safer. She didn't often travel to *Frukthagehus*—Orchard House —but she remembered the way.

Sometime in the afternoon she spotted the familiar red house with white shutters on a rise overlooking the fjord. Rows of apple trees marched down the slopes on both sides. Please, she thought as she reached the drive. Please say yes. *Please.*

When Solveig knocked, the front door opened quickly. Her older sister's eyes went wide with surprise. "Solveig! What are you doing here?" She glanced at the empty drive. "Are you alone?"

"I am." Solveig set down her fiddle case and her bag, and flexed stiff fingers. "Helene, I need your help." Tears threatened for the first time. If her sister turned her away…

But Helene stepped back, gesturing her inside. "Of *course*." Once the door was closed, she wrapped her arms around Solveig. "What's happened?"

THIRTY

"So," Roelke said when they reached the car. "What happened?"

Chloe was grateful that he'd given her time before asking. "I'm not entirely sure."

Roelke checked for traffic and pulled out. "Start with why you disappeared with Torstein without saying anything to *me*."

Chloe shifted in her seat, vainly trying to find a comfortable position. Skidding full-tilt boogie down a scree-filled ravine was not something she'd have chosen to do the day after surviving a car crash. She also felt emotionally exhausted, and really was not up to an argument.

"I'm truly sorry I scared you," she said at last. "Torstein and I enjoyed dancing that Springar." She'd thought that Markus, her Swiss ex, had been a good dancer—but oh my, Torstein was in another league. Even though the local nuances were new, he'd intuited every move.

"Chloe?" Roelke's voice was tight. "I know you had a good time dancing with Torstein. What I'm waiting to hear is why—"

"I'm trying to explain," she protested, holding up one hand. "Dancing with Torstein was so effortless that I felt myself just kind of… disappearing. It was genetic memory, I'm sure of it. During the final series of turns, out of the corner of my eye I could see all the women's skirts flaring out."

"Most of the women weren't wearing skirts."

"That's my point."

He took that in, keeping his gaze on the road. "Ah."

"I've been folk dancing for years, Roelke, and I'd never felt so much joy. It was wonderful, but also overwhelming. When the music stopped I felt dazed. Torstein looked happy, but all of a sudden his face crumpled. He looked horrified, and said, 'Dear God, how can I dance after Klara…'"

"I'm glad he didn't completely forget that his girlfriend was brutally murdered."

Chloe bit her lip. Roelke was even more pissed than she'd thought. "When we left the floor, he turned away from where you were waiting. I didn't know what to do. I was worried, and I had to make a decision, fast, or I would have lost sight of him. I *did* try to catch your eye, but you weren't looking."

A wordless sound—half grunt, half growl—rose from Roelke's throat. His facial muscles were hard. His hands showed a strangling grip on the steering wheel.

When he didn't speak, she kept going. "So, Torstein went into the trees and I followed him. When we came out on that outcrop, I thought for one sick moment that he was going to do something terrible." She swallowed hard. Grief could make people do all kinds of things.

Roelke finally unclenched his jaw. "Torstein said you were standing on the ledge and zoned out. Was that another moment of genetic memory?"

"I don't know." She winced, trying to ward away the visceral memory. "All of a sudden this sense of fear slammed into me like a mallet." She considered. "No, not fear. Pure terror." It had welled within her. She'd tried to retreat but couldn't. She remembered clawing at her blouse, trying to ease a crushing pressure.

"So it was more like what you feel sometimes in old buildings."

She shrugged helplessly. "All I know is that I walked into something very dark. Someone who once stood on that ledge was so terrified I could still feel it."

"Someone afraid of heights?" Roelke suggested. "Maybe someone got drunk at a dance, wandered too close to the edge, and realized at the last moment what was happening."

"Maybe."

Roelke blew out a long breath and put one hand on her leg. "I'm sorry that happened."

"I should be used to it by now."

"No. I'm sorry because it was my fault."

Chloe turned to look at him. "What on earth are you talking about?"

"It was my fault." A pull-out appeared on the side of the road, and he swerved into it. He cut the engine before facing her. "I watched you dancing with Torstein, and … well, it bothered me. A lot. I'm ashamed, but it's true. That's why I wasn't paying attention when you tried to catch my eye."

The pain in his eyes twisted Chloe's heart. "Oh, Roelke …" She unhooked her seatbelt so she could rest her head on his shoulder. She should have known that watching her dance with another guy might be hard on him. "I'm the one who needs to apologize. You have been amazingly supportive and patient on this trip, and I'm grateful."

He stroked her hair. They sat in silence as cars passed on the road. Chloe thought about how much folk dancing had meant to her over the years. It had meant a *lot*.

But it didn't mean as much as having Roelke in her life.

"I won't dance anymore," she murmured into his shirt.

"Don't say that." He traced her cheekbone with one finger. "When you were dancing this afternoon, you looked so happy. I would never take that away. This is my problem, not yours."

As long as I have Roelke, Chloe thought, everything will be okay. She straightened. "Roelke, as soon as we get home, let's just go find a justice of the peace and get married."

His eyebrows rose. "Is that what you really want?"

"A courthouse wedding? No. That's not what I want. But what I *really* don't want is to spend more time not being married to you."

Roelke wanted to detour to the hospital in Odda. "That will take all night," Chloe moaned.

"You might need stitches."

"Let's see how it looks." When they checked the gash, she was grateful to see the sterile gauze come away clean. "Your butterfly bandages did the trick. Please don't take me to the ER. I'll be very careful with it, I promise." She dared a bad joke. "No dancing."

He didn't smile, but he did concede. "I'll put a new dressing on it. If that wound starts to bleed again, though—"

"Absolutely."

Chloe and Roelke stopped at a café in Kinsarvik before catching the ferry back to Utne. Once in their hotel room, Chloe headed for the shower. Warm water felt good. After the jolt of her fall and one initial heart-stopping tumble, she'd skidded most of the way on one hip. Her thighs were badly scraped, and her left forearm. Her favorite skirt was toast. Still, once again, things could have been a *whole* lot worse.

Once she'd gingerly dressed in a pair of loose chinos, they stopped at the hotel desk to check for messages. The clerk handed over a fax and one phone slip.

"My dad called." Chloe read the short note several times before daring to smile. "Aunt Hilda is showing some signs of improvement."

"What kinds of signs?"

"He doesn't say. I'm going to call him." A few minutes later she shook her head and replaced the receiver at the pay phone. "No answer."

"You can call first thing in the morning." Roelke put a hand on her shoulder. "For now, let's just focus on that encouraging news."

The fax was from Rosemary Rossebo. *I found an attest from a pastor, giving character reference for one Solveig Sveinsdatter prior to her emigration. Dated 1920. Don't know if that's helpful or not. Still no record of Amalie.*

"Hmm." Chloe twisted her mouth, trying to remember the *Bygdebok* pages she'd skimmed. "Maybe Solveig was a sister or an aunt. I haven't had a chance to comb through all the information about other occupants of Fjelland." What with the car wreck and mountainside tumble and all.

"Not quite what you wanted," Roelke said. "But research can wait for tomorrow."

"Actually, I'd like to go to the museum."

Roelke looked exasperated. "Chloe, it's seven o'clock! The museum closed two hours ago. What could you possibly want to do there?"

"I want to talk to Sonja about the symbols in my hand cloth. Ellinor said she was working this evening. I doubt she'll be working tomorrow, on a Sunday. She might even take Monday off."

"What do you think Sonja can tell you?"

Chloe frowned, trying to tamp down frustration. "She said the woman who stitched my hand cloth was conveying a message, remember? Since then, I've realized that some of the designs on Hardanger fiddles are similar. And then we saw that heart-shaped swirly design carved into the house at Fjelland."

"I don't get the connection."

"The whole topic keeps nagging at me. It's understandable that in the old days, illiterate people used specific designs to convey certain ideas. But someone deliberately made that circle mark on Klara's forehead. It's got to mean something, and maybe Sonja can tell us."

"We can't talk about that with Sonja." Roelke leaned close as another couple passed. "As far as I know, the cops haven't released that detail. They'll want to keep the killer guessing, wondering what they know."

"Well, maybe we could simply ask if a circle has some particular significance. I doubt the cops would have thought to ask her. If I hadn't seen how Sonja reacted to the embroidery on my hand cloth, it wouldn't have crossed my mind either."

She could tell that Roelke was torn. In the end he nodded. "Okay. But we're driving. You need to stay off that leg as much as possible."

Fifteen minutes later he pulled into a parking spot near the Hardanger Folkemuseum's front door. Two tour buses were parked nearby. Inside, the young woman at the counter affirmed that Sonja was on duty. "But she's upstairs, where one group is enjoying a fiddle program. If you want to wait for her, feel free to slip into the back of the auditorium and listen. The other group is touring the open-air division."

Chloe and Roelke took the elevator upstairs and peeked into the auditorium. Sonja stood off to one side, stylish as ever in a silver sweater, black pants, and high heels. Visitors were listening with rapt attention as the fiddler with garnet hair from Tuesday's concert discussed the *hardingfele*'s unique qualities.

The only empty chairs were in the front of the room. "Let's wait in the hall," Chloe whispered.

They settled onto a bench. "I wonder if Sonja's had a chance to develop the pictures she took of my *handaplagg*," Chloe murmured. She tried to remember the specific stitched motifs, and not the grief that someone had stolen it. *The woman who created this* handaplagg *was expressing herself, yes?* Sonja had said. But there hadn't been any plain circles on the hand cloth.

"I feel like the killer was speaking a language we don't know," Chloe said. "Probably most Norwegians today don't know it either. But in the old days, people stitched symbols into linen hand cloths. They inked them onto wooden fiddles. They carved them on log beams in their homes. They even—" She stopped abruptly as she remembered something new. "*Kroting*. Roelke, remember what Klara said about *kroting*?"

He sighed. "Just save time and remind me."

"When we were sitting in Høiegård the day we took the tour—the day Klara died in that very house—she pointed out the chalk decorations on the walls. A row of geometric shapes. I don't remember exactly what they looked like." Chloe heard Klara's voice in memory: *Some designs may have been decorative, but others were intended to protect the home.*

"Um ... okay." Roelke clearly wasn't sure why this was exciting her.

"The site's still open, right? Let's go up and—" Chloe stood and abruptly dropped back down. Shit. In her excitement she'd forgotten to favor her injured leg.

"You are not walking up that hill to the open-air division." Roelke's voice was resolute.

"I know." She looked at him, nibbling her lower lip. "But you could."

"I'm sticking with you."

Chloe was momentarily distracted as jaunty fiddle music burst from the auditorium. Evidently the lecture portion of the program had ended. "Please, Roelke? There's a tour group up there, so the house will be open."

"What purpose would that serve?"

"I still haven't figured out why that mark on the house at Fjelland seemed familiar. Maybe it's just because some of my ancestors lived there, but … I think there's more to it. I'm almost certain it wasn't on my *handaplagg*, and it wasn't on the fiddles on display. Maybe the design appears in that *kroting* up in Høiegård."

He pressed one knuckle against his forehead for a moment. "Sweetie, I think you're starting to grasp at straws."

"Maybe so. But if you could just make a quick sketch of the designs, we'd have them to work from."

"I'm staying with you."

"Roelke, I love you for that, but nothing is going to happen to me in the Hardanger Folkemuseum with thirty people in the next room. Please?"

After a bit more debate, Roelke held up his hands in grudging surrender. "Alright. You will not move from this bench until I get back."

"I will not move from this bench until you get back," Chloe repeated. He fixed her with a look. "I *promise*."

After he left, Chloe leaned against the wall. The fiddler started a new piece, this one slower and poignant. It seemed familiar, but at this point, Chloe couldn't tell if she'd heard the tune before, if she was tapping into ancestral memory, or if she was losing what little remained of her rational mind.

To distract herself, Chloe pulled from her daypack the Høiegård file she'd borrowed from Ellinor's office. She'd barely had time to peek at the contents, and she might as well put this interlude to use. She was reading a description of the *årestove*, the ancient smoke-house style with a raised central hearth, when the stairwell door nearby opened.

For half a second Chloe pictured Roelke's faceless bad guy emerging with weapon brandished. The woman who stepped into the corridor was tall, thin, erect—and she had taken the stairs, which was more than Chloe could say. But she was quite elderly, and instead of bludgeon or blade, carried only a cane and leather pocketbook. Surely this woman wearing a white-collared blue dress with sensible black shoes hadn't come with evil intent.

"Pardon me." The woman spoke English with slow care. "Are you Chloe Ellefson?"

Chloe sat up straight. The woman's thin white braids were pinned to her head coronet-style. Her eyes were a faded blue, her skin wrinkled. Chloe would swear that they'd never met before. And yet… something about the newcomer felt so familiar that a lump rose in her throat. Maybe I really am losing it, Chloe thought. "Yes, I am."

"Oh, thank God I found you." The woman's thin shoulders melted with obvious relief. "I'm Helene Valebrokk."

———

Roelke reached the open-air division just as a guide was pleasantly shooing visitors back to their bus. "Is it all right if I stop in there?" he asked the guide, pointing toward Høiegård.

"Sure," the young man said. "Sonja will be up soon to lock up for the night."

Roelke wasn't used to walking into eight-hundred-year-old buildings. It wasn't surprising that Chloe got overwhelmed here, he thought. In the empty space, devoid of tourists, even he sensed something indefinable.

A table sat against the far wall, right below the chalked designs. He pulled out his notebook and started sketching. None of the designs resembled the swirly heart thing, but maybe Chloe would make something of another symbol.

He was almost finished when he heard someone step into the entryway. "Sonja?" he called. He had no wish to be locked inside.

Torstein Landvik bent low and entered the main room. He still wore his old-timey clothes and looked right at home. But something made Roelke's nerves prickle.

He kept his tone conversational. "Hey, Torstein. I figured Sonja had come to kick me out. What are you doing here?"

Torstein stared at the small room as if he'd never seen it before. "I needed to come to the place where Klara died. What are *you* doing here?"

Roelke gestured to the notebook. "Just making some sketches for Chloe."

Torstein stepped closer and studied the drawings. His face was expressionless.

As a cop, Roelke had gotten pretty good at reading people. His read of Torstein said it was time to get the hell out of there. He stepped, ever so casually, closer to the door.

Torstein side-stepped too, keeping his body between Roelke and the only exit. He met Roelke's gaze full-on. This was not the grinning, exuberant Torstein, or the grieving Torstein. In the gloom his eyes seemed dull.

Then his hand settled on the hilt of his ceremonial knife.

———

"You're Helene Valebrokk?" Chloe repeated. Tiny fireworks exploded in every cell. "Do you mean … H. R. Valebrokk?" This was the person who currently owned Fjelland, the farm where Amalie Sveinsdatter had been living when she was baptized in 1905.

"You came to see me yesterday?" Helene prompted. "I found your note."

Chloe slid over and patted the bench invitingly. "But how did you find me? Here, I mean?"

Helene sat. "The girl at the hotel said she'd heard you say you were on your way here." She gripped Chloe's hand with surprising strength. "When I came home this afternoon and found your note, I was …" She searched for the word. "Excited, yes? You see, I never heard from Amalie after she left for America!"

"So you're related to Amalie …?"

"She was my sister."

I am staring at a relative, Chloe thought, pressing one hand over her mouth. Helene Valebrokk was her great-aunt.

"Do you know Amalie? Is she still alive?"

"I don't know. I'm sorry." Chloe could tell Helene had hoped for more. "The only thing I can tell you is that Amalie Sveinsdatter surrendered my mother for adoption in 1920 at an orphange in

Stoughton, Wisconsin." Excitement bubbled inside. "It's just *wonderful* to meet you! I have so many questions."

"But I can't stay." Helene made a helpless gesture. "The friend who drove me is waiting in the car."

Chloe barely managed to swallow a dismayed wail. "Please, what can you tell me about the farm? Has it changed hands since 1920?"

"It has been in the family since 1838."

"Oh." This was better than Chloe had dared hope.

"You've been to see the house up the hill?"

"Um …" Chloe was confused. "Your house? Fjelland?"

"No, no." Helene waved that suggestion away. "Here, at the museum. Up the hill. They use the old name, Høiegård. But the building came from Fjelland."

"*What*?" Chloe struggled to keep up. "Are you telling me that Høiegård and Fjelland are two names for the same farm?"

"Yes!" Helene nodded. "Høiegård means 'high farm.' Fjelland means 'mountainous.' A farm in the mountains."

"Oh, my, God," Chloe breathed. Amalie Sveinsdatter, and the building restored at the Hardanger Folkemuseum, had come from the same farm. That explained a lot.

But there was still much to sort through. "Are you also related to Solveig Sveinsdatter? Her name came up in the search for my mother's family."

"Solveig was my other sister. I was the oldest, and left home to work when I was fourteen. There is so much I want to tell you! About the family." Helene put both hands on the knob of her cane and pushed to her feet. "But not tonight. You will come back to the high farm? Tomorrow afternoon?"

"Of course." Chloe would get to Fjelland tomorrow if it meant crawling through the damn tunnel on her hands and knees.

“Good.” Helene paused in front of a color photograph on the wall—part of the “Folk Art in Focus” exhibit Chloe had admired earlier. “Torstein’s fiddle,” she murmured.

“Torstein Landvik? You know Torstein?”

“I do.”

Helene used the clipped tone of polite elderly people who didn’t want to speak ill of someone. Had Torstein interviewed Helene for his folk dance project and let his enthusiasm override polite behavior?

“I look forward to seeing you tomorrow.” Helene disappeared into the stairwell.

Chloe got up to study the photograph that had given Helene pause. The close-up camera angle showed the musician’s left hand on the fingerboard, including the unusual forged ring on his fourth finger. Definitely Torstein, Chloe thought. But the real star of the shot was the fiddle itself, glimmering inlay and flowing inked scrolls.

... Wait a minute.

The design included two snail shell whorls presented as mirror images, creating a stylized heart. It was the same symbol she’d seen carved into a log at Fjelland. The one she was sure she’d seen elsewhere. The image here didn’t *quite* match her memory, but this had to be it.

Chloe wished she’d noticed the photo before Roelke had headed up to the old house to check for the same double-whorl in the *kroting*. Well, he’d be back any minute, and they could compare notes. And if Sonja was ever free ...

The visitors in the auditorium burst into applause. The fiddler began yet another tune. Chloe stifled a frustrated squawk. She wanted to get Sonja’s take on the double-spiral heart.

Tipping her head, Chloe considered the design in the photograph. Something basic didn't make sense. The symbols adorning textiles, fiddles, woodenware, and walls in Western Norway were rooted in antiquity. It was hard to imagine Vikings decorating their possessions with hearts, at least not in the modern romantic sense. It was hard to imagine Vikings honoring snails, either. What else could the design depict? A ram's horns, maybe?

… *Wait* a minute.

Fragments of knowledge twirled through Chloe's mind as if someone was frantically turning a kaleidoscope, trying to find the correct picture among a million possibilities. An ashy circle. Two carved spirals. Two inked spirals. Could interpreting that design as a ram's horns provide the key to everything?

Chloe quivered with agitation as a possible answer emerged. She wanted to run her theory by Roelke, but he wasn't back yet.

He should have been.

A sudden flash of panic overruled pain. She jumped to her feet and headed toward the nearest exit. A stand near the door offered loaner umbrellas for guests in need. Chloe grabbed the tallest one and banged out the door. Leaning on the makeshift cane, she hop-walked up the hill as fast as she could.

The open-air division looked deserted. There was no sign of Roelke. Chloe opened her mouth to holler his name, but a sudden inner voice urged caution. Silence was best. Stealth was too.

She faced the back of Høiegård, where a wooden hatch had once been used for removing the dead. Some later generation had replaced it with two nine-paned windows—the only ones in the house. Chloe didn't want to be seen, so she circled wide and approached the house from the side.

At the back corner she pressed herself against the log wall. Was she being ridiculous? Was Roelke going to emerge any minute, grumbling that it had taken forever to sketch the chalked designs, and what on earth was she doing up here anyway?

But the inner voice was insistent. Chloe simply *knew* that Roelke was in trouble.

She slid along the back wall toward the window. Before daring a peek she heard Roelke speaking deliberately: "… telling you, this is a big mistake." Pause. "No, it *isn't* too late."

Chloe's heart plummeted.

"Let me talk to the cops with you," Roelke urged. Then his voice rose to a sudden bellow: "*Drop the knife!*"

Chloe looked through the glass. Torstein, a knife clenched in his right hand, gathered himself for a mighty vertical spring. Once airborne, his left leg shot out and caught Roelke in the shoulder.

Roelke went down. Torstein leapt on him. All the air disappeared from Chloe's lungs.

When Torstein scrambled away, his knife was bloody. Roelke was on the floor, leaning against the raised hearth, both hands pressed against his right side. His chest was heaving. Blood leaked through his fingers, staining his shirt.

Rage seared away Chloe's fear. Torstein Landvik had just stabbed Roelke. She believed that Torstein had killed Klara in this same room. Torstein had to be stopped.

But how? She couldn't take him down with an umbrella. She cast frantically about, and—*there.* The replacement slate shingles Klara had mentioned during their tour were still stacked nearby.

Chloe needed both hands to heft one of the heavy stones. As she hurried to the cabin door, something crashed inside. She hoped that meant Roelke was still fighting.

She stepped silently into the narrow entryway, heart slamming against her ribs. If she waited here with slate held high until Torstein bent over to leave the main room, she could brain him. But Torstein wouldn't leave unless Roelke was dead.

Grunts and thumps and a wooden clatter suggested that Torstein hadn't won yet. Chloe scrambled through the low door. The two men were grappling on the floor, rolling back and forth. Torstein saw her over Roelke's shoulder. For an instant he froze.

That let Roelke stagger to his feet. One shirt sleeve was stained with blood too, now.

"Move!" Chloe shrieked. He was between her and Torstein.

Roelke stepped back and Torstein bounded to his feet. Roelke kicked at Torstein's right hand. Torstein twisted away from the blow. Roelke wrapped his arms around the fiddler and made a half-turn before letting go.

Now. Chloe heaved the slate sideways, Frisbee-style, with all her strength. It slammed Torstein in the back. He howled and staggered to one knee. The knife clattered to the floor and skidded out of reach beneath the table.

Chloe stood panting. She had no idea what to do next.

"Get out of here *now*, Chloe!" Roelke gasped.

She didn't want to, but she did back away. Roelke threw himself at Torstein. They fell against the hearth, wrestling, punching, making furious animal sounds.

Chloe bit her lip so hard she tasted blood. Roelke was bigger than Torstein, but he'd suffered at least two knife wounds, maybe more. And Torstein had a dancer's agility. She didn't think Roelke could last much longer.

Frantic, she snatched a pewter candlestick and raised it high. But with the men writhing violently back and forth, she'd be just as likely to hit Roelke.

Help me! she begged silently of whomever might be listening.

The kettle. A heavy iron kettle hung from the ceiling over the hearth. She ran to the far side, grabbed the kettle's rim with both hands, and pulled it to her chest. "Hold him, Roelke!"

Slowly, painfully, Roelke managed to pin Torstein against the hearth, head and shoulders above the stones. Chloe shoved the kettle forward. It hit the back of Torstein's skull with a sickening thud. He crumpled like a stringless marionette.

Roelke's knees buckled. He sat down hard on the edge of the hearth, his breathing loud and ragged. Clamping a hand over the side wound, he bent double. There was so much blood now—on his shirt, dripping through his fingers.

Chloe whimpered, but just once. Roelke needed her.

His daypack was on the floor. She scrabbled inside for his first-aid kit, then crouched beside him. "Let me see." Blood flowed from the slash wound. She ripped open paper packages, layered bandages over the hole, and applied pressure with both hands.

But should she stay with Roelke, or go for help? The wrong choice could cost his life.

Then footsteps sounded in the entryway. Sonja bent low and stepped into the main room. She surveyed the scene with shocked horror.

"Call an ambulance!" Chloe implored.

Sonja gave a sharp nod, whirled, and disappeared.

"You're going to be okay," Chloe told Roelke. He managed a short chin jerk—trying, Chloe knew, to pretend that he believed her. She sent up a prayer to God, and to all the women who'd once lived in this house, that he wouldn't bleed to death before help arrived.

THIRTY-ONE

Solveig—June 1920

"I'm worried about you." Helene put water on the stove to heat for washing the breakfast dishes but kept her gaze on her sister. "What if the bleeding starts again and there's no one to help?"

"I'll be fine," Solveig insisted. She had no choice. Since giving birth she was always tired, and sometimes blood still spotted her undergarments. But nothing would keep her from attending the Midsummer dance. Jørgen would be waiting.

"Perhaps I should come with you."

"You need to stay here with the baby." Solveig glanced at her infant daughter asleep in a cradle nearby.

Helene sat down and put one hand on Solveig's arm. "You know you both are welcome to stay with me. You don't have to go to America."

The offer was sincere, for the sisters had shared a pleasant winter. Helene was a tall, capable woman who'd managed to hang on to her home and apple trees after her husband's accidental death. She hired help during busy times, but Solveig had watched Helene work the cider press, cook huge batches of apple butter and jelly and seal them in jars, and prune the trees with skill. Since Solveig didn't want anyone to know she was staying at the orchard, she rarely left the house and talked to no one else. She and Helene had grown closer as winter winds pummeled the house and blizzards packed snow almost to the eaves.

But Solveig couldn't consider changing plans. "I will go to the Midsummer dance and find Jørgen. Then we'll come get the baby and leave for America."

"But ..."

"I can't hide here forever," Solveig said gently. "Besides, I love Jørgen. We want to be together."

Traveling to Kinsarvik took more of a toll than Solveig cared to admit. But she was offered a ride up the mountain to Tollef's Danseplass in a crowded wagon, and her heart was light. She'd always dreamed of attending such a dance, of listening to music without fear of reprimand.

And somewhere, just ahead, Jørgen was waiting. She knew he was there, sensed his nearness. Heard him silently calling her name.

By the time she reached the clearing, festivities were underway. Some people were resting on blankets, nibbling treats from picnic baskets. Young men were arranging wood for the bonfire they'd light when dusk finally, reluctantly, descended. The floor was already crowded with people whirling and stomping, attired in their best traditional clothing.

But the four fiddlers and two accordion players sharing the musicians' platform were all strangers. Where was Jørgen? Solveig eeled through the crowd, jostled this way and that. He must be here, she thought. He *must*.

When the polka ended, the *kjøgemester* held up his hands for attention. "Friends, I'm happy to welcome a fine fiddler, Jørgen Riis, back to our Midsummer dance."

Solveig stood on tiptoe—and there he was, stepping up to the musicians' dais. Her knees went soft. Her eyes misted. She and Jørgen had known each other only briefly before their months-long separation, but he was her other half. She would always be incomplete without him.

Jørgen closed his eyes and launched into a tune. The piece he'd chosen was wistful, even melancholy. Tears flowed down Solveig's cheeks, coming from some well deep inside. The haunting music perfectly expressed the longing she'd felt since she and Jørgen parted.

The people who'd lingered on the floor, eager to keep moving, shrugged and departed. "Play something we can dance to!" a man yelled.

But as Jørgen played, the complainers ceased grumbling and the chatterers stopped talking. Even children ended their games and fell silent. Solveig wasn't the only listener who fumbled for a handkerchief.

When the piece ended, Jørgen lowered his instrument slowly. He blinked at the mesmerized audience as if he'd forgotten he wasn't alone.

"Jørgen!" Solveig cried, just as the crowd erupted in applause. She elbowed her way closer. "*Jørgen!*"

Somehow, he heard her. He met her gaze. Then he handed his fiddle to the *kjøgemester* and jumped from the dais to the dance floor to the ground. The next thing Solveig knew she was in his arms. She felt the longing in his crushing embrace.

But people pressed close, congratulating him, calling for another tune. He grabbed Solveig's hand and towed her through the crowd to the forest beyond the dance floor. "I know a special place where we can talk."

They took a narrow path into the woods. The *kjøgemester* must have called up another fiddler, for music sounded from the clearing behind them. Soon they emerged on a narrow outcrop. The view was splendid, but Solveig saw only Jørgen.

"You're well?" He gripped her shoulders as if needing reassurance.

"Well enough, now. Your tune—"

"I wrote it for you. The winter was so lonely…"

Solveig nodded.

"Did you like the gift I left at the *seter*?" His eyes danced.

"More than I can say. But I need to tell you—Jørgen, you're a father."

His mouth opened. His face went blank. "I'm… *what?*"

"You have a daughter. Three weeks old."

Clearly, this possibility had not entered his mind. "But… whatever will we do with her?"

He looked so bemused that Solveig had to laugh. "We will take her to America, of course!"

"Yes. Of course." Jørgen's stunned expression faded to a dawning smile. "Yes! We will take her to America. I'll make a tiny *hardingfele* and teach her to play. But… oh Solveig, however did you manage on your own?"

"I wasn't on my own. I've been staying with my older sister."

His eyebrows rose. "Amalie didn't say so."

She took a step backwards. "When did you see Amalie?"

"Last week. I traveled through Utne, stopped at the inn for a meal, and she recognized me."

Solveig sucked in an uneasy breath. "Amalie didn't know I'm still in Norway. I didn't tell my parents, either. They think I already emigrated. Did you mention my name?"

Jørgen's brow furrowed. "No, but she asked me—" His voice broke abruptly as he focused on something over her shoulder.

Solveig whirled. Her father and Gustav stepped from the trees with a gray-haired man she'd seen at her father's preachings.

Her heart made a sickening slide. How had they known? *How?*

Svein strode to them. "Father, I—" Solveig's words ended in a yelp of pain as he gripped her arm with iron fingers.

"Stop!" Jørgen tried to shove himself between father and daughter. Gustav grabbed his arms from behind and pinioned Jørgen against his chest.

"You sinful girl," Svein hissed at Solveig. His eyes glittered with the fanatical intensity of a man certain of his own unfailing righteousness. He thrust her away so roughly that she stumbled to her knees. The third man hauled her up again and jerked her toward the path.

"No!" Solveig shrieked. She couldn't make sense of what was happening.

The man dragged her beyond the outcrop, farther from the dance. Voices raised in song drifted faintly from the gathering.

Solveig fought to break free. *"Help me!"*

The man smacked her across the face, hard enough to send her reeling. But when he reached to grab her again she kicked hard, catching him in the groin. He doubled over, bleating in pain. She desperately scrambled away. Back to the ledge, she had to get back toward the ledge.

But she was too late. Before even leaving the trees she saw the men writhing on the outcrop. Jørgen was younger than Father and Gustav, but he was no sturdy laborer, and outnumbered.

One moment there were three men on the ledge. Then there were two.

THIRTY-TWO

CHLOE FOUND HERSELF BACK in the Odda hospital's emergency room waiting area.

When the first responders had arrived at the restored cabin from Høiegård, Torstein was still breathing. In a detached way, Chloe was relieved. But Roelke had lost consciousness in the ambulance. Medical staff had whisked him away upon arrival, and no one had provided an update since.

Now she sat with elbows on knees and face in hands. What would I do without Roelke? she wondered numbly. She'd already lost her mother. She wasn't sure she was strong enough to lose Roelke too. He'd become part of her, the foundation for everything else.

A heavy hand settled on her shoulder. "Chloe?"

Chloe jumped. "Why—Reverend Brandvold! What are you doing here?"

"People still call me when there's trouble in Utne." He settled heavily into the next chair. "I thought you might like some company."

His kindness almost broke her composure. "I would *love* some company. Roelke's with the doctors now. I don't know what's happening." Her forehead wrinkled. "But … how did you get here? We left your car parked at the museum."

"Barbara-Eden drove me." Reverend Brandvold leaned closer. "She wasn't sure you'd want to see her, so she's fetching coffee."

"Why wouldn't I want to see her?"

"She's learned to be hard on herself."

A few minutes later, when the young woman hesitantly approached, Chloe reached for the Styrofoam offering. "Thank you, Barbara-Eden. This is exactly what I needed."

Barbara-Eden perched on the edge of another chair and began pleating the hem of her skirt. "Is what I heard true? Did Torstein really do something awful?"

Chloe sipped the coffee, thinking that through. "I haven't given a formal statement to the police yet, so I shouldn't say too much. But … yes. He did."

"I thought he was wonderful," Barbara-Eden whispered.

"I did too." Chloe pinched her lips into a tight line. From the moment they'd met she'd been attracted to his energy, his enthusiasm for folk dance. She remembered how his intense gaze suggested that her every word was fascinating. She remembered the joy she'd felt while dancing with him that afternoon.

Her stomach roiled. She'd been dancing with the devil.

"Chloe, I …" Barbara-Eden glanced at Pastor Brandvold, who gave her an encouraging nod. "Torstein asked me questions about you. He asked if you'd brought a fiddle to Norway. I said I didn't know! But …" She swallowed hard. "But I did tell him about the heirlooms you put in the hotel safe."

Well, there's one question answered, Chloe thought. She imagined Torstein Landvik bestowing one of his smiles as he pumped Barbara-Eden for information, leaving the girl eager to share something, *anything*, that might interest him.

Barbara-Eden looked wretched. "I didn't think that he would—"

"I know," Chloe said firmly. "We'll let the police sort all that out, okay? None of this is your fault."

"Miss Ellefson?" A gray-haired nurse beckoned from the doorway.

"That's me." Chloe spilled her coffee as she jumped up, but she didn't look back. Please, please, *please*, she thought. Please tell me that Roelke's okay.

"Mr. McKenna lost a lot of blood, but he was lucky."

Chloe's knees went wobbly.

"He had several slash wounds, but those were shallow," the nurse continued. "We were most worried about the deeper wound in his side. Fortunately, the blade didn't hit any organs. He's getting a transfusion, and the doctor's stitching him up now."

"So—so he's going to be all right?" Chloe wanted it spelled out.

The nurse put a reassuring hand on Chloe's wrist. "Your friend is going to be fine."

"He's my fiancé," she whispered, because it mattered. "We're going to be married soon."

Pain woke Roelke the next morning, but he tried to put it aside. He was lucky to be alive. And instead of being incarcerated at the damn hospital as he'd feared, he was back in Room 15 at the Utne Hotel.

And Chloe was in bed beside him. *And*, she'd actually met a relative yesterday. There really was nothing to complain about.

Then he realized that she was awake too, watching him. "Hey," he said.

"You're really okay?"

"I'm really okay." They'd had that exact exchange the night before. Several times.

"When I saw you on the floor, and Torstein standing there with a bloody knife in his hand..."

They'd had this conversation last night, too. But he knew exactly how she felt. When Landvik attacked, all Roelke could think was, Thank God Chloe's back at the museum. The moment she burst into the cabin was one of the worst of his life.

Now he instinctively reached for her, groaning against a throbbing burst of pain. "Jesus. I swear the shoulder where Landvik kicked me hurts worse than the knife wounds. Is he some kind of secret ninja or something?"

"No," Chloe said soberly. "He's a folk dancer who obviously excels at the Halling."

Roelke gritted his teeth and tried again, wriggling his fingers beneath the sheet until he found hers. For a long while he was content to just be, bruised and bloodied but alive, with Chloe's warm hand in his.

Finally she pulled away. "I couldn't sleep last night, so I got up and wrote down some thoughts." She pulled her notebook from the bedside stand and handed it over.

Roelke took a careful look. She'd told him a few things last night—including the astonishing arrival of her great-aunt—but honestly, he hadn't made much sense of it.

<u>Monday</u>

- *Arrived in Bergen, met Sonja at the airport, showed her my heirloom textiles, she speaks of ideas expressed in embroidered symbols*
- *After Sonja left, someone tried to grab my pack—presumably after the textiles*
- *Torstein was in Bergen at the time (per Ellinor)*

<u>Tuesday</u>

- *Torstein arrives in Utne*
- *Rockfall while Roelke hiking up mountain*
- *Sonja returns to Utne early*
- *Klara killed in Høiegård that evening, circle of ashes drawn on her forehead*

<u>Wednesday</u>

- *Trip to Kinsarvik, Ellinor said she couldn't go, but Roelke spots her there*
- *Visit Rev. Brandvold and learn a letter from Amalie has disappeared*

<u>Thursday</u>

- *Fire alarm before dawn, our room ransacked, my heirlooms stolen from hotel safe*
- *I find reference to Amalie in Ellinor's Jørgen Riis file*

Friday

- *Get fake phone message to call home, delay kept us from getting the next ferry*
- *At Fjelland, see whorled heart symbol carved into log, I'm sure I've seen the motif before but can't remember where*
- *Someone cut brake line so we crashed in the tunnel*

Saturday

- *Librarian lies about telling no one that we were going to Fjelland the day before*
- *Met Helene Valebrokk, my great-aunt; she IDs fiddle in photograph as Torstein's, and photo shows similar whorled heart symbol*
- *Helene seems to dislike Torstein*
- *Helene confirms that the museum building called Høiegård came from Fjelland, and that Mom's mother comes from there*
- *In Høiegård, Torstein*

The final notation was incomplete.

"I couldn't even write the words," Chloe admitted. "And I left out the personal stuff too. The places where I experienced flashes of ancestral memory."

"We can hardly present that as evidence," Roelke agreed. He looked over the list again. "You left out Barbara-Eden and the necklace, too."

Chloe shrugged. "That's been resolved. But Ellinor has some explaining to do. Possibly Sonja too, since she's the textile expert and has knowledge about old symbols. Torstein is the constant, though."

Roelke couldn't grab all the dangling threads. "Let's go down and get some breakfast before taking this further." Coffee and smoked salmon and some of that odd-but-tasty brown cheese could only help.

A fax from Rosemary Rossebo was waiting at the hotel desk. *Still no sign of Amalie, but Solveig Sveinsdatter left Bergen on the steamship* Jupiter, *first stop Newcastle, England. From there she would have taken a train to Liverpool and boarded a ship to America.*

"I'm hoping Helene can help sort this out," Chloe said.

Roelke nodded. "There's a whole lot that needs to get sorted out right now."

After hitting the buffet, they were just settling at a table when Ellinor, Sonja, and Reverend Brandvold approached. It was an unlikely trio: Ellinor in jeans and a plain blouse, Sonja in a glowing emerald jacket with matching earrings, Reverend Brandvold in his usual suit.

"Are we interrupting?" Ellinor asked hesitantly.

"Not at all," Roelke assured them. "Pull up a chair."

"We're all concerned," Ellinor said. "Martin here"—she patted her friend's arm—"gave us an update late last night, and Sonja and I have been interviewed by the police again. But we still don't know what's going on."

Sonja leaned forward. "Did Torstein really stab you?"

Since Sonja had walked in on the aftermath, Roelke saw no reason to be evasive. "Several times."

Ellinor winced as if she'd hoped for a different response. "Why? *Why*?"

Chloe caught his gaze. He gave a tiny nod: *Go ahead*.

"I've been trying to lay everything out." Chloe opened her notebook to the correct page and placed it on the table. Reverend Brandvold, Ellinor, and Sonja hitched chairs closer so they could all read.

"What?" Sonja gasped almost at once. "Someone tried to steal your textiles at the airport? I didn't know that."

"At the time we thought it was a random thing," Chloe said.

"You're the textile expert," Roelke pointed out. "Did you tell anyone what Chloe had with her?"

"No." Sonja looked stunned. "But ... I did make some notes when Chloe and I first spoke on the phone, and it's possible that someone saw them on my desk. Ellinor had mentioned the textiles too, so it didn't occur to me to be secretive."

After eyeing her closely, Roelke decided Sonja was telling the truth. He turned to Ellinor and tapped the Wednesday notation. "What about this?"

Ellinor looked chagrined, but she met his gaze. "I did go to Kinsarvik. The man I met deals in antiques. He told me he might have a lead on the Jørgen Riis fiddle I've been trying to trace."

"Why be so secretive?" Chloe demanded.

"Because this particular dealer doesn't have the best reputation." Ellinor picked up a fork and turned it in her fingers. "After years of searching, I'd grown desperate for leads. But I'm not proud of contacting him. In the end, I walked away without seeing what he'd found."

Plausible, Roelke admitted silently.

Chloe, though, wasn't done with Ellinor. "Why was 'Amalie Sveinsdatter' written in some notes in your Jørgen Riis file?"

Ellinor looked startled. "Why were you reading my file?"

"Because it was in plain sight on your desk, and after you told me about the legendary Jørgen Riis, I was curious." Chloe didn't sound even a little bit remorseful. "Amalie was my mother's mother. What do you know about her?"

"Some of the notes in that file go back decades, Chloe. I didn't remember that the name was in there."

Chloe looked unconvinced.

Ellinor's forehead furrowed. "Was the name Solveig there as well?"

"Well, I don't know," Chloe allowed. "At that point I wasn't looking for that name. But I've learned that Solveig was one of Amalie's sisters."

"I've heard tales about Solveig Sveinsdatter." Ellinor nodded pensively. "Her name gets whispered when the old ones speak of that murder I told you about. Some said she was in love with Riis."

"Helene would know. Oh!" Chloe's eyes went wide. "Roelke, she's expecting us up at Fjelland this afternoon. And she doesn't have a phone, so I can't call her."

Pastor Brandvold spoke for the first time. "I'd be glad to drive you. I'm almost as eager to sort out your family story as you are."

Roelke wasn't ready to think about returning to Fjelland, and he didn't want to lose track of the conversation. "That's a kind offer, sir, but let's get back to Torstein."

"I have a theory," Chloe said. "To me, the symbols are significant. Torstein had a symbol on his fiddle that echoes one carved into the house up at Fjelland. That's the farm where the building here called Høiegård came from."

"What does the symbol look like?" Sonja asked.

Chloe pulled the notebook closer, sketched the design, and pushed it back.

Sonja nodded. "Norwegian people have expressed important thoughts in symbols like this since ancient times. They played an important role in ceremonies and rituals. They might be stamped, or embroidered, or carved, or—"

"Are you familiar with this particular symbol?" Roelke wanted the condensed version.

"Historians call these reciprocal spirals." Sonja touched Chloe's sketch with one manicured finger. "Or ram's horns."

"I knew it." Chloe looked pleased with herself.

"This ram's horns design was invoked to encourage male fertility. Horse heads too. Sometimes you see carved horse head handles on ale bowls that end in a circle or spiral." Sonja circled one hand. "Whatever the variation, the symbol is all about male vitality."

Silence descended as they thought about that. Roelke realized that the other tables had all been cleared. Even the buffet tables were empty. He appreciated the staff leaving them alone.

Finally Chloe mused, "I think Torstein is somehow connected to my mother's family, and that he didn't want me to learn that her people came from Høiegård. I think he used that symbol to express power. That's why it's on his fiddle. I suspect that's why a circle got marked on Klara's forehead after she died."

"But why would he kill Klara?" Ellinor cried. "She adored him!"

"Well, I can make a general observation." Sonja toyed with one of her dangling earrings. "Klara might have gotten caught up in something that flew out of control. On more than one occasion I have observed Torstein's powerful impact on gullible women."

Like Barbara-Eden, Roelke thought. And Sonja herself? Who knew. Instead he observed, "The librarian who identified Fjelland as Chloe's family's farm was a young woman. Perhaps Landvik asked her to let him know if we came to the library for research help."

"And a handful of young women work at the hotel," Chloe added. "He could have gotten one of them to pull the fire alarm, and to break into the safe if she'd somehow found the combination. And to give us a fake note saying we needed to call home."

"Surely Klara wasn't involved in the whole mess," Ellinor said. "She was such a lovely girl."

The director sounded sincere, but Roelke still wanted confirmation of Ellinor's relationship with Klara. "Last summer Klara worked full-time at the museum. This year, even though she loved history, she was working full-time at the hotel and just helping out at the museum. Why was that?"

"Because her younger brother is…" Ellinor turned to Sonja for help.

"Developmentally disabled."

"Yes." Ellinor nodded. "Klara wanted a job that included mornings and evenings so she could help at home during the day."

Okay, Roelke thought. Makes sense.

"Chloe, did Torstein try to kill you at the dance yesterday?" Sonja asked. "I can't figure that out. If he wanted you dead, why come running for help after you'd fallen? Why not go down the slope and finish the job?"

"I've been thinking about that too," Roelke said. "That ravine was treacherous. Since Chloe survived the fall, maybe Landvik was too scared of plummeting to his own death if he tried to follow her down the scree."

"Or maybe," Chloe offered, "I just got dizzy and fell, and he was so shocked that decent instincts kicked in."

Roelke was in no mood to give Landvik any credit for decency. "This is all speculation. None of us should repeat anything we've discussed to anyone but the police. I'll give Inspector Naess a call."

Roelke had given a statement the night before, of course. So had Chloe. But a lot of new ideas were floating around.

"Skip the phone call." Chloe leaned toward the window. "Inspector Naess just pulled up."

Roelke went to meet the inspector, and soon led him into the dining room.

"We'll leave you to talk," Ellinor said. She and Sonja and Pastor Brandvold stood.

"Pastor?" Naess said. "I'd like you to stay."

Looking startled, the minister sat back down.

Naess took one of the empty chairs. "There have been some new developments. Miss Ellefson, when we searched Mr. Landvik's room at his cousin's house early this morning we recovered what appear to be the heirlooms that were stolen from the hotel safe. You'll need to formally identify them, but they match your descriptions."

Chloe caught her breath, eyes glimmering. "That's *wonderful*."

Thank you, God, Roelke added silently. A weight slid from his shoulders.

"We can make arrangements before you leave the country. You're cleared for travel. Now, I have a few more questions." Naess looked around the table. "What can any of you tell me about Trine Moen?"

The name was familiar, but Roelke couldn't immediately place it.

Chloe looked confused too. "Trine Moen? The woman doing an exchange program in Wisconsin?"

"Trine Moen is a student at the University of Bergen," Naess said. "One of her classes last year was taught by Torstein Landvik."

Roelke remembered meeting Trine at Marit's funeral. They'd seen her again at the Stoughton Historical Society. She'd been working with Hilda on … Oh, *hell*. He scrubbed his face with his palms. "We were just talking about Landvik's apparent appeal to some women."

Naess turned to the pastor. "I understand you once employed Trine Moen?"

"I did." Pastor Brandvold looked as gobsmacked as Chloe. "I often hire students to help manage my local history collection. Trine worked for me last summer. Later, she gave me a few hours if she came home from school on weekends. And at Christmastime."

Naess scribbled. "The last time you saw Trine Moen was at Christmas?"

"No. She flew back to Norway at the end of April for Easter. She spent a day cataloging a new box of materials for me."

"When did the letter from Amalie Sveinsdatter disappear?" Roelke asked. He was out of line, but he just couldn't help it. "The one you remember even though we couldn't find it?"

"The last time I saw it," Brandvold said grimly, "was right about that time."

That afternoon, Chloe wasn't ashamed of clutching Roelke's hand as Reverend Brandvold drove his old sedan up the torturous road to Fjelland. She might have held her breath while in the tunnel, too.

"Oh my," Barbara-Eden squeaked when they parked. "That was quite a drive."

Her presence on this trip had been the pastor's idea. "She's feeling lost right now," he'd said. "An outing might help." Chloe had been happy to agree.

Today a police car followed them. Inspector Naess asked them to wait in the parking lot while he questioned Helene about Torstein. Since all Helene had been expecting was a little family reunion,

Chloe regretted the need for the inspector's visit, but it couldn't be helped.

Naess returned within half an hour. "Mrs. Valebrokk had two sisters and one brother," he reported. "Torstein Landvik is the grandson of that brother."

Torstein and I truly are related, Chloe thought. She'd suspected it. The confirmation was abhorrent, but it explained so much.

"After Mrs. Valebrokk's parents died, her brother become a traveling preacher," Naess continued. "He had no use for the farm. Mrs. Valebrokk was a widow and sold the orchard she'd inherited from her husband so she could buy the property from her brother. In recent years Landvik was a frequent visitor, but Mrs. Valebrokk gradually realized that the property meant more to him than she did. She said his charm hid a darker side. After Landvik pressured her to put him in her will, she had the locks changed and asked him not to return. And she quietly took him *out* of her will."

"So all of this was for *nothing*." Roelke's hands fisted. "If he'd just been nice to his great-aunt..."

"Apparently so." Naess shook his head and took his leave.

"I would have been overjoyed to meet Torstein as a distant cousin," Chloe said sadly. But when Torstein somehow learned that Helene had distant American relatives, he saw only a threat. He wasn't some anonymous psychopath on a random rampage. Torstein had been deliberate.

"Try to put all that aside for now," Roelke advised. "Your great-aunt must be looking for us."

Helene was waiting on the patio in front of the house. If the interview with Naess had been distressing, she gave no sign. She wore a dusty rose dress, and her white hair was again braided into a coronet. "Welcome to the farm!" She folded Chloe into a gentle hug.

"I hope you don't mind that I brought some friends." Chloe introduced Roelke, Reverend Brandvold, and Barbara-Eden.

"Oh, no." Helene gestured them into lawn chairs. "For so many years I had very little company. Not many were willing to make the climb."

"The climb?" Chloe echoed.

"The road and tunnel only went in about fourteen years ago." Helene patted Chloe's arm. "The government wanted to put some sort of tower up on the ridge, so they paid for it. Before that, we traveled on foot. Everything needed was carried up the mountain."

That meant Helene had hiked up and down until she was what ... somewhere in her seventies? Maybe even early eighties? Chloe felt the weight of her own obvious and glaring inadequacies.

Helene smiled, as if sensing Chloe's thoughts. "But you came here to talk about the family."

"Maybe Barbara-Eden and I should take a walk," Pastor Brandvold suggested. "So you three can talk."

"You're welcome to stay," Chloe assured them, then turned back to her great-aunt. "Could you start by telling me about my grandmother Amalie?"

"Amalie?" Helene looked surprised. "Chloe, Amalie was not your grandmother."

"Yes, she was," Chloe protested. Then she rubbed her temples. "Wasn't she?"

Helene patted Chloe's arm again. "I'll tell you the story."

THIRTY-THREE

Amalie—June 1920

"Wake up, Amalie." Someone shook her arm—her mother, leaning over the bed.

"What are you doing here?" Amalie mumbled. Since Solveig had emigrated to America, Britta was spending the summer at the *seter*.

"Pack your things."

"What?" Amalie sat up, ashamed to be caught napping. Father would whip her if he knew. But she'd hardly slept the night before. Ever since he had—

"Get up!"

"You want me at the *seter*?" Amalie pushed away the covers. "But I'm expected at the Utne Hotel—"

"Just do as I say! We're not going to the *seter*. I made arrangements for the livestock."

Probably the boy from the closest farm, Amalie thought as she stamped into her shoes. He'd helped out before. But why was Mother here?

Everything had turned upside-down. Her brother was off on a week-long fishing trip. Yesterday, on Midsummer, Father had disappeared for hours. He'd come home in a strange mood, sometimes sitting morosely, sometimes pacing. Then he'd dropped to his knees and ordered Amalie to join him. He'd prayed at length about the wickedness of women and fiddlers.

Afterwards she staggered to her feet, sending up her own prayer of gratitude. But Father had one more thing to say: "Amalie. You will marry Gustav Nyhus in the fall."

"Marry Gustav Nyhus?" Amalie stared blankly. Gustav had taken to visiting the hotel lately, but she'd never imagined this. "But—"

"It is decided!" Father had roared. Amalie had cried herself to sleep. The next day he'd left to hunt game in the high mountains—something he'd never done before.

Now this.

Fifteen minutes later she and Britta left the house. Amalie carried her belongings in a satchel—clothes, a hair brush, a lace collar, sewing supplies, her spoon. Britta, carrying a rosemaled *tine* filled with flatbread, cheese, and a few dried apples, headed for the trail that wound down the steep mountain.

Amalie felt even more bewildered. "When will we be back to Høiegård?" Høiegård—or Fjelland, as Father had renamed the farm—had always been her home.

Britta stopped at the edge of the clearing. "I don't know when you'll be back." Her voice trembled, but she firmed it up. "*Please*,

Amalie. Do you want to marry Gustav, or do you want to come with me?"

They caught a ride along the coast with a fisherman, then another ride from a farmer, and reached Helene's house by late afternoon. When Britta knocked on the front door, Amalie hung back. She'd been three when Helene married and left home, and they'd seen each other only a few times since.

Sounds came from within, but it took several minutes for Helene to open the door. "Mother! And … Amalie!" Helene looked astonished to see them. "Please, come in."

Once seated in the kitchen, Britta didn't hesitate. "I need your help, Helene. But first, a question. Have you seen your sister in the last year? Is she here?"

Amalie shot her mother a bewildered look. Solveig was in America … Wasn't she?

A ticking clock on a high shelf sounded loud in the silence. Then, from upstairs, came the sound of a crying baby. Helene made a gesture of futility. "Yes, she is. I'll fetch her."

Britta sighed with obvious relief before bowing her head, lips moving as if in thankful prayer.

Moments later, Solveig crept down the stairs. Her cheeks were hollow. Her eyes were red and swollen, as if she'd been sobbing. And she held a baby in her arms.

"Oh, child. I *so* hoped I'd find you here." Britta gently wrapped her arms around Solveig and the infant, rocking them back and forth.

Finally Solveig broke away and kissed Amalie on the cheek. "As you can see, things didn't happen as I'd planned." Even her voice was thin, worn out.

"Who is this?" Amalie whispered. The baby had a round face and a fuzz of brown hair.

"This is my sweet Marit."

Britta cooed at her first grandchild. "She's beautiful. But I think you should sit down, Solveig. Tell us what's happened."

By the time Solveig finished her tale, Amalie felt numb. "*Father* did this? And Gustav?" The man she was to marry.

"I watched it happen."

Amalie still couldn't grasp what she'd heard. "Are you sure Jørgen is dead?"

"Yes." The word was clipped, brittle.

"But … I saw him just before Midsummer," Amalie protested, as if that might change everything. "He stopped by the hotel for a meal. He was so happy that day. Excited." Now she knew why. He'd been on his way to reunite with Solveig.

"I don't know how Father knew we'd be at the Midsummer dance," Solveig said dully. "But somehow he did."

A memory struck Amalie like a blacksmith's hammer. "Solveig, Gustav was in the dining room the day Jørgen came."

"Did Jørgen mention me?"

Amalie tried to remember. "He said he was on his way to the dance. And … he'd said he'd written a tune for you. I thought he meant in your honor!"

"That must have been enough to make Gustav suspicious," Britta muttered.

"I got to hear the tune." Solveig's gaze grew distant, as if she heard a faraway fiddle. "At least I have that."

Amalie struggled to offer consolation. The words bunched in her throat, inadequate.

Solveig looked at their mother. "Something else must have happened. Isn't that why you're here?"

"Yes." Britta nodded. Solveig's tale had clearly shaken her, but she was calm. "Your father stopped by the *seter* yesterday to say that he's going hunting—"

"He's afraid the police might be hunting *him*." Solveig's mouth twisted bitterly.

"I expect that's true," Britta agreed. "But he also announced that he's promised Amalie to Gustav."

"She mustn't!" Helene exclaimed.

Britta closed her eyes for a moment, as if gathering strength. "Can Amalie stay here for now? I'll see if anyone I trust might know of a job available in Bergen—"

"I don't want to go to Bergen!" Amalie protested. She felt trapped.

But she certainly didn't want to marry Gustav, either. She wanted to go back in time. She wanted to sing with Solveig while doing chores at the *seter*, and to giggle with friends at the Utne Hotel. She wasn't brave like her older sisters. They'd both been eager to leave home. The thought terrified Amalie.

"At least stay here while we think things through," Helene urged.

Britta opened her little purse and dumped its contents on the table. "I brought some money for Amalie's keep."

Solveig's eyebrows rose. "That's more than a few coins set aside from the milk money."

"Perhaps." Britta hitched her shoulders, unrepentant.

Amalie stared at the money. Had Mother raided Father's purse? How else could she have saved so much?

"We don't know what Father will do next," Solveig said slowly. "He might look for Amalie here."

Amalie crimped her lips together. The thought of Father finding her was terrifying too.

"I've a little money set aside as well," Solveig said. "Added to that"—she nodded at the coins on the table—"it's enough to get Amalie to America."

Amalie's stomach lurched. No, no, no! Solveig couldn't be serious.

"America is *your* dream," Helene reminded Solveig.

Solveig shrugged wearily. "But I'm not well enough to travel. Amalie should go instead."

"I couldn't possibly!" Amalie insisted.

But one by one, her mother and sisters whittled away her objections. "You'll have to travel under my name," Solveig said. "I have a passport, and an *attest* from the pastor." A testimonial of good character was required for passage.

I'm losing my home, Amalie thought. I'm losing my name. Who will I be?

"And Amalie ..." Solveig hesitated, then leaned forward. "I want you to take Marit with you."

"*What?* No! How would I manage? I—"

"Please." Solveig went to the cradle, scooped up Marit, and slipped the infant into Amalie's unwilling arms. "I need to know that *both* of you will be safe."

Amalie stared at Marit. She smelled sweet and sour at once. "I don't know how to take care of a baby!"

"No one does, until they have to." Their mother's voice was firm. "You'll manage."

Amalie felt the baby's weight in her arms. She thought of Høiegård, long taken for granted. She couldn't imagine crossing the ocean on a ship filled with strangers, only to find more strangers in America. She would feel so alone…

Marit waved two tiny fists as if to say, *You won't be alone. I'll be there.*

Those baby fingers seemed to squeeze Amalie's heart. If Solveig is strong enough to give up her baby, she thought, I must be strong enough to take her.

That night, as Amalie lay staring at the shadows, she heard Solveig and Mother murmuring in the next bed. "Mother, I wish you could go to America as well." That was Solveig.

"There is not enough money."

"Perhaps go to Bergen, then? Surely you won't go back to Father."

A long silence passed before Britta answered. "I will go back to Høiegård. I have to protect the farm."

"Oh, *Mother*…"

"Someday," Britta said, "one of you girls might need it."

Amalie didn't think Solveig was going to answer. Finally she said, "I have judged you unfairly, Mother. I'm sorry."

At dawn the four women gathered in the kitchen. Amalie wanted more time to prepare, to get used to the idea, but the others had insisted she leave at once.

One of Helene's neighbors agreed to bring his wagon and take Amalie to Bergen, where a shipping agent would arrange her passage. Solveig gave her the travel documents and wrote down the name of Jørgen's American friend. "He'll help you get settled."

"Amalie, I have something for you." Britta's eyes were glassy, but her voice didn't waver. She pressed a square of white linen into

Amalie's hands. "For your embroidery. Whenever you get homesick on the ship or in America, work on this."

Just holding the clean new cloth was a comfort. Amalie did love creating *Hardangersaum*. The precision required would help occupy her hands—and her mind.

"I have a gift for you as well." Helene held up the embroidered *handaplagg* she'd used to cover her hands on her wedding day. "Your great-great-great-grandmother received this when she got married in 1765. It's been passed down ever since. It will help protect you."

The gifts went into the painted *tine*, tucked safe in Amalie's bag. Helene filled her own small bridal trunk with sheets and a blanket, sacks of peas and beans, three loaves of crusty bread. Solveig added the linens and clothes she'd made for Marit. "You'll need to find another new mother on the ship. Save some coins to pay for milk."

The neighbor knocked on the door. "All set?"

Amalie clung to her mother and Helene. Then she squared her shoulders and reached for Marit.

Solveig started to surrender the baby but stopped. She's changed her mind, Amalie thought.

Then her sister began to sing a beautiful lullaby that Hardanger women had sung to their babies for hundreds of years. A salty lump filled Amalie's throat. When the song ended, Solveig kissed Marit and gently settled the baby in her younger sister's arms.

I must not fail, Amalie thought. Her mother and sisters had taken risks, made sacrifices, so that *she* would be safe. That same strength was inside her. She just needed to find it.

"I love you all." Amalie raised her chin. "And Solveig, I promise to *always* do whatever I think is best for Marit."

THIRTY-FOUR

HELENE'S TALE LEFT CHLOE teary-eyed and sniffling. Roelke passed her a tissue.

"Not all family stories are happy ones, I'm afraid," Helene said.

Chloe blew her nose. "I hate knowing that my grandma lost the man she loved *and* her baby."

"Solveig was half dead herself by the time she made her way back to Orchard House that Midsummer." Helene pinched her lips into a thin line as she remembered. "In shock. Bleeding. She hadn't recovered well from childbirth."

"But why didn't she report what happened to the authorities?"

"No one else witnessed the incident. After Jørgen went over the ledge, Father and Gustav and their helper ran off. Solveig managed to scramble down to Jørgen, but he'd hit his head on a rock. He was already dead."

Chloe put her hand on Roelke's knee, just needing to know he was there.

"I told her, 'Solveig, go to America,'" Helene said. "'Rest here, gather your strength. Then take your baby to America.' But she didn't have the heart for the journey anymore. Not without Jørgen. She died a month after Amalie left."

"And your mother?"

"She did go back home. I saw her only a few more times before she died." Helene spread her hands, palms up. "Somehow she managed to live with my father, and to keep this place. She loved it so." She nodded, clearly remembering days long gone. "I did my best to keep the orchard I inherited from my husband going, but it was too much. I don't know what I would have done if my mother hadn't clung to this mountain."

Chloe stared over the lawn, trying to imagine them all. "You never met Jørgen, right?"

Helene shook her head. "No. He must have been special."

"What happened to the fiddle he made for Solveig? The director at the Hardanger Folkemuseum has been trying to track that down for decades."

"It was the only thing Solveig had left of him, and I think she desperately wanted to cling to it. But as Amalie settled in the wagon that day, Solveig called for the driver to wait. She fetched the fiddle and gave it to Amalie." Perplexed, Helene looked at Chloe. "Didn't your mother end up with it?"

"No. I found the Hardanger doily, the blackwork *handaplagg,* and a little Hardanger bride doll tucked in a painted *tine.*"

"A doll?" Helene repeated thoughtfully. "Amalie must have purchased that for the baby in Bergen. I never saw a doll."

"Well, I never saw a—"

"*Chloe.*" Roelke gave her a meaningful look.

It took a moment, but she caught on. “Oh, my, God. Hilda’s fiddle.”

“I’m thinkin’,” Roelke agreed.

Chloe pressed one palm against her forehead. *That’s* where she’d seen the ram’s horns symbol. On Hilda’s fiddle.

Then she explained to Helene, “I think Mom gave Solveig’s fiddle to her best friend.”

“It has devils on the sides?”

Chloe frowned. “No, the sides are rosemaled. But…” She thought that over and winced. “Mom was a skilled painter. She could have created a design over the devils.” To Chloe’s curator heart it seemed a sad desecration, but perhaps Mom hadn’t approved of the devils. Or maybe Mom had simply wanted to put something of herself into the gift to her dearest friend.

“Solveig believed the devils were Jørgen’s way of…” Helene paused, searching for the right words. “Of standing up against men like our father.”

Thumbing his nose at the zealots, Chloe thought. “My mother’s adoptive parents were wonderful people. My mom had a good life. Still, I so wish she could have known Jørgen and Solveig.”

“Solveig adored her daughter.” Helene’s voice trembled. “What was left of her heart broke when Amalie and Marit left.”

Chloe nibbled her lower lip before asking, “And you don’t know what happened to Amalie?”

“She said she’d write when she reached Wisconsin. I never heard from her again.”

Tragedy piled on tragedy. “I’m so sorry,” Chloe said. “We’ll probably never know why she decided to go to the orphanage that day, or what happened to her after that.”

"Perhaps." Reverend Brandvold broke his long silence. "Don't forget, I believe I had a letter from Amalie in my possession. Perhaps her letters went astray because she addressed them to Solveig, who was first in hiding and later, deceased. Anyway, if Trine Moen found the letter *I* had, and passed it on to Torstein, it's possible that the police will recover it."

"That would feel like a miracle. I will wait and see." Helene smoothed her skirt and looked at Barbara-Eden. "Young lady, would you come with me? I have a pitcher of lemonade in the refrigerator."

After they disappeared inside, Roelke reached for Chloe's hand. "You must feel overwhelmed."

"Kinda," she admitted. It would take time to process everything she'd learned.

Barbara-Eden returned with a tray holding the lemonade, glasses, and a plate of cookies. Helene followed and handed a small leather-bound book to Chloe. "This is my dearest treasure. Solveig wrote down family stories she learned from our mother."

Chloe's eyes went wide. Easing the book open, she found lines of fading script covering brittle pages. Everything was, of course, written in Norwegian. Still. No way am I getting on an airplane without a copy of this, she thought.

But ... no. It was impossible. The book was far too fragile to photocopy.

"I could transcribe it for you," Barbara-Eden offered, as if reading Chloe's mind. "Mrs. Valebrokk, might I come back to work on that?"

Helene looked delighted. "That's a lovely idea."

"I'll do as much as I can before you leave," Barbara-Eden promised. "If I don't finish, I'll mail you the final pages."

"That would be perfect," Chloe said. "Thank you."

"Now." Helene smiled. "I want to hear about *you.* You're getting married?" She looked from Chloe to Roelke. "When?"

"We haven't quite worked that out," Chloe admitted. "But soon."

"Why don't you get married here?"

Chloe sighed. "Actually, Aunt Helene, Roelke and I did think about getting married while we're in Norway. But there's not enough time to make the arrangements."

"I'm afraid that's true," Reverend Brandvold added sadly.

"Then perhaps you can come back," Helene suggested.

When police officers and museum curators earn a whole lot more money than we do now, Chloe thought. "Perhaps."

Roelke reached for her hand. "Helene, do you mind if we take a walk?"

Helene did not. Roelke led Chloe across the lawn to the high overlook. Having fallen from one cliff already, she almost balked. But he spotted a flat stone back from the edge, perfect for sitting.

"I'm sorry the conversation took that turn," he said. "Helene didn't know it's a sore subject."

Chloe gazed ahead. Beyond the sun-dazzled fjord far below, white-frosted mountain peaks scraped the sky. Veils of water plunged down stony clefts. "This place is beyond beautiful."

"It is."

She turned over a new thought, examining it from different directions, and felt a tiny bubble of excitement rise inside. "Roelke, let's get married here. Right here in Helene's front yard."

He frowned. "Chloe, you know we can't—"

"I've got an idea." She took a deep breath. "Neither one of us wants to get married at the courthouse. So let's make our commitment to each other here. It won't be legal, but I simply can't believe that God would take offense."

"But…"

"Have you ever seen a more holy place? A more magnificent cathedral?"

Roelke regarded her, rubbing his chin.

"We can write our own vows. And when we've exchanged them, in our hearts we'll be truly married."

"It's a nice idea. But I want our marriage to be official."

Well, I do too, Chloe thought. "So… when we get home we'll go to the courthouse and make it legal. At that point it will be a formality, so I won't mind. And after *that*, we can have a reception for our family and friends at the Sons of Norway lodge." She stopped then, giving Roelke time to catch up. If they were going to do this, it had to be because they *both* wanted to.

He looked away for a long moment, thinking. Then he grinned. "Let's do it."

Three days later, Chloe and Roelke dressed in their best: Chloe's only remaining skirt and a blouse; Roelke's dark trousers and a white dress shirt. "I wish we could just go to the farm," Chloe murmured as they left their room.

"Inspector Naess said this wouldn't take long," Roelke reminded her. "And I'd like an update."

Officer Naess was waiting in one of the hotel's side parlors. "I have good news," he said without preamble. "Torstein Landvik has given a full confession."

"Wow." Chloe tried to take that in. She felt more sadness than relief.

"I'm surprised," Roelke admitted. "I'd expected him to fight all the way."

Naess offered a hard, satisfied smile. "He tried, but we had a lot of evidence. First, Trine Moen has admitted to Wisconsin police that she collaborated with Landvik."

"Oh." Chloe had hoped that Torstein had duped Trine.

"She confirmed she'd found a letter from Amalie Sveinsdatter in Pastor Brandvold's things, and passed it on to Landvik," Naess continued. "And she confirmed that Landvik believed that your *real* goal, Miss Ellefson, was to claim his inheritance and steal heirlooms he thought should belong to him."

Chloe clenched her teeth. That part still really hurt.

"How did Landvik learn that Chloe was a distant relative?" Roelke asked.

Naess glanced at his notebook. "Klara Evenstad and Trine Moen *both* helped Landvik search for family history. And once Moen was in Wisconsin, she began searching records there. She knew she'd made an astonishing find when she got a good look at Hilda Omdahl's fiddle."

"Trine had worked at the Hardanger Folkemuseum," Chloe observed. "She'd certainly know that a Riis fiddle would be an extraordinary find."

"Mrs. Omdahl told Trine that it had been a gift from your mother." He nodded at Chloe. "And the details you provided to Ellinor Falk and Sonja Gullickson about your family search, and the heirlooms you were bringing, enraged Landvik."

Torstein Landvik was gunning for me before I ever decided to come to Norway, Chloe thought. It was creepy-horrible to imagine him scheming about her while she was oblivious to his existence.

"*And*," Naess continued, "we have the silver necklace—"

"The necklace?" Chloe frowned in confusion. What did the necklace have to do with anything?

"After Barbara-Eden Kirkevoll confessed to taking it from Klara's locker, we returned it to Klara's mother. She found a note inside—"

"It's a locket?" Chloe blurted. Roelke put a hand on her knee. "Sorry. I don't mean to interrupt."

"It's an antique bridal locket," Naess explained. "Brides carried the pastor's fee inside for safekeeping. When Klara's mother identified the locket, she showed me a hidden catch."

Well, shut my mouth, Chloe thought. Inspector Naess was the first cop to school her in historical detail.

The inspector leaned forward, elbows on knees. "Klara had found a letter from Trine Moen in Landvik's things. It referred to the letter from Amalie Sveinsdatter that Moen stole."

Chloe waited until she was sure he was finished. "Have you recovered the letter?" She longed to find out what it said.

He nodded. "It is evidence, but in time, it will be returned to Pastor Brandvold."

Roelke stroked his chin with thumb and forefinger. "So, Moen knew what Landvik was doing, and helped him."

"Yes," Naess confirmed. "But Klara Evenstad assumed Torstein's interest in family history was completely innocent."

Why wouldn't she? Chloe thought. Klara had loved history. She'd understood that heritage and traditions were important for their own sake, not for financial gain.

"Landvik told Klara that he wanted to surprise you with the discovery that you were distant cousins of some sort. But after you arrived, she found Trine's note and discovered that Landvik had completely misled her. She confronted him about it."

"She must have been shocked to discover she was involved in something unethical," Roelke said.

"And to realize that she was not Torstein's one and only," Chloe added.

"Landvik's reaction frightened Klara. When she got upset, he begged her to meet him in that cabin, Høiegård, later. Said he'd explain everything. Evidently they'd met there before. Landvik knew it had come from his old family farm, so that must have appealed to him."

"A part of Klara must have still believed, or at least hoped, that Torstein could provide some kind of explanation." Chloe grasped her shoulders. She hated picturing Klara daring to meet Torstein—only to be murdered.

"But part of her also feared the worst," Naess said. "Before meeting him Klara wrote a note about what she'd discovered, hid it in the locket, and left that in her locker."

An employee carrying a bucket of cleaning supplies appeared, spotted them, and backed out. Naess continued, "Moen's relationship with Landvik had become strained. She hoped that if she could actually present the Riis fiddle to him, she'd win his affection."

Chloe looked at Roelke. "Kent said Trine was having boyfriend troubles, remember?"

Roelke looked revolted. "I do not get why so many women went gaga for that guy."

"Trine Moen went to Hilda Omdahl's house the night of Marit Kallerud's funeral," Naess said. "She tried to talk Mrs. Omdahl into selling the fiddle. Things got heated."

"And Hilda ended up in a coma," Chloe said bitterly.

"Moen panicked and fled without the fiddle. She hoped the problem would go away." Naess's mouth twisted with disgust. "That's a quote. But she really panicked when Hilda showed signs of improvement."

"Which, fortunately, she did." Chloe had enjoyed a brief but wondrous telephone conversation with Aunt Hilda the day before.

"Moen called Landvik, and all he did was criticize her for not finishing the job. I think that's why Moen was so eager to talk to the police."

"A woman scorned," Roelke murmured.

Naess leaned back in his chair. "As you see, we had a lot to lay out to Landvik. He knew he was caught. He confessed to trying to grab your pack at the airport, to killing Klara Evenstad, to ransacking your room in search of any other heirlooms, and to stealing your textiles from the safe. He enlisted the help of a female employee here for that."

Somebody's in big trouble, Chloe thought.

"Landvik also confessed to tampering with your rental car. He knew that once you had Amalie's birthplace narrowed down, it would be easy enough to find the farm name. His librarian friend had promised to give you false information, but another librarian was there?"

Roelke confirmed that with a nod.

"So," Naess continued, "all she could do was tell him that you'd identified the family farm and were going to visit. Landvik's hotel friend left the 'call home' message to delay you, drove Landvik up to

Høiegård, and left him there. He hid, waited until you'd left the car, and damaged the brake system. Then he made his way down the mountain on foot and hitchhiked back to Utne." The inspector closed his notebook, tucked it in a pocket, and stood.

"Thank you," Chloe said. "It's good to know all this before we leave."

Roelke shook hands with the inspector but glanced at her. "Chloe, would you mind waiting outside?"

She shrugged. "Um … sure." Roelke probably wanted to wrangle some final detail from the inspector.

Chloe went out to the front porch and stared over the fjord. Laughter drifted from the dining room where guests were enjoying breakfast. A car door slammed. Then Roelke joined her.

Whatever he'd learned could wait, she decided. "I don't want to talk about Landvik any more today."

"Me neither," Roelke agreed. "Let's go get married."

When Chloe and Roelke arrived at the mountain farm, Helene and Barbara-Eden soon whisked Chloe inside. "It's tradition for friends and relatives to help a bride prepare for the ceremony," Helene said. "Our *stabbur*, where women used to dress for weddings, was torn down years ago. But my bedroom will do."

When Helene opened the door, Chloe's mouth dropped open. Draped on the bed were the components of a *bunad*: red skirt with colorful trim, a white apron with cutwork embroidery, blouse, dark jacket, and a beaded bodice insert.

"I hope you will wear these," Helene told her. "You've brought joy to this farm and made me a happy woman."

The makeshift bridal attire Chloe had pulled on that morning didn't stand a chance. "I'd be honored."

Even with help, it took some time and several safety pins to get Chloe dressed. "This is similar to my mother's favorite *bunad*," she said wistfully. "I love it, but I do wish she was here."

"I think your mother will be smiling down," Barbara-Eden said. Surprisingly, that thought helped.

"You must wear my *sølje* too," Helene murmured, fastening a lacey pin with quivering teardrops at Chloe's throat. "Dangling silver frightens evil away."

After the week she'd had, Chloe welcomed help from any quarter.

"And the final touch." The old woman removed a crown from a faded black hatbox. "Many brides in our family have worn this."

"Oh *my*." Chloe took a deep breath. This was all becoming real. She'd worn *bunads* when dancing, or at special functions, but she'd never imagined wearing a bridal crown. Helene carefully positioned the heavy crown, tied the ribbons beneath Chloe's chin, and smoothed the long blond hair flowing loose.

"You mustn't let the crown slip," Helene advised. "That's bad luck."

"I'll be careful."

Barbara-Eden held out a small, flat box. "We have another surprise."

Chloe accepted it and removed the lid. "My *handaplagg*! I thought the police still had it!"

Helene smiled. "You have Mr. McKenna to thank for this."

That's why Roelke wanted a moment alone with Inspector Naess this morning, Chloe thought. He must have talked the other officer into bringing the cloth.

Helene arranged the *handaplagg* over Chloe's hands. "We don't have the proper muff, but it looks lovely."

Roelke was waiting in the living room. When Chloe walked in, he sucked in an audible breath. "You," he said huskily, "have never looked more beautiful."

"You look amazing yourself," she countered. "Where did those come from?" His trousers and dress shirt were now topped with an embroidered red vest and a frock coat.

"Ellinor knew what Helene had in mind and offered me the loan of a folk costume from the museum," he explained. "I hope you don't mind that I passed on the breeches."

"Not at all." Roelke did look *very* good in the vest and coat. Best of all, Roelke McKenna, uptight cop, looked happy. "And thank you for this." She raised her hands, indicating the cloth.

Pastor Brandvold, who'd happily declared himself *kjøgemester* for the day, poked his head in the door. "Your other guests have arrived." Through the window Chloe saw Ellinor and Sonja waiting on the patio.

"Ready?" Roelke took her arm.

Chloe nodded. "Absolutely."

They led the others across the lawn to the stone overlook. A misty morning drizzle had cleared, and sun shone on the mountains. It's a fine day for a wedding, Chloe thought. For *our* wedding.

The pastor had asked if he might say a few words. "Let's begin with the *bryllupsfred,*" he boomed in his preaching voice. "The wedding peace. It is tradition to cast aside all hurts and grudges that might be troubling those in attendance. There have been too many of those in recent days." He paused. "I declare this to be a gathering of love and joy."

Chloe blinked back tears, feeling ridiculously emotional. Pastor Brandvold had set the perfect tone. She didn't want to think about anything but making a forever commitment to Roelke.

With the sun on their shoulders, she and Roelke faced each other and exchanged the wedding vows they'd written together. "I promise to be your devoted companion, to nurture you, to go adventuring with you, to share life's joys and sorrows, in sickness and in health, for as long as we both shall live." Roelke leaned in to seal the deal with a lingering kiss.

Pastor Brandvold closed the ceremony by singing an old Norwegian folk song in a rich baritone. Barbara-Eden snapped photographs. Aunt Helene dabbed her eyes with a handkerchief. Ellinor beamed. Even Sonja looked moved.

This is the most wonderful day of my life, Chloe thought. She wanted it to last forever. Roelke smiled at her: *I feel the same way.*

When the song ended, Reverend Brandvold offered a prayer before congratulating the happy couple. "May God shower you with blessings." He clasped his hands together. "Now, refreshments will be served on the patio."

Chloe stepped carefully from the stone, keeping her head still. The bridal crown was heavy, but in a good way. The weight connected her to all the women who had worn this crown on their wedding days. The weight also demanded that she stand straight and tall. Based on the stories Barbara-Eden had transcribed so far, that felt appropriate too.

Barbara-Eden had baked a luscious chiffon cake with strawberries, which she served with champagne on the patio. She'd also gathered mountain wildflowers to decorate the table. "Everything is perfect." Chloe kissed the girl's cheek. "Thank you."

They lingered, savoring the celebration. All too soon, though, it was time for Chloe to change her clothes and say her farewells.

Ellinor gave Chloe a warm hug. "I couldn't be happier for you two. Please keep in touch as you develop your exhibit and program in Wisconsin."

"I will," Chloe promised.

Ellinor hesitated. "Chloe, did you ever wonder why I'm so interested in Jørgen Riis?"

"Um … not really," she said honestly. Museum people often had some singular passion.

"Gustav Nyhus was my grandfather."

Chloe had not seen that coming. "I see."

"When I was growing up, I heard hushed whispers about some horrific trouble he'd had with Riis. It became obvious that my grandfather was involved in something awful." Ellinor rubbed one hand with the other. "I wanted to find Riis's story. I felt the need to atone, I guess. The one thing I heard over and over, as a child and later doing interviews, was that Jørgen Riis had a rare talent. I wanted to give him the credit he was due."

"You still can," Chloe said. "I won't forget to send photos of the Riis fiddle that ended up in Wisconsin." She'd already told Ellinor about Hilda's fiddle. "And do come visit. You can document it yourself."

Ellinor brightened. "I'll do that."

Sonja's farewell was more restrained. "Chloe, I'm sorry that you had reason to think I might be involved in the theft of your textiles."

Chloe tried not to squirm. "It was just a passing idea. Roelke is trained to consider all possibilities."

"Hold on to him, Chloe. You know what they say. A good man is hard to find." For a moment Sonja's gaze was unguarded. Chloe read longing there, and regret. Then the curator smiled, and the moment passed. "I'm glad you were able to carry the *handaplagg* today."

"Ever since that day we met at the airport, I've been wanting to ask you about it!" Chloe darted to her daypack, extracted the box, and returned with the cloth held over her palms. "You said the woman who did the embroidery was expressing herself. What do you think she was trying to say?"

Sonja leaned close. "Actually, I think more than one woman contributed to this cloth. The stitching is excellent, but there are some minuscule variations."

Okay, even better, Chloe thought, but that wasn't what she wanted. "What about the symbols? What do they *mean*?"

"Well, this figure"—Sonja pointed—"probably represents the *disir*, ancient spirits who guarded women and families. The tiny stitches in these squares represent seeded fields, and the hope that the bride be blessed with many children. Crooked lines were added to confuse malicious spirits, and this sun to celebrate all that is good. My favorite is the tree of life, with roots in the earth and top branches in heaven." Sonja smiled. "I think the women in your family wanted to protect their daughters and granddaughters from evil, and to bless their lives with love and balance and holy light."

Love and balance and holy light, Chloe thought. Who could ask for more?

Barbara-Eden was next. "Thank you, Chloe. You were kind during a—a bad time."

"If I helped, then I'm glad. And I'm so grateful to you for transcribing my family stories." The tales had filled a void, reminding

Chloe that even though daughters and mothers sometimes misunderstood each other, even resented each other, bonds remained. "What you said about my mom earlier—you were right. I could feel her presence here today."

Barbara-Eden looked pleased. "And I want you to know that I'll keep an eye on your great-aunt Helene, Chloe. I like coming here, and she said I'm welcome any time."

Chloe put her hands on the girl's shoulders. "You have no idea how reassuring that is. We'll stay in touch."

The hardest good-bye came next. "Aunt Helene," Chloe began, "meeting you has been a dream come true. And having our wedding here..." Her voice trailed away. She couldn't find the right words.

"When I was a child, this was still considered a poor farm," Helene said. "But now..." She waved an arm toward the vista. "You've reminded me how special this place really is. I hope to transfer the property to a preservation group so that after I'm gone, people can come learn about the old days."

"I *love* that idea!"

"And I'm officially changing the farm name back to Høiegård." Helene smiled. "I should have done it long ago. It wasn't appropriate to change it in the first place! I'm sure my father renamed it just to make himself feel powerful."

"I'll always think of this place as Høiegård." Chloe wrapped her arms gently around Helene's thin shoulders.

Helene took Chloe's hand. "Will you take advice from an old woman? To escape my father, I left home at fourteen and married at fifteen. My husband was a good man, but I did not love him. I don't know what that feels like."

That made Chloe sad.

"But I do know what true love *looks* like. I saw it in Solveig's eyes when she spoke of Jørgen. I see it when you look at Roelke, and when he looks at you. Don't ever take that for granted."

"I won't," Chloe whispered. "I promise."

Roelke was waiting nearby. "Ready? Pastor Brandvold has already gone to the car." The minister would drive Chloe and Roelke back to Utne, where they would spend a final night at the old hotel before heading home.

Chloe took one last look over the farm. "It's so hard to leave."

"This place will always be a part of you."

She nodded, then leaned against his shoulder. "Just like you."

THIRTY-FIVE

A MONTH LATER, THUNDEROUS applause greeted Chloe and Roelke when they walked into Stoughton's Sons of Norway lodge hall for their reception. "Oh my," Chloe murmured. The room was packed with friends from high school, friends from Old World Wisconsin, friends of her parents. Cops from the Eagle and Milwaukee Police Departments were there, and Roelke's cousin Libby with her kids and her steady, Adam. Museum director Ellinor Falk had even scheduled her trip to Wisconsin to coincide with the event.

"What a great space!" Roelke murmured. The lodge hall had retained most of the original church windows, including a huge work of stained glass that lent a warm golden glow to the gathering.

It took a long time for well-wishers to pass through the receiving line. Kent Andreasson was one of the last to greet them. "Congratulations!" he exclaimed before leaning close. "I'm so sorry about everything that happened. Both over there and here. With Trine. I feel just horrible."

"None of it was your fault," Chloe said. "Let's try to forget about all that right now."

"Of course." Kent looked relieved. "I'm truly happy for you both." He moved on.

After the last handshake, Roelke shook his head and murmured, "Holy toboggans. I didn't expect quite so many people."

"It means a lot, doesn't it?" Chloe laced her fingers through his and took her first good look around. "And the lodge members have done an awesome job. This party is more Norwegian than the one we had in Norway." The hall was adorned with Norwegian flags and banners. Many people wore *bunads*, and some of the Old World staffers wore period clothing. Sprightly folk music played on a sound system. Chloe's sister, Kari, had baked a *kransekake*—the traditional cake made with almond meal and powdered sugar, baked in rings, stacked high and decorated with icing, flowers, ribbons, and tiny flags.

"The lodge members have been great," Roelke agreed. "And now, I could use something to drink."

Before they could reach the refreshments table, Kari joined them. "The cake is amazing," Chloe told her sister, while Roelke headed toward the punch bowl.

"You two did make it legal, right?" Kari asked. "There are eighteen layers in that cake, Chloe. I went to a lot of trouble." Then her teasing look disappeared, and she surprised Chloe with a quick hug. "I wanted to do it. I'm so glad you and Roelke found each other."

"Our marriage is absolutely legal," Chloe assured her. "But listen, I've got something to show you." She pulled Kari out of the traffic flow. "Guess what came in the mail today? A copy of the letter Amalie wrote from Stoughton. Want to hear it?"

Kari hesitated only briefly before nodding. "At this point, yes. I do."

Chloe pulled a folded piece of paper from her purse. "The original was in Norwegian, of course, but Pastor Brandvold sent a transcription. Let me share the most important part." She found the appropriate paragraph and began to read.

Solveig, before we parted I promised that I would always do my very best for your precious Marit. Before we left Bergen I bought a bride doll for her, to one day help remind her of the country where she was born. On the journey I often felt overwhelmed with the responsibility of her care, but I have also come to love her as my own. I often sing to her, and whisper stories about her brave mother.

Now I am trying to be brave. You see, I have promised myself to a wonderful man. Rasmus and I met on the ship and already I can not imagine life without him. He had no prospects in Norway and is very poor, but has accepted a job with a railroad company. It will be his job to travel throughout the West to inspect ongoing work projects and consider new ones.

Rasmus already loves Marit. When we began speaking of marriage we imagined becoming a family of three. But Solveig, since arriving in Wisconsin, and talking with his brother (who already works for the railroad, and made arrangements for the job), I have come to realize that the life Rasmus and I will lead is no life for an infant. We will be moving from here to there, not making a permanent home for who knows how long. After much anguished thought and prayer, and many tears, I have decided that Marit's best chance for a happy life does not lie with me.

Many Norwegians have settled in Stoughton, Wisconsin. Tomorrow I will take sweet Marit to an orphanage, with the request that she find a home with a well-settled Norwegian couple.

My heart breaks as I write these words. Please don't think of me harshly. It is not laziness that has led me to this decision, but only love and my promise to you to always put Marit's needs first. I will leave several family treasures with her in hopes that one day she can rediscover her true homeland.

"There's more, but that's the main bit." Chloe folded the paper back away. When she looked up, she saw a tear trickling down Kari's cheek. "I know." She'd had time to think about Amalie's decision, but re-reading the letter still brought a lump to her throat. Would I, Chloe wondered, have been strong enough to make that decision? She wasn't sure.

"Well, now we know," Kari managed. "Chloe ... thank you for that. For persevering. You were right all along."

Before Chloe could answer, Roelke approached with a crystal cup of cranberry punch. "Everything okay?" he murmured as Kari swiped at her eyes. Chloe nodded, sipping gratefully.

Dad stepped up to what had once been the church chancel. After tapping a microphone, he waited until the room fell silent to thank everyone for coming. "My family is blessed to belong to such a community." He paused to clear his throat. "And we're blessed to welcome Roelke and his family and friends to our community."

"That's a long speech for my dad," Chloe whispered. "He's going to make me cry."

Dad offered a toast to the newlyweds, and everyone raised glasses of punch or *akevitt*. "And now," Dad concluded, "we have a special surprise." He looked toward a side door just as Kent walked in—with Aunt Hilda on his arm.

Chloe gasped. "I didn't think she was coming!" She had visited Hilda, now recuperating at home with full-time caregivers, several times. Chloe had found the tiny telltale letter *R* that identified the fiddle maker as Jørgen Riis, and she'd explained what she'd learned about Hilda's fiddle. Hilda had confirmed that it had been a gift from Marit, but a private conversation had been impossible.

Kari smiled. "She wanted to surprise you."

Kent helped Hilda to a chair on the dais, then handed her the Hardanger fiddle that Jørgen Riis had made for Solveig. As Hilda began to play, Roelke put his arm around Chloe's shoulders. She closed her eyes, hearing not just Hilda's beautiful music but Grandfather Jørgen's too, and Grandmother Solveig's. It was magical.

After the tune, Roelke cocked his head toward the front. "You go say hello."

Chloe greeted Hilda with a kiss on the cheek and pulled another chair close. "I am overjoyed to see you here, and to hear you play."

"I'm grateful to be here," Hilda said fervently. "But—there's something we need to talk about."

"Okay." Chloe scooched her chair even closer.

Hilda's eyes were troubled. "Chloe, I'm sorry I never told you that your mother gave me the fiddle. We were fifteen, I think. I'd heard someone play at a lodge meeting and was crazy to learn how. And Marit told me she'd painted the sides, which made it even more special. I didn't know she'd inherited the fiddle." She lifted a palm, let it drop back to her lap. "I did wonder where she got it… but that was a different time. Back then farmers stored cattle feed in their grandparents' rosemaled trunks. Ale bowls and *ambars* disappeared into attics. Heirlooms represented the past, and the immigrants' children wanted to be American. But … I should have asked."

"Aunt Hilda, you have nothing to feel bad about," Chloe assured her.

"When you and Kari were in high school, I tried to give the fiddle back to Marit. I thought it should go to one of you girls. But Marit said no, that she hadn't changed her mind about the gift."

Chloe snorted. "Mom was not one to change her mind."

"But," Hilda continued, "she *did* say that if it troubled me, I should leave the fiddle to you in my will."

"To me?" Chloe repeated. "Why me? Kari was closer to Mom."

"Marit didn't say. Maybe it was because she never really knew how to connect with you."

Or maybe, Chloe thought, Mom trusted me to figure everything out.

"I almost told you," Hilda said. "The day of your mother's funeral."

Chloe nodded, remembering.

Hilda leaned forward and clasped Chloe's hand with surprising strength. "I want you to take the fiddle now."

Chloe placed one palm on the fiddle. She'd seen it many times, but now it told new stories about people and places she couldn't have imagined. The pearly inlay and black inked designs held new meaning. Jørgen had included the twin spirals she'd remembered, but also the squares representing fertile fields, and an ornate sun. The designs were balanced and spoke of his dreams of a happy family. It was a precious artifact.

But it was not one she wanted to possess. "Thanks to *you*, Aunt Hilda, that fiddle brings people joy. That's as it should be. I can't accept it."

"Well, I have to do something," Hilda fretted. "Now that we know who made it, it seems too important for me to keep."

"It would be nice to have an expert remove a bit of Mom's painting, to expose a devil or two," Chloe mused. "Both Jørgen's handiwork and Mom's painting are part of this fiddle's story now. But Aunt Hilda, all I want is for you to enjoy playing it for many more years to come. Leave it to the Stoughton Historical Society or the Hardanger Folkemuseum in your will. In fact, the Norwegian museum director is here. I'll introduce you later."

The older woman hesitated, considering the fiddle. Then her facial muscles eased. "All right, dear. That's what I'll do."

"Pardon me." Kent approached, looking apologetic. "Hilda, people are hoping you'll play a dance tune or two. Only if you're up to it, of course."

Hilda smiled. "I am indeed."

She began a schottische, and couples moved to the open area in the middle of the room. Chloe rejoined Roelke, who was watching from the side.

"Everything good?" he asked.

"Everything is wonderful."

It was fun to watch the dancers—young and old, skilled and not, happy people wearing folk costumes and immigrant attire and everything in between. After a few sprightly tunes, Hilda began a slow piece.

Roelke held out his hand. "May I have this dance?"

"But you—you don't dance," she stammered.

He led her onto the floor and pulled her into his arms. They swayed back in forth in time to the melody. "This is the extent of my ability," he warned her. "No Hallings or Springars for me."

Chloe had never been happier on a dance floor. "This is *perfect*."

After a moment he said, "I've been thinking about our Norwegian wedding all day. You know what my favorite moment was?"

She shook her head. The day had overflowed with favorite moments.

"The part where we promised to go adventuring together."

Chloe tipped her head to meet her husband's gaze. "I think we have *lots* more adventures ahead of us."

"That," Roelke said, "sounds very good to me."

Vesterheim Norwegian-American Museum and Heritage Center, 1979.044.009

1. Porcelain doll dressed as a Norwegian bride, purchased in Bergen, Norway, 1911.

Vesterheim Norwegian-American Museum and Heritage Center, 1970.006.001

2. Square Doily with border of elaborate white Hardanger embroidery with cutwork.

Hardanger Folkemuseum, HFU 17931

3. Hand Cloth (Handaplagg, Handaklede), linen cloth with silk blackwork embroidery, 1700s.

Vesterheim Norwegian-American Museum and Heritage Center, LC5632

4. Bridal Crown made of silver with gold wash, glass, and enamel, Bergen, Norway, ca. 1740. Embroidered silk ribbons hang from the bottom section.

Vesterheim Norwegian-American Museum and Heritage Center, 1977.058.016

5. Silver Bride's Locket with filigree work covering the front, leaf-shaped dangles with an engraved decoration, and Maltese-style cross with three additional leaf-shaped dangles.

Vesterheim Norwegian-American Museum and Heritage Center, 1976.036.001

6. Hardanger Fiddle (Hardingfele) with devils painted on the sides, made by Otto Rindlisbacher, Rice Lake, Wisconsin, 1930–1970

Vesterheim Norwegian-American Museum and Heritage Center, 1976.036.001

7. Hardanger Fiddle (Hardingfele) with devils painted on the sides, made by Otto Rindlisbacher, Rice Lake, Wisconsin, 1930-1970.

Vesterheim Norwegian-American Museum and Heritage Center, 1995.004.015

8. Carved printing block with spiral motifs, Hallingdal, Norway, nineteenth century.

Vesterheim Norwegian-American Museum and Heritage Center, Eklund10001 - A.V. Eklund

9. Midgard's Studio, Marie Maurseth Egge and daughter Helen, Stoughton, Wisconsin, 1915. Marie's folk costume is from the Hardanger area. Helen holds a bride doll with folk dress from Hardanger.

Photographer Nils Løyning, Kraftmuseet, Norway

10. Bridal Party approaching the Kinsarvik Church.

Hardanger Folkemuseum, HFU F.03799

11. The Utne Hotel, with the Utne Church visible to the left, 1929/30.

Acknowledgments

Vesterheim, the National Norwegian-American Museum and Heritage Center in Decorah, Iowa, has been a wonderful partner since I began researching the first Chloe Ellefson mystery, *Old World Murder*; the fourth mystery, *Heritage of Darkness*, is set there. *Fiddling With Fate* was born when my husband and I traveled to Norway with Vesterheim in 2015. Warm thanks to Vesterheim's dedicated staff members and volunteers. Special thanks this time to Chief Curator Laurann Gilbertson.

I am indebted to Agnete Sivertsen, Director of the Hardanger Folkemuseum in Utne, Norway, who provided insight into the Hardanger area's extraordinary folk traditions and material culture; and to guide Maria Folkedal, who sang for us in the open-air division's oldest building. Thanks also to everyone at the Utne Hotel who continue to welcome guests with rare hospitality.

Many people have helped me glimpse Stoughton's Norwegian-American community. I'm grateful to Susan Slinde, one of the first Norwegian Dancers; Vicky Goplen, Sons of Norway, Mandt Lodge Vice President; Nancy Hagen, Stoughton Historical Society President; and genealogist Dee Grimsrud, who helped me imagine the complicated task of tracing Norwegian ancestors.

Thanks to Jeff Dunn for sharing his knowledge about 1980s Volvos.

I'm grateful to my agent Fiona Kenshole, and to Brian Farrey-Latz, Terri Bischoff, Amy Glaser, and Nicole Nugent for championing the series. Huge thanks to Laurie Rosengren for editorial assistance; and to Katie Mead and Robert Alexander, Write On Door County, the Council For Wisconsin Writers, and Ernest Hüpeden's Painted Forest, for providing space to write.

I'm especially grateful to my family for a lifetime of encouragement, and to my husband and partner Scott Meeker. Most of all, heartfelt thanks to my wonderful readers.

Geri Gerold © Kathleen Ernst

ABOUT THE AUTHOR

Kathleen Ernst is an award-winning author, educator, and social historian. She has published thirty-six novels and two nonfiction books. Her books for young readers include the Caroline Abbott series and *Gunpowder and Teacakes: My Journey with Felicity* for American Girl. Honors for her children's mysteries include Edgar and Agatha Award nominations. Kathleen worked as an interpreter and as curator of interpretation and collections at Old World Wisconsin, and her time at the historic site served as inspiration for the Chloe Ellefson mysteries. *The Heirloom Murders* won the Anne Powers Fiction Book Award from the Council for Wisconsin Writers, and *The Light Keeper's Legacy* won the Lovey Award for Best Traditional Mystery from Love Is Murder. Ernst served as project director/scriptwriter for several instructional television series, one of which earned her an Emmy Award. She lives in Middleton, Wisconsin. For more information, visit her online at https://www.kathleenernst.com.